DOUBLE DARE

Michael Curless

mAcinSF

Book Cover by Joleene Naylor

Second edition 2024

eBook ISBN 9781005400859

Paperback ISBN 9798990747609

To Gene.

Whose love of art, literature ... and me,
manifested my greatest joy in life.

A NOTE TO THE READER

THE DOUBLE DARE TRILOGY portrays a chosen family of gay men living in 21st Century San Francisco, a city long revered for encouraging its denizens to live their best, authentic lives. The men chronicled here are striving to do just that. Which means there are occasional, frank scenes of sex between men. Loving, devoted men, some of whom enjoy exploring new and growing subcultures in the modern world. As the title should imply, some of these scenes may be, for the uninitiated, a bit daring.

As Luke hovered between consciousness and that delicious dream state, he suddenly realized what Raphael's next dare would be. Should he? Could he really? But what if... Then, within seconds, both men were asleep.

One

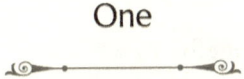

THE FIRST DARE

RAPHAEL SLID INTO THE booth, stuffing his and Luke's gym bags under the seat. He was still slightly damp from the post workout shower at their gym around the corner. Even though they'd both spent Christmas earlier in the week with their respective families, they were faithful to their workout routine: Tuesday, Thursday and Saturday. Of course, part of the routine included protein shakes and chicken salad sandwiches at their favorite neighborhood café after their workout. They took turns buying, and this evening was Luke's turn.

As Raphael pulled his nearly shoulder length hair back, to let a little air under the damp locks, Luke slid into the other side of the booth with the shakes. "Food will be here shortly," he said, smiling at Raphael's efforts to dry out his shiny, black hair. "Now, see, if you'd get a cool cut like that guy's, your hair would be dry by now," Luke nodded his head to the booth across the aisle where two guys were sharing a loaded pizza. One of them sported a high 'n tight that must have been only a few hours old since far more skin than hair gleamed on the sides and back of his head. The fact that the skin was nicely tanned indicated it wasn't a new high 'n tight, either.

"Right," replied Raphael. "Like you'll ever see me with a flattop." He lowered his voice, "It looks good on him, I have to admit ... in fact, he's pretty hot, but not me. No way."

Luke reached up and brushed the back of his head, feeling the soft nap of his own week-old flattop. "Don't be too sure, Raphael, my boy. I never thought I'd have short hair either, but since I got buzzed, I love it. And, I get plenty of compliments and come-ons, too, so it must not look too bad."

"It looks great, Luke, and you know it. But that's you. I'd look like hell. My hair's my best asset. After my ass, maybe."

"Your ass, my ass. Your baby-smooth pecs are your best asset. These workouts are paying you much bigger dividends than they are me."

"Yeah, right. So why did that hunk in the practically see-thru body suit find it necessary to "spot" you on the bench press tonight? You're looking great."

"He was just looking out for my safety."

"Safety? Give me a break. He was looking for something, all right." Raphael rolled his eyes and rubbed his leg up against Luke's and left it there. Both men were showing progress from their devotion to the gym, and they both knew it. In fact, Luke now wore many of Raphael's shirts because Raphael had outgrown them over the past few months.

A familiar counterman walked up with their sandwiches, deftly sliding their plates in front of them. He knew Raphael had the fries and Luke the onion rings. "Another shake?" he asked Luke, noting his tumbler was two thirds empty.

"That'd be nice," Luke responded.

"Yes, Sir," was the comeback. The man turned to the table across the aisle and picked up the empty pizza pan, giving the hot guy's high 'n tight a brisk, flirtatious, rub as he left.

"See, a manly cut commands respect," said Luke as he tore into his sandwich.

"Which are you referring to — the subservient 'Yes, Sir' or the awfully familiar noogie he gave Mr. Skinhead over there?"

"Both. I find both to be admirable."

After the boys finished their meal, they sat back to relax a minute before heading home. They lived on the same block, but in different buildings. Raphael had briefly thought about suggesting they move in together, but he didn't want to rush Luke. They spent plenty of time together, at the gym and on weekends either rollerblading Golden Gate Park, at the beach or hiking the nearby hills. And, more and more, in bed. God knows, the sex was better than it had ever been with Larry, but still. Luke was sometimes something of an enigma. Raphael cared too much for him and the growing relationship to do anything to spoil it. You could say Raphael was waiting for a sign, a spontaneous sign, from Luke to indicate how he felt.

"What should we do for New Year's?" Raphael asked, assuming, hoping, they'd do something together. Maybe go to the bars, or find a party.

"Hmmm," Luke grunted. "Good question. I'm not sure I want to start another year off in a noisy, crowded bar." Luke hated most bars and usually got hoarse trying to yell over the ubiquitous loud music. Why the hell did they have to play it so damned loud, anyway?

"I dare you to go to the Powerhouse and do that little strip tease on the bar again," Raphael chided, smirking as he grabbed another napkin to pat down his forehead. The hair closest to his scalp was still a little damp, the humidity held in by his thick hair. Raphael was referring to an impromptu performance Luke gave on the night the two met. Luke was 'in high spirits' and had acted on a dare Raphael dealt him. That was before Raphael learned how uninhibited Luke was, especially when it came to his own body. The studded leather codpiece Luke stripped down to, before the bartender ended his performance, was his second clue that there was more to Luke than first met the eye.

"Really? Well, I'll do it in a flash, if I get to dare you, too. If I do your dare, you'll have to do mine."

"Yeah, right. Like you'd really mind stripping in front of a bunch of horny guys. Some dare. Besides, I don't know." Raphael pulled back his hair and waved it a couple of times to allow cooling air around his ears. Finally, in desperation he pulled a hair band out of his pocket and tied it into a man bun. "You've got a devious streak. I mean, it's one of the things I love about you, but ... what if I didn't do your dare?"

"Then I'd know you didn't really love me." Luke smiled. He suspected that would get Raphael's attention.

"So, if you give me a dare," Raphael asked a little breathlessly, "and I do it ... you'll know I love you?" Interesting turn of events. Maybe Luke felt as much for him as he did for Luke. This could be a better holiday than he'd imagined.

"We'll, it would certainly say a lot, don't you think? Your willingness to put yourself totally in my hands, so to speak. Trust like that is usually only found among soldiers and lovers."

The word 'lovers' caused Raphael's heart to pause, then race a few beats. Strip off a couple of consonants, and you had the word he'd been waiting months to hear from Luke. Another of Luke's words gave him a small thrill, too.

"What do you mean, 'totally'?"

"Hey you started this. You dared me. I kind of like the idea of starting the new year testing our devotion to each other. You test me, I test you back. Dare and double dare."

"Not fair. If I dare you and you double dare me, then you get to one up me. You come out ahead, especially considering how creative you can be sometimes. I don't think I like this."

"I do. I like it a lot. And, I think I have more guts than you, too, so, I'll tell you what. It doesn't stop with the double dare. You can triple dare me, then I get to come back at you. And so on."

"And so on? When does it stop?"

"When one of us can't meet the other's challenge. When one of us admits his pride is greater than his devotion to the other."

Raphael sat back and thought over the conversation, sipping the last of his shake. Luke just stared back, that mischievous little-boy smile on his face. "You know," Raphael finally said, "you said if I couldn't do your dare..."

"Dares, Raphael. Dares. We're talking multiple jeopardy here."

"Dares. Whatever. You said if I couldn't do them, then you'd know I didn't love you." Raphael paused and made it look like he was swallowing some shake when in fact he was simply anxious. Finally, he took a deep breath, looked back into Luke's almost clear blue eyes and asked, "How do I know if you love me?"

"Easy," Luke responded coolly. He stared back, lifting his left eyebrow in that sexy/sinister way he had. "I won't be the one to stop the dares."

New Year's Eve. Raphael got home early from work, as he and Luke had discussed, so they'd have plenty of time to psych up for the evening and, hopefully, the night ahead. He had no idea what to expect, although he had thought about what would be happening tonight almost non-stop since their conversation in the café. Raphael had tried to joke about it at their workout last night, but Luke wasn't cooperating. He'd simply said, "We made a deal and that's that. Talking about it will just take the edge off of what I intend to make a perfect New Year's Eve."

Raphael had spent hours trying to come up with dares that he thought Luke would refuse to do. This was going to be tough. Oh, sure he had a few wild ideas, but, hell, he didn't want to get Luke arrested. He wanted to get him into bed ... for good. The bad news was that, of most of his ideas, none were things he thought Luke wouldn't be willing to do. Except, maybe one. Just in case things got out of control, Raphael had what he hoped would be his trump card. A dare that, if Luke did it, would make Raphael the happiest guy in town, and if he didn't, well, Luke had said he wouldn't be the one to stop the dares. "God, I hope not," Raphael muttered to himself.

An hour later Raphael was finishing blowing his hair dry in front of the full-length mirror in his bedroom when the door buzzed. Except for Luke, Raphael wasn't expecting anyone, and that wasn't for another half hour or so. He put down the blow dryer and wrapped the bath towel around his waist. The white towel contrasted nicely with his smooth, tanned torso. Luke was right; his pecs were looking pretty good lately. A second buzz woke Raphael out of his short, narcissistic reverie, and he padded through the living room to the front door, bunching up the towel in front to hide his half-mast erection.

On the other side of the door stood Luke, grinning from ear to ear. "Hey, Raphael. I see you got all dressed up for me."

"I was just getting ready. I thought..."

"You can stop thinking, my boy. This is double dare night, remember, and I plan to keep you off balance all night."

"Oh really," Raphael feigned confidence. "Maybe I plan to knock you off balance first. In fact, I think I do go first, don't I?"

"Yeah, you get to go first," Luke said as he dropped his oversized gym back to the floor. Something inside clinked as it hit the carpet. "But, remember, I go second. And fourth. And so on." With that, Luke slid his hand between the towel's knot and Raphael's smooth, flat belly and pulled, freeing Raphael's semi-hardon. Luke grinned, then brought Raphael close by placing one hand on each bubbly little butt cheek and pulling him tight. His lips touched Raphael's as they both exhaled together. Then, pulling his face back enough that he could look into Raphael's eyes, Luke said, "Do it. Test my devotion, Raphael. Dare me."

"I'd rather just do this all night," Raphael replied. Luke looked hot. And, there was something sensual about being naked when Luke wasn't. It made him feel kind of subservient. It made him feel good.

Luke let go of Raphael's ass and flopped onto the couch. "Your bidding, Sir?" he asked.

Raphael was ready, at least for this first dare. He was pretty sure Luke would do it, but he was concerned it might piss him off, too. But he also knew Luke was just waiting to spring a dare on him, so Raphael figured, what the hell. Might as well get the ball rolling in a big way.

Luke loved parading around naked in the locker room and steam room at the gym. He was proud of the progress he'd made and he liked being watched. His cock was a little bigger than average, and certainly bigger than Raphael's, and no one ever complained about Luke's inhibition. Luke was uncut, and that alone made him stand out from the crowd. Raphael was ready with his first shot.

"Strip, Luke. Stand up, strip, then, put your hands on your head and spread your legs," Raphael commanded. Luke just smiled.

"Hey, you're supposed to make me do something I don't like."

"Just do it, mister. There's more after you're naked."

"I hope so," Luke said. Obediently, he stripped off the fleece sweatshirt he was wearing, then his shoes and socks and finally his tight, black 501s. As usual, he wasn't wearing any underwear. Slowly he raised his hands to his head and slid his feet apart, to shoulder width. Now, both men were naked. Luke smiled and said, "How's this, Sir?"

"Perfect," Raphael replied. "Now you must stand absolutely still." With that, Raphael left the room and returned with a small brown bag which he placed on the coffee table. He stared at Luke a moment, admiring his naked body. Raphael began to have second thoughts. What if Luke got mad at him over this first dare? How would he retaliate? Worse yet, what if he simply left? He couldn't bear that.

"What are you waiting for, Sir? I am still at your command, Sir," Luke barked, pretending to be a new recruit or something. Obviously, Luke was enjoying this. What the hell. It was Luke's idea, after all, to do this. Raphael reached into the bag and pulled out a new pair of barber scissors. Luke did a slight double take, but remained at attention. Raphael hesitated only a second, slowly dropped to his knees and reached for Luke's thick, ginger bush.

Holding the curly red and blond hairs with his left hand, Raphael began snipping them close to the skin with his right. Fuck, he thought, Luke's going to hate me. He'll have to wait for weeks before he can run around the gym in front of the other guys. Dreading Luke's certain disapproval, Raphael kept his eyes locked on Luke's diminishing pubes. He moved his cock and balls from one side to the other as he clipped the hair down to stubble, all around Luke's crotch. Then, as he reached into the bag for the shaving cream and razor, he looked up to see how Luke was taking it.

Nothing. Luke was looking straight ahead, stone faced. Shit, shit, shit, Raphael thought. I knew I shouldn't have done this. I knew it. Man oh man oh man. Quickly, wanting to get this over with before Luke said something, or worse yet, started to leave, Raphael smoothed the gel shaving cream around Luke's crotch, all around his cock and up under his balls, clear back to his ass. He pulled the tray of water out from under the couch that he'd stashed earlier, and began to shave Luke down.

With each stroke, foam and hair rolled away from Luke's crotch, revealing fresh, smooth skin, much like the rest of Luke's slightly furry body. In a sexy contrast, his pubes really were dense. The skin underneath was pale white next to his otherwise all-over tan. After several strokes, most of the pubes were completely gone. Raphael turned and selected a new disposable razor, not wanting to cut Luke with a dull blade. When he turned back, Raphael was greeted with a surprising sight.

Luke was at half-staff, more than half staff. He was turned on. He was getting hard! Raphael looked up and instead of the cold look he'd displayed earlier, Luke was grinning. He looked down at Raphael and winked. He winked! Heartened, Raphael carefully worked around Luke's horizontal shaft, slowly freeing it of every vestige of manhood. He glided over Luke's balls, swath after swath peeling away the stubble he'd left a few moments earlier. Then, becoming braver with Luke's still raging hardon, Raphael lifted cock and balls and shaved down that wonderful patch of grooved skin between Luke's balls and his ass. Raphael had spent hours licking these sparse little hairs as they'd made love; now he was whisking them off in an instant.

Finally, he was done. Raphael stood up, looked Luke in the eye, smiled, then silently turned and left the room. He returned with a warm, wet towel and proceeded to rub Luke's truly naked endowment clean of remaining foam and loose hairs. Just when Luke might have thought the ordeal was over, truly emboldened now, Raphael said, "Whoops, missed one," and reached for the razor again. He took his time to carefully inspect every inch of Luke's silkily smooth genitals, scraping off an errant hair here and another one there. Back to the warm towel and another rubbing of Luke's still hard cock.

At last Raphael stood up and, this time, it was Raphael who put his arms around Luke and pulled him close. Luke's smooth cock slid up Raphael's belly, giving both an exciting new sensation. Luke's arms dropped from his head and circled around Raphael's naked back. His right hand slid down to Raphael's ass and squeezed it firmly.

Raphael let out a long, deep breath. The touch of Luke's naked body always made him feel so relaxed. "Thanks for not getting mad, Luke," he whispered into Luke's ear.

"Mad? Raphael, I'm not mad. I love what you did. I just hope you love what I'm about to do as much as I love what you just did." And, with that, Luke took Raphael's head in his hands and gave Raphael a long, deep, sloppy wet kiss. Both men moaned as Raphael's cock began to rise, sliding up Luke's legs until it rested under Luke's baby smooth balls. Many shared breaths later, Luke pulled away from Raphael's mouth, looked deep into his brown eyes and said, "My turn."

Two

Raphael's Journey Begins

RAPHAEL CONTINUED HIS EMBRACE of Luke, reveling in the smooth, warm feel of his torso and back. He was so relieved that Luke wasn't angry over the crotch shaving that all he could think about was pulling him into the bedroom and making crazy, non-stop love to him all night long.

Luke, however, had other plans.

"You must think my devotion to you is mighty weak, Raphael" Luke said as Raphael's hands circled Luke's back, occasionally brushing the top of his tanned, muscular butt.

"What do you mean?" Raphael asked, pulling his head back far enough to look into Luke's eyes.

"I mean that wasn't much of a dare, shaving my pubes. Now they fit the rest of me ... well, most of the rest of me." Luke rubbed his trimmed pecs and grinned.

"Well, I really thought you'd be pissed. I thought it was a pretty good test, Luke." Raphael was relieved Luke was taking it so well, but he was a little disappointed that Luke thought Raphael's test was lame, or worse, that he might have implied Luke's devotion was lacking. Raphael wanted Luke to understand that not only was his devotion to Luke beyond measure, but that he hoped Luke's was, too.

"Pissed?" Luke laughed. He released his hold on Raphael and walked into the bedroom to admire Raphael's handiwork in the mirror. He returned, rubbing his balls with his right hand while scratching his flattop with his left. "It looks pretty hot to me, Raphael, and I love the way it feels. I think I'll keep it this way. It'll look better once it's tanned, don't you think?" Luke reached out and gently fondled Raphael's right nipple. Luke's touch made Raphael shudder.

"Yeah, maybe, once you get used to it," Raphael replied. "I gotta admit," Raphael said as he reached out and cupped Luke's smooth balls in his hand, "it does feel pretty cool. But you won't be able to strip at the gym now, until it grows back out."

"Weren't you listening, Raphael? I'm going to tan it and keep it smooth. Those guys won't care. Hell, I'll have more guys rubbing up against me in the steam than ever. This was your gift to me, Raphael, your test of my devotion, and I plan to prove my devotion by keeping it just the way you wanted it."

Raphael smiled, a sucker for Luke's sweet talk, and he began stroking Luke's erection, closing his eyes slightly.

"Slow down, Raphael, my boy," Luke murmured. "Don't get me too hot. I still have plenty of work to do before midnight. And, I'm assuming you do, too."

"You mean we can't enjoy ourselves as we go along?" Raphael almost whined. Raphael may not have been as uninhibited as Luke, but, once he got started, Raphael could make sex last all night long. That was one of the things Luke loved about him.

"Oh, I'm already enjoying myself. I just don't want to peak before we get to the really good stuff. Speaking of which, it's still my turn now." With that, Luke slipped out of Raphael's embrace, took him by the hand and pulled him into the bedroom. Luke walked to the chair in the corner that served as a clothes horse more than a seat, pushed the stack of discarded clothing to the floor, and lifted the chair, plopping it down about three feet in front of the full-length mirror. Luke returned to the living room, picked up his gym bag, and rejoined Raphael in front of the mirror. Luke took Raphael by the left biceps and said, "March over to that chair, boy. You're in the army now."

"The army?"

"Just march. Remember, letting me have my way now, as I just did with you, proves your devotion. How deep is your devotion to me, Raphael?"

"As deep as yours Luke," Raphael said, a bit warily. Then, with more force, "Deeper than yours. Sir."

Luke smiled. "That's my boy. But we'll see whose devotion is deepest, won't we, Raphael? Now, sit." They'd reached the chair. Raphael sat as Luke turned up the lights in the room. Then, as he bent over and unzipped the gym bag, giving Raphael a breathtaking view of his bare tanned ass in the mirror, Luke said, "I won't ask you to put your hands on your head. In fact, I want them straight down at your sides."

Raphael obliged. Luke turned around, holding a six-foot length of white rope. "This is cotton rope," Luke said, "so it won't hurt. Trust me, I know. In fact, if you cooperate, this should all feel pretty good."

"What are you going to do?" Raphael asked.

"Just relax." Luke gave Raphael a devilish look in the mirror, then he approached with the rope. Luke squatted and knotted the rope around Raphael's wrists, passing the rope under the seat of the chair so that Raphael couldn't stand or even raise his arms. Then, Luke reached back into the bag and pulled out another length of rope. He positioned himself in front of Raphael, his face inches from Raphael's bobbing erection, and he proceeded to tie Raphael's ankles to the chair legs. Finished, he leaned forward and blew a soft, warm fount of air over the tip of Raphael's swollen cock. Raphael moaned. "Raphael, I want you to feel better than you've ever felt before," Luke said.

"I feel great," Raphael responded. "This is kinda hot."

Luke smiled, then he stood, walked around behind the chair and stared at Raphael in the mirror. "I want you to look better than you've ever looked as well."

Luke reached into the bag again and, this time, he pulled out a gleaming object, barber's clippers, the kind Raphael had seen in barbershops when he was a kid. They hadn't been anywhere near his prized head of hair for years.

Oh fuck. Raphael was now beginning to understand what Luke was up to, but he couldn't believe Luke would really do it. Stripping in a gay bar was not much of a challenge. Losing your pubes, when you already trim your body hair to stubble isn't much of a stretch, either. Besides, nobody but Raphael and a few guys at the gym or Marshall's Beach would even know about the pubes. But, this ... barber clippers?

"Oh, no," Raphael started to blurt out, then stopped.

"What's that?" Luke asked. He turned and moved his head down, close to Raphael's. "Did you say something, Raphael?" Raphael remained silent. The look on his face, reflected in the mirror, said enough.

"Were you about to comment on the depth of your devotion?" Luke asked. Luke squatted down on his naked haunches, putting his face level with Raphael's. "Go ahead, I'm listening," he whispered.

Raphael took a deep breath, looking into the mirror at his freshly shampooed hair. Naturally, it was at its best, gleaming in the overhead light. Slowly, he turned to Luke, forcing an almost convincingly brave smile and said "I was about to say, please, Sir, test my devotion." After a pause, he continued, "It knows no bounds, Sir."

Luke grinned and leaned forward to touch his lips to Raphael's. After a shared breath he stood, placed his hand on the back of Raphael's neck and switched the clippers on.

Raphael snapped to attention. This was it. Luke was going to buzz off his hair into a flattop to match his own. He should have seen it coming. Luke's comments the other night came back to him as Luke lowered the clippers to his neck. Raphael knew how he'd look when Luke was done, too. Terrible. He'd had one flattop in his life, at the age of twelve, and everyone had made fun of him. He'd immediately grown it back out and had never had it shorter than near shoulder length ever since. This was *not* what Raphael had hoped for this evening. As Luke pushed his head forward, Raphael could see his own erection going limp. Fuck. This was going to be the worst New Year's ever.

Luke lifted a handful of Raphael's hairs and touched the clippers to the nape of Raphael's neck, gently resting them just below the hairline. He slowly moved them up a couple of inches, before lifting them away from Raphael's head. Raphael's hair was so long and thick he couldn't see what he was doing very well. Some of the hair fell onto Raphael's shoulder, then his thigh. The rest went straight to the floor. Raphael remained stoic, unmoving. Luke didn't even have to keep his hand on the back of his head.

Luke returned the clippers to Raphael's neck and glided them slowly up again, overlapping the first spot to cut a wider swath. The scalp showing through was exactly what Luke was yearning for. It looked hot, and his hard cock bounced in appreciation as he moved around behind Raphael's chair.

Again and again, Luke ran the clippers up the back of Raphael's head, removing only a couple of inches of hair with each pass. He loved the effect his work was having on Raphael's head, and he was enjoying it. When he glanced at Raphael's reflection in the mirror, he saw that Raphael was definitely not enjoying it with him.

Luke clicked off the clippers and sat them on the bed behind him. He put his hands on Raphael's muscled shoulders and gave them a little rub. Raphael, surprised, lifted his head and looked at Luke in the mirror. "That's it? You're done?"

"If I stopped now, you'd look like one of those scary club kids, so I'd better not stop. It's just that you're not enjoying this, like I am, and that makes me sad."

"I can't believe you're doing it," Raphael said. He tried to keep his voice even, natural.

"Okay, so you *do* want me to stop? Have we finished our dares?"

Raphael almost said 'yes, please stop.' But, as he looked at Luke's reflection, he saw the white, naked patch around Luke's still hard cock and remembered how happily Luke let him have his way with Luke's pubes. Maybe Luke loved him more than he loved Luke. Could that be true? Oh, please make it so, Raphael thought. Let Luke love me as much as I love him. With that, Raphael looked at his own reflection one last time, then closed his eyes and said, "No, Sir. Please do not stop, Sir. Do not stop until you are satisfied with the way I look, Sir."

Luke smiled and rubbed Raphael's shoulders again, reaching down to tweak his caramel nipples. Then he retrieved the clippers. As Luke snapped them on and moved them to the base of Raphael's neck again, Raphael voluntarily lowered his head. Again, Luke began sliding the clippers up Raphael's scalp. Although Luke seemed to be moving them just as he had before, something was different. Raphael noticed their warmth for the first time. The deep vibration he felt as Luke moved them over his head was nice, too. Almost erotic. As Luke worked, his fingers touched Raphael in a spot where the clippers had already passed, and Raphael gasped at the feel of Luke's touch on stubble. Noting the response, Luke bent close and licked the buzzed back of Raphael's head.

"Oh, god," Raphael groaned. Luke blew on the spot he'd just moistened, sending a chill down Raphael's back that re-ignited Raphael's cock. It began to swell again, rising among the pile of Raphael's now forsaken locks.

"Feels, good doesn't it, Raphael?" Luke asserted.

"That's unbelievable," Raphael replied.

"It just gets better. Go ahead, you can lift your head now. I'm done with the back for a while. Why don't you watch?"

Raphael did. He watched as Luke deftly moved the clippers up the sides of his head in even, metered strokes. Moving from the back to the front on first the right side, then the left. Watching Luke's erection bob around as he worked was almost as hot as watching his hair fall away from his head in stroke after stroke after stroke. Luke finished the left side, then snapped off the clippers again and put them down. He left for the living room.

Raphael looked totally bizarre now. Although most of the hair on the top of his head was untouched, what he could see of the sides and back was buzzed down to less than a quarter inch in length. He could see much of his scalp through the hair. The strangest part of all was that it really looked kind of hot. It sure as hell felt great. He could feel the air moving around the room, touching his scalp as it passed. Another chill went down Raphael's spine.

Luke returned with the same scissors Raphael had used on his pubes. "Since I'm going to let you keep some on top, I want to make sure I don't mess up," Luke announced. He grabbed a handful of hair right in the middle of the top of Raphael's head and snipped it off, about an inch from the scalp. "There," Luke said. "Looking better already."

It wasn't long before Luke finished his scissoring, leaving Raphael with the equivalent of a spiky punk look. Damn. Even that looked hot to Raphael. Apparently, Luke liked it, too. "I thought you said you'd look terrible with a buzzcut," Luke said.

"I did. I mean, yes, I did say it and I did look terrible with a flattop. At least I think I did. But then, I also said you'd never catch me with a flattop."

"Funny thing, devotion, huh?" Luke replied. Raphael smiled. Things were looking up, after all. "You were right about one thing, though," Luke continued.

"What was that, Sir?" Raphael was getting back into the spirit of the moment.

"I won't catch you in a flattop."

"What do you call this?" Raphael asked.

"A haircut. Until it's done, it's still just a haircut." With that, Luke snapped the clippers back on and proceeded to buzz the top of Raphael's head down to a very smooth, very even, very short quarter inch. Several times Luke stopped, bent down, brushed the hair this way and that, and then resumed his handy work. Finally, he snapped the clippers off, rested his left hand on Raphael's shoulder, and once again squatted to face him eye to eye. "How does that look, Raphael?" he quietly asked.

"It looks fantastic, Sir. I love it, Sir." Raphael responded. Damn, it really did look hot, just as hot as the guy they'd seen in the café. And, although the experience had become very sensual and enjoyable, Raphael was glad it was over. Now maybe he and Luke could climb into bed and really have some fun.

"What kind of haircut would you say it is, Raphael?" Luke smiled. "Wouldn't you call it a flattop?"

Confused, Raphael looked again at this reflection and nodded. "Yeah, I guess it is a flattop. A fucking hot looking flattop, Sir." Raphael grinned. Who would have ever thought he'd be smiling at his reflection without his sexy mane?

"But, Raphael," Luke quietly continued, "you vowed I'd never see you in a flattop and, to further prove my devotion to you, I will not leave you with a flattop."

"What?" Raphael blurted. "What do you mean?"

"Just what I said, Raphael, my boy. This is to further prove my devotion. And yours."

Luke walked into the bathroom and started the water running. He returned with a steamy towel, which he wrapped around Raphael's head, obscuring his view of the mirror. It felt incredible. As he let it rest there, Luke again rubbed Raphael's shoulders. Raphael began to relax again.

When Luke lifted the towel, Raphael was not surprised to see a can of shaving cream in his hand. Luke squirted the gel into his palm and began rubbing it into a fragrant white foam. As he smoothed it onto the sides and back of Raphael's head, Raphael groaned with pleasure. Damn, Luke could do anything tonight, as long as it ended with the two of them in each other's arms. As the foam began to do its work, Luke moved around in front of Raphael. Quietly, he brushed the long, loose hairs off Raphael's crotch and thighs. Raphael had been fully erect again for some time now, and some of the hairs stuck to the precum on his cock head. Luke leaned forward and licked them off.

"God, Luke, untie my hands and let me touch you," Raphael moaned.

"Soon, Raphael. I'm almost done with this dare." Luke again left the room and returned with a bowl of hot water from the bathroom. He set it on the bed, then pulled a brand new razor out of the gym bag and unwrapped it. After a couple of swishes in the bowl, Luke carefully positioned the razor at Raphael's right temple and slowly, carefully pulled it down, leaving a shocking wake of smooth, naked skin. Even though, being Filipino, Raphael had a naturally brown complexion, it was paler than Raphael's face and ear.

"Oh, Raphael, you are going to look so hot," Luke said. "A couple of hours on the beach and you'll be perfect." Then, he fell silent, concentrating completely on each swath of the razor. After four or five strokes, he swished the razor in the tub of warm water and continued, slowly moving around Raphael's head. Raphael was hypnotized, both by the incredible new look Luke was producing and simply by Luke's intensity. He'd seen such intensity before; that's how Luke often was at the gym. But Raphael's look was not at all familiar. Raphael had never thought of himself as a military kind of guy, but that's what he looked like now.

Finally, Luke put the razor down and rubbed Raphael's head with the still warm, damp towel. He stood behind Raphael and put a hand on each of Raphael's naked, hairless temples. He turned Raphael's head from side to side and smiled in admiration. "Damn, Raphael. I've never seen a Marine look as hot as you look right now. Almost done."

With that, Luke pulled different clippers out of the bag, plugged them in and set them humming. Carefully, he held them right in the middle of Raphael's head, just behind the crown and slowly pushed them forward. These had a different sound and feel. As Luke lifted them off Raphael's head, just short of his forehead, Raphael saw why. These clippers left virtually nothing behind. Luke made three more passes to widen the landing strip. He blew across the top of Raphael's scalp, and Raphael nearly came on the spot. He couldn't believe how horny he was right now.

Luke switched off the clippers and laid them down. He squatted behind Raphael and untied him, first the wrists, then the ankles. He stood between Raphael and the mirror, and pulled Raphael to his feet. As the two men embraced, Luke reached up and began to massage the shaven back and sides of Raphael's head. Helpless, Raphael came, shooting between Luke's legs and all over the mirror.

"I take it that means you like your haircut, Raphael," Luke grinned, holding Raphael's body tight against his own as it spazzed with his orgasm.

"Like it? I only have one request," Raphael said between breaths.

"Yeah?" Luke asked.

Raphael ran his tongue behind Luke's left ear, biting down on his earlobe. This was one of Luke's helpless zones. "Promise me you'll do this every week."

Luke laughed and squeezed Raphael harder. "Every week, hell. This kind of cut requires daily attention." Raphael moaned, pressing his thigh against Luke's throbbing cock. As he kneaded Luke's ass with both hands, Raphael realized that Luke's dare was finally done.

"So that's it," he said. "Dare and double-dare."

"That's it? You mean you're going to be the one to end the dares? So. Your devotion to me has its bounds after all?" Luke gave Raphael the kind of look a guardian would give a naughty puppy. "I'm disappointed, Raphael. I thought you really loved me. At least as much as I love you."

There it was. The word Raphael had been waiting for ... 'I love you.' Luke had said 'I love you.'

"You mean that, Luke? You *love* me?" Raphael asked.

"Oh, yeah, I love you, Raphael. More than you could possibly know. You think I'd do this for just any guy? You and I are magic, Raphael ... and what we just did proves it."

Raphael continued to hold onto Luke as though he might suddenly slip out of the room again. Luke again rubbed Raphael's bare scalp and said, "Your turn, baby. Test me again. But, this time, make it challenging. I promised I wouldn't be the one to stop."

Three

LUKE (ALMOST) LOSES IT ALL

RAPHAEL TIGHTLY SQUEEZED LUKE, again. The naked side of his head rubbed against the short stubble on Luke's head, producing yet another new, but exciting, sensation compliments of Luke's deft barbering. Add that to the warmth of Luke's buffed chest, and the pressure of Luke's hard cock against his abs, and Raphael couldn't imagine feeling any better.

"Before the next dare, we've got to get you off, Luke," Raphael whispered as he ran his tongue behind Luke's ear one more time. Then, without warning, he dropped to a squat, sliding his hands down Luke's back until they stopped, each around one of Luke's squat-hardened butt cheeks. Of course, this also put Raphael's face right where he'd intended — facing Luke's smooth crotch. The smell of the shaving cream he'd used on the pubes still lingered on Luke's skin, mixing with the scent of sex.

Raphael slid his mouth over Luke's erection, pushing the foreskin back with his lips. The familiar taste of Luke's precum spilled onto Raphael's tongue. Luke, his hands still rubbing Raphael's freshly shaven head, sucked in a deep breath and clenched his ass. Raphael responded by moving his fingertips into Luke's delicious divide and sliding them down, toward another of Luke's helpless zones. Enough dares for one night, Raphael thought. This will mellow Luke out, and get him into bed, where he belongs. Raphael's fingers had nearly found their mark when Luke reacted.

"Whoa, boy," Luke said, realizing exactly what Raphael was up to. "Not yet, Raphael, not yet. I want it as much as you do, but we're on a hell of a roll here, and we can't stop now. Your job is to test me, not seduce me." With that, Luke slid his cock out of Raphael's oral embrace, then pulled Raphael's head forward, tight against his thigh. Some of

Raphael's cum was still there, and it smeared onto Raphael's cheek and chin. Raphael whimpered.

Luke pulled Raphael to his feet and grinned at the sight of Raphael's face. Holding Raphael still, his fingers interlocking at the now hairless back of Raphael's head, he licked Raphael's face clean, then kissed the boy again, his tongue finding its way to Raphael's molars. This is what Raphael wanted now. Not another dare, but warm, wonderful sex with the man who had just vowed his love for him.

As they kissed, Raphael slid his right hand up the back of Luke's neck, into the nap of his flattop. Wow. Luke seemed to have so much hair now, compared to Raphael. That was when Raphael began to get the idea for his second, unplanned dare. He definitely shouldn't play his trump card yet. Things were going too well. Luke's admission of love made it more of a possibility, all right, but love meant different things to different people. And Raphael, being the worrier he was, wasn't convinced yet that Luke felt as deeply for him as he did for Luke.

He needed to get Luke to a point where he was willing to end the dares, or at least, maybe, put them on hold a while. Playing with the nap of Luke's flattop helped him realize what just might help get Luke there.

"Okay. I never realized when I agreed to this that dares and double dares could take so much time," Raphael said.

"Really? This is just what I expected. Besides, we're together, aren't we? We're naked and in each other's arms. And, I don't know about you, but I'm having a wonderful holiday. And, Raphael, my boy, you've never looked better."

Raphael looked up to catch his reflection in the mirror again. Except maybe for the relative paleness of the naked scalp, he had to agree. Even though he now had less hair on his head than most guys shaved off their face after a long weekend, the look was hot. He grinned at himself, thinking about what he was about to do to Luke's appearance.

"We're both a little messy," Raphael said. "How about we shower together before my next dare?"

"Raphael, I love wearing your cum, but if that's what you want, you're in charge now. Let's go." Luke slapped Raphael on the ass with one simple open-palmed smack. It stung at first, then, after a few seconds felt warm and pleasant. Raphael hardly noticed; he had already begun planning his next move.

"You go ahead and start the water. I'll get fresh towels," Raphael said over his shoulder as he headed out of the bedroom. Luke obliged, stepping into the shower stall and turning on the tap. Luke started with his hair, as always, lathering up with the shampoo he and Raphael often shared. Raphael slipped in behind him, and began soaping up Luke's back and ass.

For at least fifteen minutes the two acted out what was usually an after-sex ritual for them, soaping and scrubbing each other. It wasn't unusual for Raphael to end up on his knees, bringing Luke off yet again, before the shower would end. Not this evening, though. Luke wanted to wait and Raphael had other plans, anyway.

The first time Raphael stepped under the showerhead, he couldn't believe the rush he felt as the steamy water splashed off his naked and nearly naked scalp. All his insulation was gone now, and the water directly assaulted his head. Although it felt fine on the rest of his body, it seemed too hot for his head. At one point, Luke grabbed him and held him under, laughing as Raphael sputtered and struggled. Before, Raphael would have retaliated by shaking his head, whipping his hair from side to side, sending shampoo and water into Luke's face and holding him at bay. Not tonight. There was nothing to shake.

"All done, Raphael?" Luke finally asked, turning off the water. He started to step out onto the bath mat.

"Not yet, Mister," Raphael replied. "Get your ass back in here."

"Yes, Sir," Luke complied. "At your command, Sir." Luke knew the next dare had begun.

"You've made me into a recruit to suit your desires, and for that I am grateful. Now I must mold you into a fantasy of mine."

"And, what is that, Sir?"

"You'll see soon enough, Mister. Now, sit down and cross your legs."

"Of course, Sir." Luke sat down in the middle of the shower stall, crossed his legs as commanded and waited. Raphael dashed into the bedroom then stepped back into the shower, shaving cream and razors in hand, and moved behind Luke.

"You're gonna be a pro at this before you're done, Sir," Luke said.

"If not today, within a week or two, I'm sure," Raphael replied. "Do I need to tie you up like you did to me, Mister?" Raphael asked.

"If you'd like, Sir, that would be really nice, Sir. But, it isn't necessary for your task, Sir. I am at your command, Sir."

"Very well. We'll save the rope for later, then." With that, Raphael squirted gel and began lathering up Luke's head.

"Please, Sir, if you're going to shave my head, may I watch, Sir? Could we get a mirror, Sir?"

"Nope. I knew you'd want to watch. This first time, as part of the ordeal, you may not watch."

"Yes, Sir," was Luke's response. "I understand, Sir." Raphael could hear the disappointment in Luke's voice, and almost gave in. But, he didn't. He wasn't sure how to do this, and he didn't want Luke to watch him fumble. Damn, he'd never shaved anything but his own face before, and now he was shaving Luke's head. My god, Luke was going to have to go work and out in public, displaying Raphael's handiwork. Or, lack of it. If nothing else, Luke must really love him a lot to demonstrate such trust in him. Raphael's cock again began to swell with that realization.

Raphael was grateful for having watched Luke denude his own scalp. It was his only exposure to a head shave and he mimicked Luke's technique, starting at Luke's right temple, then moving toward the back, peeling Luke's already buzzed hair away in stroke after stroke. Like Luke, Raphael moved slowly and deliberately, careful not to nick Luke. He was especially worried around the ear, where Luke's hair sprouted almost down to where the ear emerged. When he had made it about two inches behind Luke's ear, he stopped, replaced the blade cartridge and began fresh at Luke's left temple.

Luke's left ear was easier. Luke was right, Raphael was getting to be pretty good at this. Again, about two inches beyond Luke's left ear, Raphael stopped. He turned on the shower to cleanse Luke's head. Then, more gel, more lather.

This time, Raphael started right at Luke's hairline, just above the center of his right eye. Slowly, carefully he pulled the razor back and down in a diagonal path towards Luke's ear. Then, a couple more strokes eliminated the island patch of hair that had remained above Luke's eye.

Luke had no idea what Raphael was up to. He feared Raphael was trying to shave some bizarre pattern into the remaining hair. Yikes ... He didn't mind a shaved head at all. In fact, he was looking forward to one; he had hoped Raphael's cut would invoke retaliation like this. But this was not a typical head shave. Despite that, Luke wasn't about to protest. Not at this point.

Raphael continued his efforts, moving from the front of Luke's head all the way to the base of his skull. Then, he retraced his path, carefully shaping the edge of what he'd left of Luke's hair, into a sharp, defined line. Luke's nappy flattop was just the right length for a perfect mohawk.

Satisfied, Raphael began again at Luke's forehead, centered over his left eye. Stroke followed stroke, gel and hair rolled away, dropping in globs onto Luke's naked legs and crotch and back. Luke was fully erect by now, realizing what Raphael was up to. A mohawk! Far fucking out. Luke had a friend who'd worn his hair in a mohawk for over a year now, and Luke had always loved it. He hoped that Raphael wasn't going to do a full head shave after all. A mohawk would be a very cool way to start the new year.

Luke's reverie was broken by the blast of hot water as Raphael sprayed him down again. A couple of touch ups, then Raphael moved around Luke, stepped out of the shower and turned to look down at Luke.

Luke looked up without lifting his head, giving Raphael the full benefit of his mostly-shaved, nappy mohawked head. Raphael grabbed his own cock and began slowly pumping it, a vast grin spreading across his face. Luke stood up and reached out to grab Raphael's balls with one hand while reaching up to his head with the other. He loved what he found there.

"At last," Raphael said, "I have a Braveheart of my own. And, a strong, fine, hairless example of a brave he is." Luke leaned forward to lock lips with Raphael, keeping his hand on Raphael's balls. Then he released Raphael and quickly moved to the mirror over the vanity.

"Wow, Raphael, you did an incredible job. This is too fucking much." Luke couldn't help himself, he was pulling on his own cock, too, aroused by his own strange, yet familiar reflection. Raphael stepped behind Luke, putting his arms around him, his left hand fingering Luke's right nipple while his right hand slid down Luke's torso to his balls. Raphael's fully erect cock was where it was happiest, between Luke's thighs, pushing against the same scrotum his hand was caressing.

After another moment of indulgent self-arousal, Luke released his grip on himself and turned around in Raphael's embrace. Raphael's cock eventually found its way next to Luke's. Luke instinctively moved his hips apart, then together, to allow Raphael's member to slide into formation, beneath his own. Each man had one hand on the other's freshly shaven head. They kissed, with lips locked, breathing through each other's noses, even taking breaths from each other's lungs. They shared each other completely.

Finally, Raphael pulled back enough to say, "Will you be keeping the mohawk as well as the shaven pubes, Braveheart?"

"Of course, Sir. Until you stop shaving it, I will continue to wear it as another sign of my devotion ... my love ... for you. And, your high 'n tight, Raphael?"

"Until you stop shaving me, Sir," Raphael responded, effortlessly sliding from the dominant to the subservient role. "I will keep it exactly as you want it, Luke." The middle ground. Luke and Raphael, each commanding and each joyfully bearing service to the other. This was indeed the finest New Year's each had ever had.

Four

RAPHAEL'S TRANSFORMATION

WHAT A NEW YEAR'S Eve this had been so far. Although it was only ten p.m., already Raphael had shaved off Luke's pubes, and left him with just a two-inch wide Mohawk. Luke had taken all of Raphael's long, dense locks, leaving only a thin, stubbly horseshoe of hair, an extreme regulation high 'n tight. Raphael had laid the razor on Luke in two sessions; Luke, so far, only had one turn at his dare allotment. Even though both men were eager for an afternoon on the beach to add some color to their pale, naked scalps, (and Luke's bare crotch) both surprisingly, especially in Raphael's case, were very happy with their new looks ... and with each other's.

Raphael had been transformed into Luke's subservient recruit and Luke was now Raphael's loyal, if edgier, Scottish warrior. Each man's fantasy had become reality. And, both had vowed to keep his new look to please the other. Raphael was more than ready to end the dares, to call it an incredibly successful evening and pull Luke into bed for a night of exploration and passion. He wanted to experience every inch of Luke's more hair-free body, to feel it, taste it, become one with it.

Luke, however, was ready for more.

"There's just enough time left before midnight to squeeze in my next dare, Raphael," Luke said.

"It's going to take you two hours to shave my body?" Raphael asked. "I assume that's what comes next?"

"Well, actually, no. As happy as it made me to see you lose the hair on your head, I kinda like your body hair, what little there is of it. So, for the most part, I'm going to let you keep it, although we might have to 'groom' it at some point. But I have something even better in mind to improve your appearance and help you declare your devotion to me boldly and permanently."

"Permanently?"

"Yeah, permanently, Raphael, my boy. You *do* always want to be my boy, don't you?"

Raphael pulled Luke's chest against his own again, his right hand seeking Luke's shaved scalp while his tongue wrestled with Luke's. "You know I do, Luke," Raphael mumbled through their locked lips. Luke's nappy strip of hair felt so erotic next to the smooth scalp that surrounded it. Raphael hoped Luke would really keep the mohawk; just touching it initiated another Raphael erection.

Luke pulled his lips and tongue away from Raphael's and replied, "Good. Then you're ready to do my next bidding, whatever it might be?"

"Whatever, Sir. I am at your service."

Luke extricated himself from Raphael's embrace and walked to his gym bag and reached in. He pulled out a couple of items and tossed them at Raphael.

"Put those on, we need to go out for a while."

Raphael held up what Luke had tossed him, then looked at Luke in amazement. Although he was ready ... maybe even eager ... to appear in public bearing Luke's razor work, he was not so sure about parading around in this outfit.

"Put them on, Raphael. If I could, I'd take you out just like you are, to show everyone you're Luke's boy and you do what I say. But, now that total nudity is no longer legal on the street most days, we don't need to accrue any citations on our way to our, uh, destination."

Raphael hesitated, turning the flimsy material over in his hands, a concerned look on his face.

"It's part of my dare, Raphael."

"Yes, Sir," Raphael responded, still looking at what he was holding. With that he stepped into the black lycra shorts, which seemed to be a couple of sizes too small. They felt like bike shorts, only thinner and more giving. Because they'd been designed to display his cock and balls, they were far more provocative than any of his bike shorts, however. But that was only half of it. Numerous slits had been sewn in as well, exposing long strips of skin on his hips and ass. Only the crack and his basket were solid material. The second item was a leather vest with no buttons or other hardware. When he put it on, it barely covered his nipples, leaving a wide gap over his chest and abdomen. Raphael looked up to see Luke smiling from across the room.

"Fuuuck, Raphael. You are sooo hot."

Raphael stepped in front of the mirror and looked. Of course, Luke was right -- he looked incredible, if he could think of his reflection as someone else, someone you might see at one of the leather bars. He certainly didn't look like a recruit anymore.

"I thought you wanted me to look like a new recruit," Raphael said. "Not that I'm complaining, I think I like this better, but..."

"You're my boy, Raphael, no matter what kind of look I give you. And, I love having you as my boy. More than you know."

Raphael's heart skipped another beat. Luke was becoming freer with his feelings with each passing hour. If only Raphael had realized handing control over to each other would have resulted in this much sharing, he would have suggested it a long time ago.

"Here, put these on so we can go." Luke said as he pulled a pair of short, black boots out of the bag. "I got these for you today at a used leather shop. That way, they won't look brand new." One of the boots had a pair of white crew socks in it. As Raphael pulled the boots on and began lacing them up, Luke pulled his jeans and sweatshirt on as well. The boots fit perfectly. Luke, not surprisingly, had thought of everything.

"Ready?" Luke asked.

"Where do I put my wallet?" Raphael asked. Luke smiled. Raphael, of course, was being practical.

"Actually, there are a couple of pockets inside the vest, down here." Luke pulled the vest open and slid his fingers into the pockets. He moved his lips nearly to Raphael's and quietly said, "But, you won't need your wallet, Raphael. This little treat's on me. Let's go."

Luke took Raphael's right hand in both his own and pulled Raphael toward the door. Midway through the living room, Luke swung his left arm over Raphael's leathered shoulders and gave him half a squeeze. "I love you Raphael. You're turning into exactly the man I dreamed you'd be the first night I met you."

That stopped Raphael dead in his stride. He turned and grabbed one of Luke's biceps in each hand. Looking into Luke's clear, blue eyes, Raphael said, " That's all I want, Luke. To be your dream. 'Cause you sure as hell are mine."

Luke pulled Raphael close, one hand on Raphael's back, the other slipping into one of the many slits in Raphael's body shorts, caressing the skin on Raphael's ass. "Then it looks like we both get what we want, Raphael, my boy." Then, just as quickly, he drew back and began marching Raphael toward the door again. "But I'm not done yet. Let's go."

They were almost out the door when Raphael stopped and said, "Wait. I forgot something."

"You don't need anything, Raphael. Just your body. And me."

"No, really. Just give me a second." With that, Raphael ran back into the bedroom and returned almost as quickly, straightening the vest. "Okay, I'm ready now, Sir."

Luke nodded, grabbed the back of Raphael's naked neck and pulled him out the door. At the sidewalk Luke turned them both to the left.

"Aren't we taking MUNI?" Raphael asked. He'd expected to be able to enjoy some degree of privacy in the J-Church trolley.

"Nope. We're walking, Raphael. Only about six blocks."

Uh oh. Not what Raphael was expecting at all. Granted it was dark, but still. He was half naked, parading around in leather, with a freshly shaved, and still pale head on a chilly New Year's Eve. What if one of his friends saw him? How would he explain it?

"But, Sir, it's very cool out here ..." Raphael started to protest when his greatest fear suddenly materialized dead ahead. There, coming around the next corner, was Niki, a neighbor, but more importantly someone he'd grown up with. Not only had they gone to the same schools, with Niki a couple of grades behind Raphael, Niki had lived with Raphael's family for a few years, becoming his adopted brother. And, even worse, Niki, wasn't alone. He was with his boyfriend Steve, another of the guys from the gym they all belonged to. Raphael steeled himself for whatever was about to transpire.

"Raphael?" Niki said, both eyebrows practically disappearing under his hairline. "My god, Raphael, is that you?"

Luke took charge. "Hey Niki ... Steve. How are you guys?"

"Not as good as you guys, obviously," Steve replied. "Damn! You both look hot tonight." He reached out and ran his fingers along Raphael's naked temple." Raphael reacted with an embarrassed grin. "Raphael, you look incredible. I didn't even recognize you. I mean, I don't mean that you didn't look fine before with all that hair, but .... wow, I can't believe it. You, too, Luke. Great mohawk. You guys going to a costume party or something?"

"What are they gonna say at work?" Niki asked, before either Luke or Raphael could reply to Steve's question. Niki hadn't yet expressed his disapproval, but he didn't have to. He didn't look thrilled with Luke's or, especially Raphael's, transformations. This could well be the first of many of the unhappy encounters that Raphael had tried not to think about over the last couple of hours. The shaving, the hair cutting, the erotic leather gear were all things he was happy to share with Luke, but there was another world out there to deal with. Just how *would* he deal with it? Raphael had never been one to make waves. But, if making waves was a way to cement Luke's love, this was as good a time as any to start.

"I'm not worried about work, Niki" Raphael answered. "They all know I'm gay. Hell, Luke and I were the most popular people at the company holiday party. And, nobody does my job better than me. They'll just have to get used to it."

"Yeah, they'll get used to it," Luke confirmed. "And a whole lot more."

"Man, I hope so," Steve said. Then, looking at Raphael he continued, "You look too hot to grow your hair back, now. Keep it like this. Hell, get another job if you have to." Steve put a hand on each man's shaved scalp and rubbed, a big grin breaking out on his face. "I love it. Nice shorts, too, Raphael. Man, I figured you guys were pretty basic. I stand corrected."

With that, each couple continued on their way. Raphael could hear Steve's voice trailing off: "Let's get our hair cut like that, Niki. You wanna?" He couldn't hear Niki's reply, but he knew it was most assuredly negative. Niki, he knew well, definitely was 'basic.'

After another block, Luke finally spoke. "You OK, Raphael?"

"Yeah. Better than OK. I mean, Niki was blown away, but Steve was great. I guess that's what it's going to be like. Some will like it, some won't."

"And, for those who don't?"

"Fuck 'em? I only serve you, Sir."

"Good boy." Luke rubbed the back of Raphael's scalp. Raphael put his arm around Luke's waist. Luke followed suit. This was what love, and devotion, was all about. The men traveled the remaining blocks in relative peace, with only a couple of wolf whistles from guys heading in the opposite direction. Good or bad, their new looks definitely attracted guys' attention.

Finally, they arrived at a typical looking Victorian. Luke led Raphael up the steps to the front door and pressed one of four doorbells. Almost instantly a voice on the intercom uttered, "Yeah?"

"Happy New Year's, Jake. It's Luke."

The door buzzed and the two men entered a dim hallway. Luke walked toward the door with "A" on it opposite the stairway that presumably led to the other three apartments. The door opened before they reached it, the light from inside blocked by the silhouette of a naked man who greeted them with a hearty, "Luke!" And, to Raphael, "Yo, boy. Come on in." The man put his arm around Raphael's shoulders and pulled him into the apartment.

Once inside Raphael could see the man wasn't actually naked after all, at least not completely. In fact, he was dressed exactly the way he'd been dressed the last time Raphael had seen him, when Luke had urged him to go back to Luke's favorite leather bar a couple of months back. Despite an impressive beach ball belly, the man obviously worked out and liked everyone to know it. His pumped pecs were highlighted by the leather harness he wore, the cock strap disappearing behind the codpiece that bulged between his thighs. Smooth leather boots completed his ensemble. All leather, all black, all hot.

Raphael remembered being astonished at how comfortable the guy seemed, walking around the bar, chatting with friends, slapping guys on the back, all the time with his ass out there for everyone to see and slap back. Obviously, he was so comfortable because this was how he always dressed.

"So, this is your boy, Luke?" Jake asked as he grabbed Raphael's shoulders and squared them up. Raphael tried to smile as he straightened his back. Jake smiled back and said, "Nice material. You do the high 'n tight?"

"Yeah. Just a little while ago. Tonight's his night."

"Looks like it's your night, too, bud," Jake said, moving closer to Luke and rubbing his fresh mohawk. "Nice look for ya'll. Gonna keep it?"

"As long as I keep the boy," Luke responded. "Maybe for life."

"That's cool," Jake replied. "Think he's worth it?"

"Oh, yeah. He's worth it all right. He's the best."

"The best, huh?" Jake seemed impressed. He walked close to Raphael, who was still standing at attention while Jake and Luke discussed him as if he wasn't even there. Jake stood so close Raphael could see individual tiny hair stubble on Jake's recently shaved chest. The stainless-steel rings in his nipples were joined by a fairly heavy gauge steel chain that sparkled and moved with each of Jake's movements. Each tit ring had a dark magenta bead in it, matching the bead in his septum ring and the beads in each earring. The guy was totally coordinated with captive bead rings. Raphael wondered how much body jewelry was hidden under the leather codpiece.

"So, you want to be Luke's boy, huh?" Luke asked.

"Yes, Sir. Very much, Sir."

"And you'll give up your hair to be his boy, huh boy?"

"Yes, Sir, with honor, Sir. Forever, Sir"

"What else will you do to become his lifelong boy?"

"Whatever he asks, Sir. With pleasure, Sir."

Jake turned to look at Luke and smiled. "You're right. He's okay." Jake turned back to face Raphael. "This is gonna be fun, boy. For both of us." With that, he rubbed Raphael's remaining stubble and turned and walked out of the room. His voice came from around the corner. "Follow me, boy."

Raphael glanced at Luke who was looking at Raphael in the way a father looks at his kid just before he gets on the bus to go to camp for the first time ... proud, a little nervous, but excited for him, too. Raphael smiled, then walked to the door Jake had disappeared into.

"Hold it," Jake yelled. "Nobody comes through that door unless they're naked."

Raphael froze. He paused only an instant before he slid the vest off his shoulders, then unlaced and pulled off the boots. By then Jake was back in the doorway, holding an eight-inch hunting knife. Before Raphael realized what was happening, Jake slid the blade between Raphael's waist and the shorts and pulled the blade down his thigh, ripping the shorts from seam to seam. Raphael was naked again.

"That's better," Jake said. "A boy as fine as you ought to be naked all the time anyway." Jake grabbed Raphael's balls and pulled him down a narrow hallway toward a door. As he entered the door, and looked down an even narrower flight of stairs to the basement, Raphael could hear Luke stripping in the living room behind him. Apparently, Jake was serious about mandatory nudity.

Jake urged Raphael down the stairs ahead of him, his callused hand cupped around Raphael's hairless nape. The room below was almost pitch dark, with only a dim spot illuminating the end of the stairs. By the time they reached the bottom, Luke had caught up, his cock already beginning to swell in anticipation of Raphael's next display of devotion. Jake noticed Luke's excitement and grabbed Luke's cock, then Raphael's and said, "Happy New Year's guys. Hope it's the first of many..."

With that, Jake flipped a switch, bathing the room in red light. Raphael audibly gasped. As he'd sort of suspected, this was a bona fide dungeon, with a sling, a rack, dozens, maybe hundreds of toys and implements hanging on the walls. Crops, hoods, paddles, chains ... it was all there, waiting. How much of it was waiting for him?

"You look surprised, boy," Jake grinned. "Like what you see?"

"Yes, Sir. I think so, Sir, but..."

"But, nothing!" Jake cut Raphael off in mid-sentence. "Luke has arranged a special initiation for you tonight, which you either must accept in toto, or reject completely. That's my understanding, so it's your understanding. What will it be, boy?" Jake moved into Raphael's face, his warm breath flowing over Raphael's face and scalp.

"I was only going to say that I don't think we have time for everything here I want to experience, Sir," Raphael affirmed. As Jake hesitated, surprised at Raphael's remark, Raphael continued. "I want it all, Sir. I want everything."

Luke stepped up behind Raphael and put his arms around Raphael's chest in a bear hug, pinning Raphael's arms against his sides. Luke's fully erect cock pressed into its familiar spot just above Raphael's ass. Luke was proud of how Raphael was handling the situation. "You'll have it all, Raphael, my boy, eventually. But we only have a little time left tonight." He squeezed again. "Damn, I love you, Raphael."

"That's enough, men," Jake interjected, pulling Raphael away from Luke. "I have work to do. Here, sign this." Jake handed Raphael a piece of paper, folded so that only the bottom two inches were visible.

"What's this?" Raphael asked.

"Your consent form. Most guys help me fill it out first, of course, 'cause they know what I'm going to do. But, the lucky ones, like you, belong to someone else who decides all that for them. Legally, I gotta have you sign it, but, for Luke's sake ... and yours, boy ... it'll be better if you don't read it now."

"Yes, Sir." Raphael signed the paper and handed it back to Jake.

"Good boy. Now, step up on this platform here and relax." Jake moved aside and Raphael stepped up onto a wooden platform where a variety of chains and shackles were dangling and attached in seemingly random fashion. As Raphael stood there, his arms at his sides, his cock at half mast, Jake buckled each of his ankles into leather restraints that pulled his feet about a yard apart. Next Jake buckled restraints to Raphael's wrists and biceps, then clipped the restraints to chains suspended from the rafters above.

"How's that feel, boy?"

"Fine, Sir. Like I belong here, Sir," Raphael replied.

"Just about ready for your prep work, Luke," Jake said, walking behind Raphael. Just as Raphael lowered his head to look down on his captive, naked body, Jake came up behind him and pulled a leather hood over Raphael's head that not only blocked all vision, but covered everything all the way down to his neck. The hood had an opening for his nose, so he could breathe, but Raphael doubted he could talk if he wanted to. As Jake began lacing the hood in the back, pulling it tightly around his face and head, Luke stepped close to the right ear hole and whispered, "I'm very proud of you, Raphael." Luke rubbed Raphael's firm right pec and continued, "Just relax and enjoy yourself. If you like this, there'll be plenty more to follow."

Jake finished with the lacing. Before Raphael could wonder what was to come next, he felt Luke's hand on his side. Then, he felt hands all over his body, as Luke and Jake massaged a scented lotion of some kind all over his restrained arms, legs and torso.

"You have such a perfect inny belly button, Raphael. I know what to get you for Valentine's Day." Despite the unfamiliar restraints, what Luke and Jake were doing felt good, especially when they worked over his cock and ass at the same time. Then, nothing again.

Raphael began to relax into the combination of several new sensations. There were the feelings of sensory deprivation and bondage. His whole body tingled from the massage and lotion. He was terribly aware of his own body, as the hood amplified the sound of his breathing. He couldn't imagine feeling any more erotic when, suddenly, he felt more leather enveloping his body. As hands and leather encircled his chest and crotch, Raphael moaned in anticipation. He didn't know what was happening now, but he didn't care. It felt wonderful.

"This is a suspension harness, boy, to take some of the pressure off you," Jake muttered into his right ear hole. Raphael felt a couple of buckles being tightened further around his chest and back.

"Okay, go limp for me," Jake commanded. Raphael let his knees relax. Amazingly, he remained upright without any effort on his own part at all.

More silence. Raphael was enjoying the sensation of leather touching many parts of his body, especially the naked skin on his head. Wearing a leather cap would be a great turn on now, he decided. Except for the ability to move his head slightly, Raphael was completely immobilized. He was also fully, happily erect. There was no question that Raphael was going to let Jake do whatever Luke wanted him to do.

Raphael felt a hand on his chest again and instinctively knew it wasn't Luke's. Jake's voice in his ear confirmed it. "Okay, boy, I'm ready. Are you?" Raphael nodded his head imperceptibly. "I want an answer, boy."

"Mmmph thrrh," Raphael responded. Jake rubbed his chest and pinched Raphael's right nipple so hard that Raphael managed a gasp through the hood.

"I'm going to take you places you've never been, boy. Sometimes it'll hurt. But once we get past that, you'll never want to go back to where you were yesterday. Or, an hour ago. Or, right now, even. I'm doing this for you, boy. Remember that."

More silence. Then, just as Raphael began to relax again into the harness, he heard a loud smack, and felt a sudden warmth on his ass. Smack. Smack. Smack. Raphael was rigidly upright now, straining at his ankle restraints and yelling as best he could through the hood. Jake was attacking his ass with something, something small and fast. A crop maybe. Whatever, it hurt like hell. Smack. Smack. Smack.

Raphael twisted in the harness, but he couldn't really move more than an inch. Jake had full control. So, this is what Luke wanted, huh? To have someone beat him? Smack. Raphael couldn't even finish a thought before another blow fell on his warming ass.

Sweat began pouring into Raphael's eyes, a combination of heat from the hood, the lack of hair to absorb it and the pain of Jake's lashing. It burned his eyes, diverting his attention from his ass for a moment. Then, as he wondered what to do about his eyes, suddenly he heard another smack, only this time he felt a sting on his right nipple instead of his ass. Smack, sting. Smack, sting. First his right nipple, then the left. Jake was an excellent shot; the blows landed perfectly on target each time.

Raphael continued to wince, to jerk, to scream, to sweat. To burn and sting. Then, eventually, surprisingly, Raphael realized he was raging hard again. Suddenly he realized his ass didn't hurt so much as it felt warm, felt touched, loved, attended to. As Jake's blows continued, Luke began touching Raphael's naked, leather-bound body. Luke's touch was reaffirming ... soothing ... overwhelming.

As someone - Luke? - took Raphael's cock in his hand, another hand squeezed his right nipple sharply. Any other time he would have protested in pain, but Jake had conditioned him well, by now. He felt the sting, but not as pain. It was a touch of ... of what? Domination? Ownership? Attention, certainly. The two hunks in the dungeon were totally focused on Raphael and he knew it. He relished it. He loved it. His Luke had gone to great lengths to arrange this experience. The thought of Luke's devotion, the feel of Luke's hands on his cock took Raphael to an even higher plane. Before he realized it, he was shouting through the hood, "Mmoorrph. Mmmoree. Pltth thrrr. Mmmoore." And, for now, that's exactly what Raphael got.

Again, Jake grabbed his nipple. Again, the sharp pain. Suddenly, between lashings on his now ecstatic ass, a new sensation hit Raphael in a flash. One of them was massaging his cock. Squeezing it. Raphael wasn't all that surprised when he heard the sound of electric clippers and felt their warmth on his crotch. After all, he'd completely denuded Luke's pubes, so this was payback, no doubt. Then, he felt more manhandling of his cock. Someone was forcing it into a too small cock ring? Then, more manipulating of it. And his balls. Except for the fondling earlier, this was the first time his cock had even been acknowledged, except by himself. Then, just as suddenly, all activity stopped.

Silence. Motionlessness.

Raphael again became aware of his breathing as it slowed. He'd been panting, straining, operating at a high aerobic rate for ... what, hours? Minutes? Whatever it had been, Jake was right. He'd gone places he'd never been to before.

But, now, Raphael heard nothing, felt no new touch. His body was still ablaze from the session, however. Waves of warmth flowed over him. His ass was alive as it had never been before. He was amazingly aware of his nipples. He could feel air passing over them, much as he'd noticed the air on his newly shaven scalp. His body, his being, was surrounded by leather that gave him the support he needed right now just to stay upright.

As the waves of warmth continued, Raphael suddenly felt a hand at the back of his head. Jake was unlacing the hood. Soon, it slid up and over his nose. In the dim light, Raphael jumped to realize Luke's face was centimeters from his own, smiling, maybe even adoring. Luke's lips touched Raphael's. Luke pulled back to lick his lips. "Mmmm. Nice and salty, Raphael, my boy. You taste good after a workout."

Raphael smiled. "I feel pretty good, too, Luke."

"I know just how you feel. You look pretty good, too, Raphael. Here, let's get you down." Luke slowly unbuckled Raphael, releasing the arm and leg restraints first, then the suspension harness. As Luke removed the last straps, Raphael realized for the first time that Jake wasn't in the room.

"Where's Jake?" Raphael asked as he nearly collapsed into Luke's arms.

"He left a while ago. His work was done. He's out celebrating the New Year. It's almost midnight, you know."

"Almost midnight? Feels like I've been here twenty-four hours."

"Yeah, it's great, isn't it? Let's go over here, Raphael. There's something I want you to see." Luke led Raphael, who was still a little uncertain on his feet, to a wall mirror. Luke twisted a dimmer that controlled a couple of spots overhead. Raphael saw his glistening reflection. He first noticed his naked head. He'd never seen it covered in a sheen of sweat before. Damn, it needed some sun bad. Then, he saw a flash of light emanating from his chest. Hallucination? No, a new reality that shocked him. Raphael reached up to touch the stainless-steel ring in his right nipple.

"What?" Raphael gasped. "When did this happen?"

"When you were in ecstasy, Raphael," Luke replied. He put his arm around Raphael's waist and gingerly touched Raphael's newly adorned nipple. "It's one of your marks as my leather boy. This is the other." Luke reached down and cupped his hand around Raphael's cock and lifted it to the light. A cock now safely secured in a baby blue Holy Trainer chastity cage.

Raphael was too numb from the workout to react immediately. He fingered the nipple ring, then looked down at his cock. He looked back into the mirror at a man that barely resembled who he'd been just hours before. There stood a proudly naked, buzzed and shaved, pierced and caged leather boy, who'd just been bound and gagged and whipped. He swallowed, cleared his throat and looked intensely into Luke's eyes. Luke smiled, but didn't show any other emotion. He was waiting, perhaps a little uncertainly, to gauge Raphael's reaction to his new modifications. His new status as a caged boy. Possibly even his rejection of such.

"I'm not sure I understand," Raphael said, as he reached down and fondled his now useless cock. It felt weird, to say the least. He'd never seen something like this, let alone actually worn it. He had questions. Lots of them. Was this just for tonight? Could he pee with it on? How the hell was Luke going to suck him with it on? What the hell? Then, he looked up again, into Luke's transparent blue eyes, the eyes that always melted him. Luke's smile broadened as he reached out and pulled Raphael into a tight embrace.

"Is there more?" Raphael asked. "To this dare, I mean?"

"I hope so, Raphael, but not tonight. I'm finished for now."

"I'm not, Luke. Wait here. I have a lot of questions about all this, but first, I have a last dare for you tonight. I'll be right back." Raphael disappeared up the stairs, and immediately returned, carrying his leather vest. "My next dare will only take a minute. I got a ring for you, too. Not as sexy as what you got me, maybe ... I didn't realize what we'd be doing tonight when I got it. But, it's my last dare for you tonight. Please don't fail to accept it."

Raphael reached into one of the pockets inside the vest and pulled out a small object that glittered in the spotlight. He handed it to Luke. It was a gold wedding band. As Luke held it up, he noticed something inside the band. On closer inspection he saw it was an inscription that read, 'Love U Always, Raphael.' Luke handed it back to Raphael, who immediately looked crushed.

"No, Raphael. No, don't look so sad. It's perfect. It's beautiful and it's totally you. It's exactly what I was hoping for. I want you to put in on my finger. I want you to take possession of me, just as I did to you tonight."

Raphael, tears brimming in his eyes, took Luke's left hand and slid the ring into place. The two naked men embraced again under Jake's spots as Luke whispered into Raphael's ear, "Here's to a life of mutual ownership and devotion. I love you, Raphael, my boy."

Five

RAPHAEL COMES OUT — AGAIN

JUST OVER THREE WEEKS had passed since Raphael's initiation into leather life on New Year's Eve. Both men had been through much in that short time. Raphael's co-workers were speechless when he returned to work after the holiday. Most everyone knew how much he liked wearing his hair long, particularly those with whom he worked most closely. Raphael took the easy route and told them the truth ... that he'd gotten it shaved on a dare. He saw no reason to enlighten them about the other 'dares' he'd taken that night, however. Even more shocking to his colleagues was the fact that, after weeks, his hair wasn't growing out. Each night Raphael and Luke sat naked together in the shower and shaved each other's scalps. And, each Friday night, before heading out to dinner and the clubs, Luke buzzed down Raphael's horseshoe and carefully groomed his landing strip. Raphael trimmed Luke's mohawk in kind, keeping the nap at a velvety quarter inch.

Raphael's explanation for the look was simple. "I've decided I like it this way, okay?"

Nobody argued, and work went on as usual. Another guy in the office even showed up with a flattop about a week later. Everybody blamed Raphael for 'corrupting' him.

Although his hair was actually longer than Raphael's, Luke's mohawk was even more radical to most people. Too radical for his boss at the newspaper, where Luke ran a press.

"Either shave it all or grow it out, Luke. You're too distracting to the other employees," he'd said.

"Sorry, Jim, this is how I wear it, now," was Luke's response. "Besides, mohawks are not exactly rare in San Francisco these days."

"You want to keep your job?" Jim threatened.

That night, as Raphael carefully lathered and shaved Luke's scalp, keeping the edges of the mohawk crisp and straight, they talked about it.

As usual, Raphael was sitting behind Luke, with his legs wrapped around Luke's waist, his heels planted in Luke's hairless crotch. Raphael's caged cock pressed against Luke's furry, trimmed ass as Raphael worked and, occasionally, as Raphael leaned forward, the cold steel of his tit ring would graze Luke's back. The sensations reminded Luke of Raphael's willingness to be his leather boy. That realization, and the sensation of Raphael stripping the day's growth from his head, always kept Luke hard. The best sex they'd ever had always followed their evening shaves.

"He can't fire you over your hair, Luke. It's not like you meet with customers or anything."

"I know. I could fight him if he tried, but I don't think it's worth it. I've been thinking about looking around, anyway."

"With a mohawk? That might be challenging. That might take some luck."

Luck was with Luke, however. That weekend, at what was becoming their favorite hangout — the leather bar where Raphael had first seen Jake — Luke was describing his dilemma to a casual friend. One conversation led to another and Luke was offered a job on the spot at a printing company owned by one of the bar's more loyal patrons. It even offered better pay and more benefits.

Luke especially enjoyed delivering his resignation to his boss's boss the following Monday.

"Listen, Luke, let's talk about this. I don't care how you wear your hair. Hell, you can shave your whole body if you want to, for all I care. You're a damn good pressman and I want to keep you. Let me talk to Jim and everything will be fine."

"No thanks, Mr. Jasper. I wouldn't be comfortable knowing you'd made Jim keep me on. It would only be a matter of time before he'd find some trumped up reason to fire me."

"You're not being fair to Jim or us, Luke. He's not that kind of guy; he'll get over it."

"Maybe. Maybe not. I don't need the grief. If I'm not wanted, I'm not gonna stick around."

"That's my point, Luke. You are wanted here." Jasper came around the desk and put his beefy arm around Luke's shoulders. "You belong here, kid. We need good people like you." Jasper almost rubbed Luke's mohawk as a show of good will, then thought better of it.

"I appreciate that, Mr. Jasper, but I've already taken another job. I wouldn't want to go back on my word to my new employer."

"They paying you more?"

"A lot more."

"Damn. Well, I respect your decision. Make me one promise, though. If it doesn't work out, call me first. You'll have a job waiting here, with a raise."

"I promise. Thanks, Mr. Jasper. Take care." Luke shook the man's hand and started for the door.

"One last favor, Luke. When you go back to the press room, would you ask Jim to come up here? Now?"

"Sure thing, Mr. Jasper." A big grin danced across Luke's face as he closed the door. It looked like the Hair Police was in for a surprise. Maybe more.

"How's it going?" Connie, Mr. Jasper's secretary, asked as Luke headed out of the outer office area.

"Couldn't be better, Connie. Couldn't be better."

So work was cool for both of them. Then, of course, they also had to face their first day back to the gym. They'd waited until they'd had a chance to hit the beach a couple of times since New Year's Day and both had picked up nice color on their bare scalps and crotches. The first time out Raphael was understandably self-conscious about his cage, which made his buzzed crotch seem inconsequential, but Luke, as Raphael had expected, didn't think twice about ripping off his jeans and shirt and stretching out nude, and hairless, for all to see.

They'd spent about an hour at Marshall's Beach, and several guys had found it necessary to come over to 'check the time' in order to get a better look at Luke's smooth crotch and Raphael's captive cock. A couple complimented Raphael on his tit ring, apparently uncertain how to approach the topic of the cage. Until one guy, who apparently had fewer boundaries, sat down next to Raphael and simply said, "That's amazing. What is it and why are you wearing it?"

"It's a chastity cage, a Holy Trainer v.3 small, to be exact," Raphael, who had already rehearsed a response to the question he knew would come sooner or later, replied. "My cock belongs to my fiancé, Luke, who keeps the keys. It's one of the ways I show my devotion to him."

"Wow. So, you can't touch your own dick?"

"No. Only Luke can."

"How often do you get, uh, 'uncaged'?"

"Well, it's been on for almost three weeks now."

"Three weeks without touching yourself? You must be crazy!"

"I am. Crazy for Luke."

"Wow. I don't know. Is this a Master/slave thing with you guys?"

"More like mutual ownership," Luke spoke for the first time. "Raphael has a reasonable amount of control over me, too. We like it that way."

"Well, okay. Thanks for sharing. It's pretty sexy, I guess. Pretty radical. Wow." With that, the guy stood up, brushed off some of the sand from his not too shabby naked ass and walked away.

"He'll have one before the week's out," Luke laughed as the guy sauntered away, slowly growing erect as he headed for the surf.

After a while, Raphael concentrated on getting his scalp evenly tanned and pretty much forgot about how his body looked. He didn't know any of these people anyway. By mid-month they had both picked up enough color that their heads and crotches matched everything else. Their shaved scalps looked much better, and, Luke's long-tanned cock and the skin around where his pubes had been was vastly improved. They decided it was time to hit the gym again.

They wore their workout gear into the gym straight from the beach, so it wasn't until after their workout that they had to strip in the locker room. Both had already received plenty of jokes and noogies from fellow members who admired or otherwise commented on their smooth scalps. Now it was time to bare all.

Luke dropped his shorts, pulled his tank top over his head and stood there, rubbing his smooth crotch and absent-mindedly pulling on his cock as Raphael fumbled with his T-shirt. Luke's crotch tingled a bit from the day's sun. He hoped it hadn't burned.

"Come on, Raphael, my boy, let's steam," Luke prodded. Three or four other guys were in the locker room and all managed to notice Luke's denuded crotch. Raphael kept stalling.

"Geez, Raphael," Luke exhaled as he reached over and pulled Raphael's shirt up and over his head, pulling his arms up in the air. Without pausing, Luke immediately pantsed him, too, leaving his shorts around his ankles. With a half-hearted smile, Raphael kicked off the shorts, peeled off his jock, rolled his eyes to the other guys nearby and followed Luke into the steam room.

At first, they were the only two there. Raphael stretched out on a top bench, where the heat was hottest, and he slowly began to relax. Luke laid on the bench below, his left hand resting on Raphael's smooth thigh. After a few minutes a couple of guys entered and took the benches opposite. Luke, as usual, kept his hand on Raphael's leg. After a couple of minutes of self-consciousness, Raphael again began to relax and closed his eyes, enjoying the wet heat and the feel of Luke's hand on this leg. The other guys were chatting about this and that, apparently oblivious to Raphael and Luke. Soon, another guy entered, then two more. Raphael was completely at ease.

"You guys lose a bet or something?" It was one of the last two guys to enter.

"Who, us?" Luke asked. Raphael tensed.

"Yeah, what happened to your hair. All your hair."

"Well, he shaved mine off and I shaved and buzzed his off. It was a bet, kind of, but nobody 'lost.'"

Silence. Then, surprisingly, Raphael spoke.

"Do we look like we lost?" he asked, rising up on his elbow so his cage would be in full view.

"No. I just wondered."

Raphael laid back down. More silence. Then, another voice, from one of the first guys to follow Luke and Raphael in.

"Your name's Luke, right?"

"Yeah, Luke. This is Raphael."

"It works. The smooth look, I mean. You know, it's kinda like Michelangelo's David or something. I like it."

"Thanks. You should try it. It feels good, too."

The guy looked at his companion, then back to Luke and replied, "Hmmm. Maybe I will." Although Luke couldn't see it, Raphael smiled. And, he started to get a little hard. Not that anyone could detect it inside the HT v3.

Then, with impeccable timing, Niki entered the steam room, with a towel wrapped around his waist, as always. It wasn't until he'd sat down that he realized Raphael and Luke were already there.

"Oh my god. I forgot you guys shaved your heads," he exclaimed. Everybody turned to Niki. Raphael started to sit up, then, too late, realized what he'd just done.

"Oh my god, you pierced your nipple!" Niki was off the bench and standing over Luke staring straight at Raphael's pecs. Niki's crotch was just above Luke's face, hidden behind the towel. Niki reached out and touched Raphael's nipple, then quickly drew his hand back. That's when he glanced further down and saw Raphael's cage. "What are you guys into?" he practically shrieked.

"Each other, Niki," Raphael replied. He was nearly mortified that Niki was making a scene in front of the other members in the steam room. "What's the big deal?" Raphael asked.

"Yeah, his nipple is pierced and his cock is caged, Niki. Check it out." Luke said, as he reached up and lifted Raphael's locked cock and balls.

"Luke!" Raphael barked, grabbing his cage away from Luke's grasp. Luke laughed.

"Oh my god," Niki whimpered, heading out the steam room door. "Oh my god." The door slammed. More silence. Raphael, no pun intended, was steaming.

"Are you out of your mind?" he accused Luke.

"Hey, he might as well get over it all at once, Raphael. He'll get used to it."

"I don't think so," one of the other guys offered. Then he laughed. So did Luke. So did the others, until finally, Raphael had to laugh, too.

"Is the cage a sometimes thing or a long-term thing?" one of the guys on the other bench asked. "My boyfriend locks up now and then."

"Well, it hasn't come off since it first went on," Raphael answered. The question made him stop and think. How long would this dare last? Wearing it had been hell at first. He seemed to have far more frequent erections than usual, and he was intensely aware of each one thanks to the cage. But there was something delicious about being Luke's total bottom boy. And, Luke was paying way more attention to Raphael's bottom and his unpierced nipple, too, and both were becoming more erogenous, doing their best to make up for the inability to manually stimulate his own cock. So far, it hadn't been all that bad, he thought.

After everyone had gone back to their silent reverie or their own conversations, Raphael leaned over and looked down into Luke's clear blue eyes. "You don't know Niki. Trust me, we haven't heard the end of this." Luke squeezed Raphael's thigh and just smiled.

Six

A Double Pierce

In the intervening weeks, Raphael's nipple piercing had pretty much healed, allowing Luke to give it a little more attention during their nearly daily 'naps.' Raphael hadn't said anything to Luke, but he had feared the piercing would diminish the sensitivity of his nipple, but to his surprise if anything it was more sensitive, more erotic than ever. Even better, it was plumper than the other nipple, too. As usual, Luke had known what was best for him. Since he couldn't touch his cock any longer, Raphael found himself frequently touching his nipples for pleasure, even in public at times. It felt so good, and no one would have guessed he was actually playing with himself in the only way he could.

Not that everything was perfect. Raphael was used to jerking his cock while Luke fucked him, often managing to come simultaneously with Luke. They'd learned how to read each other's breathing cues and moans and pace each of themselves to the other. Raphael was hardly coming at all now. He still loved being fucked by Luke, loved having Luke inside him, loved falling asleep in Luke's arms, still impaled by Luke's beautiful cock, but now, rather than being spent and helpless after sex, Raphael was hornier than ever. Luke, too, was aware of Raphael's frustration.

After one very long, but one-sided fuck, Luke pulled out of Raphael's sweet, caramel ass and turned him so they could continue to embrace facing each other. Luke lightly kissed Raphael, then pulled his head back far enough that they could look into each other's eyes.

"Are you happy, baby?" Luke asked. Raphael nodded and whispered, "Mmm hmm."

"I want you to be the happiest boy in the world, Raphael." Luke bowed his head so he could gently lick Raphael's pierced nip. Raphael shuddered. "I think it's time for your next dare. You haven't come in a while, I know. It's harder now for you, but it doesn't have to be. Maybe we should unlock you, not just for your weekly hygiene, but for sex, too."

"No!" Raphael said, leaning closer and pressing his tongue between Luke's lips to silence him. "I've been your locked boy for over a month now. Weeks with only you touching my cock to clean it and shave me down."

"Yeah, and every time I do it you're hard as a rock."

"I'm hard as a rock right now, you just can't see it. Luke I've never been hornier. I've never been so conscious of my cock before. I've never gotten so much pleasure out of touching my nipples before. The weird thing is I don't think about jerking off anymore, but I think about your cock *all the time*. I have always loved sucking you off, always loved feeling you inside me, but now, it seems like it's all I think about. I think I'm becoming your boy toy and I think I like it. I wish we didn't have to ever remove the cage, even for cleaning. I just wish I could come at the same time you do, like we used to do."

"Okay, okay, baby. I understand. I love seeing you caged, too. I just want you to be happy with yourself, with me ... with us. So, I think we need to create as many triggers for you to come to as possible. Your next dare is to get the other nip pierced, now that I can play with this one." Luke flicked the ring in Raphael's plump nip with his tongue. Raphael pulled Luke's face up from his nip, leaned forward and buried his tongue in Luke's mouth. After a few shared breaths, Raphael pulled back and said, "That hardly seems like a dare to me. You're laming out on me, Sir."

"Fear not, my love," Luke replied. "I have other dares in mind, just waiting their turn. I've made an appointment with Jake for tomorrow after work, figuring you wouldn't be willing to say no to my next dare just yet."

"Seriously? You think I'd say no to a dare from the handsomest Braveheart in San Francisco? Clearly you underestimate me. I can hardly wait."

Raphael met Luke at Jake's BodyMod studio after work the next day. Raphael stripped off his polo shirt and laid back on the table.

"Ready to make this a matching pair, Raphael?" asked Jake as he pulled on the nitrile gloves.

"Yes, Sir," Raphael responded. "More than ready." Jake manipulated the ring in Raphael's right nipple, testing for easy movement. "Looks like this one is healing nicely. You've been following the aftercare protocol like a good boy, I see. Too many guys start to play with them too soon, and that just slows down everything."

"Luke has made sure we followed your instructions. He's paid extra special attention to this other guy, here, to help keep me distracted."

"Good for Luke. Okay, then, let's make some symmetry happen." Jake, being experienced with nipple piercings, didn't need to mark the targets on Raphael's left nipple. As he clamped the forceps in place, Luke took Raphael's right hand in both of his and squeezed, knowing the pain would be intense but quick.

"Okay, Raphael, take a deep breath," Jake said. "Now take another … and let it out." And, that was the instant that he passed the needle through the nipple with one quick push. Before Raphael could finish another deep breath, Jake had threaded the new ring through, pulling the needle out. Seconds later the bead was in place and Raphael was the proud owner of two pierced nips, one still flat and one now plump, perky even, and finally ready for Luke's fingers, lips and tongue.

"All done," Jake announced, as he tweaked Raphael's healed right nip. You're a real trooper."

"You make it easy," smiled Raphael. "Looks really good, Jake. Thanks."

"My pleasure, always, sweetheart," Jake replied. "Okay, Luke, your turn. Drop your pants and hop up on the table."

"Excuse me?" Luke said, looking wide-eyed at Jake, then at Raphael, who leaned forward from his perch on the table and planted a kiss on Luke's lips that were still parted in surprise. Raphael slipped down off the table, pulled his polo back on over his head, and smiled at Luke, with a bit of a sheepish look on his face.

"Well, Luke, I, uh, thought as long as we were going to be here, uh, that, well, we might as well take care of my next dare for you. Call it a flash dare."

"Flash dare?"

"Flash dare … no warning, no time to think about it."

"Ohhh kay." Luke looked inquisitively at Raphael, then at Jake, who was looking expectantly at Luke. "What might this 'flash' dare be, Raphael?" Luke's voice was almost quivering. Almost.

"Well, since my best chance at having regular orgasms now kind of depends upon your fucking me, I thought, well, enhancing your cock, your beautiful cock that I love so much, that I love sucking, that I love having in me all night, that …"

Luke cut Raphael off in mid-sentence, "Baby, don't torture me. What is your next dare?"

"I want Jake to give you an ampallang."

"Oh. Oh," Luke repeated. "Wow. Hmmm. I have to say, I'm impressed, Raphael. I didn't even think you knew what that is."

"I did a little research, Luke. Sir."

"That is definitely taking it up a notch, isn't it? And, with no notice … to me. Obviously, you thought this out already, and discussed it with Jake."

"The boy already paid for it," Jake said. "You guys really have something interesting going on here."

"We do," Luke said. "We really do, don't we, baby." Luke pulled Raphael into a tight hug, tight enough that Raphael pulled back, wincing.

"Oooh, my nipple."

"Oh, sorry, sorry, baby. I'm sorry." Luke turned to Jake, "What's the healing time on an ampallang, anyway?"

"A month, give or take, sometimes longer. Depends on whether Raphael can leave it alone 'til it heals."

"You really want to go a month without my cock?" Luke asked Raphael, trying to look stern and serious. And, thinking about the consequences for himself as well.

"What do you think? Of course, not. But, this little guy here." he tapped his right nipple, "has been all but abandoned for that long, so, I think we're getting used to a little sacrifice for the good of the team. So, how about it, Sir, is this the dare you finally find you can't accept?"

Luke placed his hands on either side of Raphael's face and pulled him into an embarrassingly long kiss in front of Jake. Or, maybe not, considering how familiar Jake was becoming with each of their bodies. Luke released Raphael, unbuttoned his jeans, pulled them down to his knees, hopped up on the side of the table, looked Raphael in the eyes and said, "You'll have to do better than this to get me to say no to a dare from the man I love."

Seven

NECESSITY, THE MOTHER OF INVENTION

A MONTH HAD PASSED since Jake had installed Raphael's second nipple ring and Luke's ampallang. He had given Luke a selection of different size treaded balls for the post, and a shorter post for after the healing was complete, so he and Raphael could experiment to see which was ideal both for anal stimulation for Raphael and for comfort when deep throating Luke's newly outfitted cock. Since neither piercing was completely healed and had not yet been given Jake's seal of approval for fully functional sex, both men were basically horny as gay rabbits in neighboring cages. Kissing, always a favorite sideline had been the main attraction lately. Luke was beginning to understand better what Raphael got out of nipple play, but still his nips weren't wired directly to his dick like Raphael's were.

One evening while the two were lounging on Raphael's sofa, naked as usual, Raphael landed on an idea he thought might bear fruit. He decided to try bringing Luke off by squeezing Luke's cock shaft while sliding his tongue into Luke's piss slit and massaging his cock from the inside. It definitely got Luke hot in no time. While Luke gently massaged his own nipples, Raphael's tongue tried every dance move he could conjure. Soon he was rewarded with Luke's sweet precum, first a drop, then another, then a nice, syrupy spool of what Raphael had been longing for. As Raphael's cock grew hard inside his Holy Trainer prison, he too began dripping long denied precum. He reached down and coated his index finger with it, and lifted his finger up, sliding it into Luke's slightly open lips. As Luke sucked in Raphael's finger, wrapping his tongue around Raphael's sex coated digit, Raphael decided it was time to go for broke and pressed his tongue as far up Luke's slit as he could, twisting his tongue as he drove it in.

Luke was helpless as he came, weeks' worth of salty, sweet cum spraying into Raphael's waiting mouth, Raphael almost giggled with delight and a sense of accomplishment. He raised up and took Luke's head into both hands and locked lips with Luke, snowballing a mouthful of nectar with Luke, who was no stranger to the taste of his own cum. Luke, in turn, drove his tongue down Raphael's throat, fucking his face the only way he could at the moment.

Lips still locked together, the men curled up together and held each other tightly.

"That was a first for me," Luke finally said.

"Me, too ... Sir," Raphael replied. "I kind of made it up as I went along."

"That's what I love about you, baby ... one of the many things I love about you. You're always ready with another surprise."

"Well, I could say the same about you, Luke. Never a dull moment."

"Hardly, love. No, never a dull moment. The question now, is 'Can Luke bring Raphael off tonight given our current situation?' My cock is out of commission, one of your nipples is off-duty for the interim ... what to do. What to do. ... Hmmm. I wonder..."

"Oh, don't worry about it, Luke. It's my fault you can't fuck me yet anyway. I'm the one who dared you to get pierced. It'll be worth the wait, I'm sure."

"Always the giver, aren't you, baby. No, I don't want you to be denied tonight. After what you just did for me, you deserve to come."

Luke gently played with Raphael's good, right nipple, while lightly kissing him, tasting the lingering coating of his own cum there. After a few delicious minutes, Luke pulled his lips free and said, "Ah, I have an idea. Don't move, baby." Luke leapt up and dashed into the bedroom, returning with the gym bag he'd brought the night the two started their now seemingly endless series of dares. He'd stashed it under Raphael's bed that night and almost forgot about it. Raphael had forgotten about it as well.

Luke dug around and pulled out a small black bag and a pump bottle of lube. Raphael watched with curiosity as Luke opened the bag to reveal a stainless-steel butt plug. "Ok, now what are you thinking of doing," Raphael asked, his almond eyes widening, just a little. "That looks pretty big."

"It's not as big as it looks, Raphael. I want you to come tonight, too. I can always bring you off with my "dick of death," to quote Pansy Division, but this will have to do. Now, lay back, close your eyes, and let me enter you as I always do. Well, kind of like I always do." With that, Luke lowered Raphael back on the sofa, with his ass near the edge. He lifted Raphael's legs up, onto his shoulders exposing his second favorite of Raphael's orifices. In this position Raphael's caged cock laid flat against his belly, and the sight made Luke's cock swell, in spite having just come.

If only he could use it, instead of the plug, to pleasure his locked cock boy. Luke squirted lube on the tip of the plug and smoothed it all around the plug's circumference, then pushed his coated index and ring fingers into Raphael, to lube him up, too. Raphael faintly moaned, just as if he was preparing to accept Luke's familiar cock.

Luke rolled his fingers around, coating Raphael completely, then withdrew his fingers and began inserting the plug. True, the main part of the plug was bigger than Luke's erect cock, but the stem was much narrower, so he just had to ease Raphael through the insertion phase.

"I know this is more than you're used to, baby, but once it's in, it will feel wonderful. Be brave for me." Luke moved slowly, watching Raphael's face to judge when to press and when to stop. "Deep breaths, baby. Deep breaths." As Raphael breathed out, Luke pushed, and to his surprise, after only a couple of breaths the plug slid the rest of the way in. As Raphael's sphincter locked the plug in place, Luke let go and moved his hands up to caress Raphael's chest. As he gently rubbed Raphael's healed nipple, he asked, "How does that feel, baby?"

"Ohhh, it feels good. Weird, good. Like I somehow swallowed you up completely."

"All right! Well done, baby. You're a champ. You never disappoint me, Raphael. I'm impressed."

"We aim to please, Sir. So, uh, about that promised orgasm ..."

"Oh, so now you're going to be my needy bottom, huh? From one extreme to another. Okay, just relax, play with the plug, with your ass, wrestle with it against your prostate. You know like you always do with my cock in you." Luke watched Raphael's face as he followed Luke's instructions. A faint smile began to appear, indicating Raphael knew exactly what he was doing. He was an experienced bottom, capable of overpowering any top if he wanted to, and after weeks of abstinence, this butt plug didn't stand a chance. Raphael's breathing clued Luke in to his progress, as did the pool of precum dripping out of the tip of the cage. Luke knew he was getting close. Not wanting to be left out, Luke leaned forward, pressing his pubic bone against the plug as he squeezed Raphael's nipple. When Raphael's lips parted in a last gasp moan, Luke slid his tongue into Raphael's mouth and down his throat.

Blast off! Raphael shot a month's worth of cum onto his belly, his chest, on Luke's chest and the underside of his chin. Luke couldn't help himself as he laughed at the impressive performance, his tongue still in Raphael's mouth. Raphael had to laugh, too. "That was amazing," he said. "I mean, I don't know if it was the plug or the weeks without coming or ..."

"I think I know what it was, baby."

"What, Sir?"

"I was your first orgasm as a locked cock, plugged at both ends, pierced and ... and loved and worshipped leather boy."

Raphael, still glowing, flat on his back, feeling the warmth of Luke's cummy chest pressed against his own, looked deeply into Luke's transparent blue eyes and smiled. "Oh, yeah, that's what it was. This leather boy needs another kiss, Sir. A long one, please."

"At your command, baby," Luke said as he moved in for the kill.

Eight

LUKE SPLURGES

JULY IN SAN FRANCISCO. Six months since Luke and Raphael had discovered the excitement of daring one another to explore each other's limits, and their own. One thing that seemed limitless, so far, was their devotion to one another. They were spending virtually every free moment together, and never taking the other for granted. With his cock locked, Raphael needed Luke to satisfy himself more than he ever thought would be necessary from another man. Luke, in turn, was dedicated to making sure Raphael received all the attention he deserved. Things were going better than either could have hoped just months earlier. In fact, Luke decided it was time to risk a dare that Raphael just might decline. He was sure of Raphael's love for him, he just wasn't sure about Raphael's comfort as an out and proud leather boy. One thing he was sure of was Raphael's commitment to the cage. More and more, Raphael resisted the weekly cleanings, insisting everything was just fine.

Luke decided it was time to resolve this dilemma. During one of these cleaning sessions, as he finished shaving Raphael's barely visible pubic stubble, he surprised Raphael by jumping out of the shower before replacing the Holy Trainer.

"Hey!" Raphael exclaimed. "Where are you going? I'm still unlocked!"

"It's okay, baby, I'll be right back." And he was, with a length of string, a marker and a ruler.

"What are doing, Sir?"

"Science, my boy, science. Call it an experiment," Luke said as he wrapped the string around the base of Raphael's cock and balls, where a cock ring would reside. With the pen he marked the loop of string, then took it off and laid it along the ruler, noting the length.

"Okay, this is bizarre," Raphael muttered, slightly amused.

"Bear with me, baby. I just want a couple more measurements before this little peepee of yours gets hard." Luke used the string to measure the length, then the girth of Raphael's smooth, brown cock.

"Are we ordering a new suit for my 'little peepee,' Sir?"

"Ha, yeah, that would be cool, wouldn't it, baby? No, I prefer it caged. Actually, I'm interested in seeing if the myth that permanent chastity shrinks the cock is true or just wishful thinking. We'll compare these measurements to your size in a year or two to see if you really do shrink."

"Oh. So, some guys shrink?"

"Some claim they have, yeah. Does the possibility of your cock shrinking disturb you? Would that be bad?"

Raphael remained silent a moment, while Luke reinstalled the Holy Trainer. "No, not bad. Not disturbing. Not really relevant, is it, since your cock is the only cock I want to worship. As long as your cock is my cock, it's the only cock I really need. Does that make sense?"

"Perfect sense, baby," Luke replied, then slid his tongue into Raphael's waiting mouth. "Mmmm, baby you taste so good. Let's dry off, get dressed and go get a Little Star pizza."

"Yum, you talked me into it."

Later that week, Luke texted Raphael, telling him to meet him for an early dinner at a favorite South of Market Italian restaurant. Raphael thought it was a little odd, since they usually did Italian at the Sausage Factory on Castro Street, but didn't think too much of it, since it was sort of on his way home from work. After the dinner, however, the real plot of the evening began to unspool as they left Rocco's hand-in-hand on Folsom Street. As they approached 8th Street, instead of heading west on Folsom, towards Raphael's apartment, Luke pulled Raphael onto 8th and into Mr. S.

"Ah," Raphael smiled, "so this is why we ate at Rocco's. Let me guess. I'm about to be the recipient of another challenging dare from my Braveheart lover."

"Oh, no, nothing so exotic, baby. It's just that you enjoyed the butt plug so much the other night, I wanted to get you one that you can wear full time. Here, over here." Luke led Raphael to the extensive ass toy section, where they located a Master Plug. "This is designed for long term wear. The narrow stem won't strain your delicate sphincter."

"Yeah, so delicate. You certainly don't treat it delicately, Sir. Not that I'm complaining." Raphael planted a teasing kiss on Luke's lips as he took the package from Luke to examine it closer. "What's with the slots?"

"Oh, those are so you can thread the ass strap of a full body harness through it, to insure it stays in place. Not that you need to. This plug won't pull out unless you want it out."

"Well, doesn't matter. I don't have a body harness."

"Hmm, you're right." Luke smiled as he gifted Raphael with a kiss of his own. "We should remedy that while we're here. Come over here." He took Raphael by the hand and pulled him over to the harness section. Luke was browsing, pulling one, then another off the rack when one of the store's staff walked up, clad in 30-holer boots, lace up codpiece shorts and a skin-tight Mr. S tee.

"Hey, guys. I'm Rob. Interested in a harness this evening?"

"Yes, Rob" Luke replied. "For my fiancé, Raphael. Full body, leather, snap, not buckles. Maybe custom fit."

"Ah, a man who knows what he wants. Well, let's see." He looked Raphael over approvingly, then reached behind Luke and lifted a harness off the rack and slid it off the hanger. "This should fit you perfectly. Want to try it on?"

"Sshh, sure," Raphael replied. He was a little intimidated by Rob's confidence and nonchalance at being so sexily clad ... at work. "Um, where is a fitting room?"

"Oh, Raphael, baby, fitting rooms are for wannabes. Here, give me your shirt ... and pants." Rob smiled as Luke reached over to help Raphael wiggle out of his polo shirt. Knowing this was turning Luke on, Raphael unbuttoned his pants and slid them down to reveal his pink jock. He'd given up tighty whities shortly after being caged, for comfort. And because Luke loved touching his bare ass. Stepping out of the jeans, Raphael looked at Rob a bit sheepishly, then pulled off the jock and handed it to the very attentive clerk.

"Whoa. Perfect. This harness was made for you, but I'm going to have to get a bigger cock ring so it will fit over that pretty little cage of yours. I assume it doesn't come off."

"That would be correct, Rob," Luke said proudly.

"Go ahead and slip into the harness, I'll be right back."

As Luke began fitting the harness on the now totally naked Raphael, Raphael noticed a couple of guys watching intently from the chaps section. They were talking quietly, but furtively looking over at Raphael. As Luke positioned the upper harness on Raphael's torso, adjusting the snaps for a tight fit, Rob returned with a selection of chrome and rubber cock rings.

"Would you like to do the honors, Sir, or shall I?" he asked Luke.

"Oh, by all means, you are the expert," Luke smiled.

"My pleasure," Rob replied and as he knelt down, eyes level with Raphael's cage. He worked one of the rubber rings over Raphael's cage, a tight fit, but it worked. He threaded first the front strap through the ring, then the ass strap, and snapped both in place. The ass strap was tight against Raphael's pussy, instantly bringing on a caged erection.

"I think that's about perfect," Rob said, taking Raphael by the shoulders and turning him around 360 degrees. "Yes, I like it. How does it feel, Raphael?"

"It feels awesome, Rob," Raphael responded. "What do you think, Luke?"

"I think it's almost perfect," Luke said, grinning bigger than he had all evening. It's just missing one thing." Rob looked surprised. "No, the harness is perfect, Rob. You know your stuff. We need to make one more stop, here, and, ah, Raphael will wear the harness out, so if you can take the sales tag to the counter for us, and this Master Plug, we'll be ready to settle up in a few minutes."

Rob untied the tag from the harness, took the plug from Luke, and asked, "Would you like me to take Raphael's clothes to the checkout counter as well, Luke?"

"Yes, please, Rob. Thank you." Luke handed the clothes to Rob, took Raphael's shoulders in each hand and pulled him close for a long, deep kiss. He pulled his tongue free, looked Raphael in the eyes and said, "Okay, I lied. Just a little. We did come here for your next dare. Are you ready?"

"Um, you mean stripping me naked in front of a store full of strangers, and letting another stranger feel me up while fitting me in a body harness that I'm apparently wearing home isn't the dare?"

"Nope. Those are just well-deserved gifts from your adoring Luke. So, ah, ready?"

"This oughta be good. Sure, it's been a while since our last dare. Test my devotion here in Mr. S."

Luke grinned again, kind of devilishly, Raphael thought, as he took Raphael's hand and led him through the store, over to the high-end island counter, where the most expensive and exotic toys and implements were kept. The staffer behind the counter seemed unsurprised to be approached by two men, holding hands, one naked, harnessed, and caged.

"Evening, men, how may I help you?"

"I'm Luke, this is Raphael, and you are holding an item for us to try on."

"Ah, yes. Of course. We've been expecting you." As he reached beneath the counter, Raphael looked at Luke in surprise and admiration.

"You sure know how to make an evening special, don't you, Sir," he said.

"Nothing is too special for my boy. I just hope this dare pleases you as much as it will please me." With that, the staffer presented a stainless-steel collar. A locking Talon collar, to be precise.

"This is the fifteen and a half size you specified, Sir. If it's not the right fit, we can select another."

"Let's try it," Luke replied. At that the staffer, unlocked the collar and handed it to Luke. Raphael, meanwhile was stunned. He no longer was aware that he was still naked and harnessed in a room with a number of strangers. All he could see was the intense look in Luke's eyes as he fitted the collar around Raphael's neck. Luke turned Raphael around so he could fit the second segment in place and then lock the collar on. He turned Raphael around again, stepped back and sighed. "Raphael, if only you could see yourself right now as I see you. Come here." Luke took Raphael's hand and led him to a full-length mirror. Raphael had a sudden sense of déjà vu, to the night Luke had revealed the new him to himself in Jake's dungeon. Only this time he was not just caged, but harnessed, and collared. Collared by Luke.

The collar didn't look like the collars you see on most guys these days, the dog collars with tags, or the chains with padlocks. This looked like an expensive piece of jewelry. It *was* an expensive piece of jewelry. Raphael was almost speechless. This was totally unexpected. And, really, as he stood there looking at himself, totally right. And, so beautiful. Discreet, tasteful, profound.

"Well, baby. Will you accept my dare, to wear my collar, twenty-four seven to announce your devotion for me to the world?"

Raphael turned away from the image in the mirror and pulled Luke close. "Seriously? Need you ever ask, Luke?"

"I am so proud of you, Raphael. Thank you, well, for being you. And for being with me. And, for making me the happiest man in the world." Luke wrapped his arm around Raphael's waist and the two walked over to the counter. "We'll take it," Luke said.

The staffer nodded, handed the sales tag to Luke, then, turning to Raphael, he said, "Wear it proudly. It was made for you." Raphael smiled, nodded his head in thanks, then he and Luke walked to the cashier. When he saw the total as Luke was paying, he realized this had been a very expensive evening for Luke. As he reluctantly pulled on the clothes the clerk had handed him, he began to form an idea for a perfect next dare for Luke. He touched the collar, feeling closer to Luke than ever.

"Oh, one more thing," Luke said to the cashier. "I opened one of your keyholder accounts under my name."

'Yes, I see it here."

Luke handed the key to Raphael's collar to the clerk. "You can hold this for us, then. We won't be needing it any time soon." The clerk nodded, took the key and placed it in an envelope. Luke turned to the now fully dressed, but still harnessed and collared Raphael, put his arm around his waist and said, "Let's go to your place. You're looking very overdressed, don't you think?"

Nine

───◦◦───

RAPHAEL GETS AN UPGRADE

IT DIDN'T TAKE LONG for Raphael to feel totally at ease wearing just the collar, cage and harness at home, whether Luke was there or not. He'd even taken to sleeping in the harness, enjoying the feeling of it hugging his body, tugging up on the Master Plug. Just as he'd grown so accustomed to the Holy Trainer that he was only aware of it when an erection drew attention to it, soon the collar, plug and harness just felt natural, too. He regretted that he couldn't wear the harness to work, but took solace in at least being plugged, caged and collared there, without anybody being the wiser. Everyone knew he was Luke's boyfriend, and a few knew he was Luke's fiancé, but so far, no one knew he was Luke's leather boy.

And, as for the collar, well, that quickly became a source of pride for Raphael, and he was always aware of its weight around his neck, especially when it shifted during his workout routine at the gym. Several co-workers had complimented him on his new 'necklace,' and one had referred to it as a 'choker.' Raphael liked that designation and adopted it when answering any questions about it. "Yes, this choker was a gift from Luke. Isn't he the greatest?" Raphael no longer doubted Luke's commitment.

His own feelings for Luke had now deepened to the point he felt it was time to take the next step. After their Thursday workout, as usual they headed to Raphael's apartment to shave, shower and 'nap' before deciding on dinner. After stripping off their gym gear, Raphael knelt down in the shower so Luke could buzz his high n' tight first. He'd long ago figured out that if he knelt before he sat in the shower, he was much better positioned to suck and tease Luke's cock while enjoying Luke's touch up.

"Mmmm, you taste so good, Sir."

"Why thank you, boy," Luke replied, playing along. "Must be all your great cooking you've been feeding me lately."

"I love cooking for you, Luke. I love doing everything for you, not that you are any slouch in that department."

"What do you mean," Luke asked as he sat and reached for the razor to take care of the sides and back of Raphael's head.

"Well, exactly what you're doing right now, making me look as good as you do. Every night. That's dedication."

"You do know I enjoy every minute of this, don't you? I enjoy every minute we share like this."

"As do I, Luke, which is why I have decided on your next dare."

"Okay...?"

"Come around, so I can see your face." Luke put down the razor and moved around in front of Raphael, pulling close, wrapping his legs around Raphael, their locked and unlocked cocks touching. He put his hands on Raphael's waist and said, "Dare me, baby."

"I, uh, I don't think this is going to be such a challenge, future husband." Raphael paused and looked longingly into Luke's clear blue eyes. "I want you to move in with me. I want you be here every night, every morning, all the time. Heck, you practically live here, now. And, think of the money we'd save. And, I'm sure your roommates won't have any trouble replacing you ... not that you are replaceable, but that ..."

Luke cut Raphael off in mid-sentence, "Raphael, baby, sweetheart, love of my life, my beautiful boy ... you had me at 'future husband.' Raphael, I thought you'd never ask. Of course, I will move in. Of course. I'm paid up through the end of the month, but I can move my stuff in this weekend. Yes! Easy dare, Raphael, my boy!"

"I'm so glad you agree," Raphael sighed. "But, um, actually it would be better to wait until the end of the month."

"Why? Are you planning to redecorate first?"

"No, I can't tell you why yet, but I have a good reason. Steve and I have already reserved two Zipcars so we can make the move in one trip. So, you just have to wait a couple of weeks."

"So, Steve is helping?"

"Yeah, with three of us it'll be a breeze."

"Couldn't you get Zipcars this weekend?"

When Raphael hesitated, Luke's light bulb flashed. "What, is there another dare involved?"

"Maaayyybe," Raphael smiled, unable to produce a believable poker face.

"Ah, working ahead on the dares, sweetie? God, I love you," Luke said before planting a big one on Raphael's waiting lips.

"Mmmmmm," was all Raphael could reply. When they pulled apart, Raphael continued, "Okay, time for the part I hate. Taking off the cage for clean up."

"Actually, Raphael, I have a dare for you right now, that I think you're going to like as much as I like your dare for tonight."

"Oh really? Goody, goody, Sir."

"Silly boy, Here, let's get the cage off." Luke unlocked the baby blue holy trainer, pulled off the tube and then began to ease off the cock ring.

"Oh, come on, leave the cock ring on at least, Sir. I don't want to be completely uncaged."

"Well, we have to take it off, so we can put this on instead." Luke leaned out of the shower, pulled a black bag out from under the waiting towel, and handed it to Raphael.

"For me? Is this the dare?" Luke nodded. Raphael undid the tie and pulled out a shiny, metal cage. "It's beautiful, Luke! What is it?"

"It's a Looker 01, from Steelworxx in Germany. I had it custom made for you. Remember when I measured your pretty little peepee? It wasn't to see if you were shrinking; I needed the measurements so this could be a perfect fit. It's way more open so you can stay clean without ever having to remove it again. It can be permanent ... if you want."

"If I want? Seriously? You know that's what I want. You are so amazing, Luke. I love it so much!" Needless to say, Raphael's exclamation ended with another long, juicy kiss. "But what is this thing here?"

"That is a urethral tube that will side up inside your cock, so the cage will squeeze you from the outside and the inside when you get hard."

"Oh ... Really? Won't that hurt?"

"You've heard of sounding, right?"

"Of course."

"Well, baby, you're going to be caged and sounded twenty-four seven for the rest of your life."

"I think I must be dreaming. Put it on me quick, before I wake up, Luke. I love it!"

Luke finished shaving Raphael's pubes and balls, then took the cage out of Raphael's hands. He'd been fondling and admiring the cage all throughout the shave. Luke pulled the keys out of the bag, unlocked the cage from the ring and worked the cock ring into place. It took a little doing.

"It's tighter than the Holy Trainer," Raphael said.

"Yeah, remember this one is custom made just for you, baby." Luke then reached under the towel again and pulled out the sterile antibacterial spray.

"What's that?"

"This will make sure the urethral tube won't introduce anything to give you a urinary tract infection."

"Infection?!"

"Relax, baby, this is just a precaution. Not to worry." Carefully Luke slid the tube up Raphael's now slightly tumescent cock, as he worked the cock itself into the cage."

"Mmmm," Raphael muttered.

"You okay, baby?"

"Yeah, it just feels, I don't know, a little weird."

"When was the last time you were sounded?"

"Uh, that would be never."

"Until now. Enjoy it, baby, it'll just get better." With the cage now fully in place, Luke reached for the keys and locked the two parts together. "This looks fantastic, Raphael."

"Let me see, let me see," Raphael chirped as he stepped out of the shower and into the bedroom to stand in front of his full-length mirror. He turned this way and that, as if modeling a new jock. "It does look really cool, Luke. And, it feels pretty amazing. Not as heavy as I thought it would when I first saw it."

"That because it's perfectly fit to you, Raphael, my beautiful, now permanently caged boy." Luke took Raphael by the shoulders and turned him so they faced one another, and pulled him close for yet another kiss. Suddenly, Raphael pulled back.

"Wait a minute. How do I pee with this in ... on ... in?"

"Like always, baby, except now you won't always have to sit down to pee. The tube is hollow, so you should shoot a narrow, sharp stream again."

"Cool. Let me see." Raphael started for the bathroom. Luke grabbed him by the arm and pulled him back. He again turned Raphael to face him, then got down on his knees, his face level with Raphael's shiny new cage and said, "Okay, baby, pee."

"What? Here? No!"

Luke, for once, was the one looking up into Raphael's dusty brown, almond eyes. "Pee, dammit, pee on me, Raphael and watch the stream. Please, do it for me."

"Luke, are you kidding me? That's gross!"

"Um, so say you. I think it's pretty awesome, pretty intimate, and it's pretty tasty, too."

"I don't think so." As Raphael turned and headed into the bathroom, where he would observe his new piss stream in what he considered a more appropriate venue, he looked over his shoulder and said, "I just never know what to expect from you."

"I'm counting on that, baby," Luke said as he stepped behind Raphael, who was now standing in front of the toilet for the first time in months. He embraced him from behind and waited to speak until he heard Raphael's initial, manly splash. "You're welcome, baby," he whispered into Raphael's ear. Raphael chuckled, leaned back into Luke's embrace, and continued to splash.

A couple of days later, as Luke arrived at Raphael's apartment for their daily shave, shower and nap, Luke asked Raphael how the new cage was working out.

"Is it as comfortable as the Holy Trainer?"

"Um, yeah, it's fine. It's very comfortable, but, um, it's a little more … powerful than I was expecting."

"What do you mean?" Luke asked as he stripped off his 501s and shirt, to join the already naked Raphael.

"Well, I have a confession to make, Luke."

"Oh, yeah?"

"I had sex today at Safeway."

"What?"

"Yeah, in the checkout lane."

"Whaaat?"

"Yeah, kind of with the cashier, that cute guy who works out at the gym."

"Are you kidding me? In the checkout lane … at Safeway?"

"Okay, not exactly. Here, sit down so I can shave your sides. I'll explain." Raphael splashed some warm water on the sides of Luke's head and began rubbing shave gel all around Luke's head. "It's all your fault, you know."

"Of course it is," Luke said as he laughed. "It's always my fault, my faultless boy. So, start at the beginning and don't skip anything."

"I was in line, you know, a 20-minute line, 25 minutes … it's Safeway. So, I was bored and instead of reading the tabloids like some people do, I started edging myself with the Master plug I was wearing. You know, Luke, you were right, it *is* perfect for long term wear. I love wearing it."

"I know. I notice you're wearing it now. Back to the 'sex at Safeway story,' baby."

"Okay, so there I am, edging away with no one the wiser. Then, of course, this evil cage you got me, which is so beautiful by the way, starts playing with my cock as it gets harder. All this feels really good. So, I keep edging. Waiting in line, edging."

"That part I got. Get to the sex, baby!"

"I finally get to the head of the line, and I guess I over did it, because when that cute guy looks at me as he picks up my shopping bag, he says, 'Hey, handsome, good to see you.' And, I came."

"You came?"

"Yeah, right there, in the checkout lane, in front of the cute guy."

"Okay, that's ... funny. That's ridiculously funny. And, it's so like you. You have an amazing prostate, you know. Did he notice?"

"Oh, I think so, Luke."

"Why?"

"Because as he handed me the receipt, he said, and I quote, 'It was good for me, too. See you next time, sweetheart.'"

"That is amazing! I'll bet no one has ever had sex in the checkout lane at Safeway before."

"I wouldn't count on it, Luke. This is the Castro. But, uh, yeah, it was a first for me. And, like I said it's all your fault."

"You're welcome, baby. You're welcome. But this probably means we're going to have a pretty one-sided nap this evening."

"Don't count on it. Like you said, I have an amazing prostate. And, uh, a very sexy Sir."

Ten

RAPHAEL'S BEST DARE YET

MOVING DAY FINALLY ARRIVED. It was hard to tell who was more excited, Luke, Raphael, or for that matter, Steve. He had never been in on one of the dares, and he felt special to be included in this one. And, it was a doozy.

Raphael and Steve knocked on the door to Luke's shared Edwardian, then went on in without waiting. Luke was dressed in just a pair of shorts, knowing this was going to involve a little sweat. Raphael and Steve each were carrying broken down packing boxes and a roll of shipping tape. Raphael handed his to Luke and said, "You're in charge of your kitchen stuff since we don't know what's what. Steve and I will pack up your room."

"Yes, Sir," Luke replied, smiling at Raphael's in charge attitude. "Anything else, Sir?"

"Not at this time, Luke," Raphael smiled back. He was so excited about the coming dare it was going to be hard to concentrate on the task at hand.

While Luke toiled in the kitchen, Raphael and Steve packed and loaded boxes into the two cars. Then they joined Luke in the kitchen, who was just finishing up. "You guys done already?" Luke asked.

"Well, there were two of us," Steve answered. "And, I was working with the 'boss' here."

Luke looked around and said, "I guess I'm going to miss this place. But not for long." He planted a kiss on Raphael's cheek, then one on Steve's, who looked a bit surprised. "Hey, thanks for helping out, Steve. You didn't need to do this."

"Oh, I wouldn't have missed this for anything," Steve replied. "Happy to help. Very happy." Steve wasn't much of a poker player.

"Okay, men, let's do it," Raphael announced.

"Let me double check the bedroom," Luke said. "Be right out." In a gesture to placate his roommates for his sudden departure, Luke had decided to leave his bed and dresser behind for them to keep or resell. As Raphael and Steve went down the front stairs, they turned and grinned at each other. Everything was set for Raphael's most brazen dare yet.

Steve arrived first at Raphael's (and now Luke's) apartment. By the time they arrived he'd already unloaded everything ... almost. He helped Raphael and Luke carry in the boxes from Raphael's Zipcar, then the three were left standing in the living room.

"It's customary when someone helps you move, to feed them well," Raphael announced. "So, as soon as we return the cars, let's meet at Wooden Spoon, my treat. But first, ah, Steve, a little drum roll if you please." Steve drummed a short burst on the coffee table, then Raphael said, "Follow me, Sir. It's time for your next dare."

As the three walked into the bedroom, Luke said, "Hmm. We've never had a witness before ... well, except for Jake that first night. And, he was necessary for your first transformation."

"Just as Steve was instrumental to this dare, Sir. Behold, I have rearranged the closet for us. I have the left side and you shall have the right side." As he spoke, Raphael did his best impersonation of a game show hostess as he slid the closet door open to reveal ...

"What is this?" Luke asked, genuinely confused and surprised.

"This is your new wardrobe, Sir. I present to you eight kilts. Four Utilikilts, three Stumptown kilts and this, for special occasions." At that Raphael pulled out a genuine, Scottish-made regulation plaid kilt made with nine yards of wool.

"Is that what I think it is?"

"Yes, Sir, this was your grandfather's kilt in your family tartan. I called your Dad to get help on identifying your tartan, and he was thrilled to help. He'd been holding onto this, planning to give it to you one day as a family heirloom, so instead of directing me to someone who could make a kilt in your tartan, he sent me this to give you instead."

"Wow, you really went to a lot of work. You outdid yourself, Raphael. Thank you. This is ... this is really very thoughtful. I love it." Luke took the kilt from Raphael and found it was heavier than he expected. "I'll always cherish this. But, uh, why so many kilts? This one was more than enough." Steve, standing behind Luke, couldn't help but grin and wink at Raphael.

"Oh," Raphael said, "I guess I wasn't clear. This," he said, motioning to the kilts in the closet, "is your new wardrobe. No more pants, Sir, no more shorts, you are now my kilted Braveheart ... full time."

"Full time?"

"Correct. On the street, in the bars, at the Symphony, in the park, at the beach ... that's what this camo one is for, all kilts, all the time. Well, except you can still wear workout gear at the gym. No need to scare the natives when you lay down on a bench." At that, both Steve and Raphael laughed. Luke was still a bit behind the curve.

"No. More. Pants? Ever?"

"Yes, Sir, unless this is the dare you cannot accept." Raphael's face suddenly became quite serious. Had he gone too far? "Here, take off those shorts and try this on." He held out a black and grey Stumptown kilt. Luke looked over at Steve, who nodded gently and reached out to take Luke's tartan kilt, then his shorts. Luke wrapped the kilt around his waist and fumbled, not knowing how to fasten it. Raphael stepped forward and closed the snaps on either side of Luke's waist. He took a belt from the closet and threaded it through the belt loops and fastened it, while Luke stood still. Then Raphael stepped back, next to Steve and said, "Well, Steve?"

"Damn. Luke. You look hot as shit. Er, I mean, well, to quote Billy Crystal, 'you look mahvelous.'"

"He does, doesn't he?" Raphael stepped up to Luke and turned him to face the oft-used full length mirror. "You have to admit, Luke, you've got the legs for it."

Luke stared at himself, not quite believing what he was seeing. It did look sexy. He'd seen plenty of guys wearing kilts in the neighborhood, some on occasion, some exclusively. But, he'd never in a million years considered wearing a kilt himself. Let alone wearing kilts full time. Like, everywhere.

"Just to be sure I understand, baby. I don't get to wear pants anymore? Ever?"

In hopes of sealing the deal, Raphael looked into Luke's eyes as he reached up his right hand to fondle the stainless-steel collar around his neck. "How deep is your love, Luke?"

"You got me. You got me, you beautiful, brazen, too clever by a mile ... sneaky, I might add ... owner of my heart. I, uh, I guess I have no choice, do I?

"This is so beautiful," Steve spoke up. "Man, I wish I'd filmed that."

Ignoring Steve, Raphael took Luke in his arms and whispered in his ear. "Thank you, Sir. I knew you could do it." Then speaking normally, he said, "Okay. We can unpack later. We need to return the cars and take that awesome kilt for a test drive. And, then, as promised, lunch!"

Raphael and Luke returned their car in a different location from Steve's, and had a five-block walk to the restaurant. Luke was pensive.

"I think I now know how you felt the first time you went out in public with your collar. I feel very conspicuous. Is this your revenge?"

"Revenge? Hell, no. I wouldn't give up my collar, my cage or anything else for anything. They're all emblems of my love and devotion to you. I hope you'll feel the same way, you know, once you get used to it."

"Yeah, right, in a year or two."

Raphael laughed and fake punched Luke's biceps. "Grow up, big boy. You look great." Raphael's case was almost instantly supported as they walked along Market Street. Between the car and the restaurant, Luke was the recipient of 'nice kilt,' 'love the kilt,' 'awesome, man,' a couple more 'nice kilts.'

"Okay, this is nuts," Luke finally said. "Did you pay those people off?"

"No. And, you'd better get used to it, because ... you look mahvelous." For the first time since Raphael slid open the closet door, Luke laughed. A real laugh. "I'm glad you're laughing, Luke, because while we were returning the car, Steve was donating all your pants to the thrift store."

"Oh, really? Pretty sure of yourself, weren't you?"

"No. Pretty sure of you."

"Ah." Luke put his arm around Raphael's shoulders and said, "I guess this is why I love you. You make my life better, every single day."

"You're welcome, Sir. Let's go eat."

Eleven

Two Can Play This Game

Not a lot had changed since Luke had moved in with Raphael. He'd practically been living there the past few months anyway. Luke had taken a little ribbing initially at work about the kilts, but people in San Francisco are accustomed to the unusual, so the novelty quickly passed. Besides, going commando in kilts felt even better than in 501s. At home, both men had taken to wearing just their harnesses, when not completely naked, if you could describe Raphael in harness, collar, cage and plug as naked. It certainly made flirting and playing with each at a moment's notice easier.

It struck Luke as unfair, one night at one of their favorite leather bars, that Raphael, in leather codpiece shorts and tank was, in some ways, more 'normally' dressed than himself, in his camo kilt and leather vest and or t-shirt. Not that he minded wearing kilts anymore. The comfort, the attention were worth it, not to mention Raphael's somewhat lame trick of dropping something in the bar, just so he could crouch down and then raise up under the kilt to suck Luke's cock. Raphael thought he was being discrete, but nobody mistook what was really happening. One night, just to pimp Raphael, Luke fed him a little piss, right there in the middle of the bar. To his surprise, there was no reaction from Raphael. He just stood up and planted a big kiss on Luke that was a little juicier than usual. The boy could give as well as he took. Sometimes better.

Raphael's wardrobe dare was instrumental in helping Luke formulate his next dare for Raphael. An hour or so online was all it took to set the dare in motion. He texted Steve to get permission to have a couple of packages delivered at his and Niki's place until he was ready for the big reveal.

It was barely a week later, while Raphael and Luke were relaxing in the steam room after another intense workout, when Steve wandered in.

Luke scooted over on his bench to make room, and Steve stripped off his towel and placed it next to Luke, then sat down on it.

"Where's Niki?"

"He's finishing up his cardio. How are you guys doing?"

"Excellent." Raphael sighed from the adjoining bench.

"You still liking that new cage?" Steve asked.

"You kidding? I love it."

"Especially at Safeway, right baby?"

"Luke!" Raphael slapped Luke's glistening thigh.

"Safeway?"

"Never mind, Steve. It's nothing."

"It doesn't sound like nothing. Come on, what about Safeway and your cage?"

"Another time, Steve, in a more private place. Maybe after a bottle of Cab." Raphael laid back on his bench, eyes closed, enjoying the steam.

"I'll hold you to it, Raphael," Steve said in a normal voice. Then, leaning over to Luke's ear he whispered, "Your packages are here."

Luke nodded, then whispered back, "Free tomorrow evening? Around six?" Steve nodded. "Bring them then." Steve nodded again. That's when Niki entered the steam room and sat down next to Steve. He kept his towel around his narrow waist in case someone else entered the room. After all this time he was still self-conscious about being naked at the gym.

"Hi, guys," he said.

Raphael sat up and responded, "Niki! How was your workout?"

"Fine thanks. Yours'?" Luke and Raphael both nodded wordlessly.

After a few moments of silence, Niki spoke again. "So, do you ever take that collar thing off?"

"No, Niki. Like the cage, it's permanent."

"I see," Niki replied, almost sadly. Raphael looked at Luke and rolled his eyes. Not knowing quite what to say, Raphael let it go. Someday he'd have to have a real heart-to-heart with Niki about his relationship with Luke but not here and not now. Raphael got up and, unlike Niki, wrapped his towel around his neck as he walked naked out of the steam room, proudly displaying his caged cock to anyone who cared to see. Luke followed, putting his arm around Raphael as they entered the crowded locker room.

Niki, one tier below where Steve was still sitting, moved closer to Steve and put his arm on Steve's thigh, brushing Steve's cock in the process. Steve reached down and massaged Niki's head. "Hungry, babe?"

"Yeah, I guess so. Mama Ji's?"

"Yeah, Mama Ji's."

The following evening, Luke got home before Raphael. He'd stripped as usual, slipped into his harness and opened a bottle of Sauvignon Blanc to go with tonight's delicious dare. As he was unwrapping a wedge of St. Andre triple cream cheese, Raphael opened the door.

"Mmmm," Raphael said through the kiss with Luke. "This is wrong, me clothed, you naked, Sir."

"Not wrong, babe, just premature. Let's get you out of those awful street clothes." Luke reached down and grabbed Raphael's polo shirt at the waist and pulled it up as Raphael lifted his arms to assist.

"Oh, oh," Luke said.

"What?"

"Look ... there's a hole under each of the arms of your shirt."

"Yeah. I guess I need to find a less toxic deodorant."

"I don't think it's your deodorant. You wear your shirts until they fall off of you in despair."

"I guess. I just hate shopping. You know that." Raphael proceeded to pull off his street pants and jock, and walked to the bedroom and opened the closet to retrieve his harness. He was already plugged and had been all day. The two walked into the kitchen where Luke handed Raphael his glass of wine. Just as Raphael sliced off a bit of cheese to go with it, the doorbell rang.

"I'll get it," Luke said punctuating the sentence with a wine flavored peck on Raphael's cheek. He walked into the living room and opened the door to a broadly smiling Steve. "Steve!" Luke said in mock surprise. "Come on in."

Steve handed the packages to Luke and walked into the apartment a bit tentatively. Raphael entered the room at the same time, holding his glass of wine. "Hey, Steve. Want some wine?"

"Oh, I probably shouldn't stay. Looks like you guys are, um, busy."

"Not at all," Luke offered. "Stay, I'd like you to be here for this, just as you were for my, ah, wardrobe premiere."

"What?" Raphael said, sitting his glass down on the coffee table while eyeing the packages in Luke's hands. "Is this what I think it is? Are you two colluding on ... a dare?"

"Busted," Luke laughed. "Baby, get Steve a glass, and Steve, don't make us feel self-conscious. Take off your clothes."

"Do you guys ever wear clothes at home?"

"Only when we have company, and you're not company. You're family. Strip, sit, here have some wine and enjoy."

"Well, if you insist." Steve was naked in a flash. He took the glass of wine from Raphael and settled into a spot on the couch.

"So, Luke, tell us about this next dare," Raphael directed to Luke who was still holding the packages. He set them down, took Raphael by the shoulders and grinned what could only be described as a diabolic smile.

"Raphael, my boy, you really took things up a notch with the kilts. Not that I'm complaining, but I have to say it was genius. Very impressive. I didn't know how I could top it ... but, I just may have succeeded. As you were saying before Steve got here, you hate to shop for clothes, so I decided to do it for you."

Luke took the cheese knife from the coffee table where Raphael had placed the snack for everyone to enjoy, and cut open one of the packages. He pulled out a stack of t-shirts in a variety of colors and handed a hot pink one to Raphael. "Here try this on."

Raphael fed his arms through the arm holes and pulled it over his head, As he smoothed it over his torso, he looked over at Steve who's eyes widened to saucers. Raphael looked down at himself and saw there was a black inked graphic on the front of the shirt, but he really couldn't tell what exactly it was. Luke was smiling broadly. Steve simply said, "Oh, boy."

"What?" Raphael asked. "What?"

"Come look in the mirror, baby." Luke took Raphael by the hand and led him into the bedroom. Steve leapt up and was right behind. Raphael stepped in front of the full-length mirror and there, looking back at him was a half-naked caged man wearing a hot pink tee with a graphic that he'd never seen before ... a bird cage with a rooster inside.

"I don't get it." Raphael looked at Luke. Luke looked at Steve, who put his hand over his grinning mouth.

"Luke, you are evil," Steve said.

"What?!? What?" Raphael pleaded.

"Raphael, there's a caged cock on your shirt," Steve explained. "Oh, wow. It's awesome, Luke!"

"Ohhhhhhh. Of course. You *are* evil, Luke," Raphael said. "Cute! I love it. Very clever. I love it." Raphael walked back into the living room, trailed by Luke and Steve. Raphael picked up the stack of other tees, seeing that every one had the same caged cock graphic. "This'll be fun to wear at the bars. But you shouldn't have bought so many."

"Well, baby, I had to, since these are the only casual shirts you'll be wearing from now on. To the bars, to restaurants, SFMOMA, the beach ..."

"Oh, no. You don't mean..."

"I do. You kilted me for everywhere. I've shirted you for everywhere, too, baby. In fact, let's see what's in this package." Luke ripped open the second package and pulled out a dozen classy, two button, cotton polo shirts, each with a small caged cock logo right over the left nipple, where a Tommy Hilfiger logo would be.

"This is your new work wardrobe, Raphael. A couple of long sleeve dress shirts, appropriately embroidered, for more formal occasions are on their way, too."

"Fuuuuck. I mean, whoa. Seriously?" Raphael stood there, holding the stack of shirts.

"It's none of my business," Steve finally spoke, "but, I think it's you. It's totally you, Raphael."

"I guess I asked for this, didn't I, kilt boy?"

"You did," Luke replied. "You really, really did. But. Steve's right. It's totally you. Now, put on some shorts and let's take that hot pink shirt for a test drive, well, test walk, to Sausage Factory. Steve, you and Niki wanna join us?"

"You bet. I'm dying to see if anyone notices."

"Oh, man," Raphael said. "I'll never live this down."

Not surprisingly, no one took a second look at Raphael's tee. Every other guy on the street and in the restaurant was wearing a graphic print of some sort. After a while, Raphael relaxed. Since even he hadn't caught on right away to the meaning of the caged cock, it stood to reason that the uninitiated wouldn't either. Unlike the many acknowledgments Luke received every time he left the house in one of his kilts, Raphael's shirt was basically unnoticeable.

The next morning, Raphael debated, then selected a teal polo with a dark blue embroidery. The caged cock was most subtle in this color combination. "If anyone asks, just tell them it's a popular Australian brand that I got for you. People expect unusual things like dingoes and wallabies from there," Luke advised, prior to his goodbye kiss for the day. Raphael thought that sounded plausible. And, he did get a few comments, if only because it was unusual to see him in new clothes. Perhaps it was common knowledge that Raphael was not much of a shopper.

Raphael's flight under the radar came crashing down mid-afternoon, however, when one of the tech support guys came by to add a new app to Raphael's PC. They'd interacted many times in the past, so Raphael automatically stood up when he arrived at his cube.

"Hey, Raphael, how's it going."

"Fine, thanks, Alex. Busy, of course. Should I take a break, or will this be quick?"

"Less than five," Alex said as he glanced down at Raphael's shirt. Alex's smile widened, and he looked directly into Raphael's eyes when he said, "Why don't you stay right here and keep me company."

"Sure." Raphael didn't mind. Alex was everyone's favorite tech guy, often requested by name. And, it wasn't just because of his technical skills. Women in the office, and more than a few of the guys, never seemed to mind when Alex came around with an update.

Without looking up from Raphael's monitor as he navigated the PC, Alex asked, "So, Raphael, plastic or metal?"

"Huh?"

"Are you wearing plastic or metal?"

It took a second for Raphael to switch gears and realize Alex wasn't talking tech. Alex was getting very personal. Raphael cleared his throat, then knelt down level with Alex so he could reply without being overheard.

"How did you know? Is ... is it that obvious?"

"It is to me, Raphael. I'm locked in a V3 Nano. Have been for, well, since it came out. I've been locked for over three years now."

"Seriously? That's awesome! I never would have guessed,"

"Me, either. But, it's good to know. I love your shirt. Know where I can get one?"

"No, but Luke does. Maybe you should come by sometime, you know, for drinks or something."

"I'd like that. Can I bring my husband ... he's also my keyholder."

"I think you should, He and Luke can compare notes while we do the same."

"I'm really looking forward to it, Raphael." Then louder and more professionally, Alex said, "You're all set, Raphael. Thanks again for letting me disturb you."

"Anytime," Raphael grinned in return. "Anytime."

"By the way, Raphael, you didn't answer my question."

It took Raphael a second to realize what Alex meant, then smiled and said, "Metal. Of course."

"Awesome. We do need to compare notes."

Twelve

MORE OF A BRAVEHEART

BY THE BEGINNING OF September Raphael hardly gave a thought to the locked cock shirts, just as Luke had adapted to wearing the kilts full time. Luke still got plenty of affirmation from people everywhere he went, and that's something he would probably never get used to. He was accustomed to guys checking out Raphael instead. Now, the attention was more equally shared, and that was just fine with Luke. Who doesn't enjoy being noticed?

Raphael got a kick out of it, too. He liked being seen hand in hand with a handsome guy who garnered comments and high-fives. Not that he needed to be reminded that there was more to Luke than his heart, his mind and that very much appreciated 'dick of death.' They'd been living together more than a month now, and it was all good. In fact, it was so good, Raphael was having trouble coming up with a new dare to spring on Luke. Everything was fine, just the way it was.

Then, one afternoon, as they were finishing up their workout at the gym, Raphael noticed a guy he'd seen before on occasion. He was tall, like Luke, with a similar complexion. And, he sported a full, lush Nordic-like beard. On Raphael, it would have looked ridiculous, if he had even been capable of growing that much facial hair. But, on this guy, it looked damn sexy.

That evening, as they were midway through their daily head shave and shower ritual, Raphael made his move.

"Ready for your next dare, Sir?"

"Finally. I thought maybe now that you've ensnared me in your nest, that you had no more use for devotion testing dares."

"Well, yeah, I don't think either of us questions how we feel about each other any longer. Do we?"

"No, baby, I don't think so. It's pretty clear to me, and I think to everybody we know, that we were meant for each other. Not to sound cliché, but you really do complete me."

"And, you, me," Raphael said as he bent forward and locked lips with Luke. As he pulled away, he continued, "But I do love playing games with you, testing you, stretching you, making you into an even sexier guy than you already are."

"Well, that goes double for me, even though you were already a "ten" when we started."

"You are such a comedian. We both know I was only a nine point nine." Both men laughed. Despite his looks, Raphael was anything but vain. "Anyway, your dare, Sir, is to stop shaving your face for a month. I want to see how you look with a beard."

"Really? That's unexpected. Are you sure? What if it looks horrible?"

"Then I'll never want to be seen in public with you again." Luke laughed. "No, really, I think you would look really hot, and if not, we shave it off. Unlike my cage, my collar, my piercings ... which by the way I seem to have accumulated more than you ... your piercing, oh, and of course your kilt wardrobe, the beard doesn't have to be permanent. If I don't like it, it goes. But if I do ... you can't shave it off. That's your dare. October 1 will be decision day.

"Can I at least trim it during that time?"

"Nope. Well, maybe, but I decide. It may be growing on your face, but it's my beard."

"Yes, Sir."

The first week or so was the worst for Luke. His ginger/blond hair made his face look more dirty than butch initially. He really hated how it looked, but Raphael was enraptured, so what could he do. Raphael liked to stroke it with his hands and even with his cheeks.

"Mmmm," he'd say. "Feels so scratchy, but manly. My manly, Braveheart man." Then he'd kiss the fuck out of Luke. It really seemed to turn Raphael on, so, at least there was that.

"It looks like shit."

"It's not done! Just be patient. Only three more weeks to go."

Then, "Only two more weeks to go."

Followed by, "Only one more week to go."

Of course, by then it had really filled out. Pretty nicely too. Luke had to admit, it didn't look bad. And, Raphael couldn't leave it alone. He made love to the beard almost as much as he did to Luke's cock, maybe because it was no longer scratchy, but soft and cuddly. Whatever, Raphael was enraptured, and that was just fine with Luke.

As the deadline on the fate of the beard approached, so did the date of the Folsom Street Fair, the leather/kink street fair that attracts 250,000 kinksters from around the world. It hadn't come up in conversation yet, but Luke was fully aware, having been several times.

So it was, one night, as the two were falling asleep, spooning in bed, with Luke behind Raphael, his arm draped over Raphael's chest, as he lightly fingered the ring in Raphael's left nipple, and Raphael reveled in the feel of Luke's beard brushing the back of his neck and shoulders, that Luke muttered, "You know what this Sunday is."

"Judgement day for the beard, right?"

"Almost, and actually I think that ship has already sailed. But, no, what I meant was it's the Folsom Street Fair."

"Oh, right. Why, do you think we should go?" Luke and Raphael had only been casually dating at the time of last year's fair.

"You've never gone, have you?" Luke asked.

"No, I mean I've wanted to, you know, been curious, but one thing or another has always interfered."

"Well, baby," Luke said as he pulled Raphael into an even tighter embrace and kissed the back of his shaven head, "of course I think we should go. Where else should a collared, caged, plugged and harnessed boy and his mohawked and dick-pierced fiancé go on a sunny Sunday in September in San Francisco?"

"Welllll, when you put it like that, the question pretty much answers itself, doesn't it, Sir?"

"Then it's a date. It'll be fun sharing it with you. I think it'll be a very memorable day for you."

"Mmmmm. Sounds good. Should be fun." Raphael yawned and sank further into Luke's embrace. As his breathing slowed, Luke, too, drifted off to sleep.

Thirteen

RAPHAEL'S FIRST FOLSOM

As they finished brunch out that Sunday, Raphael asked Luke, "When did you want to go to the Fair? And, what should we wear? Anything goes, right?"

"I think for your first outing we should go relatively early. It won't be as crowded as it will be later in the afternoon, and not as hot either. Maybe one. Let's go home, relax for an hour, then get ready and go."

And so they did. At twelve-thirty, Luke found Raphael in the bedroom, with an array of clothing items on the bed. A little lycra workout gear, short shorts, several tank tops, his leather lace up codpiece shorts among them. "What do you think, Luke? I don't want to stand out."

"First of all, you're going to stand out, trust me, despite the fact there will be a couple hundred thousand people there. Besides the harness you're already wearing, those codpiece shorts will be perfect. Here, wear this mesh tee over the harness for the MUNI ride, but once we get there, you'll probably want to take it off. Before you dress, though, take off the harness so I can coat you in sunscreen, head to toe."

"Good idea." A full body coating seemed unnecessary, but Raphael wasn't about to turn down a full body rubdown from Luke. "Mmmm, now I smell tropical. So, what are you wearing?"

"I'm thinking my body harness, too, and the camo kilt. We'll make a striking couple, don't you think? Okay, my turn, here, give me the works." Raphael applied a generous coat of sunscreen to Luke's naked body, giving special attention to his thickening cock. "I don't think that's going to get much sun, baby."

"You can never be too careful, Sir," Raphael said, as he knelt down to be sure he didn't miss an inch. He licked the tip of Luke's pierced cock, because that's what good boys do. "Okay, we'd either better get dressed, Sir, or get on the bed. Your choice."

"Dressed. We'll save the bed for later. I'm excited for our first Folsom together."

"Me, too," Raphael tossed over his shoulder as headed into the bathroom for a last-minute pee. Luke snapped his body harness in place then quickly strapped on his mesh codpiece thong jock before wrapping the kilt around his waist. Raphael returned, snapped on his body harness and pulled on and laced up his codpiece shorts. Luke also stuffed his and Raphael's IDs, Clipper cards and some cash in a leather wrist band and snapped it on his left arm. He and Raphael pulled on almost matching mesh tees and boots and headed for the door. On the way, Luke grabbed one of his backpacks. "Why are you taking that?"

"Oh, just in case we see some things in the booths that we just can't live without. You, know, a giant dildo or a latex corset."

"They'll have those there?"

"Sweetie, they'll have everything there."

"Maybe I should get my American Express card, too."

Luke laughed and pushed Raphael toward the door. Arm in arm, and rather spectacularly clad, they made their way to the street car stop. As they boarded the car, few eyes even turned their way. It was Folsom Sunday, and everyone in San Francisco had seen it all before. In fact, there were several guys in bare-assed chaps, and even less, already on board.

In no time they arrived at their stop on Market. Along with a dozen or so other leathered passengers they made the three-block walk to one of the entrances to the Fair. After paying their donations to the two Sisters of Perpetual Indulgence on duty at the gate, Luke re-snapped his wrist band and took Raphael by the hand.

"Okay, Sir, where to first?"

"Our first stop is right over here." Luke led Raphael to a canopied booth sporting a banner that read "Clothing Check." Luke stopped, slid his backpack to the ground and opened it. He then pulled off his shirt and stowed it in the bag. Raphael did the same. Then Luke unsnapped the kilt, revealing the codpiece and placed the kilt in the bag.

"Oh, you're kind of doing the full Monty, eh, Sir?"

"As are you, my boy. Take off your shorts."

'But, I'd be naked."

"Not really. You're harnessed, collared and caged, and plugged as I recall. But, not naked."

"Umm, that's pretty naked."

"Oh, sorry, I forgot to say, 'Welcome to your next dare, baby!' You're doing Folsom naked."

"You bastard! ... Sir. Seriously? What if, what if..."

"What if what? You're at Folsom. Half the people here are naked, or damn close. What's the worst that could happen?"

"The worst? That I'd run into my Mama? Okay, that's pretty unlikely. Run into somebody from work?"

"And? If you run into somebody from work, what does that tell you about that somebody?"

Raphael hesitated before answering, "That they're just as kinky as you, I guess."

"As kinky as us, Raphael. Exactly. You go to the beach caged and naked all the time. You relax in the gym steam room naked and caged all the time. This is no different. Except we're with hundreds of thousands of other naked kinky people." Luke put his hands on each of Raphael's naked shoulders, pulled him close and kissed him. "Relax, baby, and enjoy. Now, give me those shorts."

And he did. Luke handed the backpack to the volunteer in the booth, received the ticket and put his arm around Raphael's shoulder as the two walked away from their clothes. "How come I always have to be the naked one?" Raphael asked, with just a little whine in his voice.

"Because you're the beautiful one, baby. I bet you dinner you get at least a hundred compliments today."

"Deal. And, uh, what if they lose your backpack back there?"

"Then you'll probably get another hundred compliments on the walk home."

"Ha. Small comfort."

As they strolled the Fair, Raphael began to relax. There really were plenty of naked people, guys in skimpy jocks, in bare-assed chaps and bare-assed shorts. Guys in puppy gear, complete with puppy tail butt plugs, so he didn't feel so exposed any longer. True, his exposed cock was caged rather than totally naked, but they even encountered a few other guys who were clearly caged. Some were as naked as Raphael; others' cages were half-heartedly hidden under flimsy jocks. It was more than Raphael had expected, and soon he was totally at ease. The fact that Luke was right, that hardly two minutes passed between compliments, or requests to take a picture of the two of them or of Raphael alone, certainly helped. Folsom was awesome.

After an hour or so, Luke suggested getting a couple of beers. As they stood against the wall of a building to escape the crush of the already growing crowd, two men in matching leather jocks walked up to them. The one wearing the leather 'lone ranger' style mask grinned broadly and said, "Raphael, you look fucking amazing!"

"Uh, thanks. Do I know you?"

"Sorry, it's me, Alex," Alex said as he pulled off the mask.

"Alex! Oh, wow! You look great, too. Alex, this is my fiancé, Luke. Luke, this is Alex from work."

"And this is my husband, Greg." Greetings and hand-shakes followed.

'Damn, Raphael, you have more guts than I ever would have imagined, walking around naked like this."

"Well, it's not like I had a choice."

"How's that?"

"This was Luke's decision."

"Whoa. What other decisions has this handsome man made for you?" Greg asked, giving Luke a big grin.

"Quite a few, actually."

"So, Luke is your fiancé, and your Master?"

"No, it's not like that. I make quite a few decisions for Luke, too. We think of it as kind of a mutual ownership thing."

"That's interesting," Alex said. "Tell me more!"

"Maybe another time ... it's kind of a long story."

"And obviously an interesting one. I'll hold you to that. Raphael, can I look at your cage closer?"

"Oh, sure." As Alex squatted down to take the Looker in his hands to examine it, Raphael turned to Luke. "Alex is caged, too, with a Holy Trainer."

"Fair is fair, Alex," Luke said. "Let's see your cage."

"Here, on the street? I don't think so."

"Alex, you're standing there, bare-assed in a crowd of naked and nearly naked people. Nobody's going to notice."

"Okay ... I guess I can't argue," Alex said, as he stood up and unsnapped his codpiece and pulled it aside.

"Very nice," Luke said as he squatted down to inspect Alex's locked cock more closely. "I see you shave, too."

"Yeah, once a week when the cage comes off for cleaning."

"Looks great. Do you shave, too, Greg?"

"No, Alex likes my bush. So, Raphael, how long have you been caged?"

"Nine months, since New Year's."

"Cool. Alex has been caged, what, over three years now. Raphael, how often do you take your cage off for cleaning and shaving?"

"It doesn't come off. And, Luke shaves me, head and pubes. And I shave him. Head and pubes. It's kind of a ritual for us."

"That's sweet," Alex said. "But seriously, your cage never comes off?"

"Nope. We don't even have access to the keys to the cage or my collar."

"You're kidding!"

"They're stored at Mr. S, with their keyholder service," Luke explained. "I started Raphael in a Holy Trainer similar to what you're wearing, but he was always complaining about not wanting to take if off for cleaning, so, I got him the Looker 01 so we could keep him clean and caged permanently. He's a lot happier now."

"So, you guys shave each other every week? That's really hot."

"Oh, no, Alex, we shave each other every day. At least the heads. The pubes every few days. Yeah, like I said it's a ritual for us. Before, Luke had to take off the Holy Trainer and clean me every week. So, this is a time saver."

"Wait, Luke does your cleaning?"

"Yeah I haven't touched by cock since New Year's. Only Luke touches it. Only now, even he doesn't."

"So that must put a crimp in your sex life," Greg said, looking at Raphael.

"Hardly," Luke replied. "You feel deprived, baby?"

"Hell, no. Luke is an amazing lover. I wouldn't change a thing. His cock is all the cock I need."

"Okay, this is an incredibly personal question, Raphael, but I'm going to ask it anyway, considering our surroundings. Do you really come often enough permanently caged," Alex asked.

"He comes all the time, usually more than I do," Luke laughed. "Even in line at Safeway." Raphael made a cringing face at that, and looked sheepishly at Alex.

"Ignore him."

"Not likely," Greg said. "You gotta explain that to us."

"Some other time," Raphael said. "You guys are embarrassing me. But, seriously, Greg, I have no complaints. Our relationship, our sex life, is more than anything I ever thought I'd be lucky enough to experience. And, it's all because of Luke."

"Listen," Alex said, "you guys are just amazing. I mean, look at you both. Raphael, I never would have dreamed the cute guy in Cubical 83 was this harnessed, pierced, collared, cock locked beauty, brave enough to show it all off with his hunky fiancé on the streets of SOMA."

"Look who's talking? You're the reason all of the women and half the men make up tech issues just so they can spend time with you. I certainly wouldn't have guessed you were locked."

"Yeah. I guess we can thank Luke for that, huh?"

"What do you mean," Luke asked?

"The locked cock wardrobe you got me," Raphael explained. "A dead giveaway to Alex, here."

"See, I told you it would be good for you, baby."

"Raphael, tell me more about this bit about staff making up tech issues ..."

"Another time, Alex. You know what, I think we have a lot of subjects to talk about. We should get together for brunch or dinner or something sometime."

"Yes, we should," Greg responded. I'd love to get to know you guys better."

"Let's work it out, Raphael," Alex offered as he strapped his codpiece back on.

"You know there's a clothing check down that way, Alex," Luke suggested. "You really look better with that codpiece off."

"Aw, thanks. But I don't think so. Maybe next year. I'm not as uninhibited as Raphael."

"Something to work on," Luke said, pulling Raphael closer.

"Maybe you can give me some pointers," Greg laughed as he and Alex started walking away. Greg slid his arm around Alex's waist as they walked. He looked over his shoulder and shouted, "Nice meeting you! See you soon!"

Luke looked at Raphael, and they both smiled. "Raphael, my boy, I think you could be a good influence on your colleague Alex."

"Could be. I think they could become good friends. And, as usual, I owe it all to you."

"You're welcome, baby." And with that, Luke planted a sunscreen flavored kiss on Raphael's waiting lips.

Fourteen

———✦———

FANCY MEETING YOU HERE

LUKE AND RAPHAEL FINISHED their beers and set out to further explore the Fair. For a first timer like Raphael, it was overwhelming. The crowd alone was worth the price of admission. He'd never seen so many bare asses in one place in his life, including the beach. And, much like the beach, they came in all shapes, sizes and colors. There were plenty of topless women, too, lesbians and straight, which further added to the kinkiness of the experience.

Then, there were the experiences. Naked twister on an elevated stage, emceed by a naked guy with an unflagging boner. Flogging demonstrations. Spanking demonstrations. Go-go boys in suspended cages over a side street dance floor. Musicians on stages, many of whom were in kinky attire themselves.

And hundreds of booths selling and promoting everything imaginable, just as Luke had said. Luke insisted Raphael try on a ruby red leather corset in one booth. The attendant took his time lacing Raphael up in the back, winking at Luke as he did so. Raphael was his first naked cock-locked customer of the day, and he saw no reason to rush. Once corseted, Raphael modeled it around the booth, doing a couple of three-sixty's in front of the tall mirror.

"Looks damn good on you, man," the attendant said.

"Oh, you say that to all the boys," was Raphael's reply.

"He's right, baby. As a wise and lovely man once said, not that long ago, 'you look mahvelous.'"

"Your turn, Luke I want to see one on you. How about this black one ... would that fit him?"

"Let's try this one," the attendant countered, pulling one from further back in the rack. "Turn around, Sir." Even though he'd never met them before, he intuitively knew to call Luke 'Sir.'

Laced up, Luke looked perfect. "God, Luke, it makes your back look even more V-shaped than usual. And, it really highlights your ass!" Raphael cupped each of Luke's ass cheeks in his hands and rubbed. Luke's mesh thong jock bulged in response.

"Better stop that, boy, you're going to get us in trouble."

The attendant laughed. "Trouble is fine with me. You guys both look great. Will you be wearing them home?" Both Luke and Raphael laughed. The corsets were sexy, but they covered a lot of flesh, flesh that was better exposed and accessible to touch and kiss and to lick.

"Let us think about it," Luke replied. "You've been great. We still need to see more of the Fair first." The attendant was a good sport, as he unlaced the guys. Feeling badly for him, Raphael gave him a big hug before leaving the booth, along with a peck on the cheek. "Thank you and have a good Fair."

Later, as they stood watching someone who was tied up facing a St. Andrew's cross, getting paddled by a guy in a leather jock who might have been his partner, Luke leaned over to Raphael and said, "Remember how good that felt?'

"Mmmm. I do. It was pretty incredible."

"Wanna do it again, here, for all your fans?"

"Do I want to do it again? Yeah. But, not right now. There's still a lot of Folsom to see."

"Fair enough ... no pun intended."

"Ha ha." Before he could say anything else, a guy in the paddling booth walked up and handed Luke a paddle. Luke took it and landed a couple of smacks on his naked boy's butt, before handing it back. "Thanks," Raphael said to the man, "but we're just looking today."

"Ha," Luke said "Now who's the funny one." They turned and started away from the booth when they saw Niki and Steve walking toward them. Steve was modestly attired in leather shorts, but was at least bare chested. Niki was in jeans and white mesh crop top, so showing a little skin, but not much. Steve was smiling broadly; Niki was not.

"Hey, guys, looking hella sexy as always. I see you're wearing your house coat, Raphael."

"What?" Niki asked.

"Umm, nothing," Steve replied. He put his arm around Niki's waist and pulled him closer. "Enjoying the Fair?"

"We are!" Raphael said, taking notice of Niki's facial expression as he spoke. "It's my first time, and I love it."

"Well, you certainly don't look like a first timer." Steve laughed.

"Aren't you even a little embarrassed?" Niki said, making it sound more like an accusation than a question.

"About what?" Raphael directed back.

"Oh, I don't know. Maybe being naked in public, where everyone can see that chastity cage?"

'No, Niki, I'm not embarrassed. I have nothing to be embarrassed about. I'm proud to be Luke's locked cock boy, and I want everybody to know it."

"Oh, Okay. Whatever. See you guys later." At that, Niki slipped out of Steve's hold and started walking away.

"Sorry guys. I think you look awesome. I better go catch Niki before he gets lost. Again." Steve took off after Niki as Luke and Raphael turned to each other.

"What is wrong with Niki?" Luke pleaded. "I haven't seen him smile in a long time."

"Yeah, I know. I really need to have a talk with him."

"I think you're right. But for now, we either need to find an indoor space or go visit the sunscreen booth and get another application."

"Hmmm. You mean have some hunky guy smear lotion all over my body while you watch?" Luke nodded. "I vote for that!"

Fifteen

NIKI SENDS A TEXT

THE FOLLOWING SUNDAY LUKE and Raphael were stretched out on the couch, drinking coffee and munching bagels as Luke flicked through his tablet and Raphael, old school, dug through the Sunday *Chronicle*. Although their heads were at opposite ends of the couch, each man had a playful foot in the other's bare crotch, so they felt very connected.

Raphael's phone chimed a Temple Bell, announcing a text from his brother, Angel. Raphael unlocked and retrieved the text. It took a few seconds for the message to sink in. "Holy shit."

"What?" Luke looked up. "What happened?"

"Niki sent a text to Angel. He forwarded it to me." Raphael handed his phone to Luke.

"Jesus. Looks like you didn't have that talk with Niki soon enough."

"No doubt. This. Sucks."

The text in the message was brief. The real stunner was the accompanying pic, which showed an essentially naked Luke smacking an essentially naked Raphael on the ass with a paddle, on a public street. At least Raphael's crotch was facing away, concealing his cage. The text read:

'Did you know Luke has made Raphael his sex slave? Collared, chastity cage, kept naked and on a leash.'

Angel's comment in the message was even briefer: *'Should we talk?'*

Luke handed the phone back to Raphael, who clicked on Angel's contact icon. "Want me to leave the room?"

"No, please, no. I need you here for this." When Angel answered, Raphael didn't even say hello. "Thanks for the text. Luke's here, too. Let's talk. I didn't know you and Niki kept in touch that much."

"We don't, really. Not as much as we should. So, it was kind of a surprise. So, what exactly is going on?"

"Well, first of all, you do realize where that photo was taken don't you? And, without permission, I might add."

"I guess I didn't look that closely. I barely recognized you without your hair. When did you cut it?"

"Months ago. Long story. Luke and I were at the Folsom Street Fair when Niki took that photo."

"Ah, sure, now I see. That explains all the kinky people in the background. I thought maybe you guys were, you know, hosting an orgy."

"Yeah, that would be us," Luke said. "Gay equals orgy, right?"

"I was kidding, Luke. So, you guys were fooling around at Folsom. Makes sense. But, why would Niki say you've become Luke's sex slave? And, uh, where's this famous leash?"

"There is no leash. Niki's embellishing. A lot. I'll be honest with you, Angel, Luke and I have been exploring some things that, uh, well, let's just say they're not 'vanilla.' But, it's all consensual. Slavery is definitely not involved. We're falling in love, Angel. In fact, I wasn't ready to announce it yet, so please don't say anything ... I want Mama to hear it from me, but we're engaged. I'm going to make this man my husband!"

"Whoa! Seriously? That's awesome! Congratulations, guys!"

"Thanks," Luke and Raphael said in unison.

"You know," Angel said next, "I think I know what's going on here ... with Niki. You've always been his hero, Raphael, his big brother. His idol, really. I don't think I ever told you, but Niki and I talked a lot when Mama and Pop first took him in after his parents threw him out. You know, he came out because of you."

"What? What did I do?"

"You came out. At fourteen. To everybody. And, nothing changed. Mama and Pop didn't judge you. In fact, Mama told me shortly after you came out that she always knew you were gay, and was finally glad you were being honest with her. Funny thing, she told me it would be okay if I was gay, too."

"Sounds like Mama."

"Anyway, Niki saw how much happier you were, and how well things went for you, so he got the courage to do the same thing. Except, his parents weren't our parents."

"Wow. So, he went through hell because of me."

"It wasn't your fault. You were just an ideal role model in an imperfect world. On the bright side, we all saved him. Mama didn't hesitate to take him in. He traded a dysfunctional family for a loving one. Even though he and I were the same age and in many of the same classes, you're the one he felt closest to, you both being queer and all."

"Well, he always was my favorite brother."

"Fuck you,' Angel laughed. "But my point is, I do think that's at the heart of this text. He's losing his queer brother. You were always there for him back then. He probably never would have made it without you. It's hard being young, black and queer. You helped a lot."

"Angel, I feel awful. I was getting tired of his mopey attitude, and then this text ... I was pissed when I read it. Now, I just want to hug the little bastard."

"You should, but maybe without the bastard reference. A little too close to home."

"You know what, Angel? I'm glad Niki texted you. It was a cry for help, one that I needed to hear. I've been so focused on Luke that I've been oblivious to what's really going on with Niki."

"He's still seeing that guy, right?"

"Yeah, Steve. Steve's a great guy, and they're getting pretty serious. Serious enough that they're living together. I just need to fix things between Niki and me, so Niki can be more like his old self with Steve. I have some work to do."

"Well, I can't think of anyone better than you to fix Niki. He'll do anything you ask."

"By the way," Raphael said, "speaking of changes, when did you get that awesome little septum piercing?"

"Septum piercing?" Luke exclaimed. "Let me see!" He and Raphael scooted together on the couch so Luke could look at the screen.

"Are you two naked? And wearing leather?"

"Yeah, we're always naked at home. Like I said, we're having fun and exploring. And, it's consensual!"

"Okay! No judgement here, just, you know, a little surprised to see naked guys on my phone."

"You should see my phone."

"Ha, ha. No doubt. No, I got it pierced a few months back. Like it?"

"Very much. It's sexy."

"Only a gay brother would call his straight brother sexy."

"As well as his gay brother-in-law-to-be," Luke chimed in. "It is sexy, Angel."

"You guys are too much. Maybe you should think of getting a piercing, Raphael."

'Ha," Luke barked, grinning at Raphael. "Maybe he should, Angel."

"Alright, you guys. We should go, we have to figure out what do about Niki. Thanks again, Angel. Love you."

"Love you too, Raphael. You too, Luke. Don't forget to invite me to the wedding!"

"Hell, you'll be in it, Angel," Luke shot back. "Bye." Raphael put the phone down. "That was intense."

"Not as intense as the night Niki's parents threw him out. I guess I never realized the impact I had on him. I remember that night. Niki, who was still going by 'Nicholas' at the time, showed up at our door in tears. He didn't know where to go, what to do. Luke, he was this little 14-year-old queer black boy suddenly on his own. Huh, I hadn't thought about it before ... he came out at the same age I did."

"Angel's right. He emulated you."

"I guess. Mama was pissed. Not at him, at his parents. She was amazing. She held him in her arms and told him everything would be fine. That he wasn't alone. We all sat around the table while she fed him warmed up dinner 'cause we'd already eaten. She said things like, 'you home now. We your family now.' Her English wasn't as good then as it is now. You know I hadn't thought about it since then, but the first couple of nights, until Pop was able to get an extra bed for Angel's room, Niki slept in bed with me because I had a bigger bed."

"And because why not put the two queer boys in the same bed?" Luke offered.

"I don't think that was the motive, but who knows. At any rate ... and it all makes sense now that Angel opened my eyes. Even then I slept naked. Mama had given Niki a pair of pajamas, and he wore them to bed. Needless to say, he was surprised when he pulled the covers back to see me naked. I told him I always slept naked, and not to worry. He was a little wimpery still, so I pulled him close and cuddled him. He snuggled up against me like a puppy. The next night, wouldn't you know it, he was in bed first and when I crawled in, he was naked. Angel said he slept naked in their room, too, which didn't surprise him. He probably figured it was in the gay boy handbook. I never realized what influence I must have had on Niki."

"He was lucky, Raphael. He couldn't have had a better role model."

"Seems like I've failed him lately, though. I'm not sure what to do now."

"I think we should start by talking to Steve. He's closest to Niki. Let's text him and see if he'll come over."

Steve showed up around one, on his way to the gym. Comfortable with the protocol by now, Steve stripped off his gym gear, and sat down on the floor, near Raphael's and Luke's feet.

"What's up, guys?"

"You tell us, Steve. What's up with Niki?" Luke asked.

"Huh?" Steve looked genuinely blank.

"What has Niki said to you about Raphael ... and me. And the dares we've been sharing?"

"Oh, not much." Steve looked over at Raphael. "I really do think you guys look great like this."

"What does Niki think?" Raphael now asked. Steve looked visibly uncomfortable. He was searching for words when Luke spoke up.

"He doesn't like it, does he?" Luke pressed. "Don't worry about hurting our feelings. What we need right now is the truth."

"Well ..." Steve began, then halted.

"Here," Raphael said as he handed his phone to Steve. "This is why we asked you over."

Steve studied the text for a moment, looked up at Raphael and Luke, handed the phone back to Raphael and sighed.

"Man, I'm really sorry guys. This pisses me off. I respect what you guys have going with each other. I really do. Niki is just so, uptight I guess. I don't know why he thinks he has to act so ... 'straight' all the time, especially for a gay man. I like so many of his qualities, but, damn, he's anal. And, I don't mean that in a good way." Steve began to loosen up and told Raphael and Luke about how Niki had obsessed for days about how they looked when they ran into each other New Year's Eve.

"He kept saying, 'Raphael's beautiful hair.' I think he's gotten over the haircuts by now, and, not your fault, but you guys keep throwing new curve balls at him."

"But you do care for Niki, right?" Luke asked.

"Oh yeah, absolutely. I love the little fucker. He just needs to figure out what's important and what isn't. I mean, when I told him I thought he was being ridiculous about you guys' hair and that I was thinking about getting pierced myself, he acted like I was crazy. Which is really weird, you know?"

"Why is it weird," Raphael asked. "That's Niki."

"Well, I'm not so sure."

"What do you mean?"

"Like I said, he acts so vanilla, but that's not the real Niki, not the secret Niki."

"There's a secret Niki?"

"Oh, yeah, Raphael. I probably shouldn't tell you guys this, but considering what he did with that text, maybe it's best that I do. Niki managed to download a virus a few weeks back, so, of course, he asked me to fix his laptop. It was nasty, so he didn't have a chance to delete his browser history or hide his bookmarks. I don't know, maybe that didn't even cross his mind. So, okay, maybe I shouldn't have, but I took a little tour of his computer once I'd cleaned it up."

"And...?"

"Lots of porn, no surprise there. But what was surprising was most of it was leather stuff, pretty hot, really. I could tell he must have gotten off on it, too. Especially the stuff featuring pierced and tattooed guys. Some shaving stuff, too. But, most of it, believe it or not, was puppy play."

"You don't mean cute little dogs, do you?" Luke asked.

"Oh, no. I mean cute guys plugged with dog tails, wearing puppy hoods and dog mitts. Eating from dog dishes, leashed and kenneled. All the elements of a pup's life. Hundreds and hundreds of bookmarks."

"Oh, this is crazy," Raphael said. "He pretends to hate Luke and me shaving and me getting pierced and caged, but he secretly gets off on guys role playing as dogs? Now I don't know what to think."

"Here's what I think," Luke said. "He's a lot more like us than we thought. He's as kinky as us, but he's afraid to admit it. Afraid to live it. He knows what happened the last time that he came out as gay. He's afraid to risk what happiness he has now if he were to come out as kinky. As a puppy. He feels forced to live a double life. This is awful, really. This is why we don't see him smile anymore. He's in love with you, Steve, but he sees you as much more vanilla than us, and he assumes you only want a vanilla lover. He wants to continue emulating his hero, Raphael, but he's afraid to, especially around you. Am I crazy, or does this make sense?"

"It makes perfect sense," Steve replied.

"So," Raphael said, "we're at a very fundamental juncture here. Niki loves Steve. Steve loves Niki. Niki is kinky as shit but thinks Steve is too vanilla to accept kinky Niki. So, Niki is in hiding and miserable. He doesn't want to break up with Steve, but he wants to be a puppy. Steve ... how would you like to have a puppy?'"

"Jeez, I never thought about it." Steve stared up at Raphael and Luke a moment, thinking. "Well, that's a lie. I started thinking about it after what I found on Niki's computer. Oh, and last Sunday at Folsom, we had to stop by the puppy park not once, but twice. He was clearly obsessed. I wanted to say something to him then, but I didn't know how to without admitting that I snooped while fixing his laptop."

"So, you're open to helping him explore his puppy persona?"

"Look, I do love Niki. I want him to be happy ... happier than he is now. As happy as he used to be. So, if letting him explore puppy play, or any other kinks for that matter, will bring back the happy, giggly boy I fell in love with then, sure, I'm all for it."

"And what about you, Steve?" Luke asked. "Are you ready to get a little kinky, too?"

"You mean, be a puppy with Niki?"

"No, I mean be his handler, his trainer, his owner. His human when he's being a puppy."

"I don't think I have a choice, do I? But I'll need a tutorial, or something. I wouldn't know where to start."

"I do."

"Of course you do," Raphael laughed. "Luke to the rescue."

"Well, I do have an idea. Or, two. Hand me my tablet."

While Luke worked over the tablet, Raphael motioned to Steve to turn around and put his back up against the couch, between Raphael's legs. Raphael gave his shoulders a good massage. "Are you sure you want to release Niki's inner pup?"

"Well, the more I think about it, the more I like the idea. To be honest, I'm probably just as jealous of what you two have going as Niki is. So, yeah, I'm ready to do a little exploring with Niki … probably with help from you guys."

"You can count on us," Luke said, putting down the tablet. "But we're going to need to work fast. There's a great opportunity to kick this whole thing off as early as next weekend. I just made a tentative reservation, so we've got a lot of planning to do."

"Reservation for what?" Steve asked.

Luke ignored the question and directed one to Steve. "Can you take a week off, as early as next week?"

"Uh, maybe. I'll have to ask. For what?"

"Let's discuss it over food. After all the drama this morning, I'm starving. Let's put on some clothes and head out. Lots to discuss. Can you skip the gym today?"

"Sure. Niki takes priority. Let's go."

Sixteen

NIKI'S INTERVENTION

LATER THAT DAY, AFTER an intensive planning session over brats and beers at Willkommen, Raphael and Luke headed back home to relax and prepare for what was to come, while Steve met Niki as he was getting off work, to corral and deliver him to the session they'd planned earlier.

"Steve, what are you doing here?" Niki nearly shrieked as he exited the coffee shop. Steve pulled him into a hug which immediately quieted him.

"I came to see my sexy little lover, obviously. Is that okay?" Niki sighed and squeezed Steve back.

"Very okay. I'm glad you're here. I missed you."

"Missed you more." Steve held onto Niki a bit longer than usual, but Niki didn't pull away. Finally, Steve pulled back a bit to look into Niki's eyes. "I confess I have a surprise. Let's take a little walk." Niki was quiet as they walked, typical of him. Steve avoided any small talk and just enjoyed holding Niki's hand as they headed for Raphael and Luke's flat. They were almost there before Niki realized their destination.

"Why are we going to Raphael's place?"

"Well, it's sort of a surprise. You'll see. I'm excited, and I hope you will be, too."

"We'll see, I guess."

Luke answered the door when Niki and Steve arrived. "Come on in. Make yourselves at home." Luke was naked and harnessed, of course. Steve immediately began removing his clothes, instigating a frown from Niki who stood still in the middle of the living room. Raphael entered from the kitchen, also naked and harnessed, and handed Niki his favorite flavor of Kombucha. "Have a seat, Niki. Steve, what can I get you?"

As Niki sat down on the floor, still in his knee length nylon shorts and Warriors Curry 30 jersey, Steve sat down beside him. "I'm fine, Raphael. Maybe later." Luke and Raphael sat down on the couch, facing Niki and Steve.

"Niki, we asked Steve and you here so we can have a talk. An important talk," Raphael began.

"Is everything okay?" Niki asked. "You look serious."

"Let's just say things could be better." Raphael paused a few beats, then continued, "You could be better."

"Me? What? What have I done?" Niki started to look even more morose than ever.

"Well, Niki, you did this." Raphael picked up his phone, clicked a couple of icons and handed it to Niki. It took Niki only about two seconds to realize what he was looking at.

"Oh, no. I can't believe Angel sent you that!"

"What did you expect him to do?"

"I ... well ... I ..."

"And, Niki, where's the leash you accused Luke of using on me? I don't see it in the photo."

Niki looked up into Raphael's face as his own disintegrated into a puddle. "Raphael, I'm ... I'm so sorry!" Tears began to fall down his cheeks as the corners of his mouth dragged down to his chin. His shoulders began shaking as his whimper became sobs. "I'm ... I'm ... Oh, fuck ... Oh fuuuuck ..." The sobs drowned out any further attempt Niki made to speak.

Luke sat silent, watching Niki, and Raphael's reaction, letting Raphael manage the situation. Steve put his arm around Niki's shoulders, but Niki seemed oblivious to his touch. Raphael slid off the couch and sat down next to Niki, silently urging Steve to give Niki some space. As Steve pulled away Raphael wrapped his arm around Niki's shoulders himself. As Niki continued to sob, Raphael rocked him gently, as if soothing a crying baby. After a few minutes, Niki quieted a bit, as Raphael began softly talking.

"Niki, I want you listen to me, listen very closely. Everything I'm going to say is true. I want you to understand it and believe it. Okay?"

Niki sniffled, but nodded. Luke leaned forward and handed Raphael a tissue, who handed it to Niki, who immediately desecrated it. Luke handed Raphael another.

"Niki, I love you. I will always love you. As much as I love Angel. You are our brother, our chosen brother, and you always will be. We will always be there for you. Steve loves you. He loves you in a way even I will never do. We all want the same thing for you, and that is for you to be happy. Niki, love is not a zero sum equation. If I love Luke, that doesn't mean I love you less. Luke is not stealing me away from you. I'll always be there for you, but I will also always be there for Luke. You're my brother. Luke is my lover, and one day he'll be my husband. One day Steve may be your husband, and if so, would that diminish your love for me?"

Niki sniffled, and blew into the tissue, then quietly said, "No. 'Course not, Raffi." Luke and Steve looked at each other and simultaneously mouthed "Raffi?"

"Exactly. So, Niki, I've probably not been there for you lately as much as I should have been, and for that I apologize. Luke has become the center of my universe, and that makes me very, very happy. But that doesn't mean I don't have time for you, when you need me. You just have to ask. Can you do that?"

"Yes."

"I also need you to stop judging me and Luke. It's not fair, Niki." Niki's face began to crumble again. Raphael pulled him closer, "Niki, we're here because Luke, Steve, and I all miss the sweet, fun-loving guy we all know and love. I haven't heard you giggle in forever."

"I don't giggle," Niki argued.

"Oh, yeah? Then what do you call this?" Raphael, conjuring up an old trick from their adolescence, slid behind Niki's back, put his legs around Niki's body and began tickling both sides of Niki's torso.

"Stop it! Stop! Stop it now." Niki protested half sobbing, half choking. Raphael took advantage of his position behind Niki to reach down, grab the waist band of his jersey and yank it up and over his arms and head, giving him direct access to Niki's vulnerable belly and sides. As he continued tickling, he leaned back, taking Niki with him, as the cries melted into groans, then slowly, giggles. Steve, seeing the opportunity he'd been waiting for, grabbed the waistband of Niki's shorts and pulled.

"Stop. No, Steve, dammit! Don't! Stop!" But it was too little, too late. Raphael forced out a couple more giggles, and Niki, at long last, was as naked as everyone one else.

"You guys ... you perverts. Give me my shorts!" The one man in the room who was not in the scrum was the one man who had never seen Niki naked before. Luke, alone on the couch, finally spoke.

"Holy moly." Raphael flashed Luke a discouraging look and shook his head. Luke ignored him. "Niki!" Luke exclaimed. "You're ... you're a god!"

"Not helping, Luke..." Raphael warned. Niki finally pulled his arms free from Raphael and tried to cover his crotch. Luke was having none of it. He leapt off the couch and crawled between Niki's spread legs. He literally pulled Niki's hands away from the most impressively massive cock he had ever seen ... and he'd seen some beauties.

"Luke..." Raphael again cautioned. Niki was looking at Luke as if he really wanted him to go away.

"Ok, look," Luke said, looking up at Raphael from his vantage point between Niki's legs. "Raphael, you just blew me away with the love and support you have for Niki. That was incredible. And, what you said is exactly right, we're here to help Niki be happy again. So, let me have my say for a moment, okay? Okay?"

"What do think, Niki? Should we let him talk?" Raphael asked. He was still holding Niki's now naked body from behind in a brotherly embrace. Luke was still holding Niki's hands away from his endowment.

"Umm, if he'll let me have my shorts back."

"No, not yet," Luke firmly said. "I want to do my part to help. Niki, are you really embarrassed for guys to see how big you are? Is that why you won't get naked in the steam?"

"No. Well, yeah, but..."

"But what?"

"Look, Luke. I don't think you can understand this. I'm black, okay? I'm queer, and sometimes even a little fem. But, I'm me, okay? I'm a real person, with real feelings. Steve says I have a big heart. Maybe I do. But, what I'm not ... I'm not a fucking big, black cock! I got so sick of guys reacting exactly the way you just did ... they didn't see me for me. They didn't want my mind, my heart, my anything ... except my big, black cock! Admit it. You'll never see me the same way again, will you? Will you?"

Luke looked devastated. He let go of Niki's hands and put one of his own on each of Niki's thighs as he lowered his head between Niki's calves, his face on the floor. Steve looked over at Raphael looking for a clue as to what to do or say. Raphael just shook his head. Niki stared down at the top of Luke's head. Finally, Luke lifted his head enough to look into Niki's eyes.

"Niki, I am so sorry. Niki, I will never see you as anything but one of the best people I have ever had the honor to know. I already know your heart, and your mind. And I look forward to becoming your brother-in-law. I just hope I can help you accept a gift you have that should give you pride and confidence, not shame. Is that okay?"

"That would be quite a challenge, Luke. It hasn't exactly brought me a lot of happiness."

"I like a challenge, Niki. Just ask 'Raffi'." That actually elicited a chuckle from Niki. "Seriously, Niki, and I mean this, if I can help you come to accept all of you with the pride and confidence you deserve, then I'll die a happy man."

"Oh, man, it's getting pretty deep in here," Raphael offered, squeezing Niki again from behind. "But I have to say, Niki's been naked for a good ten minutes now, so I guess you're already making progress."

"So, can I have my shorts back?"

"The answer is still no," Luke smiled. "We haven't even started on the most important issue of the evening."

"Luke's right," Raphael said as he let go of Niki and scooted around to face him, letting his naked thigh rest against Niki's naked thigh. "Niki, we said earlier that we want you to be happy again, actually happier than you've ever been. We want you to get the most fulfillment possible out of life. We want you to be as happy as Luke and I are together."

"I know. I shouldn't have sent that stupid text. I don't know, maybe I was just jealous of how happy you guys are. How much fun you always have."

"You're happy with Steve, aren't you?"

"Totally."

"Totally? Or could, maybe some things change to make you even happier with Steve?"

"Like what?"

"You tell me. You said you were maybe a little jealous of Luke and me. Does that mean you'd like a little more spice in your love life? A little adventure? A little more excitement? Maybe a leash?"

At that everyone, including the still naked Niki, laughed. Except Niki thought Raphael was referring to the leash in his very unfortunate text.

"Look at you right now. You're naked with your lover, your brother and brother-in-law, and you're laughing. You're actually enjoying the moment. Now, we haven't shaved you or pierced you or put a harness on you, which would look fucking awesome on you, but you've taken a little baby step here. You've let your guard down with three guys who love you and want you to blossom into the man you were meant to be. Will you let us take you further into that future?"

"This is all so weird. This is all about me, isn't it? You aren't talking about punishing me for the text. You're doing ... what?"

"We're asking you to become the real you," Steve finally spoke up. Niki turned to him, putting his hand on Steve's nearby thigh. "We want you to forget trying to be what you think everyone else expects you to be. We want to unveil the real Niki in all his glory."

"And if that includes being proud of a big black cock, so be it." Luke chimed in. Raphael shot him daggers. "Hey, it's part of the package!"

"Luke ..." Raphael started.

"It's okay," Niki said softly. "No, Luke's right. I shouldn't let shit-heads determine what I like or don't like about myself. So, this has been interesting all right. Are we done? Is there more to this 'let's fix Niki' intervention of yours?"

"Oh, there is a lot more to come." Luke said, once again placing his hands on Niki's thighs. "And, again, forgive me for getting distracted by your ... awesomeness. I promise to control myself in the future, since, it's official, like the rest of us, you're not allowed clothing in this house. As to 'is there more,' indeed there is. Steve is going to be the guy in charge of what we hope will be the best month of your life ... so far. Starting tonight."

"The best month ever, huh? Are we going to Tahiti?"

"Better. But, before we start, we need you to promise to do everything Steve says, for the next thirty days. If you're not the happiest you've ever been at the end of those thirty days, any and everything we've done can be undone. But, in the meantime, you can't say no to anything. Deal?"

Niki looked first at Steve, then Luke, then at Raphael, who smiled and mimed him a kiss. Then, back to Steve who silently asked with his eyes, "Well?"

"I can't say no to anything? What if ..."

Steve cut him off. "I won't ask you to do anything that will hurt you."

Niki thought a moment, then sighed. "Deal."

"Awesome!" Luke exclaimed. He, Steve and Raphael scooted up and encircled Niki in big, naked, group hug.

Raphael, whose mouth was inches from Niki's ear, quietly asked, "Remember what Mama used to say when we were kids and you, Angel and I would head out with our skateboards?" Niki shook his head slowly. "She'd say, 'Be good, be safe. You take care of each other.' We're going to take care of you, Niki. Trust us."

Steve pulled out of the hug first. "Niki, your first task will be to give a week's notice at work tomorrow." Luke and Raphael, pulled loose, too, to give Niki some space. His smile had disappeared.

"What? Why? I can't quit my job."

"Why? Because we have big plans for you, sweetie. That job isn't good enough for the new, improved Niki."

"New and improved? You make me sound like a detergent or something. Besides, I need the money."

"Like I said, we have plans for you, including a new job, with better money, but first you have to give notice tomorrow."

"What is this new job? Who gets someone a job without discussing it first?"

Raphael spoke next. "Niki, people who care about you do. Look, you don't even like your job. This is all part of what we have been talking about. Just. Trust. Us. All will be revealed in due time. Think of the next thirty days as a movie you've never seen before, but you are the star. We've written the script. Just read your lines. And enjoy."

"Enjoy, huh?"

"Trust us. Can you do that? Please? Otherwise, we'll be forced to just find Steve another cute boyfriend."

Steve stood up and said, "Nobody is finding me a new boyfriend. I like the one I've got just fine. Niki, let's get dressed. I've made a reservation for dinner to celebrate the first day of Niki's New Adventure." He reached down and took Niki's hand and pulled him up into a hug. Luke and Raphael remained lounging on the floor as Steve and Niki dressed. Goodbyes were exchanged and after the door closed, Luke scooted over to Raphael and pulled him into an embrace. As their lips parted, Luke spoke.

"I meant what I said about you being incredible with Niki. Most guys would have yelled, would have angered him, been pissed off. You weren't. You were compassionate, understanding. You know, as I watched I realized something new about you. Raphael, you'd make an amazing father."

"What? Seriously? I was just being a good brother."

"You were being you. Each passing day I find more reasons to love you even more than I did yesterday. And, that comment about me being your universe? Baby, that made my heart sing."

"Well at least one part of you can carry a tune, then."

"That was harsh. I have other talents, you know."

"Indeed you do. You know how to take a simple Filipino boy and turn him into a proud leather boy. Not a sex slave, mind you, but a loving, proud leather boy."

"Okay, first of all, there's nothing 'simple' about you. Because, in fact you made it easy. Baby, I had great material to work with." Raphael batted his eyes in response. "Is my proud leather boy hungry?"

"I'll say. This intervention stuff is exhausting, Let's not cook. Let's go out."

"My treat. You did all the heavy lifting."

"Deal."

Seventeen

THE MUTUAL FLASH DARE

As LUKE AND RAPHAEL dined on shrimp fajitas at West of Pecos, they continued to talk about Niki's intervention, and the next steps they were about to take to help Niki submit to his true needs and nature.

"So, have we covered all the bases for next weekend?" Raphael asked. "I feel like we should be writing all of this down so we don't forget anything. And, is it fair to keep Niki in the dark until the last minute?"

"Maybe you should make a list, baby. I think we've covered everything, but it wouldn't hurt. You and I have the most responsibilities this week, but once Saturday arrives, it'll all be in Steve's hands. And, yeah, I think it's best to wait until next weekend to reveal all to Niki. Otherwise, he'll have time to fret and get cold feet. Better to have him plunge in headfirst than to come up with reasons to back out. Remember, we're doing this for his own good in the long run."

"Oh, I don't disagree. You think Steve is really, totally on board?"

"Yeah, love conquers all, right? And, remember, we told Niki if he wasn't happy, it could all be undone. I think the same should apply to Steve. As long as they both agree."

"Well, I can't argue with that." After finishing dinner, the two walked back home, hand-in-hand as always. As they approached Valencia on 16th, Raphael broke the comfortable silence with an announcement. "Mutual Flash Dare, Luke."

"What?"

"It's time for our first Mutual Flash Dare."

"Is it? I have no idea what you're talking about, baby. And, I'm not sure I like that evil grin on your otherwise saintly face."

"You mean the face that is about to become 'new and improved' just like the pre-puppy Niki?"

Luke stopped and looked into Raphael's eyes. "Sorry, I'm still in the dark."

"Ok, let me spell it out for the uninitiated in our audience. Mutual dare, because we both have to do it. Flash, because it happens right now, without any warning, well, except for the warning I just gave you."

"So, you're giving me a dare that you're going to do, too?"

"Yep."

"And we're doing it right now?"

"Yep."

"Ooookay. Am I doing the dare right now?"

"Almost." Raphael pulled Luke across Guerrero Street and up the block until they stopped in front of the entrance to Body Manipulations. "Here. We're here."

"Because?"

"Remember how sexy we thought Angel's little septum ring was?"

"Ah. Ah ha. Let me guess ... no, I don't have to guess. I'm getting a tiny little septum ring, aren't I?"

"We both are. *Mutual* flash dare. You. Me. Both. Now. March, mister." The march order was unnecessary, as Raphael was still holding Luke's hand as he pulled him through the open door. He was holding his hand again as they exited, thirty minutes later, each with what some would describe as 'a sexy little septum ring.' The rings were tiny, just brushing the bottom of each of their septums. Discrete. Tasteful. And, yeah, sexy.

As they continued on the walk home, Luke muttered, "Just when you think it's safe to take a little walk with your fiancé in the big city..." Raphael laughed and put his free arm around Luke's waist and pulled him close.

"I thought that was pretty clever. Inventing a new kind of dare on the spur of the moment. Serendipity, you know. It was perfect ... like you."

"Well, the dare was perfect, I'll give you that. But it does open up new possibilities. I just might have to come up with a counter mutual flash dare ... whatever ... for you, after this."

"I'm counting on it."

After a couple more blocks, Luke rubbed his itchy nose and was instantly reminded it had just been poked. "Damn, I forgot already. We're gonna have tender noses for a while, aren't we?"

"I guess. No Eskimo kisses for us for a while. But, that's okay. I prefer the 'suck Luke's tongue down my throat' kind better anyway."

"As do I, baby. As do I."

"By the way, did I mention, you look ..."

Before Raphael could finish, Luke joined him in unison to say, "mahvelous!"

Eighteen

BOUQUET FOR THE BEAUTIFUL

ALMOST EVERY WAKING MINUTE outside of work had seen Luke and Raphael finalizing everything for Niki's big day on Saturday. They'd kept in touch with Steve, who was plenty busy himself. He'd relayed that Niki had followed through on his first command, and would finish his last shift on Friday. His boss was sad to see him go, as so many customers had developed a great rapport with Niki, but this was retail in the city, and she was used to turnover. So, all in all, it would be an amicable parting. Niki was bugging Steve every other minute for details on just what the heck was going on, but Steve held firm.

"I love you too much to spoil the surprises," he'd finally said.

"Surprises? As in plural?"

"Well, yeah. I mean, there are many components to what is going to happen in the next few weeks, or what I like to think of as Niki's Great Adventure."

"God, Steve, you're driving me crazy."

"Um, actually, Squirt, it's you who are driving *me* crazy. I'll tell you what, this wasn't part of the plan, but any time you bring the subject up between now and next Saturday, you have to strip naked, just like Raphael and Luke live. And every time you bring it up and you're already naked, and we both know that's always going to be the case, you have to suck my dick ... for five minutes ... no matter what else we're doing."

"Seriously? Come on..."

"You might as well strip right now. You know I'm right."

"I guess you don't know me very well. Just watch."

Needless to say, Steve watched Niki strip within the hour, and the blow jobs ... plural ... were just fine, thank you. Between two visits to Mr. S by Raphael and Luke and visits to neighborhood pet stores by them and Steve when Niki was working, a nice little collection of bags and boxes had accumulated in Raphael and Luke's living room.

"Kinda looks like Christmas or Hanukkah, doesn't it?" Luke pointed out. "Without the wrapping."

"That's what we forgot," Raphael yelled, dramatically slapping his forehead. "We didn't get a tree ... you know, for Niki to lean against when he pees."

"Boy, you're taking this all the way, aren't you?"

"That was a joke. Nobody gets my humor. But I do wonder just how far we should take this. I wonder how far Niki will want to take this. What if Steve ... and we ...are overreacting to Niki's web surfing habits?"

"Remember his visits to the puppy play area at Folsom? Multiple visits. I have no doubt we're doing the right thing."

Despite all the time, attention, and money that Steve, Luke and Raphael were investing on Niki's behalf, Luke still found time to arrange a little surprise for Raphael.

"Raphael, I have something for you," Clifford, the intern, sing-songed as he walked up to Raphael's cubical with a big smile on his face. "Somebody certainly likes you." He handed Raphael a too-big-for-his cubical bouquet of white roses and lavender alstroemeria. They smelled intoxicating. The card envelope was addressed: Mr. Malaluan.

"Okay, this is weird, but thank you Cliff." Raphael pulled the card out of the envelope and read, 'Thank you, baby. Love, Luke.' As Raphael admired the flowers – alstroemeria were his favorite, partly because they lasted forever in a vase – Alex walked up and said, "Somebody's been a good boy."

"Yeah, so it seems. I wonder what possessed Luke to do this?" Alex leaned over to smell the blooms. "Hey, don't move. Let me take a picture of you admiring them, so I can send it with a text to Luke."

"Shouldn't you be in the pic?"

"Well, here, let's both get in the frame." Not being a prodigious self-ie-taker, it took Raphael a couple of tries before he was happy with the shot. He sent it along with a text to Luke: *I love them. Alex loves them. I love you. What did I do???*' Alex wandered off and Raphael resumed work. A few minutes later, Luke's response arrived. *'Love you, too. Glad you like them. Say hi to Alex for me.'* Which didn't really answer Raphael's question.

That evening, Raphael was home, harnessed and naked, the bouquet on the dining table since it really was too big for his office space, when Luke arrived. Raphael greeted him with a big hug and a bigger kiss. He always got off on being naked when Luke wasn't, although that didn't last long, as Luke began shedding street clothes as soon as the hug ended. After dinner, where the flowers were as much admired as Raphael's curry, Raphael and Luke retired to the shower, for the evening's shave and shower session. "What was the occasion for the bouquet, Sir," Raphael posed as he denuded the sides of Luke's head. "It was a big hit at the office."

"If I was rich, you'd get a bouquet every day, baby. But it occurred to me this morning, as I was walking and getting a couple more 'nice kilts' from strangers, that you did me an incredible favor when you took away all my jeans. Thanks to you, I get affirmations every day. I'm used to people noticing you, you sexy thing, you, but now I get noticed even without you."

"I think I detected two compliments in there, and I appreciate them, both. You are so welcome about the kilts. So, you agree, it's not just me that thinks you look amazing in them? Especially with that magnificent beard I created?"

"I guess I can't argue with popular opinion, can I?"

"No, Sir, you can't," Raphael kissed the newly smoothed, hairless side of Luke's head. "And, as long as we're exchanging gratitude, I have you to thank for limiting me to my caged cock wardrobe. I probably would have never started a friendship with Alex if you hadn't."

"Probably right. That was a cute pic of you two, by the way. We really should make an effort to get to know them better. I think we probably have a lot in common, you know, what with Alex's cage and all."

"Yeah, that encounter at Folsom was promising. I'll talk to Alex tomorrow about setting up a dinner." Raphael and Luke switched places and Luke nestled his cock into the space between Raphael's butt cheeks as he reached for the razor and shave gel.

After a couple of text exchanges the next day between Raphael and Alex, and Alex and Greg, Alex stopped by Raphael's cube. "Tonight or tomorrow both work."

"Then let's do tonight, just in case something comes up tomorrow. Luke and I have kind of a busy week. We'd like to host. Is seven good?"

"Perfect. Just text me the address and we'll see you later. I assume it won't be formal."

"Far from it, Alex," Raphael smiled. When Alex and Greg arrived, there was a freshly opened bottle of Cab on the coffee table, along with a couple of cheeses, crackers, a medley of olives and hummus. Raphael opened the door to admit them, and Luke was on the couch. Both were harnessed and naked, of course.

"Oh, are we early?" Alex asked.

"Nope, right on time," Raphael smiled. "Let me take your jackets. Oh, I get it. No, we always dress like this at home, except when we have company. You're not company ... we'd like to think of you as family, if that's alright."

"Alright by me," Greg said. "Where should I put my clothes?" Raphael led him into the bedroom, where he put their jackets on the bed. Greg's clothes immediately followed. Alex wandered in, looking sheepish.

"You guys slay me," he said. "You really live naked?" Raphael nodded and smiled. "Well, Raphael, you've already seen me basically naked at Folsom, so, gee, why not." Raphael stood by and took each item of clothing as Alex stripped.

"That's better, Alex. We locked cock brothers always look better naked, don't you think?"

"You certainly do, Raphael. I have to admit, I wish I was as uninhibited as you are. I'd never dream of stripping in front of a co-worker."

"You just did, sweetie," Greg said.

"Oh, yeah, well ..." Alex trailed off.

"We may be co-workers, Alex, but more importantly, I want you to think of me as a friend," Raphael said as he put his arms on Alex's and Greg's shoulders and led them back into the living room. Wine was poured, appetizers sampled and light conversation ensued. After a while, apropos of nothing, Alex said, "If we'd known, Greg and I would have worn our chest harnesses." Greg nodded, a mouthful of hummus preventing him from speaking.

"Next time," Luke said. "And, there will be a next time. We've been wanting to spend more time with you guys. This is great."

"You both always look like you just stepped out of a barbershop," Greg replied. "So damn hot."

"We shave each other's mohawk and high 'n tight every night," Luke responded. "In the shower. Maybe that's partly why we're always naked."

"Like I said, 'so damn hot.' You guys are an inspiration. We just have to get Alex here a little more comfortable with his body. I was all ready to check our clothes at Folsom, you know."

"We know," Raphael said. "That's one reason we decided to do dinner here. To take some baby steps with Alex and his body issue."

"I don't have a body issue," Alex protested. "I, uh, it's just ..."

"He's not totally comfortable letting people see his cage." Greg deadpanned.

"Really?" Luke asked. "Alex, are you really self-conscious about that?"

"It, uh, isn't exactly what people expect to see, is it? So, I probably am, yeah." Alex defended.

"Oh, Alex, you shouldn't be. Raphael and I go to the beach, we're in the locker room and steam at the gym. It's no big deal, believe me. We even have guys come up to us at the beach, curious and admiring."

"Well, I haven't had that experience myself."

"Then, we need to make that happen, Alex. You're too damn cute to keep your assets under wraps." At that point the doorbell rang.

"Dinner's here," Raphael announced as he hopped up from his spot on the floor and went to the door. The regular DoorDash guy handed him the packages, and Raphael said, "Hang on a sec," and put the packages on the dining table, grabbed some waiting bills next to the still vibrant bouquet, and walked back to the open door and handed the tip to the waiting delivery guy.

"Thanks, amigo. Always a pleasure," he smiled as he turned and headed down the stairs.

"Fuuuuck," Alex said. "See, you have balls I'll never have."

"What?" Raphael asked.

"You have no shame. I don't mean you should be ashamed, but just that you were so matter of factly naked and caged in front of a stranger!"

"Yeah, why not? It's my home. And, a little confession here ... he likes delivering here. I think he makes sure he always gets our order."

"Yeah," Luke chimed in. "He has the hots for Raphael."

"Who doesn't," Alex said before thinking. He immediately blushed and looked sheepishly around the room.

"You're too sweet," Raphael laughed. "Come on guys, let's eat."

As they downed dinner, Luke made a proposition. "Alex, I haven't cleared this with Greg, so Greg, stop me if I'm out of line, but I think we should make it our mission to get you 100% comfortable being naked and caged anywhere. You saw how simple and natural it is for Raphael. I propose we do this once a week until you're comfortable ... no ... eager to answer the door. Meanwhile, let's make a few outings to the beach. You know, one step at a time. Then, when you're ready, join us as guests at the gym for a steam."

"Oh, man, I don't know."

"I say yes," Greg spoke up. "Alex, let's do it. What do you have to lose?"

"My dignity?"

"Alex," Raphael said, taking Alex's hand in his as he got out of his chair and knelt down next to him, "please be my out and proudly naked locked cock brother. I will be with you every step of the way." Raphael looked pleadingly at him with those dreamy, almond eyes. "Come on ... it'll be fun, I promise."

"How do you ever say no to him?" Alex asked Luke, who was smiling away with a mouth full of pasta.

Luke swallowed and admitted, "You can't. Don't even try."

Raphael rose up, planted a kiss on Alex's cheek and exclaimed, "Saturday should be a good beach day!"

Nineteen

NIKI'S GREAT ADVENTURE BEGINS

SATURDAY MORNING FINALLY ARRIVED and, as far as they could tell, Raphael and Luke were ready. They'd made plans to hit the beach early that afternoon with Alex and Greg. But first, and far more importantly, they were needed to help Steve begin Niki's indoctrination into what they all hoped would be his new, happier, more open and uninhibited life. When they arrived at Niki and Steve's place, the tension was palpable. Niki, who'd been naked at home most of the week due to his inability to not pester Steve, was beside himself and Steve's cock most definitely needed a rest. He regretted ever issuing such a clearly foolish ultimatum.

"Niki has been driving me crazy, guys," Steve said as he opened the door. "I'm so glad today is finally here."

"I don't know about you," Raphael said as he and Luke took a seat on the couch, "but I'm kinda nervous."

"Yeah, well, we've gone this far, so let's just hope it all works out," Luke said, putting his arm around Raphael's shoulders. "We're doing this for Niki."

"Doing what," Niki asked as he entered the room. He was dressed in nylon shorts and a sweatshirt, which he'd quickly donned upon hearing the doorbell. Yes, he'd lost the right to clothing already this morning, yet again.

"Sit down, Niki. It's time we told you everything."

"Finally!" Niki sighed as he sat on the couch next to Raphael. "My tonsils were getting sore."

"What? Your tonsils? ..." Luke asked.

"Never mind. A bad idea," Steve replied. Then, turning back to Niki, he continued, "We've kept you in the dark about what's about to happen to and for you, so that we could get everything organized."

"Sounds ... complicated. So, tell me! The suspense is killing me!"

Steve sat down next to Niki, put a hand on his thigh and the other on the side of his cheek, turning his head so they were looking into each other's eyes. "Niki, you're about to become my human puppy."

"What!?!" Niki started to get up, but Steve held him down.

"Niki, when I cleaned up your computer a few weeks ago, I, uh, inadvertently discovered how interested you are in the pup world." Niki looked down at his lap, not meeting anyone's gaze. "Then, at Folsom, it became painfully obvious that you were enamored with the guys in the puppy play space." Not able to help himself, Niki smiled at the memory of that day.

"Niki, I was out of line to look at your bookmarks and history, but I'm glad I did. You might never have told me, told any of us, of your ... interest." Niki remained silent. "Am I right?" Still no response. "Do you think it's something to be ashamed of?"

Raphael decided to speak up. "Niki." He waited for Niki to turn and look into his eyes. "I understand, believe me, how difficult it is to 'come out' about something that you fear might not be understood or appreciated. You have nothing to fear. You were a brave little fourteen-year-old when you came out as queer. Tell me, has your life been better since you did that?"

Niki stalled. Raphael just continued to look intensely into his eyes. "Would you take it all back if you could?"

"God, no!" Niki finally answered.

"Yeah, exactly," Raphael smiled. "We wouldn't be the family we are if you hadn't come out. You wouldn't have Steve. You wouldn't have Angel, or Luke, or Mama and have had Pop, and *worst* of all, you wouldn't have me." That was met with a meek smile and eye roll from Niki. "Niki, you learned it's okay to be gay. You're a fabulous queer boy, and I'm absolutely certain you will be the best damn puppy our community has ever laid eyes on."

After a moment of silence all around, Steve still holding Niki, quietly urged, "So, what do you think?"

Niki looked at Raphael again, then at Luke, and finally at Steve. "I think you were a jerk for snooping. I think you were a jerk not telling me you snooped. I want to be mad at all of you. Other than that, I honestly don't know what to think." He fell silent for a couple more minutes, then looked back at Steve. "I still don't know what it is you had to 'organize.' Why I had to quit my job. Okay, yeah, I get off on seeing guys pup out. The thought of being treated like a pup makes me horny. I'll admit it, since you already know. But, how does that change anything?"

"It changes everything," Steve replied. "Today begins a week of very intense ... training. You and I are headed off to BPOS ... Beginning Pup Obedience School ... in just a little while. It's a week of intensive pup training for twelve pups and their handlers at a resort up in Guerneville. You'll live the entire week as a pup, with other pups, and with me learning alongside you about how to be your handler."

"Are you kidding?" Niki protested. Steve stood up, left the room and returned with the gym bag he, Raphael and Luke had assembled. He sat back down next to Niki, partially unzipped it and pulled out a stainless-steel chain choker and handed it to Niki. As he unspooled it, Niki saw it had a bone shaped tag that read 'Niki.'

"You know, most human pups adopt a cute puppy name for use while in puppy head space. You won't need to do that. Niki is the perfect pup name for you," Steve said.

"Sounds like you know as much about puppy stuff as I do."

"Well, sweetie, if I'm going to have the sexiest pup in San Francisco, I figure I'd better know what I'm doing. So, yeah, I did a little research. The real learning will happen starting today at BPOS."

"So, assuming I say yes, what exactly will happen at this B ... P ... O ... S?"

"Well, first, let's see how this looks on you. Raphael, will you do the honors? Niki, take off your sweatshirt. Pups don't wear shirts, except maybe at Pride." Raphael, who had helped Steve obtain the collar, knew exactly how to lock it on with the tool that would remain in Steve's possession. Niki wouldn't be able to remove it on his own. Once it was on, Raphael zipped into the bathroom and returned with a mirror, so Niki could see how it looked on him.

"It's a perfect fit," Raphael admired.

Luke chimed in with, "Niki, you look great." Steve, who saw no need for words, simply locked lips with Niki. And kept them there. Until Luke cleared his throat.

"Okay, I kinda like it. Feels good, too. About this obedience school...?"

"This is the real deal. As real as it can be. You'll be naked, collared, as you are now, wearing a pup hood and a pup tail at all times. Your hands enclosed in pup mitts. You'll eat, drink, play, sleep, piss and poop as a pup. You won't speak like a human, only bark, woof, whimper and whine, hopefully not too much whining. I will be the one to bath you, feed you, water you, pet you, adore you and help train you, as I will be trained myself. You'll sleep kenneled with one other pup at night, changing kennel mates each night, so you can establish rapport, and learn from each of the other pups. Oh, I forgot, you'll be caged like Raphael as well."

"Caged? Pup mitts? Kennels? Okay, now I know you're making this up. What's really going on?"

Steve reached into the bag and pulled out a small draw-string black felt bag and handed it to Raphael. "Raphael, you're more experienced than me with these things. Niki, stand up, please." Steve pulled Niki into a standing position and immediately pulled his shorts to his ankles. As Niki protested while stepping out of his shorts, Raphael pulled the steel cage out of the bag and began unlocking the tube from the cock ring.

"It took some doing, but we were able to get a cage that should fit you perfectly," Luke joined in. "You know, for your ..." There was no need to finish the sentence.

"You guys are really serious."

"Everything I've said is true," Steve took Niki's hands in his. "This is all for you, Niki ... puppy."

Meanwhile, Raphael was working Niki's cock and balls into the cock ring. "Steve, hand me the coconut oil. In the bag." Steve rummaged in the bag and handed Raphael a small squeeze bottle. Raphael coated Niki's shaft and balls and finally worked the ring into place. He recoated the shaft and began working the tube up Niki's slightly hardening cock. "Don't make this harder for me, Niki. Think of something really awful."

Niki looked down at the unfamiliar sight of Raphael manhandling his privates and asked, "Like what?"

"I don't know ... kale? Vomit? Maybe ..."

"Enough!" Niki protested. "I don't need to be any more nauseous than I am right now."

"Sorry. Almost there, big guy. I'm not as experienced at this as Steve thinks. You're my first caged puppy."

"You're doing great, baby" Luke offered. He was enjoying the show. Finally, tube and ring were aligned and Raphael reached down with his free hand, grabbed the key and locked the two parts together.

"Whew," Raphael sat back and admired his accomplishment. The cage looked great on Niki. "What do you think, Niki?"

Niki reached down and lifted his locked cock away from his body, then let it fall into place. He wiggled his hips to make it sway back and forth. "It looks smaller, doesn't it?"

"One of the benefits of getting locked up, yeah." Raphael smiled. "I thought you'd like that."

"It's cool, I guess. It's awesome that it's smaller, Raffie."

Steve pulled Niki into a tight embrace. "Niki, I'm so glad you like it. We weren't sure if this was the right thing to do, or not. It does look great on you. Now I can't wait to get your mitts and tail in place." After another moment in Steve's arms, Niki pulled slightly away and looked down at his locked cock.

"That's weird. It's getting heavier."

"Um, that's your caged erection," Raphael mentored. "I think the idea of mitts and a tail sounded pretty good, huh? Better get used to the feeling of a caged erection, puppy, 'cause I think you're going to have a lot of them in the next week. That's probably one reason the Obedience School requires the cage. If all the pups were naked and kenneled together, you probably wouldn't get any sleep. But, especially for you, the cage does have this one special benefit. Although, you'll probably still look bigger than all the other pups."

"Of course he will," Steve interjected, "but they'll be too busy learning to be good pups to pay much attention to each other's cages. Especially since they'll all be on all fours the whole time. And locked in mitts."

"I still like how it looks so much smaller. If nothing else, I'm happy about that, guys." Luke and Raphael stood up and with Steve encircled Niki for a group hug. Both Niki's and Raphael's cages got a little heavier as they lingered in the embrace. That's when Steve's cell sounded an alert. He broke from the hug and picked up the phone.

"Our ride is pulling up, Niki. Say goodbye to Raphael and Luke. When you see them again next week, you'll be a well-trained puppy."

"But I haven't packed anything!"

"I have everything we need right here. Just put your shorts back on for the walk out to the van." Steve grabbed a backpack of his own belongings from the bedroom, and returned to zip up and lift the well-stocked gym bag. Niki, looking excited, nervous, and maybe even a little fearful, pulled on his shorts and ran to the bathroom for a last-minute pee. Steve whispered, "I'll text you guys updates as often as I can. Wish us luck." Niki was back, and gave Raphael and Luke one last hug, then followed Steve to the door.

"Have fun you two," Luke said. Raphael just smiled nervously.

"Lock up after you leave," Steve reminded them. "Thanks for looking after the place." And with that, they were out the door. Raphael sat back down on the couch and let out a heavy sigh. Luke sat next to him and again put his arm around Raphael's shoulders.

"Everything's going to be fine, baby. Don't worry."

"I think so, too. I hope so. He did like the collar, and he *really* liked the cage. That surprised the hell out of me, considering how he reacted the first time he saw mine. Jeez, what a one-eighty."

"He liked seeing his cock half its usual size, Raphael. I think the cage was incidental."

"Imagine that. A guy sees his cock locked up for the first time, and he doesn't even focus on the cage."

"He will. It really hasn't sunk in yet, I'm sure. I kinda think another reason he likes it so much is that it is one more thing that you two have in common. Once again, he's following his hero."

"You think?"

"Yeah, I do. By the way, tell me about this 'Raffie' nickname."

"Oh, that. Remember, he was 'Nicholas' before his parents disowned him. When we were in bed together that first night, with me comforting him, I just instinctively called him Niki ... he seemed so vulnerable. He said something like, 'My name's Nicholas, not Niki,' and I said, 'Who named you Nicholas?' and of course he said his parents. And, I said, 'I'm your big, queer brother now and I'm naming you Niki.' He said something like, 'Then I'm going to call you Raffie.' I said 'fine, I love it.' I kept calling him Niki in front of everyone and soon they were calling him Niki, too. To his big disappointment, nobody bought into his 'Raffie' nickname for me. So, he basically dropped it, but it still comes up now and then as kind of a term of endearment between us. He says it when what he really means is 'I love you.' Just like when you call me 'baby' and I call you 'Sir.'

"Do you not like me calling you baby?"

"Actually ... I love it. 'Cause I know what's behind it."

"Good, 'cause I love calling you 'baby,' baby."

Raphael smiled at that, and put his arm around Luke's torso, so he could reward him with a kiss. When their lips parted, Luke broke the mood by saying, "Well, this went awfully well. But now we need to get moving if we're going to be on time to meet Alex and Greg for the beach."

"Oh, yeah, our next victim ... making Alex comfortable being naked and caged in public. You know, we should be charging for all this."

"Consider this our community service, baby. We're leaving the world, or at least the city, a better place."

"And having a hell of a lot of fun along the way."

"Amen."

Twenty

⁂

TWO CAGES ON THE BEACH

LUKE TEXTED GREG THAT he and Raphael were on their way. They stopped at home to pick up the beach backpack, then headed to Church & Duboce, where Alex and Greg were already waiting to catch the next N-Judah train.

"Hope you guys weren't waiting long," Luke greeted them.

"No, only five minutes or so. The next N is due in three minutes, so good timing," Alex said. "How did it go with Niki?"

"I don't think it could have gone any better," Raphael replied, smiling. "You should have seen him after I got the cage on him, Alex! He was beaming. He's so self-conscious about being hung, that he loved the fact the cage makes him look smaller. I mean, it still looked big, but to him, it was an improvement. If nothing else comes out of this, I'm willing to bet we've got another permanently caged brother on our hands."

"That's really cool, Raphael. I bet you're relieved."

"I think it's all going to go well," Luke chimed in. "He really liked the pup collar, too."

"Yeah, that's true," Raphael agreed. "I hope you're right. Niki deserves to be happy. Steve does too."

"Here comes the N," Greg announced. "And, now on to your next assignment ... getting Alex naked and caged in public!" As Alex eye-rolled at Greg, Raphael got behind Luke and dug into the backpack Luke was wearing.

"Here, Alex, put this on. We brought it for you." He handed Alex a yellow tee that matched the pink one he was wearing: with a caged cock graphic front and center.

"So, the, uh, conditioning begins before we even get to the beach, huh?"

"Yup. Hurry before train gets here." Alex slipped off the backpack he was wearing, stripped off his shirt and put on the caged cock tee.

The N slowed into position, the doors opened and the four boarded. The car was half full, but there was enough seating open for Alex and Raphael to sit together on one bench and Luke and Greg together across from them. After five minutes or so, as the train rumbled through the East Portal tunnel, Raphael noticed a dreadlocked white guy with a skateboard paying more than casual attention to him, or to Alex. A few minutes later, the guy moved closer. Finally, he spoke.

"Cool shirts, dudes. Is that a band I haven't heard about?"

"Oh, this? Raphael pointed to the graphic. "Nah, more of a club. Kind of exclusive. But always open to new members."

"Cool, cool. I like it." Luke was elbowing Greg and smiling. He always enjoyed Raphael attracting attention, which made him feel a strange sense of pride, even thought it was Raphael who was getting noticed. "Does it have a special meaning? I mean, it must, right?"

"Yeah, very special, but it's, you know, kinda secret. Sorry, I can't say more."

"Awesome, dude. Really awesome..." The kid said as he departed at the next stop, probably headed north into the Haight.

"See!" Raphael turned to Alex. "Advertising really does pay. He wants to join the club."

"He wants the shirt, doofus. I seriously doubt he'd make it past the initiation."

"Yeah, well, we'll never know. He was kinda cute, though. In a scruffy skater dude kind of way."

"You're hopeless."

"Bite me." And, thus began a snark fest between the caged cock brothers-in-arms until they reached their stop at Sunset, where the four exited to catch the Twenty-Nine to Baker Beach. It wasn't long before they arrived.

"Next time we'll do Marshall's Beach, more remote and more gay, but Baker's easier to get to." Luke said as they trudged into the sand.

"Planning next time already, huh," Greg asked.

"Sure. We're going to do this regularly until Alex here is so eager to show off his cage in public that he's the one to suggest the beach," Raphael prophesied.

"Don't hold your breath," Greg offered. "I still can't believe he actually showed his cage to you at Folsom."

"Guys ... I'm right here." Alex scolded. Greg put his arm around his shoulders and pulled him close.

"I'm just sayin'," Greg kidded. "You're much too hot to be so shy. I keep telling you ..."

"Don't worry, Greg," Raphael smiled. "Luke turned me into his out and proud locked cock boy. Alex is in good hands. It's only a matter of time."

"Good luck with that," Alex grinned back. "I doubt I'll ever be as exhibitionistic as you, Raphael."

"Wanna bet," Raphael countered?

"What's the stake." Alex asked, taking up Raphael's offer. "Better make it good."

"You're on. I know what my prize will be if I win, you can decide on yours ... to be revealed upon success."

"Or lack thereof, wise guy." Alex jokingly shot back.

"This is going to be more fun than I thought," Luke laughed. "And it's time to get the ball rolling, or more accurately, to get the balls out in the open." Groans were sounded all around. They had made it to the gay end of Baker Beach. Raphael picked a spot surrounded by a few dozen towels topped by naked men, some singles, some pairs and a few groups of three or four.

"Hey, can't we set up over there?" Alex asked, pointing to a more sparsely populated area closer to the cliffs.

"We can, but we won't." Raphael replied. He dropped his backpack and immediately stripped off his shirt and shorts and raised his arms in an exclamation gesture. "See how easy this is?"

"Oh, uh ..." and before Alex could complete his protest, Greg pantsed him. Alex immediately sat down in the sand, and gave Greg a look that really needed no description.

"Watch, and learn," Greg laughed as he followed Raphael's example. Luke by then was naked, too, pulling beach towels out of their beach pack.

"You might want to stand up and let Raphael brush all that sand off your ass before you sit down on one of our blankets, shy boy," Luke advised. Alex emitted a long and loud sigh, stood up and tried to be invisible as Raphael did just that.

"It's okay if I touch your locked cock boy's ass, isn't it, Sir?" Raphael joked as he brushed away the sand.

"You have my blanket permission," Greg grinned. As soon as the beach blankets were spread Alex immediately hit the deck, belly down to hide his cage. As Luke and Raphael settled in, Greg straddled Alex just behind Alex's behind, his legs squeezing Alex's. He began squirting sunscreen on Alex's back and then giving him an all over rub down.

"Mmmm, that feels so good, Greg," Alex sighed. For the moment, the drama was over. After Greg had coated everything he could reach he raised up and did his best to flip Alex onto his back.

"Sweetheart, you can either roll over so I can rub this on your front, or you can stand up so I can do it, or you're going to have one really stupid looking sunburn."

"Fine," Alex responded as he rolled over. As Greg continued with the caged side, Luke and Raphael were busy coating each other, both standing, neither hiding anything, including Luke's semi hard on. Raphael was making sure it was well coated, so he really wasn't to blame. Since Alex wasn't about to stand up, let alone sit up, Raphael and Luke were charged with coating Greg, Luke in the back, Raphael in the front. He gave Greg the same treatment, and not too surprisingly, achieved the same tumescent result.

"I like your cock, Greg. It's very photogenic," Raphael admired. "I can see why Alex is always such a happy guy." Both Luke and Greg had to laugh at that, given that Alex hadn't smiled once since they gotten off the bus.

"Thanks Raphael. That's high praise coming from a work of art such as yourself."

"Why thank you, Sir. Much obliged."

"I'm right here, guys," Alex repeated. "Jeez." Finished with his sunscreen application, Greg bent down, slapped Alex on the ass and said, "You're both works of art, okay? And, best of all, you're mine."

"Mmmmm," Alex sighed. He was already relaxing thanks to the warm sun and the soothing sound of surf. All four men grew quiet, and they soaked up the rays. Thirty minutes in, Luke's phone beeped and he and Raphael automatically flipped over onto their backs.

"You guys set a timer?" Greg asked as he, too, flipped over.

"Yeah, it's easy to lose track of time otherwise," Luke replied. "We have the technology ..."

"Alex, time to turn." Greg prodded.

"I'm fine."

Greg sat up and looked over at Raphael and Luke, then cocked his head toward Alex. Without another word, Luke and Raphael leapt up, crossed over the blankets, Luke at Alex's feet, Raphael at his shoulders and as Greg grabbed Alex's waist the three flipped him before he knew what was happening. Alex raised half way up on his elbows and gave them his best dirty look. It did him no good. He looked around, noticed everyone on the beach was pretty much minding their own business, so he laid back down.

More quiet reverie continued as the men enjoyed the sun, the gentle breeze, the high-pitched calls of the seagulls. A flight of pelicans flew overhead. "Alex, look!" Greg suddenly exclaimed. The other three all raised up on their respective elbows and looked at Greg. "You've been displaying your cage for a good ten minutes and the earth is still revolving on its axis!" Both Raphael and Luke laughed as they laid back down. Alex had a one word response.

"Bitch."

That elicited another laugh. Then, more quiet time, until Luke's phone beeped again. He sat up and pulled a couple of metal water bottles out of the pack and handed one to Greg, taking a long swig out of the other before handing it to Raphael. Alex sat up and took the bottle from Greg and drank.

"You guys come prepared," Alex said thankfully. "I think I was too nervous to plan."

"And? What did you have to be nervous about? What horrible fate has befallen you?" Greg asked.

"Yeah, see, it's no big deal," Raphael chimed in. "Most people don't pay any attention to anything but their phone. Here, maybe they notice the view, but mostly they're oblivious. They're more concerned about who might be looking at them than who they might be looking at."

"True that," Luke added. "Besides, we learned a long time ago that the only people who notice are people who are genuinely interested and always complimentary. Right, baby?"

"Totally. Judgmental people keep their opinions to themselves. Here, I'll show you." Raphael stood up, raised his arms in a long, slow yawn, as he slowly turned a three-sixty. "Nothing, see?"

"Ha, ha," Alex fake laughed. "You are so funny."

"You know what else I am?" Alex looked at Raphael but didn't verbalize anything. "I'm very persuasive. Isn't that right, Luke?"

"Are you kidding. Have you ever heard me say 'No'?"

"Nope. This is how persuasive I am." At that, Raphael walked around to Alex and reached down to take his left hand. Instinctively, Alex let Raphael take it, not realizing what was coming until Raphael started pulling him into a standing position. When he realized what Raphael was up to, Greg stood up and pulled Alex's other arm. Once he was on his feet, Raphael took Alex's hand in his and said, "We're going to take a beach walk."

"No, no ... no," Alex protested.

Raphael looked Alex eye to eye, his face just inches from Alex's and said, "What do you think will attract more attention to you, me and our cages? A simple little beach walk, or what I'm about to do if you say no again."

Alex gave Raphael, then Greg, then Raphael again his best 'fuck you' look, then simply said, you guessed it, "Bitch."

"I'm your bitch," Raphael laughed. "I'm your beach bitch. Your naked, caged and sweaty beach bitch. Let's go get wet." He pulled on Alex's hand and started walking, Alex started to resist, Raphael gave him a silent 'do you really want a scene?' look and the two set off, hand in hand, toward the surf.

Greg sat back down next to Luke and the two watched Raphael and Alex walk away. "Have you ever seen a sexier pair of asses walking away in your life? It's like poetry in motion."

"Greg, we are two of the luckiest guys in the world. In the history of the world."

"I can't argue with that. I'm so glad Alex found Raphael and that we've all become friends. You guys have really helped open him up. Growing up in the Midwest has held him back. I really appreciate how he's becoming more confident and comfortable here. You've helped a lot. It took everything I had to get him to go to Folsom."

"What do you mean? He was wearing only a chest harness and leather jock. That's pretty out there."

"You have no idea what I had to do to convince him to do that."

"Do tell..."

"Maybe when I know you better."

"Okay, now you have to tell me."

"I promise. In due time." Alex and Raphael were now ambling in the surf, not even up their knees. Maybe it was just coincidence, but it seemed like an unusual number of men had decided it was time to get their feet wet as well. "You know, is it me or have our boys attracted a little fan club?"

"Get used to it. Raphael is like the Pied Piper, and as Alex gets more comfortable and experienced, you'll get used to it. That's the price for loving a gorgeous man. But, it's worth it."

'Yeah, it would be easy to get jealous, but I never do. We trust each other completely."

"How long have you two been married?"

"Almost five years."

"Wow. Congratulations. You should be proud."

"What about you two?"

"We've been engaged since the beginning of the year. We just haven't made specific plans."

"I can tell you two really love each other."

"I love him more than I ever thought I could love anyone."

"Well, when you do get married, I hope we're there to witness it."

"Deal. I don't think it will be that far in the future. We just need to figure out a good time and make it happen. You'll be there." Both men laid back down, and closed their eyes.

After a couple of minutes of silence, Luke turned his head toward Greg. "It's really none of my business, but how did Alex come to be caged? His idea or yours?"

Greg rose up on one elbow and squinted at Luke. "It's no secret, at least it shouldn't be between us. It's kind of funny, really. Alex looks like the boy next door, but he has a libido that just won't quit." He paused a moment. "More times than I can count, I'd come home from an errand, or pop into the bedroom from whatever I was doing and catch him beating off. Sometimes, of course, that would lead to sex together. But I'll never know how many times he beat off when I wasn't around."

"Was it interfering with your sex life?"

"You know, I don't know. In retrospect, it probably was, but I didn't realize it. I mean, he was always ready to go at it whenever I was, but at that time, it was usually me who instigated it. So, yeah, he was getting off a lot more often than I was, no question. This was, oh, a couple of years into our marriage. I was getting worried, you know, that I wasn't enough for him. So, we talked about it. He insisted there was absolutely nothing wrong between us. He had to admit, and I give him a lot of credit for this, he had to admit he was addicted to porn."

"Hey, who doesn't like porn?"

"No, this was more than that. He couldn't help himself. He said every time I had caught him beating off, he swore to himself to stop, and save all his cum for me. But, after a day or two, he was right back at it. It was an emotional discussion, to say the least. He was very contrite, and genuinely sorry. And, he promised to save himself for me. So, and I really just said this jokingly, I said, 'okay, but the next time I catch you, I'm locking that cock up in a chastity device.' He thought that was funny, and so did I. Until a couple of days later, when I caught him again. I think I said something like 'you're just hopeless' and we left it at that. But, later that night, in bed, he cuddled up to me and said he was willing to try chastity ... for me, for us. It was his way of saying, 'I'm an addict, I can't help myself, please help me.' The next evening, we went online together and did some exploring, and settled on the Holy Trainer. I can't remember now which model we started with, but we put it on him when it arrived just a few days later, and except for cleanings and upgrading a couple of times, most recently to the Nano V3 he wears now, it hasn't come off. Three years and counting. And, to your question about our sex life, after only a couple of days locked up, it wasn't me initiating sex anymore. He's been the horniest and surprisingly most adventurous Alex ever since."

"Wow. That's a great story. Thanks for sharing."

"Sure thing. Bottom line, we'll do anything for our guys, right?"

"Yep. Anything."

Greg laid back down and closed his eyes. "Now you tell me Raphael's story." And, so, Luke did.

Twenty-One

A Gift for Alex

Raphael and Alex had been walking in and out of the surf for about twenty minutes. Slowly, Alex had begun to relax. More than a few guys had looked their way, but who knew if they were noticing the cages or just noticing two attractive naked guys holding hands on the beach? Alex's HT wasn't all that noticeable from a distance, or so he hoped, but Raphael's steel Looker 01 no doubt flashed brightly in the sun. Not that he cared. Nor should he have. One hot guy, passing in the opposite direction nodded as he passed, then let out an audible "Woof!" once he was behind them. Raphael looked at Alex and grinned. "See, you have nothing to worry about."

"Maybe not. You're probably right about these things. I guess that's why I was willing to come in the first place. I really want to be as brave as you, Raphael. I really do."

"You will be ... you are!" Raphael replied, planting a kiss on Alex's cheek. "I'm glad you and Greg came. We should do this more often. The more we do it, the easier it'll be and soon you won't even think twice about it. Afterall, you've been locked a lot longer than me. You should be leading me, instead."

"I'm glad it's you leading me, Raphael. Your friendship means a lot. Yours and Luke's, both. Greg really enjoys both of you, too."

"Good. Let's make sure we all spend more time together. Here on the beach and elsewhere. It's great having you as a locked cock brother."

"Yeah, me, too." A low roaring sound that wasn't the surf began to grow louder behind them. Alex turned to see a park ranger approaching on an ATV. "Shit!" Alex said. "Just when I thought we were fine, here comes a cop. We're going to get arrested!"

"Arrested for what? It's just a ranger."

"I don't know. For being naked? Public indecency? Walking while caged and queer?"

"Alex, chill out! You were doing so well." The ranger pulled up next to them and stalled out his engine.

"Hey, guys. How's it going?" Alex looked like he'd just stolen the Hope Diamond.

Raphael grinned and said, "Doing great thanks. What's up?"

"Have you seen a Scottie on the beach?"

Raphael squinted at the ranger and said, "My fiancé is Scottish. He's with my friend's husband at the north end of the beach."

"That's great, but, no, I'm looking for a little black Scottish Terrier."

"A dog? Dogs aren't allowed on the beach."

'You know that, I know it, but not everyone knows it, or at least not everyone abides by it. Yeah, we have a report of a runaway dog from the south end of the beach, a black Scottie."

"Gosh, we haven't seen anything. Sorry," Raphael said.

"Well, if you do, do you have a phone with you?"

"Yeah, sure, back with our partners."

"If you see the dog, grab it if you can and call 311. Tell them to notify Ranger Roberto at Baker Beach and give your location. I'll come round him up from you."

"Sure thing. We'll let you know."

"Thanks, men. Enjoy your day. Stay safe now." The ranger clicked the ignition on and puttered off. Raphael looked scornfully at Alex.

"Arrested, huh?"

"Okay, you win. I'm an idiot. That was awesome. He didn't even blink."

"You're not an idiot. You're just a locked cock brother who needs to spend a lot more time with his much wiser and more worldly ... and browner locked cock brother."

"Well, if we do this every weekend, maybe I'll become as wise and as brown as you."

"A worthy goal, Alex. Let's aim for that." Alex and Raphael, still hand in hand, made their way back to Greg and Luke.

"We thought you guys had run off together," Greg said as he sat up. Raphael put his arm around Alex's waist. Alex, and this was notable to everyone, put his arm around Raphael's shoulders and continued standing, naked and caged, queerly positioned with Raphael, in full view of everyone else at the beach. Progress had definitely been made.

"We thought about it," Raphael joked, "but neither of us had our wallet with us. We'd have starved." Laughs all around. "Alex," Raphael continued, "you were great. You should have seen him chatting up a park ranger in all his naked glory."

"That's not exactly the way it went, but, yeah, it was good. I feel good. I feel great. I meant what I said about doing this again, maybe next weekend?"

"Let's do it!" Luke said, standing up and rolling up one of the blankets. "We should call it a day for now. Speaking of starving, I vote we go look for food."

"I could eat," Greg offered as he started handing Alex his clothes. Alex took the yellow locked cock tee and handed it back to Raphael.

"Thanks for sharing," he said.

"Alex, it's yours now. It was a great talisman for today, beginning with our encounter with sexy skater dude on the train. This day couldn't have gone better. I'm so proud of you, and you've earned that shirt. I hope you'll wear it next beach trip, and whenever we're out together. Besides, I have plenty more. I think Luke has a standing order for them."

"Really? Wow, this is so cool of you, Raphael," Alex said as he grabbed Raphael in a big hug. He turned to Luke who was the only one in the group dressed so far, and hugged him, too. "Thanks for a great day, Luke."

"Ahem," Greg spoke up. Alex grinned, turned to Greg, and hugged him. "Thank you most of all." He punctuated the hug with a big kiss, which elicited a resounding "wooooooo" from a couple of guys nearby, who had apparently been enjoying the show. To everyone's shock, Alex turned to them and took a bow, which was rewarded with applause by the two guys.

"Okay, cast, that's a wrap," Luke said. "Let's eat."

Twenty-Two

LUKE MAKES IT PERMANENT

THE REST OF THE weekend was fairly low key, after the tension of Niki and Steve's send off and Alex's first experience of public nudity. Both had gone really well, but the day was exhausting. Luke and Raphael spent the rest of the weekend mostly relaxing at home in typical attire: naked, harnessed, and for Raphael, also collared, caged and sometimes plugged. They skipped the gym, made out some, between streaming some Netflix, laundry and cooking, but all in all, it was a welcome relief from the stress of organizing all the preparations they'd made the previous week for Steve and Niki's trip to BPOS.

Monday evening Luke beat Raphael home by only a few minutes. He was already stripped, harnessed and lounging on the couch, sipping a Kombucha and checking some online blogs when Raphael came through the door. Raphael planted a kiss on Luke's waiting lips, then moved on into the bedroom to shed his caged cock polo and khakis from work. Moments later he was back, naked but for his own harness. Instead of taking his usual place at the other end of the couch, Raphael instead dropped to his knees in front of Luke and immediately sucked Luke's cock down to the root. As he massaged the underside of Luke's cock with his tongue, Luke put down his tablet and took hold of both shaved sides of Raphael's head and caressed them.

After what seemed like a small eternity, Raphael pulled back just enough to allow himself to breathe through his nose, then dived back in for more. A few minutes later, as Luke's now raging erection was completely satisfying what was obviously a deep and abiding need in his locked cock boy, Raphael moved both hands up Luke's torso until his fingers found both nipples. Raphael began kneading and squeezing, firmly then gently, as he played a favorite melody, over and over again, on Luke's swollen flute. As Raphael arrived at his intended crescendo, Luke submitted to his lover's oral skills and came ... and came ... and came. Raphael took it all, laughing, licking and slurping his favorite appetizer. As he pulled his mouth free, he lifted Luke's legs up and onto the couch, then piled on top of Luke, his cage against Luke's still hard but spent cock, and stuck his coated tongue down Luke's throat ... being the sharing person that he is. Spit and cum and breaths were swapped and savored, then Raphael slid down just far enough to rest his head on Luke's chest, blanketing the rest of Luke's body with his own. Luke laid his own head back on the sofa arm and began slowly rubbing Raphael's back with his hands. Not quite a massage so much as a tender and grateful thank you rub.

"That was unexpected," Luke whispered.

"Mmmm-hmmm." Raphael muttered without moving.

"Should we go shave and shower now?"

"Mmmm-hmmm."

"Okay..." But Raphael didn't move and neither did Luke. Luke looked down at Raphael's back and perfect butt, his developed thighs and gym-built calves. He could just feel the touch of Raphael's cage between his own thighs. He laid his head back again and closed his eyes. Grateful for this moment. For every moment he shared with Raphael. Soon exhaustion began to take over. As Luke hovered between consciousness and that delicious dream state, he suddenly realized what Raphael's next dare would be. Should he? Could he really? But what if ... Then, within seconds, both men were asleep.

The next day Luke made a couple of phone calls over lunch. He was excited, a little nervous, but ready to move forward. Raphael beat him home this day, but soon both were in place on the couch, this time sipping Sauvignon Blanc left over from last night's dinner. Each was checking out links on their respective tablets when Raphael put his down on his lap and said, "I'm getting a little worried."

"About?"

"Niki. We haven't heard a word from Steve. I don't know if that's good news or bad."

"I vote for good news. They're probably so involved in what they're learning that Steve just hasn't had time to text. What they're going through is probably exhausting."

"I hope you're right. I'm tempted to text Steve myself. You know, just say 'how's it going?'"

"Nah, I wouldn't. He'll text when he has something to share. He hasn't forgotten about us, and he knows we're dying to hear how it's going, so, let's just be patient a little bit longer."

"You're probably right. I so hope Niki's having a good time."

"We'll know soon enough." Luke went back to his browsing for a moment, then looked across to Raphael, smiled and said," I have something that might take your mind off Niki for a little while."

"What have you got there?"

"No, nothing on my tablet. I have your next dare."

"Oooooh. I thought you'd forgotten it was your turn. It has been a while, what with our social work projects with Niki and Alex." Raphael waited, but Luke didn't elaborate. Raphael prodded, "I can't imagine what you have in mind."

"I'll bet you can't. It's a not-so-flash mutual dare."

"Oh, man, this is starting to get complicated, isn't it?" Raphael grabbed Luke's flaccid cock with both of his big toes and squeezed. "Tell me, tell me, tell me. It's mutual right? You have to do it, too?"

"Yep. And, it's not-so-flash because it's permanent. You'll want to think about it a little."

"Okay ... now I'm getting worried. Did you say permanent? Hmm, you look serious."

"Well, it's not really 'serious' but it is permanent." Luke tortured Raphael with a pregnant pause, flashed him a wicked grin and then rushed through his announcement, "We each have to get a tattoo. Your appointment is for tomorrow at four. Jake gave me a recommendation for a really good artist. I booked two hours for you, just to be safe. You get to pick what you get and where you get it. You just have to get it."

Raphael took a moment to absorb what Luke had just said. "Wow. You're right. That is permanent."

"The idea came to me last night when you were laying on top of me, falling asleep. You looked so beautiful. So sexy. The cage, the collar, they define you and make you a work of art, but they can be removed. A tattoo, like our love, is forever."

"Ahhh, what a nice poetic speech to make to someone you've commanded to alter his body forever."

"Are you upset?"

"No, just being snarky. It really was a nice speech, Sir. And, I would be honored to wear your mark forever."

"Oh, no, no. no, it isn't 'my mark.' I really want it to be all you. Your decision. Your design. This could be kind of exciting, don't you think?"

"Yeah, I guess. I mean we're probably two of maybe six guys in the hood who don't have tattoos. I'm surprised we haven't been wrestled to the ground and forcibly inked before now.'

"Yeah, not a big deal in general, but for us, a big deal. Because we're doing it for each other. I already know what I'm doing. My appointment is for day after tomorrow, so I get to see yours first, since it's my dare."

"Well, okay then. I guess it's settled. Let's eat, and then I have some thinking to do." Just as Raphael got up to head to the kitchen, his phone sounded the alert for a text from Steve. He scooped up the phone, unlocked it and sat down again. Luke slid into place next to him so they could both read it.

The text was minimal, but there was a link to a video. The text read: *'We're not supposed to do this, but I knew you'd appreciate seeing this. Safe to say we did the right thing.'* Raphael clicked through to the video, which immediately showed two human pups from a standing height vantage point, so the camera was looking down on them. Despite both wearing pup hoods, mitts and knee pads, it was obvious which one was Niki. The pups were playing with each other, barking, sniffing each other's butts, wrestling a bit, tails wagging furiously. At one point Niki caught Steve filming him and he mugged for the camera as a pup might, turning his head sideways and 'arfing' in a questioning way, as if he didn't know what Steve was doing. The other pup took advantage to roll Niki over on his back, displaying his new cage prominently. Niki retaliated, rolling the other pup over, displaying his cage, one not nearly as impressive as Niki's. The video lasted only about a minute, but the message was clear. Niki was having a blast. He was learning fast and was clearly in his element and clearly unabashed at last about being naked in a group. Raphael turned to Luke and did something he almost never, ever did. He high-fived him.

"That. Was. Incredible."

"See, I told you he'd be fine. Fine, hell, he's on cloud nine."

"I'm going to respond to Steve." Raphael typed out, *'We're soooo happy for you two! Please keep us posted.'* Then, he turned back to Luke and said, "That's a load off. Now I can sleep."

"You, uh, didn't have any trouble sleeping last evening, while using me as a mattress."

"That was nice, wasn't it? Maybe I'll do that again tonight."

"Baby, you can do a repeat of last night any time you want." It wasn't clear if Luke was referring to the nap or the spontaneous blow job, but it really didn't matter. Odds were, both would happen again. Dinner was cooked, eaten and cleaned up after. As usual, Raphael cooked with some prep help from Luke, and afterwards Luke handled the clean-up. Luke was capable of cooking, but he hadn't had Mama to teach him, as Raphael had, so he was really no match in the kitchen. Once done, the men retired to the couch. An hour later, Raphael really hadn't said much, intent on his tablet. Luke put his down and asked, "You're not working are you?"

"Oh, no. Research, Sir. For your dare. This is permanent after all."

"Have you made a decision?" Raphael clicked his tablet off, put it aside and slid across the couch to once again settle on top of Luke who instinctively wrapped his arms around Raphael's back. Raphael laid his head on Luke's chest and made a happy moaning sound.

"I think so. I just have to sleep on it."

"That's great, baby, but if it's okay with you, let's do our sleeping in bed." Luke slid out from under Raphael, who rolled over on his back. Unable to resist, Luke slid his arms under Raphael, picked him up and carried him into the bedroom. They both slept that night, but ... not right away.

Twenty-Three

EXCEEDING EXPECTATIONS

RAPHAEL LEFT WORK EARLY the following day and reported to the tattoo studio as Luke had arranged, but two hours earlier than Luke had planned. Raphael had phoned first thing that day to expand his session to hopefully accommodate his design. The shop was very modern, clean, almost clinical, which made Raphael feel at ease.

"Hi, I'm Raphael Malaluan, and I have an appointment with Peg," Raphael said in greeting to the receptionist.

"Welcome, Raphael. Have a seat. She'll be right with you. There are refreshments over there if you'd like anything."

"Thanks." Raphael helped himself to a water and took a seat. Needless to say, he was nervous, excited, but mostly nervous. Almost immediately, a tall striking woman in a bleached buzzcut, septum piercing and fabulous tribal gauged ear lobes approached with a big smile, and extended her hand.

"Raphael? I'm Peg. I'll be your artist this afternoon. And, you'll be my canvas?"

"I will," Raphael responded, taking her hand. She had the kind of personality that immediately put one at ease.

"Let's go back here so you can show me what you have in mind. I understand it's more complex than what your partner had anticipated?" Raphael and Peg walked midway back into the studio and sat down opposite one another at a small table. Raphael pulled his tablet out of his shoulder bag, turned it on and opened the photo he'd saved from the internet.

"This is one of the two tattoos I want."

"Ah, Leo Zulueta! I've met him, he's wonderful."

"You have? Oh, man, I'm so jealous. The first time I saw this photo years ago, I immediately knew that if I ever got a tattoo, this is what I'd want. He's Filipino American, too, so that kinda made it perfect. You don't think he'd mind if I got the same tattoo, do you?"

"I'm sure he'd be honored, Raphael. You're a beautiful canvas, and it will look stunning on you. Did you say two tattoos? This one alone is going to take quite a bit of time, and it's going to be very intense for you."

"Here's the other one. I tried to draw it up, myself ... it's my own concept." Peg took the piece of paper from Raphael and studied it a moment, then smiled. She looked up at Raphael who was trying hard to look innocent.

"I take it Luke is your ... partner?"

"My fiancé. My lover. My whole life, really."

"He must be if you want me to do this. Are sure? Really, really sure, Raphael?"

"I'm sure. Please, Peg. It's exactly what I want."

"Okay. You're the canvas. I'll be your artist. But, these two pieces are going to take a lot of work. I'm thinking we may need some help to do this in the time we have. How good are you at handling pain?"

"Well, my piercer says I'm a trooper. Why?"

"It would help if two of us work on your back at the same time. Could you handle that?"

"I don't know. I'll do whatever it takes, Peg. I want this very much, and I really want it done today, so Luke sees it completed, you know, not just partial or outlined."

"Simon!" Peg yelled to someone further back in the studio.

"Yeah?" A thirty-something guy with more tattoos than Raphael could count came out of nowhere.

"Simon, this is Raphael. We want to do these for him this afternoon." She showed Simon the designs. "He's a trooper and willing to have both of us do this one at the same time. What do you have lined up for the next three hours?"

"Nothing yet, just here for any walk-ins. Awesome designs. Is that Bornean?"

"Yeah, Zulueta. Raphael's got good taste."

"Wicked, too, from the looks of this second one," Simon said, looking directly at Raphael. "Are you really?"

"Yeah, Simon, I am. Proudly so."

"That's cool. Can I do the second one?"

"We'll see. We better get started. We have some work to do. Raphael, you can put your clothes on that chair over there and then lay down on that table. Simon and I will start prepping."

Raphael was a trooper. Most of the time. There were a few muffled screams. Okay, more than a few. And an occasional tear. Peg and Simon took a break every twenty minutes or so, to give Raphael and themselves a chance to relax. Whenever she sensed things were getting too intense, she'd pause, but Raphael would respond, "I'm fine. Ignore the screams. Really, I'm fine."

Finally, just over three hours in, the buzzing stopped and Peg did a final wipe down on Raphael's back. She moved to the head of the table Raphael was laying on and squatted down to his face level. "Normally, I'd wrap your back now, but I have a hunch you want Luke to see it before I do, am I right?"

"Yes. I want to blow his mind. Can I see it?"

"Of course. We'll need to turn you over anyway to do your second design." She and Simon helped Raphael sit up, then stand up. This was Simon's first opportunity to see the cage.

"You weren't shitting me, Raphael. That is one mean cage, man."

"Thanks. It's hard to explain to someone who doesn't understand the lifestyle, but it's very integral to me and to Luke. And, to our relationship," Raphael said, as they guided him to a large mirror at the side of the room.

"Sure, I get it," Simon said. "It's not all that different from ink, maybe. It, uh, suits you, you know. Peg, I really want to do the front, if Raphael doesn't mind." Raphael looked at Peg. Afterall, it was her that Jake had praised so highly.

"Simon does excellent work, Raphael," she assured. "In fact, I'd say he does lettering better than I do, so if it's okay with you, it's okay with me."

"Okay," Raphael agreed. "You guys know best." Peg handed him a large hand mirror and he turned around so his back faced the wall mirror. He raised the hand mirror and tentatively looked, half afraid of what he was about to see.

"You guys are amazing!" he shouted. "Sorry ... it's awesome ... it's exactly what I envisioned. Luke will die. Thank you, thank you. Oh wow..."

"It does look amazing on you, doesn't it, with your broad shoulders and narrow waist?" Peg said. "You chose wisely. You will never be the same after today, Raphael. Simon and I are honored to have played a part in your transformation. If you're smart, you'll never wear a shirt again." She laughed at that idea.

"That's really not so funny," Raphael said. "We both live naked most of the time anyway, at home, at the beach..."

"Yeah," Simon pitched in. "I can tell. You've been naked the whole time you've been here. Most clients request a towel."

"Wannabes," Raphael laughed.

"Wannabes?" Peg asked.

"Private joke. From one of the many times I've been naked in public."

"And, how comfortable will you be to be naked in public after this next tattoo?" Simon asked, quite seriously.

"Even more comfortable ... and prouder ... than before. It's what I am, Simon. And, always will be."

"Then let's do it!" Simon whooped. "Back on the table, 'boy'." Raphael grinned and followed Simon's orders. Just as he approached the table, his phone sounded Luke's text alert.

"Excuse me just one second. Sorry," Raphael said as he went to the chair and pulled the phone out of his pocket. He read and responded to the text, then jumped up on the table. "I told him to come by in an hour. Is that good?"

"Should be," Simon responded as he positioned Raphael and pulled on fresh gloves.

Tattoo number two took just under an hour. Raphael had time to admire the second tattoo, walk up front and settle up the additional charge for the extra time he'd booked and leave generous tips for both Peg and Simon. Typical of him, he hadn't realized he was still naked until one of the waiting clients said, "Wow! Look at that piece." Raphael wasn't sure if the 'piece' he was referring to was the ink on his back or himself. Either way, it was nice to hear.

Just as he returned to the table where he'd spent the last four hours and a considerable amount of sweat, tears and money, he heard Luke's voice in the lobby area. Peg, who was passing through smiled and asked, "Is that your ride?"

"That's Luke. Is it okay if he comes back?"

"Of course, hon. Get ready for the unveiling. I'll show him back."

Raphael moved closer to the center of the room his back to the entrance, and waited. He heard Luke's footsteps and then, "Whoa! Oh my ... Raphael ... you ... that's amazing!" This was Luke's first view of the tattoo, really two tattoos on Raphael's back. Each image, redolent of a tropical frond, started just above the center of each butt cheek, then went all the way up each side of his back, gradually tapering wider and wider until each was about three inches wide at the shoulder blades. Then, these fronds curved down, tapered quickly narrower until they came to a point again, near where Raphael's arms met his back.

"It's ... it's beautiful," Luke praised "It's ... audacious? If that's a word?"

"You like it?" Raphael turned just his head and coyly asked, a good-sized grin on his face. He already knew the answer.

"Like it? I was not expecting anything like this, baby. A little flower on the wrist, maybe, but this? I'm speechless."

"Maybe this will inspire some words," Raphael said, turning around to face Luke. Luke was looking into Raphael's dreamy, almond eyes at first, but when Raphael's grin grew even bigger, he realized he was a victim, yet again, of Raphael's mischievous, dare we say, evil, powers over himself. Raphael couldn't wait any longer for Luke to catch on. "I decided to get two tattoos," he said, as he looked down at his cage.

Luke looked down, wordlessly opened his mouth and dropped to his knees in front of Raphael. There on Raphael's hairless pubic area, just above his cage, in an arc were the words in a crisp, bold font:

Luke's Locked Cock Boy

Luke, still eye level with Raphael's cage, looked up at Raphael, stunned. And, this time, truly speechless. Finally, he stood up, looked back down at Raphael's new ink, then, putting his hands on either side of Raphael's waist, he said, "But ..."

"But?"

"What if we, someday, ever break up?"

"Luke, that's not going to happen."

"No, but what if you decide, someday, to have me unlock you? You know, give up the cage."

Raphael looked intensely at Luke. "Not going to happen."

"Okay. What about when we're, I don't know, in our sixties?"

"Luke. I will *always* be your locked cock boy. Today, tomorrow and always. Regardless of how gray we may get, I'll always be your locked cock boy."

Luke let out a long sigh, then pulled Raphael into a fierce embrace. Never had he expected this. But, of course, he shouldn't have been surprised by the intensity of Raphael's willingness to display, now permanently, his devotion to Luke. Luke felt overwhelmed, and frankly, unworthy. He pulled back enough that the two could look into each other's eyes and said, "I don't deserve you."

Raphael looked right back at Luke and said, "Of course you do. After all, you made me who I am, Sir. Now take me home and fuck my brains out. After today, I've earned it."

It was at that point Luke and Raphael realized they'd had an audience the whole time, as Peg and Simon both whooped and clapped.

"He's not exaggerating, Luke," Simon exclaimed. "He just went through hell for you. Go fuck his brains out, man."

Peg was the adult in the room. "Boys, I need to wrap, well, most of Raphael's body. We've discussed the aftercare, Raphael, please follow it to the letter. I want this masterpiece to last forever, okay? And Luke, I'll see you tomorrow."

Luke let out yet another heavy sigh. He still hadn't fully digested what Raphael had done. "Um, yeah. Tomorrow. I've got to totally rethink what we're going to do, though. I mean, talk about raising the bar, Raphael..."

"That, he did," Simon agreed. "Raphael, when you're all healed, I'd love to get pics of your ink for our book. Including the cage, if that's okay. It is so fucking radical."

"Sure, I'd be honored. Thanks."

Once Peg finished up, Raphael gingerly pulled on his work pants. "It's a good thing you guys live naked. You're going to hate clothes for the next couple of days," Simon said with a laugh.

"It'll be just like any other day," Luke laughed, as he took Raphael's hand and led him out the door.

Twenty-Four

LUKE, YOU'RE UP!

THAT NIGHT LUKE AND Raphael enjoyed a light supper, as Raphael was still buzzing and not very hungry. In fact, he did something he very rarely did ... he took a pain reliever. Since his back and pubic area were covered in bandages, the men skipped their daily shave and shower routine.

"But, Luke, I can still shave you," Raphael protested.

"No way, baby. I want you to just rest. In fact, you need to call in sick tomorrow, and just stay home and rest. When I get home from Peg's, I'll remove your bandages and give you your first antiseptic rub down."

"I'll be fine."

"You're more than fine, but at least give it day before you try to put any clothes on. You won't be able to hide the bandages on your back anyway, no matter which shirt you wear. You have plenty of medical leave saved up, this is a perfect time to use it."

"We'll see. I am kinda tired anyway. I think I'll go to bed early." And they did. For the first time since Raphael could ever remember, he wore a t-shirt to bed, one of Luke's workout shirts, since he didn't want to risk ruining the sheets or one of his caged cock shirts. Normally Luke would have been spooning Raphael, one arm under Raphael's neck, the other over and around his waist, but tonight, they reversed, with Raphael snugged up against Luke's back. His right arm draped over Luke's waist. Occasionally his right hand brushed against Luke's cock. When it hardened, he wrapped his fingers around it playfully.

"Is somebody horny?" Luke dreamily muttered. "Even after his big day?"

"Ummm, a little," Raphael whispered back into Luke's ear. "But actually, I just want to hold my cock. It feels so good on you."

"Okay, baby. You do that. Sweet dreams." It wasn't long before Luke could feel Raphael's sleep breathing, slow and steady. He was relieved. He worried the it might be a sleepless night for him. Even as he slept,

Raphael still had hold of 'his' cock, which made Luke smile. Once again, Raphael had inspired Luke. The thought carried Luke off into sleep.

Not surprisingly, the following morning Raphael agreed Luke was right, and called in sick. He planned to spend the day at home, as naked as was possible with the bandages on both front and back. The itching from the tape and maybe the tattoos themselves was irritating, but he promised to be a good boy and not remove them before evening. As Raphael had done, Luke left work early to make it to his appointment with Peg.

"How's Raphael doing?" she asked as Luke sat down across the desk from her.

"A little sore, a little itchy," Luke replied, "I talked him into staying home today."

"For the best. Once the bandages come off, he'll feel better. I'd never recommend that much coverage in one go, but he was insistent. He wanted it all done before you saw it. He's quite a guy."

"Yeah, but I'm the lucky one."

"Well, I'd say you both lucked out. So, what have you got to show me?" Luke laid two pieces of paper on the desk, that he'd finalized over his lunch hour.

"Oh, two for you, too, huh? Let's see..."

'Well, neither is anything close to what Raphael had you do."

"No. Not as massive. But, just as provocative, I'd say. And this one is sweet. You guys are so in love it makes my teeth hurt."

"Huh?"

"You know, sweet as candy. Bad joke. Raphael said you're engaged. When's the date?"

"We haven't set one. I guess we should, but it hasn't been a priority. Weddings can get so, you know, messy and complicated."

"They don't have to be."

"Maybe. What about you. Do you have a partner?"

"I do. That's my wife working the reception desk. Wives and business partners."

"That's awesome. Congratulations."

"Thanks. Maybe I should talk her into getting inked like this design of yours. That'll prove her love, don't you think?"

"Most definitely. I'm glad you like it."

"Knowing Raphael, it's perfect. You know, I do have one thought about this second one, speaking of Raphael. Since it has his name on it, what about 'queering it up' a little. What if we put six dots, each a few millimeters in diameter in an arc above the text, each in one of the pride colors. The counterpoint of that on your studly body with his name attached works for me. Here, like this." Peg quickly drew her idea onto Luke's design.

"Yes! Oh, Peg, this is why Jake recommended you. That makes it a hundred times better, and you're right, it's so 'Raphael'."

"Let's do it. Get naked and jump up on the table. Put your kilt and shirt on that chair." A moment later she walked up to Luke with clippers and razor in hand. "Well, I guess I won't have to shave down there, will I?"

"No, Raphael keeps it nice and smooth."

"Just as you keep him smooth, too, huh? You guys should write a book. Okay, I do need to shave here, though, where you just clip it to stubble."

Two hours later, give or take, the deed was done. Peg gave Luke a hand sitting up, then he leapt off the table and skipped over to the mirror. He turned slightly taking in his reflection from a couple of angles.

"Well?"

"Peg, it's perfect. It's all perfect. And the pride dots were genius! Raphael will be blown away."

"Will I?" Raphael said, from the other side of the curtain.

"What the hell are you doing here?" Luke exclaimed as he turned around from the mirror.

"I, uh, bribed Peg to text me when she was about to finish, so I could head over to see what you did." Raphael smiled as he walked past the curtain and up to Luke, who grabbed his shirt from the chair and held it at his waist, a modesty move that was totally out of character and didn't fool Raphael ... or Peg. Raphael, being shorter than Luke, was at the right height to admire the first tattoo. In a perfect ring around his left nipple were the words:

My ♥ Belongs To Raphael

The lettering was in black, except for the heart symbol, which was a vibrant pink.

"Pretty corny, huh?" Luke asked, skewing up his mouth in fake disdain.

"If you think I'm going to dis the sweetest words I've ever seen inked on the breast of the hottest Braveheart living or dead, you need to think again, Sir. These words mean everything to me. Thank you, Luke." Raphael leaned up to plant one of his signature kisses on Luke's lips, then turned to Peg and said, "It's beautiful, Peg. Thank you." Then, he dropped to his knees and yanked the shirt out of Luke's hands and said, "And, what is hiding under here?" Raphael fell back on his heals. Luke had done his best to outdo him, and perhaps he had. Inscribed above

Luke's ample, shaved and pierced member in a neat, bold arc were the words:

Raphael's Cock

And above that, another arc of six dots, each in a different pride color, Raphael's cock was flying its pride colors, out and proud for all to see.

"That pretty much clinches it, doesn't it!" Raphael whooped. "We've permanently dedicated our cocks to each other, haven't we?"

"Well, baby, they were your words. Last night in bed when you wouldn't let go of me. I realized then, that you're right. This is your cock. Everybody should know it." Raphael got to his feet and wrapped his arms around Luke in another one of the rare instances in which Luke was the only naked one.

"Okay, guys let me wrap up Luke, so you two can go get a room somewhere."

"Sorry, Peg," Raphael said as he let Luke go.

"No apologies necessary, Raphael. You two put on a great show. I should have sold tickets. Speaking of which, Simon and I are serious about the pics. In fact, now that we've done Luke, it would be amazing to shoot the two of you together … your pubic tattoos are really a set, you know."

"You got it," Luke answered. "Anything to help you guys out. We couldn't be prouder of your work."

"Hey, the concepts were yours. We were just the technicians."

"You made it art, Peg," Luke continued. "I can't wait to show your work off."

"You do that. Now, let's get you on your way."

Twenty-Five

THE OBEDIENCE SCHOOL GRADUATE

LUKE AND RAPHAEL HAD begged off the irregular Saturday beach day with Alex and Greg, both because their ink wasn't quite ready for primetime yet and because Niki and Steve were due back from Obedience School. They were excited to see Niki in person (in pupson?) and to hear all about the experience from both Steve and Niki. It was early afternoon when they finally got a text from Steve, inviting them over to their place. They rang the bell when they arrived and immediately heard barks coming from inside. Steve opened the door and stepped aside to let them in. Before they could even move, pup Niki was there, on all fours, caged, collared, hooded and tailed, his only clothing item a chest harness. Steve, too, was naked and wearing his matching chest harness.

As Niki scampered back and forth, sniffing Raphael's and Luke's crotches as they pulled off their respective shorts and kilt, Luke said, "So, he's still in pup head space, eh?"

"Oh, yeah. Here, give me your clothes. Have a seat and I'll fill you in." Steve then clapped his hands and sternly said, "Sit Niki. Sit! ... Good boy."

Niki's tail wagged a few times, then he sat, whimpering slightly.

"He's really glad to see you guys," Steve said as he returned from putting the clothes in the bedroom. "I know he wants to tell you all about his week, but, he can't as long as he's in pup space. In fact, he hasn't spoken a word since last Saturday."

"Seriously?" Raphael asked. "So, total pup mode, even after the van dropped you guys off here? Is that like a rule or something left over from obedience school?"

"Not a rule, but they told us some of the pups just don't want to leave pup space. At least for a while. Sooner than later for most guys, of course, they have to resume human tasks."

"So ... when do you think Niki will leave pup space and socialize with us as human?"

"We made a deal, even though he wasn't speaking. You can talk to him, of course, even in pup mode, but he doesn't answer back. So, I said he can be a full-time pup Sunday and Monday which will be his days off, and anytime he has a pup play date with other pups. I haven't told him about his job yet. I thought you guys would want to take part in that. But, the other days, I get my sexy human boyfriend back." Pup Niki was listening intently to Steve, and at the mention of 'job' he perked up, turned his head sideways and trotted over next to Steve on the couch and panted.

"Is Niki ready to learn about his job? Is he?" Steve addressed Niki. Niki barked affirmatively.

"Okay, but first," and Steve looked at Raphael and Luke, who were sitting cross legged beside each other on the floor, "what the hell have you two been up to?" He exclaimed. "Stand up and let me look at you two."

"Oh, yeah," Raphael grinned as he stood and extended a hand to Luke, "we, uh, had a little mutual dare action this week." He walked over closer to Steve to show first his pubic ink, then turned to showcase his back. Luke followed suit, dropping to his knees so Steve could better see his pec ink. He patted Niki on the ass, who had trotted over for a closer look. Niki's tail wagged vigorously.

"You guys never do anything half-way, do you?"

"Nope." Luke asserted. "As usual, Raphael set the pace on this one. I just tried to keep up."

"What have they said at the gym about it? You're already a steam room sensation."

"We haven't gone yet," Raphael responded. "We're still letting the ink set. Maybe next week. We skipped the beach, too, today. We wanted to see you guys more than anything." Niki rubbed up against Raphael.

"He's showing his affection, Raphael."

"This is so weird," Raphael responded.

"Said the caged, collared, plugged, inked and surprisingly for the moment, not harnessed leather boy," Steve countered.

"Touché. That wasn't a judgement. I just mean I'm not used to Niki like this. I miss his face. Don't you miss his face?"

"Yes, but I've never seen him happier or more animated. You should have seen him at the school. He was the star of the place. All the pups loved him, and so did all the other handlers. And, he was so unabashed, you know, totally naked and caged in front of everyone. He has no inhibitions as a pup. He's just fun and loving."

"That's wonderful. But, is Niki the human going to be uninhibited and fun and loving, too?"

"I think so. Yes. You'll see Tuesday evening when we come over for our regular dinner. Which is probably a good segue to the topic I mentioned earlier. Niki! Attention!" Niki left Raphael's side and sat attentively at Steve's feet. "Are you ready to hear about your new job?" Niki arffed affirmatively and put a paw up on Steve's knee.

"We've arranged a job that's perfect for a happy, sexy pup like you. You'll be working bar back at the leather bar where Raphael and Luke like to go." Niki's head turned sideways and he sounded a questioning, arrruff? "We know you don't know bartending, but that's fine. At first, you'll be helping behind the bar, you know, washing glasses, getting ice, bottled beer for the bartenders, picking up empty glasses and bottles around the bar. They'll teach you how to pull draft beers so you can quickly start serving some of the customers. In time you'll learn to mix drinks, too. You'll not only be earning a higher wage than you were making, you'll no doubt earn pretty good tips, too. Want to know why, puppy?" Niki barked affirmatively, at least that's how Raphael and Luke interpreted it.

"Niki, the best part is you'll be working dressed exactly as you are now, except, of course, you'll have to stand on your hind legs." Another questioning arf from Niki. His tail began wagging for the first time in a while. "Oh, and for legal reasons, you'll have to wear this, too," Steve said as he jumped up and ran into the bedroom. He returned sat down and held up a see-through loose woven black mesh jock that would pretty much appear invisible on him in a darkened bar. The mesh would clearly display his cage anytime one of the spots over the bar hit it. "You start Tuesday evening. Luke and Raphael helped arrange it, so say thank you, Niki."

Niki bounded over to where Raphael and Luke were sitting and jumped on Raphael, knocking him over on his back. Raphael wasn't sure how he managed it with the puppy hood on, but Niki was licking his face like crazy. He then turned on Luke, who got a similar dose of gratitude. Niki's tail was slapping Raphael then the coffee table in glee. Raphael sat back up giggling despite the abuse. As Luke sat up, Niki immediately bent his hooded face down and begin sucking Luke's cock. Luke pulled Niki's head off his crotch and said, "No Niki! Bad dog! Bad puppy!"

Still giggling, Raphael said, "Is this what you mean about being 'unabashed?'

"Yeah, since you caged him, he's been the horniest little fucker. But ... I'm not complaining."

"I know what you mean," Luke grinned. "It had the same effect on Raphael." Raphael stuck his tongue out at Luke and grinned back.

"I don't recall any complaints from you, either, Sir."

Luke leaned over and kissed Raphael. "No, baby, and you never will. I love you best when you're horny ... which is pretty much always."

The rest of the afternoon was spent with Steve filling Luke and Raphael in on the events of the Obedience School experience. He made fettucine in clam sauce and a salad that the humans ate, while the pup ate something unrecognizable from his shiny bowl on the floor. Steve said it was a recipe that had been found to be easiest to prepare and be eaten by human pups. Niki certainly seemed to like it.

"So, I just have to comment on the fact you're naked but harnessed, matching Niki's harness. Is this just because you're both still decompressing as it were, or is this the new Steve and Niki?" Raphael asked hopefully.

"Well, I think it's the new us. I don't think I'm exaggerating when I say you two have had a profound impact on Niki and me. I always liked the fact you two live naked, but of course the old Niki ... the uptight Niki ... didn't, so it wasn't an option. But thanks to the cage, and to a week of gloriously naked Niki at Obedience School, I'm thinking, yeah, this should be the new normal." Niki arffed a loud affirmative.

Raphael scooted over to Niki, lifted him up into a fairly upright posture and put his arms around him in a bear hug. Looking into those sweet brown eyes that were the only recognizable part of Niki's face, Raphael cooed, "I'm so happy for you, Niki. Welcome to your new world." Niki arffed again and put his mitted arms around Raphael. The hug was so tight, Luke and Steve could hear their cages clink.

The afternoon melted into evening, and Luke and Raphael retrieved their street clothes so Steve and Niki could relax. They made plans to see each other, all as humans, Tuesday evening as usual, then shared hugs all around and parted.

Once home, situated in their regular spots on the couch, Raphael looked up at Luke at one point and said, "I'm so glad you're not a puppy. Your face should always be on display and your lips should never be inaccessible to me." Luke put his tablet down and crawled across the couch, pushing Raphael prone and laying on top of him. He licked Raphael's lips, and before plunging in, said, "You took the words right out of my mouth. Let me see if I can find them." And thus began another long, sweaty nap.

Twenty-Six

WE MEET MR. DOORDASH

BECAUSE NIKI WOULD BE starting his new job Tuesday evening, everyone gathered a little earlier than usual for dinner at Raphael and Luke's. Alex and Greg were already there when Steve and Niki arrived. They headed into the bedroom and emerged moments later both naked and in their matching chest harnesses. Niki's cage and collar were permanent, but he was also wearing a cap and his pup tail, which was apparently becoming semi-permanent.

"Can't totally give up the pup life, eh, Niki?" Raphael asked as the hugged Niki, kissed him hard and tweaked his tail.

"I'm betting you're plugged too, am I right?"

"He's got you there, baby," Luke laughed.

"Hey, I wasn't judging, just reporting the facts. Actually, I think it's pretty cute, Niki. I like it. Why the hat?" Niki grinned and whipped off the hat to reveal that he, too, now had a shaved mohawk, only his hair was dyed in several splotchy colors to resemble an animal's coat. "Fuuuuck" Raphael shouted. He couldn't help himself.

"Niki!" Luke also exclaimed as he jumped up and ran over to admire Niki's new do. He rubbed it with his hands, then cupped Niki's face with both hands and also planted a big kiss of his own. "You look great, Niki. I mean really, really great."

"Yeah," Raphael said. "We missed you. You know, the human you."

"Thanks guys. I love you both, and I appreciate your patience. I have to say, though, it was fun playing with you Saturday." Alex and Greg looked questioningly at each other.

"Saturday?" Alex spoke up.

"Yeah, Niki was still in pup space Saturday when we went to see them. This is the first we've seen his face since before Obedience School. Take it from me, Niki makes a pretty fun puppy."

"Oh, yeah?" Greg said. "When do we get to meet this puppy?"

"We'll make plans, Greg," Steve offered. "He is pretty amazing. He was a hit at Obedience School. Of course, you can also see him in full regalia later tonight at Powerhouse. He starts his job tonight."

"He's working at Powerhouse as a pup?" Alex asked. Steve nodded. "Oh, I can't wait to see you, Niki!"

"Please don't come down yet," Niki begged. "I won't know what the hell I'm doing. Not for a while. Give me a couple of weeks first, okay?"

"Well, okay, but I want to play with this fun puppy." Alex was adamant.

"Like I said, we'll have you over real soon on one of Niki's pup days. We have to ration him, or he might just go total pup a hundred percent of the time," Steve promised.

"Dinner should be here, soon. We don't want Niki to be late on his first night," Luke said as he carried plates and utensils into the living room, so he could turn the coffee table into the regular Tuesday night buffet. Raphael was opening a bottle of wine when the doorbell rang. "Raphael, your secret admirer is here," Luke teased,

Raphael put down the wine and went to the door. It was indeed their regular guy, who handed the large bags to Raphael and hesitated before saying, "Hey, new ink!"

"Yeah ... check it out," Raphael grinned as he put the bags down and twirled to give the guy a view of his back. "What do you think?"

"It's beautiful ... and very risqué." He grinned back.

"I'm Raphael," Raphael said extending his hand.

"Yeah, I know, you know, from all the orders. I'm Enrique, but everyone calls me Ricky," he responded as he took Raphael's hand. "Nice to finally meet you."

"Listen, why don't you join us. We have plenty of food."

"Oh, thanks. Really, I ... I couldn't."

"Oh, sure, I guess you have other deliveries." Raphael still had hold of Ricky's hand.

"No, not yet."

"Then turn off your app, and join us!" Raphael pulled Ricky through the door, which wasn't that hard, as Ricky really didn't put up much resistance. Raphael closed the door, picked up the bags and took Ricky's hand again and pulled him into the living room. "Hey, everybody, this is Ricky and he's joining us for dinner."

"Hey, Ricky!" was the unison response.

Raphael set down the bags, but continued holding Ricky's hand. He made the introductions. "That's Luke, my fiancé, this is Alex, that's his husband Greg, that's my brother Niki and his boyfriend Steve."

Ricky was trying hard not to stare. "As you can see," Luke said, "we don't like to wear clothes when we don't have to. Don't feel obligated to join us, but you're welcome to."

"Umm, thanks, I'll stay like this, if that's okay."

"Of course," Raphael assured him, motioning to a spot on the floor next to Alex. Once Ricky sat down Raphael sat down next to him on the other side and began pulling serving containers out of the bags. Casual conversation ensued as the group ate, everyone making an effort to keep Ricky in the conversation to put him at ease. Soon he was chiming in and laughing along with everyone else.

Once everyone had eaten, Raphael stood up and began to clear what he could as Alex joined him. They returned from the kitchen with cookies and sat back down with Ricky. Niki grabbed a cookie and said, "I have to go. Don't want to be late on my first night." As Steve stood up, Niki gave everyone but Ricky a kiss, then extended his hand to Ricky and said, "Great meeting you. Hope to see more of you," then he and Steve headed to the bedroom to dress.

After they left, with fewer hot naked bodies in the room, Ricky felt a little more at ease. He casually said, "I envy you guys."

"How so?" Raphael asked.

"You're so ... I don't know ... so uninhibited, So comfortable with each other, with everyone, really. I confess the first time I delivered here, I was blown away when you answered the door naked and, you know, in chastity. Like it was so normal ... ordinary."

"Well, for us it is," Luke said. "But you kept delivering to us. Tell us why."

"Ummm, I ... you noticed?"

"Duh," Alex said. "We actually looked forward to seeing you. We called you Mr. DoorDash."

"Really? Oh, now I'm embarrassed."

"Why? You obviously didn't mind seeing us like this..."

"You kidding? You guys are so hot. Like I said, I'm kinda jealous of how you live."

"No need to be jealous. It's easy."

"Not for me."

"Oh, yeah? Watch how easy it is." At that, Raphael pinned Ricky's arms to his chest and laid back, pulling Ricky with him so Ricky was now prone. "Alex, a little help with his pants!" Ricky started laughing and struggling with Raphael, but he was no match for Raphael's workouts. Alex had his pants, then his underwear down to his ankles in only a few seconds. Raphael released Ricky, and both sat up, Raphael grabbed the waist of his tee and pulled up. Ricky put up token resistance, then raised his arms so Raphael could finish denuding him.

"Damn you're strong," Ricky laughed as he kicked out of his shorts and boxers.

"Damn you're hot!" Raphael countered. "Stand up so we can admire the total Ricky." Raphael stood, extended his hand and pulled Ricky up. He was obviously embarrassed, but appreciating the admiring looks at the same time.

"Alright, Ricky," Luke said, "you have to tell me your secret."

"Secret?"

"Yeah, your abs workout secret. Holy crap, look at this guy."

"Pretty impressive, Ricky," Greg agreed. "Damn."

"If I told you, you'd hate me," Ricky offered, modestly, looking down at his own torso.

"I can't imagine hating you, Ricky. Seriously ... crunches? Planks?"

Ricky smiled coyly, "I don't do anything. This is just how I was born."

Luke just stared, looked over at Greg, then back at Ricky. "I was wrong. I do hate you." That brought laughs from Steve and Greg. Ricky sat back down and was immediately rejoined by Raphael and Alex.

As he munched another cookie, Raphael put a hand on Ricky's thigh and asked, "So, tell us more about this handsome DoorDash guy who is intrigued by our lifestyle. Do you have a boyfriend?"

Ricky looked into his lap, then looked up and said, "No. Not anymore."

"Oh. I see. I just assumed a guy like you ..."

"That's kind of why I liked coming here. Okay, a confession. After the first time I got an order for you guys, I was, as you say, intrigued. I made sure I got more of your orders, to see if this is how you always live, or if it was just a kinky party or something. And, well, like I said, also, because you guys are hot. I admit it. But I wondered if it was really possible to live like you do. Obviously, it is. And that makes me sad. Sad and sorry." The sadness visibly washed over Ricky's face. Raphael suddenly felt terrible that he'd said anything. He scooted closer, his naked thigh touching Ricky's, and he rested his hand on top of Ricky's thigh.

"Ricky, I ..." Before he could say more, Ricky continued.

"See, I did have a boyfriend. The best boyfriend I could ever hope to have. Juan was handsome and strong, taller than me, muscles like you guys, he wore leather a lot, so, that was sexy, and he was so sweet and loving. We were together about three months, and it was heaven, you know? We did everything together. As time went on, and we got to know each other better, he revealed more of himself to me. I guess that's kind of natural. I was pretty inexperienced and naïve. I didn't catch on at first that his piercings were more than just decoration for him. He wanted us to start doing things I wasn't comfortable with. Bondage. Watersports, which I didn't even know what that was when it first came up ... and chastity. Other things. It was too much, too fast. I resisted. I still wanted to be lovers, but not like that. And, really, he was so sweet. He didn't get upset or anything. Juan just said one day that he obviously wasn't the right guy for me. That he still loved me and wanted me to be happy, and someone else would make me happier than he could.

"And, that was that..." Ricky took a deep breath, not looking up at anyone. Alex scooted over next to Ricky, so that now both of his thighs were rubbing against Raphael on the right and Alex on the left. Alex put his right arm around Ricky's shoulders and squeezed.

In a very quiet voice Alex said, "Ricky, I'm so sorry. You're still hurting, aren't you?" Ricky took another deep breath, obviously trying hard not to cry. Despite his obvious distress, Ricky, who hadn't been touched by another man in months, began to sprout an especially enthusiastic boner. Who wouldn't, surrounded by two naked, caged hotties? Everyone noticed, but no one said a word. First of all, this was no time for levity, and besides, boners on uncaged members of the group were not uncommon. All a part of the naked life.

Not to be outdone by Alex, Raphael leaned in and kissed Ricky on the cheek, a lingering, gentle kiss. Ricky smiled. "You guys are amazing," he said.

"Said the most amazing guy who ever brought us food ... again, and again, and again!" Luke finally spoke, breaking the somberness. Even Ricky laughed. "Tell me, Ricky, do want Juan back?"

"Are you kidding?"

"No, I'm very serious, Ricky. How badly do you miss him?"

"Fuck, I'd do anything to get him back. Yes, I still love him. I think about him day and night. I've never felt what I feel for him."

"Do you think ... if things were different ... that he would take you back?"

"Different?"

"Never mind. Do you think he still loves you?"

"Yeah, I think so. He likes to go to the beer busts Sundays at the Eagle. Sometimes I go, just to see him. Usually, I don't actually talk to him, because, you know, I see him with a guy, but a couple of times when he was alone, I said 'Hola.' He always hugs and kisses me, you know, seems really happy to see me."

"When he's with another guy, is it always the same guy?"

"No, always different. I don't think he's seeing anyone, just, you know, dating around."

Greg spoke up, having been intently watching Ricky, and loving the sight of Alex and Raphael doing such a gentle job of comforting him. "Ricky, is this the first time you've sat, naked, between two naked caged guys, sharing your innermost thoughts like this?"

"Are you kidding?" Ricky sniffed. "Yes, my first time."

"Feels pretty good, doesn't it?"

"Good? It feels awesome. You muchachos are more amazing than I even fantasized."

"You fantasized about us!?" Raphael exclaimed.

"Okay, I've said too much."

"You can never say too much to us, Ricky," Greg continued. "Let me say something to you. Take it for what it's worth, but I mean every word of what I'm about to say." He waited for Ricky to give him his full attention, not an easy thing considering where he was sitting. "Ricky. If you meant what you said about 'doing anything' to get Juan back, you couldn't ask for better help in doing so, than from these guys right here. Raphael and Luke have changed Alex and my lives. They've changed Niki and Steve's lives. Together, if you're serious, we can change your and Juan's lives, too. If you're ready. If you really want to become Juan's sexy, hot leather boy. You have a good start ... you've already got the abs for it."

Everyone remained quiet and still, as Ricky sat motionless, still in the arms of Alex and Raphael. After an agonizing moment for everyone, Ricky looked directly at Greg and asked, "You guys ... you guys would really do that?" Greg nodded, and Luke reached across and pulled Greg close for a sideways hug.

Raphael planted another kiss on Ricky's cheek and affirmed with a whisper in Ricky's ear, "In a heartbeat." At that point Ricky lost control and the tears rolled down his cheeks.

After a few sniffles and a couple of trademark tissues from Luke to Raphael to Ricky, Ricky asked, "How would that work?"

Luke took over for Greg, saying, "It would only work if you are mentally and emotionally ready to explore what Juan wants to share with you. This wouldn't be a cosmetic thing. It will never work if we made you look like Raphael, but, deep down, you were still uncomfortable with bondage or water sports or any of the other things Juan wants to do. Granted, it shouldn't just be about what he wants, but you do know what he wants. If you still don't want that kind of life, no matter what we do to help, it won't work in the end."

Ricky took in Luke's words, then thoughtfully nodded. No one spoke, waiting for Ricky's response. Finally, he turned to Raphael and said, "I want to be Juan's Raphael." A giant grin broke out on Raphael's face.

"Hey!" Alex exclaimed as he shook Ricky's shoulders. Ricky turned and planted a kiss on Alex, then looked at Greg as he said, "And ... I want to be Juan's caged Alex!" Everyone hooted.

"I may need some time before I'm ready to be Juan's Pup Niki, though." At that Raphael wrestled Ricky onto his back again, as Alex piled on. Ricky's boner was back, and that was a very good sign.

Twenty-Seven

─◉━━━━━━━━◉─

A HALLOWEEN DARE

DINNER HAD EVOLVED VERY unexpectedly, but had ended on an up-beat note.

"When do we start?" Ricky asked the group at large. "I don't want Juan to find 'boy right' before I'm ready to audition."

"Right now," Luke answered. "Raphael, why don't you get your old HT."

"HT?" Ricky asked.

"Holy Trainer. You'll see." Raphael was back in a flash, holding a brown translucent plastic zippered case. It looked like it might contain cosmetics. "Okay, Ricky, why don't you stand up. Alex, let's lock up that handsome cock." Raphael unzipped the Holy Trainer case and began fitting the cock ring on Ricky. Luke asked, "Ever worn a cock ring?"

"No. Am I going to fit? It's really tight."

"It's supposed to be," Raphael said. "Just relax. The first time is always the hardest, right Alex?"

"It'll seem weird at first, but you'll quickly get used to it and soon, you won't even realize you're caged, except, you know ..." Alex assumed Ricky would complete the thought on his own.

"Except?"

"Except when you get hard. Morning wood is the worst at first, but pretty quickly you really enjoy erections in the cage."

"Really?"

"When you get hard, just imagine it's Juan's hand squeezing your cock," Raphael offered. "It can be pretty wonderful." Raphael had thoughtfully brought along some coconut oil, that he was massaging onto Ricky's uncut cock. "Okay, now we lock you up." He slid the tube over the end of Ricky's slightly tumescent cock and worked it up to meet the ring. Ricky was screwing up his face in reaction. Raphael grunted a little, as Ricky's attempt at a hardon made his job more challenging, but he made the connection before Ricky reached a full-size boner. Alex moved in with the key and completed the mission. Both he and Raphael looked up at Ricky and grinned. "Hey, there, chastity boy," Raphael taunted. "Welcome to the family."

"Man, it's really tight," Ricky protested, "Is it supposed to be this tight?"

"That's because you have a raging hard on, you sex fiend," Raphael laughed. "You'll get used to it."

"Ricky, why don't you sit back down with Raphael and Alex for a minute," Luke advised. As he did, Raphael and Alex each put an arm around Ricky's shoulders, which did nothing to ease the pressure inside his new cage. "Think of this as a test ... as Step One in Ricky's Leather Boy Training. You said Juan was into chastity. This is what chastity is like. If you can't handle it, then, there's probably a good chance you won't take to bondage, water sports and all the other things coming your way if you become Juan's leather boy. If you are man enough to handle it, then that's a good sign that you'll be able to win Juan back. Does that make sense?"

"Yeah. Perfect sense. So ... do I need to do anything special to make sure I'm cut out to be," and he looked down directly at Raphael's tattoo, "Juan's locked cock boy?"

"Just be sure you sit down to pee," Alex laughed. "The rest is easy."

Luke offered a little more practical advice. "That cage isn't designed for permanent wear like Raphael's. We'll take it off next Tuesday to clean your cock, then replace it. We won't let you touch your cock. Raphael and Alex will do your hygiene. You need to get used to only touching Juan's cock."

"Dios Mio! No more touching my dick? How will I, you know, get off?"

"Ideally, only with Juan's cock, but until then, next week, Raphael and Alex can show you a substitute. Sound good?"

"Man, you weren't kidding about this not being just a cosmetic thing, were you? No touching my dick? It's gonna be a long week."

"Ricky. It's going to be a long month, or however long until you're ready to walk up to Juan and say, 'Please, Sir, make me your sexy leather boy,' or, however you want to word it. I'll leave that to you."

"Dios Mio."

"You'll be fine, Ricky. Just keep imagining that's Juan's hand down there. Okay?" Raphael smiled as he stood up. Alex stood as well and the two reached down and helped lift Ricky into a standing position. "Here, come here, take a look at how hot you look," Raphael said as he and Alex took Ricky by the hands and led him into the bedroom to the increasingly popular full-length mirror.

Greg put a hand on Luke's thigh and said, "We should get paid for this."

"It's our public service obligation," Luke smiled back. "Besides, the view just keeps getting better and better, don't you think?"

"True that. Juan's an idiot if he doesn't take Ricky back."

"I have a good feeling about this. Ricky is definitely motivated and to hear him tell, Juan's a good guy. The odds are with us."

The caged contingent came out of the bedroom, smiles on all. Ricky reached down and retrieved his clothes and began dressing. "I never, in a million years, would have dreamed this would happen tonight. Thank you all so much. I hope I'm up to your expectations ... to Juan's expectations. I'm going to need all the help I can get."

"You don't need as much help as you think," Greg said. "You already stole his heart once. It should be even easier this time, right guys?"

"Right!" was the response. Alex and Raphael hugged Ricky one last time and walked him to the door. They came back and took their places again on the floor.

"That was intense," Alex sighed. "What an amazing guy."

"Just think," Raphael piped up. "if I hadn't invited him in, we'd have never known how much he needed us."

"That's right, Mother Teresa."

"I'm just saying ... he needs help, and we can give it to him. Kudos to you, Greg, for starting the conversation. He's really sweet, don't you think?"

"Ah, Raphael's such a sucker for a cute guy, isn't he?" Greg laughed.

"That he is," Luke replied, nodding at Alex, "but you have to admit Ricky is pretty adorable. I hope we're doing the right thing."

"Of course we are," Raphael asserted. "Trust me."

The following day at work Alex breezed by Raphael's cube on his way from one technical rescue mission to another. As he brushed his hand across Raphael's shoulders in greeting, Raphael turned and asked, "You have lunch plans?"

"No, why?"

"Meet me back here when you're ready. I'll explain later. FYI, it might take more than an hour." Alex nodded and headed off. Whatever was up, Alex knew it would be interesting. Everything Raphael did was interesting. Now he couldn't wait for lunch.

Alex was back around twelve-thirty. "Is this a good time?"

"Perfect. Let's go." Raphael slung his messenger bag over his shoulder and they headed for the elevator. Raphael began to unveil his plan. "You moved here after Halloween last year, right?"

"Yeah, first week of November. Why?"

"It's the biggest queer holiday of the year, after Pride. Oh, and Folsom, of course. Anyway, it's a lot of fun. Do you and Greg have plans?"

"We haven't even talked about it."

"Good. Don't. Not yet anyway." The men hit the street and headed to the Melt for Impossible Burgers and sweet potato fries. Over lunch, Raphael pulled his tablet out of his bag.

"Are we working?" Alex asked.

"Nope, this is all fun." Raphael launched his browser, navigated a moment, then held the tablet against his chest and finally began his pitch. "I want you and Greg, Luke and me to do Halloween in the Castro together. Luke and Greg will be conquering Roman warriors, and we'll be their captive male sex slaves."

"Why am I not surprised. I guess a Wizard of Oz theme is too passé, right?"

"Totally. Here is what Greg and Luke will wear." Raphael turned the tablet around to show the web page to Alex. The half-eaten fry sticking out of Alex's mouth fell into his lap. He grabbed the tablet from Raphael and looked closer.

"Is this for a private party somewhere?"

"No, no. We'll be on Castro Street, Market. We'll go to Niki's bar to see him at work, finally. What do think? Pretty sexy, huh?"

"Exhibitionist is a better word." Alex spent another moment examining the 'Net Racing Suit' at slickitup.com that Raphael was proposing. "What will you have them wear under this?"

"Nothing, of course."

"They'll be naked!"

"They'll look awesome! They both have the body for it. And, here is where we get the Roman soldier helmets to complete the look." Raphael snatched back the tablet and displayed a page from Amazon.

"Oh. Okay. That'll make Greg much more willing to be naked in public." Alex's sarcasm was totally brushed aside by Raphael.

"Alex, if you hadn't objected, you would have both been naked at Folsom! More naked than this. There's at least ... I don't know, three ounces of fabric here."

"Totally see though fabric. Besides, that was Folsom."

"And this is Halloween. In San Francisco. In the Castro. At night. How many times have you seen naked guys walking around the Castro, naked, in broad daylight?"

"I don't know. I haven't kept track."

"Exactly. Come on! This will be epic. You've said yourself you envy Luke's and my dares. This is your chance to be included in one. One that Greg will love. You know he will."

"Okay ... but ..."

"But?"

"How do I know I'm going to like *my* costume? You are evil, Raphael. If this is what our conquering owners are wearing, what will us slave boys be wearing. Smiles?"

"I hope so. I know so. But we'll be wearing togas, of course."

"Of course. Silly me. Togas, huh? That won't be so bad." Alex looked again at the page displaying the Net Racing Suits. "These are pretty damn sexy, aren't they?"

"Yeah, And, you know, they're not some silly super hero thing, so they can be worn again for other occasions."

"Oh, yeah, so many other occasions. Sure..."

"So, we're agreed? You'll join me in this dare for Greg and Luke?"

"Sure. I can't wait to see Greg as my conqueror. This really is kinda cool."

Raphael took back his tablet, stuffed it in his bag and stood up. As Alex stood, he wrapped his arms around him and said, "Thanks, locked cock brother. This is going to be soooo much fun. Now, let's run over to Britex to get the material for our togas. I have a friend who will sew our costumes for us."

Raphael seemed to know his way around Britex, which was good since this was already turning into a longer than usual lunch hour. He dragged Alex by the hand to a spot near the back of the first floor, then released him to pull a roll from the shelf. He unrolled a couple of feet of fabric and held it up as he turned to Alex and asked with a big, big, smile, "What do you think?"

"You fucker!" Alex laughed. "You can see right through it!"

"Nothing gets past you, does it? It's only fair, Alex. If our conquerors' cocks are going to be on display, shouldn't our cages also be visible? Here, look, the material will be pleated and arranged so that it's opaque, translucent, then transparent as we move and walk. So, your ass and cage won't be on display *all* the time."

"Oh, well in that case ... you fucker. I hate you, even though I love you, too. What if I say, no thanks?"

"Then I'll never speak to you again."

"You've corrupted me more than you know, but I guess I've never regretted any of it. So ... okay. I guess." Raphael leaned the bolt against the wall and hugged Alex once again. This was one of the many things about Raphael that Alex didn't hate. He was shameless about public displays of affection. As they hugged, a clerk who tripped the gaydar meter at about twelve approached.

"Gentlemen, how may I help you today?"

"We need some of this, please." Raphael smiled.

"Will you be making sheer curtains?" he asked.

"No togas. For Halloween."

"Togas! Oh, my. Aren't you clever? For each of you?"

"Yes, please. How much should we get?"

"Hmmm. That depends, of course, on how much coverage you want."

"I'm thinking just below the ass," Raphael responded. "We want to show lots of ... leg."

"As well you should," the clerk laughed. "Just to be safe, I'd say two yards, but you'll probably have some left over. Better safe than sorry."

"You're the expert."

"Yes, I am. And, how will you accessorize these unforgettable togas?"

"Hmm, we hadn't thought that far yet."

"Will it be just the two of you?"

"No, Alex's husband and my fiancé will be going as our Roman owners."

"I have a suggestion for you. What color will your conquerors costumes be?"

"Black," Alex said. "What little of it there will be."

"Follow me." The clerk led them to the satins, where he pulled out a brilliant red bolt. "Red on black. You would look nicely coordinated and even more stunning if your conquerors wear red sashes around their waists and you wear red scarves either around your necks or as head bands."

"Wow. You *are* the expert. What do you think, Raphael?"

"I think you're finally getting into the Halloween spirit. Thank you, sir, let's do it."

As they headed back to the office, Alex laughed. "Now I can't wait for Halloween. I don't know how I'm going to keep a straight face around Greg if the topic comes up."

"First of all, you and I are genetically incapable of having a straight face. If he says anything, just say, 'I think Luke and Raphael are planning something, we're supposed to keep the date open. That way he won't even worry about it.'"

"When do we get our costumes?"

"Not sure, that's why I wanted to do this as soon as possible. I'll keep you posted. And, thanks again for going along with this. I love doing things with you guys."

"This is going to be so much fun. Thank you for including us. Come on ... Halloween!"

Twenty-Eight

RICKY'S BEACH DEBUT

WHEN SATURDAY FINALLY ARRIVED, the fog lifted early, so it was going to be a beach day after all. Greg and Alex arrived at Luke and Raphael's just after one o'clock. The routine had been established, and they both were outfitted with back packs containing water, food and sunscreen. Routine also mandated that Alex was wearing his caged cock tee. Luke and Raphael were still naked and harnessed, always avoiding street clothes until the last minute. It wasn't long before Ricky arrived.

"Hi, guys," he smiled as he entered. "Whoa, is that how you're going ... all naked and sexy?"

"No, silly," Raphael said as he gave Ricky a hug and kiss. "But you do need to take your shirt off. And, put this on." He handed Ricky one of his growing collection of caged cock tees. "It's part of the experience." Ricky did as instructed. Meanwhile Raphael and Luke stepped out of their harnesses and pulled on shorts and shirts.

"Oh, we're matching," Ricky said, taking stock of Alex and Raphael's tees. "The three musketeers, huh?"

"More like the three cagedketeers," Alex laughed. "Hey, I invented a new word. Think it'll catch on?"

"Don't bet on it," Greg chided. "Ricky, the shirt proclaims to the world that your cock is caged."

"Oh. Oh, I get it ... I don't know ..."

"Don't sweat it, Ricky." Raphael assured him. "I only wear caged cock shirts, and nobody gets it. Well, except guys who are caged or whose partners are caged. I do get some coy smiles now and then, but otherwise ... clueless."

"Speaking of cages, Ricky, how are you doing with your cage?" Luke asked. "It's been four days now."

"Well, Alex was right. Waking up is hell, and sometimes, even in the middle of the night, I wake up hard. I'm trying what you said, to tell myself it's Juan's hand squeezing me, but damn. Plus, I'm used to jacking off at least once a day or so. I'm kinda going crazy here, Luke."

"Horny, sweetie?"

"Yes! Crazy horny. Raphael, would it be okay if Luke, or maybe you Greg, fucked me today? I really, really need it!"

"What you really, really need is to save yourself for Juan," Greg smiled. He walked over and put his arms around Ricky and squeezed. "Remember, we're doing all this to make you irresistible to Juan. When you're ready to approach him, you need to be the horniest, and the hottest, you've ever been."

"I don't know about the hottest part, but I'm already there on the horny part. Dios Mio."

"We can talk more later about things you can do to help with your horniness, Ricky," Luke suggested. "Like I said Tuesday, Raphael and Alex can show you some things to help. Maybe you can talk them into taking you shopping at Mr. S for what the straight world calls 'marital aids.' What we in the queer world call 'essentials.' But, uh, no, sweetie, I only fuck Raphael. It's in our contract." Ricky looked a little disheartened, but nodded. "Let's head out guys, time for Step Two in our mission to make Ricky irresistible to Juan."

Once they got outside, they realized Ricky had arrived on his scooter, the one he used for his DoorDash deliveries. "Hey," Alex said. "Instead of MUNI, why don't we get Lyft bikes and ride to the beach? Ricky can lead the way. We might even get there faster than on MUNI." Everybody looked at everyone else, hoping somebody would quash Alex's crazy idea, but nobody wanted to be the wimp. "Excellent!" Alex took charge. "Bikes are in the next block. Ricky, meet us there."

And so, the contingent, led by Ricky, rode the Wiggle out of the Castro and outbound to the ocean. Three in caged cock shirts, two more unremarkably attired. Ricky knew the best route, not surprisingly, and they really did arrive at the beach sooner than they would have on transit. Alex was gleeful.

"All I can say, is, we're docking the bikes here and taking MUNI back," Greg said. "That was fun, but ...'

"I'm with Greg," Luke seconded. "Especially after a couple hours of sun, we'll be wasted." Nobody argued. Ricky secured his scooter and they set out to find the perfect spot for his debut on the beach. It didn't take long. Blankets were spread, backpacks dumped. For once, Alex was the first one naked. And he had a good reason.

"Alex!" Raphael exclaimed. "You got a Looker! Let me see!" Raphael squatted down and lifted Alex's new cage, a shiny, steel, Looker 01, just like Raphael's. "Yay. You got the urethral plug, too. Sweet!" Raphael stood up and wrapped his arms around Alex. Alex returned the favor.

Ricky, still sitting and still dressed, looked around expecting stares and condemnation. Neither was exhibited by the hundred or so naked men scattered on towels and blankets around them.

"You didn't have that Tuesday." Luke said.

"We just got it in Wednesday's mail," Greg responded. "Thanks for the help in ordering it."

"Do you like it?" Raphael grinned, already knowing the answer.

"I love it, Raphael. Everything about it. I love that it's not coming off again, even for cleaning. It feels great, too. And, I love how it shoots out the pee."

"Yeah, I remember the first time I peed in mine," Raphael smirked, looking at Luke as he said it. "It was a very memorable pee." Luke winked back at Raphael, but said nothing.

"Does yours ever vibrate inside your cock when you pee?" Alex asked.

"Sometimes, yeah. Feels really cool, doesn't it?"

"Yeah, freaked me out the first time." Both Raphael and Alex giggled at the memory.

Greg turned to Luke and said, "Boys and their toys." At that, Raphael reached down and grabbed Luke's handy cock.

"This is the only toy this boy needs," Raphael confessed. Luke winked again. Raphael stepped around to the other side of Ricky and warned, "Ricky, if you don't strip yourself, I will, and I'll make a big scene doing it."

"Hey, the first time is scary, Ricky, I know," Alex said. "But it really is fun." Ricky smiled, but hesitated just a bit too long. "Raphael, I think he needs our help." On cue, both Raphael and Alex pounced, each grabbing one of Ricky's arms, pulling him into a standing position. Alex pulled up Ricky's tee over his arms and head as Raphael ripped his shorts to his ankles. Then, he reached up and pulled down his boxers. Ricky sat down and pulled the tangle of shorts off his feet.

"You guys are mean."

"'Cause we love you. Now stand up again so we can smear on this sunscreen." Once again Ricky hesitated too long, so Alex and Raphael reached down again and pulled him up. "Here," Raphael handed Alex a spray can. You do the back, I'll take the front, the one with the amazing abs."

"Fine with me," Alex countered. "I get the amazing ass." As they rubbed Ricky down, he looked over at Greg and Luke, who had assumed their horizontal tanning positions, both naked, both hunky and both watching him intently. Between that and the feeling of two naked locked cock boys rubbing him down, well, poor little sex deprived Ricky didn't have much of a chance.

"Amigos, be careful ... you're going to make me come!"

"Would that be so bad?" Alex asked. "You said you needed release."

"Yeah, but not here ... in public."

"You're no fun," Raphael laughed. "But we really don't want you to come right now anyway. Done, Alex? Okay, Ricky, you and Alex can do me next." As the locked boys took care of each other, Greg and Luke stood back up and took care of each other. Soon all were buttered up and ready to enjoy the sun. Already it had been a momentous experience for Ricky. Not only was he naked in public, but with a caged cock. And, with four sexy, naked gay guys, two of whom were also caged. And the other four were totally unabashed about it. Rubbing lotion on each other in front of a hundred or more other men. It was, well, it was a lot to process. Finally, Ricky could lay down between Alex and Raphael and feel less conspicuous.

After twenty minutes or so of basking, a man in a black thong walked up and stood over the group. "Hey guys. Good to see you. Remember me?"

Everyone roused themselves from their sun induced trances and half sat up. Luke shaded his eyes with his hand and said, "Um, do we know you?"

"I saw you and this guy here a couple of months back. I asked about your cage."

"Oh, sure!" Raphael said. "Nice to see you."

"Well, I just wanted to say, thanks. I got one, too!" He pulled down the front of his skimpy thong to reveal a black HT.

"Hey, man, that looks amazing on you. Congratulations." Raphael said, as he got to his knees and moved closer to examine the cage. Alex was right behind, and then, Ricky sat up, too.

"How long have you had it," Luke asked.

"About a month. I really like it."

"So, why the thong? You should show it off." Luke admonished.

"I know, but ... I guess I'm not as brave as you guys."

"Boys," Luke said, then paused, "You know what to do." And, they did, indeed. Alex grabbed the sides of the thong and pulled down as Raphael stood up, grabbed their victim around the chest and lifted. Alex freed the thong, stood up himself and started running. Without thinking the guy took off after Alex, with Raphael on his heels. Raphael turned and signaled to Ricky to follow. Luke put his hand on Ricky's shoulder and said, "Go on, Ricky, help your brothers."

Ricky jumped up and ran, proving to be faster than all of them. He soon caught up with Raphael, who took his right hand as the two closed the distance from their victim. Once they reached him, they grabbed his arms and brought him to a slow walk. Greg and Luke watched as Alex circled back, the thong around his neck. As they were all laughing, Alex wrapped his arms around the guy from the front while Raphael and then Ricky embraced him from the back. After a moment, the group hug broke up and the four set out, hand in hand, toward the surf, the guy's thong still around Alex's neck.

Greg turned to Luke and said, "You know, I'm liking these beach days more and more all the time."

"Yeah, like I said, the view just keeps getting better and better."

"I'll drink to that," Greg replied as he unscrewed a bottle of mineral water, took a swig and handed it to Luke. After they finished splashing in the surf and walking the beach to let their skin dry, the four caged boys returned to Luke and Greg. They plopped down on the blankets, and reached for water, which was passed around among themselves.

"Luke and Greg, this is Justin, by the way," Alex said. "And he decided I get to keep the thong."

"I did not!" Justin protested, sounding less than convincing. "Please give it back."

"Why? You've been showing off the cage for almost an hour. Isn't it a little late to get dressed now?"

"Yeah, but..."

"You're much cuter naked, you know," Ricky said, obviously now into the spirit of things.

"Atta boy, Ricky," Luke laughed, reaching over and pulling Ricky close for a sideways hug. "Are you having fun?"

"I am. Thanks, Luke. Thank you all, amigos. You know, this was, uh, not what I expected."

"What did you expect?" Raphael asked, putting his hand back on that familiar spot on Ricky's naked thigh.

"I'm not sure. To be embarrassed. Humiliated maybe. I sure didn't expect to be cruised like I was by that guy on the red towel back there."

"Oh, yeah, he was pretty obvious, wasn't he?" Alex confirmed. "He can be your plan B if Juan doesn't, you know..." Alex realized he didn't want to finish the thought.

"We're not going to need a plan B," Luke spoke up. "Juan doesn't stand a chance against the new and improved, totally confident Ricky two dot oh that we're creating here. Right, Ricky?"

"Right!" Ricky laughed. It was good see him laughing, relaxed, caged and naked all at the same time. This was going better than anyone expected.

"Well, guys, we should call it a day," Greg announced. "Justin, nice meeting you. Say goodbye to your thong. You better be displaying that cage the next time we see you, or you'll be losing another suit."

"Ah, man," Justin whined, again, not very convincingly.

"I'll bring it with me the next time we come," Alex offered. "If you're naked, you get it back. Deal?"

"I'm kind of outnumbered here, so ... deal."

Alex and Justin stood up and they embraced. Alex planted a kiss on his lips and said, "You're a cool guy. See you soon?"

"I'd better! I want my thong back! Bye guys." As Justin walked away to find his long abandoned beach towel, Raphael patted Alex on the ass.

"Alex has a new friend," he teased.

"Maaaybe," Alex laughed. "He is cool. And, cute. But you're the one who corrupted him months ago. So, I think it's safe to say you have a new friend, too."

"Disciple. I have a new disciple. And, speaking of disciples," Raphael turned to Ricky, "Ricky, I can't tell you how proud I am of you. You were amazing today. Ready for the next step to steal Juan's heart again?"

"More than ready. What's next?"

"We'll talk about that Tuesday at dinner," Luke said. "When Mr. DoorDash transforms again into the amazing Naked Caged Ricky!" The last three words were announced in dramatic, fortissimo style. Ricky laughed, then hugged each companion in turn, still naked. Only then did he begin to dress. Indeed, progress had been made today. Ricky suddenly realized he only had the caged cock tee with him; he'd left his shirt at Raphael and Luke's place.

"I'll have to bring this back to you on Tuesday," he told Raphael, "I left my shirt at your apartment."

"It's yours now," Raphael smiled. "You earned it today, Ricky. I hope you're wearing it when we see you Tuesday." That initiated another hug between Ricky and Raphael, one that ended with a signature Raphael kiss.

As Ricky walked away to retrieve his scooter, Luke said proudly to the others, "Damn, we're good."

Twenty-Nine

―――⊛――・――⊛――

BEST LAID PLANS

As THEY STEPPED OFF the N-Judah at Noe Street, Luke suggested they all go home, shower and meet somewhere for dinner. "I'm too tired and baked to do dishes, and I don't want to ask Raphael to cook, either. Besides we should celebrate Ricky's accomplishments today."

"And, Alex's new friend." Raphael teased.

"Whatever," was Alex's reply. He sounded tired.

"Thanks, guys, but I think we'll pass," Greg begged off. "My guy's tired, and frankly so am I. That was my first bike ride since I don't know when. We'll see you Tuesday, though." Hugs were exchanged and the four separated.

"How about we just get something from the Whole Foods deli on the way home?" Raphael suggested. Luke agreed, and so dinner was set. They'd shaved and showered and were just finishing dinner when the doorbell rang. Raphael opened the door, expecting Steve, since Niki was probably working tonight. It wasn't Steve.

"Ricky! What a surprise!" Raphael exclaimed and immediately realized Ricky was distraught. Freaked out was more like it.

"Take it off!" Ricky cried. And he actually did cry. "Please, you have to take it off." He began pulling his pants down before Raphael had even closed the door.

"God, Ricky what's wrong?" Raphael said. Luke was at the door before Raphael had finished speaking. He took one look at Ricky and headed into the bedroom to retrieve the keys to Ricky's cage. When he returned, Ricky was in Raphael's arms, although his arms were at his sides, as if he was afraid to hug back.

"What happened?" Luke calmly asked as he unlocked the cage and pulled it free of Ricky's uncharacteristically flaccid cock. He had a little more trouble pulling the cock ring off, since it was a perfect, snug fit, but he managed. It was obvious there was no damage from the cage, so he didn't understand why Ricky wanted it off. He stood up, took hold of Ricky's shoulders and helped Raphael lower him to a sitting position on the floor, his pants still around his ankles. "What's going on, muchacho?"

Ricky relaxed a tiny bit, and looked at Luke, then at Raphael. He sniffed a couple of times before speaking. "I fucked up. When I got home, I took a shower, you know to get ready to Dash. I guess I was so happy and excited about the day, I forgot to lock the bathroom door. When I was drying, one of my roommates opened the door and saw me. Naked. He saw the cage. He blew up."

"What?" Luke spat out. "What business is it of his?"

"You don't understand. He's straight. You know, typical Mexican machismo. He pushed me up against the wall and called me a chingado marićon ... a fucking faggot."

"Yeah, we know what that means," Raphael sighed. "Fucking bastard."

"He said he didn't want any faggots in his house. And then he asked me if that's what I am."

"What did you say?"

"What could I say, Luke? I denied it. I said I lost a bet."

"And ... what did he say?"

"He said I was going to lose more than a bet if I was lying. I was scared. He and one of the other roommates are bigger than me. Meaner, too. They're assholes."

"No kidding. How many roommates are there?" Raphael asked.

"Four of us. They're roommates, not friends. I don't spend much time there, at least I didn't used to, you know, when, uh, Juan and I ..."

"Why do you stay?"

"Are you kidding? It's cheap with four of us. And I have a place to stow my scooter."

"Why don't you stay here tonight," Raphael insisted. "We have a big bed."

"Oh, no, I'll be fine."

"Bullshit. You need to get out of there."

"No, really, I'll be fine." Ricky stood up, pulled up his pants, put on his best street face and hugged Raphael. "Besides, I need to do some deliveries. You know, pay the rent." At that thought, he had to laugh. He hugged Luke. "Thanks, guys. And, I'm sorry. I'm so sorry." He turned and left.

"Fuck!" Raphael shouted after he closed the door. "Fuck, fuck, fuck, fuck, FUCK!"

Luke pulled Raphael into his arms. "I'm scared," Raphael moaned. "We have to do something."

"Maybe we've done enough for one day," Luke whispered. Raphael pulled away, enough to look Luke in the eyes. He had a shocked look on his face.

"Are you just going to accept this?" he asked.

"Raphael, we're his friends. We'll do anything he asks of us. But, at this point, it's none of our business. Ricky's a big boy ... well, he's an adult. He knows better than us what he needs to do, and what he wants us to do. He knows we're here if he needs us."

"But what if that bastard beats the crap out of him?"

"I don't think that'll happen, at least not for a while. That's why Ricky wanted the cage off. He's handling this. Let's just wait until Tuesday. We'll all have calmed down by then, and maybe we can figure out what to do, if anything."

"If anything?!"

"Raphael, or should I say, Mother Teresa, until he asks ... It's. None. Of. Our. Business."

It was clear Raphael did not agree, but he had no good counter argument. At least not yet. He looked into Luke's clear blue eyes and saw concern there. Luke was just being ... right. Dammit. He reached up and slid his tongue in Luke's mouth. He realized it was their first kiss all day. He sniffed from the near tears he'd felt earlier. He kissed Luke again and said, "I need you inside me right now, Sir. Please Sir."

"Of course, baby. I need you, too. Let's go to bed."

Even though the next day was Sunday, it wasn't a fun day. Ricky was on both of their minds. Periodically, as they lounged on the couch, a foot in each other's crotch, browsing the Sunday Chron and drinking coffee, Raphael would have a half-baked thought about how to help Ricky, but before he could voice it, he'd realize Luke would say the same thing ... wait until Tuesday. Tuesday was a long way away. The only bright spot was a text from his friend, Allyson, who announced she'd finished the togas for Halloween. He texted back his gratitude.

"Steve and Niki?" Luke asked, as Raphael thumbed his reply.

"Umm, yeah," Raphael smiled. He didn't like lying to anyone, especially Luke, but this didn't count, did it? Not when it was in pursuit of a dare.

The following day, Luke and Greg's costumes, at least the body suits, arrived at the office, where Raphael would keep them until Halloween. All they needed now were the Roman helmets, due a couple of days later.

Alex stopped by as he usually did at least once a day, and Raphael asked him to stop back when he could take a break.

"I can take one now. What's up?"

"Let's take a walk around the block." Once outside, Raphael filled Alex in. Naturally, Alex was crushed.

"Damn, this sucks. What are we going to do?"

"I don't know, but we're going to do something. Tomorrow night when we're all together, we'll figure something out. Trust me."

Tuesday evening finally arrived. Greg and Alex were earlier than usual, eager to learn more and to start discussing how they might help Ricky. Pretty much on schedule, the doorbell rang. This time Alex was right there beside Raphael, when he opened the door to welcome Ricky. But it wasn't Ricky. The delivery was being made by a guy who greeted the two naked, cock locked boys with a lot less enthusiasm than Ricky always did.

"Whoa. I wasn't expecting an orgy. Here you go." He handed over the bags and fled. He didn't even look back. Alex and Raphael carried the bags into the living room, obviously shattered.

"Where's Ricky?" Greg asked.

"It wasn't Ricky," Alex replied as he took his place on the floor. "Some freaked out straight guy." Raphael began pulling serving containers out of the bags. He put the empty bags aside, sat down next to Alex and looked up expectantly at Luke.

"Now what?" he asked. "I realized earlier today. I was going to text Ricky despite what you said about waiting until tonight. I just wanted to know he was okay. And, I realized," Raphael began to tear up, "we don't have his fucking number! Now what?"

"Oh, man. You're right," Luke sighed. "We always knew we'd see him here. Every Tuesday."

"Dammit, Luke!" Raphael shouted. "What if he's in the hospital? What if he's dead?!" Both Luke and Greg came off the couch and gathered around Raphael and Alex, who looked as bad as Raphael. Arms were slung around shoulders and no one said a word until Raphael regained control of himself. Greg got up long enough to grab the tissues. Raphael wasn't the only one who needed one. Finally, Raphael sniffed and said, in his indoor voice, "I'm sorry."

"Don't apologize. We're all upset. You're just better at demonstrating it than I am," Luke said, then sniffed. "Tissue, please," he said to Greg. Luke used the tissue, then said, "We had a hundred chances to get Ricky's number. How stupid."

"Hey, both of you. Stop being so hard on yourselves," Greg said, as he stood up and returned to the couch. "You have done nothing wrong. You're not the bad guys here. You've been nothing but wonderful to and for Ricky. This isn't over. Somehow, we'll figure out what to do. Right now, let's eat." He lifted his wine glass and continued, "To Ricky ... and to his return."

Raphael lifted his glass, and stage whispered "Please, please, please."

Thirty

GREG'S FIRST DARE

RAPHAEL'S BIG PLANS FOR Halloween seemed inconsequential in light of Ricky's disappearance. What was going to be a daring and festive evening, now seemed almost sacrilegious. He'd hinted to Alex, at work, that maybe they should just call it off.

"Absolutely not, Raphael. And I'll tell you why. You need a diversion, if even for a couple of hours. You deserve it. We all do. And, sitting out Halloween isn't going to get Ricky back any sooner. Although, who knows, maybe we'll see him there ... wouldn't that be great? Besides, I've been looking forward to seeing the look on Greg's face when I hand him that costume."

"Who said you were going to be the one to hand him the costume," Raphael chided, actually lightening up for the first time in days. "It was my idea, you know."

"Then I get to hand Luke his."

"Deal." Raphael smiled in spite of himself. For the first time, Alex hugged Raphael right there in the middle of the office. He couldn't help it. And, he knew Raphael needed it. Before parting, they finalized plans for meeting the following night for Halloween.

The topic came up that night, as Luke slipped into place, behind Raphael in bed. As Raphael snuggled his ass up against Luke's cock, Luke draped his right arm over Raphael's chest, lightly fingering the ring in Raphael's left nipple. It was something they did almost every night, when they first crawled under the covers, and it never got old. "Baby," Luke muttered, "with everything going on this week, we never even talked about Halloween. Do you want to go?" Luke knew Raphael was not likely to be in a party mood. Raphael rolled around, without dislodging Luke's arm, so he could face Luke. He put his left arm around Luke's waist and pulled him closer. Their lips met, tongues followed, breaths were shared.

Finally, Raphael broke off the kiss so he could say, "Oh, yeah. Halloween. Not to worry, Sir. Everything is taken care of." Despite the dark, Luke was able to see Raphael's smile, one that was long overdue.

"Everything is taken care of? Not to worry? Sir? Why do I feel like running? Away. As fast as possible." Raphael said nothing. He pressed his lips against Luke's in a vain attempt to distract him. It did, but only for a moment. "Am I due for another dare?" Raphael still just smiled.

"All I can say at this time, Sir, is that we won't be alone on Halloween." He rolled over again in Luke's arms, making it possible for Luke to enter him if he so desired. After the long, repeated kisses, and the realization that he was probably in line for another sexy dare, that was really the only reasonable thing left for Luke to do.

The following evening Luke arrived home, clueless but certain it was going to be a memorable Halloween. Raphael had proven, time and again, capable of devising unforgettable dares. If it even was a dare; he really wasn't sure. He was naked and harnessed, on the couch, tablet in hand and kombucha at his side when Raphael arrived. He stowed his shoulder bag, kicked off his street shoes, and knelt down by Luke to deliver his first kiss of the evening. Only then did he begin peeling off his clothes. He climbed on top of Luke and delivered the evening's second, longer kiss. That's when the doorbell rang. Raphael pulled out of Luke's embrace and went to the door, knowing who was on the other side.

"Welcome fellow trick *and* treaters," he said as Greg and Alex entered. Luke stood and hugged each of them.

"Raphael said we weren't doing Halloween alone, but that's all I know."

"You know more than I did five minutes ago," Greg replied. "I think our boys have been plotting something."

"You are correct, Sir," Raphael announced. "We have an evening of fun and frivolity planned for you. As this is your and Alex's first Castro Halloween, we wanted it to be memorable. What do you think, Alex? Will it be memorable?"

"I promise you, Greg ... and Luke, you will be talking about it for years to come. I know I will!"

"So, what are we doing?" Luke asked as Greg and Alex peeled off their street clothes. Alex tossed a backpack into the bedroom as Luke continued. "I haven't even thought about a costume."

"Costume?" Greg looked surprised. "We need costumes?" Raphael kneeled down in front of Greg who had sat down next to Luke.

"Greg, welcome to Halloween in the Castro. Everyone will be in costume. Beautiful costumes. Intricate costumes. Erotic costumes. But, not to worry. Your loving husband and I have taken care of everything. We will join the promenade around the Castro, walking the streets, enjoying adult beverages in one or more festive bars, and we'll end the night at Niki's bar where we'll finally get to see him in action. Steve will be there, too. How does that sound? Hmmmm?"

"Okay, you're starting to scare me, and I haven't even seen anyone in costume yet. Luke, should I be scared?"

"Yes ... you should. In case you haven't figured this out by now, we're in the grips of a Raphael dare. Am I right?"

"Half right. You two are in the grips of a Raphael and Alex mutual couples dare. Ta da!"

"What if I say no?" Greg asked. Seriously, he actually asked that.

"Oh, Greg, you can't say no. It's simply not possible," Alex grinned. "And, the dare starts right now." He and Raphael stood up and dashed into the bedroom with Raphael's shoulder bag. Almost immediately they returned, each with a manila envelope. Alex handed his to Luke, as Raphael handed his to Greg. "Here are your costumes for tonight."

Luke and Greg looked at each other, then at the envelopes. Luke started to laugh as Greg said, "This can't be good." Greg pulled his net body suit out of the envelope as Luke, accustomed to being abused by Raphael's dares, looked on. Greg unfolded the suit, and held it up, looking through it at Luke. "This can't be real."

Alex and Raphael looked at each other, and just smiled. Luke smiled, too. "Very cute, guys," he said as he pulled his suit out. "I bet Greg looks sexy as hell in his." Then, he couldn't help himself as he started laughing.

"I don't see what's so funny," Greg said. "You have to wear one, too."

"Yeah, I do. I will. What do we wear under this, Raphael?"

Raphael and Alex continued to smile.

"Oh, no. You're kidding, right?"

More smiles.

"Oh come on, guys."

"Do you need any help putting those on?" Raphael asked. "There is more to the outfit, but it goes on top, not underneath."

"Oh, thank goodness." Greg said. "You had me worried there for a while." More smiles. Greg and Luke both stood up and started unzipping the body suits. They were designed to be skin tight, so it took some doing to wiggle into them, but once on and zipped closed, both men looked stunning.

"Alex, they look even hotter than I thought."

"No shit. Damn, Greg, promise me you'll wear that every day!" Alex stood up and planted a kiss on Greg's lips, then ran his hands along Greg's chest, abs and ass. "Raphael, you were so right! They look amazing!"

"Let's check ourselves out, Greg. Follow me." Luke said, taking Greg's hand and leading him into the bedroom. They returned, both smiling.

"So, you chose our costumes, eh, baby?" Luke gave Raphael a well-deserved hug. "I have to admit, they are pretty sexy. Not exactly street worthy, but sexy."

"Thank you, sir. But they are street worthy, as you will soon prove."

"Yeah, but you said there was more ... to go over the costume," Greg said hopefully.

"Oh, yeah," Alex piped up. He opened the small bag he'd brought into the living room with the envelopes and pulled out the red sashes. He handed one to Raphael and then he and Raphael proceeded to tie them around their men's waists.

"That's it?" Greg asked. "This is it?" Smiles. "Guys, we're still essentially naked!"

"Greg." Luke calmly said, putting his hands on Greg's net covered shoulders. "This is what we get for not beating them to the Halloween punch. You might as well relax and enjoy it."

"I can't go out like this. Look, you can see my cock."

"And a stunning cock it is, Greg," Raphael said, still smiling. "Greg, compared to some of the people we'll see tonight, you are overdressed. Now, sit down, relax, have some wine. Your husband and I need to get into our costumes now."

"They'd better be skimpier than ours," Luke said as he sat. "Hmm, this even feels sexy sitting down." Raphael and Alex decamped to the bedroom and closed the door.

"You're encouraging them," Greg complained as he sat. "Whose side are you on, anyway?"

"Relax, Greg. Our guys are having fun, and they deserve it. The business with Ricky has torn Raphael up. If this offers them a little relief, it's worth it."

"I hear you. I'm torn up, too. But ... oh hell. You guys know what you're doing. Hand me the bottle. If I end up naked on Instagram tonight, I'm blaming you."

"You won't have to blame me. I'll voluntarily take all the credit."

On the other side of the bedroom door, Alex and Raphael got to work. Raphael pulled the bag containing their togas out from under the bed. It took only about fifteen seconds for each of them to dress. Raphael adjusted Alex's pleats and folds for maximum cage exposure, then Alex returned the favor. As Raphael was about to wrap his red scarf around his neck, Alex stopped him.

"Hold on, Raphael, I, uh, I have a Halloween dare for you ... if that's okay."

"A dare from you, for me? Alex, that's so cool. I love that you're really into this now."

"I think this will be the cherry on top of your diaphanous sundae."
As he pulled a small case out of his backpack, he said, "I participated in
drama in college. Some acting, dancing, and even make-up. I'm going
to do your eyes, Raphael. Sit down here." Raphael sat on the edge of
the bed. "I'm going for a modernized '20s silent film heartthrob. They
always had amazing eyes." As he worked, he explained what he was doing.
"Eyeliner, mascara, and some pink to red eye shadow to play off your
scarf." When he finished, he stepped back and looked Raphael over.
"Okay, one more touch." He rummaged in his bag again, and selected
a lipstick tube. "Some pale pink lip gloss that will look awesome in the
street lights on Castro." He stepped back again and smiled. "Raphael,
you are so beautiful. Luke will die. Here, look." He pulled Raphael up
and pushed him to the mirror.

"Jesus. That's amazing, Alex. You really know your stuff."

"Thanks. You would have made a fabulous 20's heart throb."

"Thank you, Alex," Raphael looked slightly embarrassed. "You were
right ... it is the perfect cherry on top of our diaphanous togas."

"Gentlemen," Luke called from the living room. "Are you painting
each other's bodies in there? I certainly hope so."

Raphael walked to the door, opened it only a crack and said, "Now
you come up with the perfect idea. Too late, Sir. Maybe next year. Give
us five more minutes." He closed the door and turned to Alex. "I don't
think I can do as awesome a job on you."

"No, that's okay, I can do it. I've always been my own test dummy."
Raphael watched him intently as Alex replicated Raphael's make-up on
himself. "I don't have 'fuck me' eyelashes like you, Raphael, so I'm also
going to add fake lashes. When he was done, he turned away from the
mirror and batted his eyes at Raphael. "Well?"

"You look pretty 'fuck me' to me, Alex. You are an 'arteeest.' Here,
here's your scarf. Let's go blow their minds. Oh, wait, let me get their
Roman helmets. We can't forget those." They approached the door and
opened it slightly as Raphael asked, "Are you ready?"

"We were ready half an hour ago," Greg laughed. "Make us proud."

Alex went first, holding Raphael's hand. They stood side by side, as
each held out the helmet to his partner. Both Luke and Greg just stared.
Raphael and Alex walked up to the couch and put the helmet on each
partner's head, then they took a step back. Alex said, "Hail, Roman
conquerors. Your captive sex slaves request an audience." Luke and Greg
looked at each other, then back at their sex slaves for the night.

"It was worth the wait," Luke finally said. He stood up, took his slave
into his arms and kissed Raphael as only a conqueror could. As he pulled
away, Raphael smiled.

"The lip gloss looks good on you, too, Sir."

"Mmmm." Luke smacked his lips. "Doesn't taste bad, either." He turned to Greg and said, "What are you waiting for? Your sex slave awaits."

"I'm just ... I mean ... wow! Alex, you've never been more beautiful in your life. I'm ... God..." He stopped trying to talk, probably a good thing, and simply pulled Alex into his arms. Soon, he too, was wearing pink lip gloss.

"I don't think I've ever seen two more beautiful guys in my life," Luke sighed. "And I've looked at a lot of porn. Greg, I don't think you have to worry about anyone looking at your cock tonight."

"I can't argue with that. We're going to be invisible. Besides, they're just as naked as we are."

"Yep," Raphael laughed. "We're a set. Conquerors and slaves. Naked and proud. So ... did we do good on the costumes?"

"Well, if there were prizes, you guys would take first, second, third *and* honorable mention. Yeah, you did good. What do you think, Greg?"

"Let me put it this way. I don't ever want this evening to end. I can't wait to show off my sex slave to the Castro. Let's go show everyone how Halloween is really done!"

"Said the guy who didn't want to leave the couch ten minutes ago."

"That was before I truly understood my role in all this. I'm ready."

"So's your cock, Sir," Raphael laughed. "You might want to get that erection under control before we get there."

"Alex!" Luke scolded. "Look what you've done to your conqueror."

"Sorry," Alex smiled. "I'll take care of that later ... after everyone's had a chance to admire it."

"Okay, men," Raphael announced. "Let's go conquer Halloween!"

Thirty-One

HAIL CONQUERORS!

BY THE TIME THE conquerors and their sex slaves reached the crowded intersection of Market and Castro, Greg had conquered his erection. Like Luke, his body, including his cock, was still fabulously on display, but coyly so. There was enough breeze to insure Raphael's and Alex's cages were easy to spot, as well as their barely shrouded asses. Hand in hand, the four strolled the crowd, but never for very long before someone, usually several someones, begged them to stop and pose for pictures. Then there were the guys who wanted a closer look at one or both of the sex slaves' cages.

"Are those part of the costume, or are they real?"

"Doesn't that hurt?"

"Your tattoo, does that mean it's permanent?"

"Is that a real tattoo, or a temporary?"

And so on. Many of the more sophomoric questions came from people who'd obviously already been over-served. But there were also some really nice people, too, who offered varying degrees of affirmation.

"Thank you for being so brave. You are fabulous and I love you."

"Now *that's* what I came to see ... gorgeous hunks!"

"Do you guys do private events? Here's my card."

"Take me home with you, please. PLEASE! PLEASE!!!"

After about an hour the four stopped at the Edge to escape the crowded streets and rest a few minutes. Greg ordered four beers, and was hit up twice before the bartender could finish pulling the drafts. Greg waved Alex over to help him carry them to Luke and Raphael. Alex batted his augmented lashes at Greg's most recent suitor, before turning away quickly enough to ensure his toga would reveal his entire bare ass, delivering his intended message. When the four had their beers in hand, Greg offered a toast. "If I ever resist another of these dares, slap me silly, or something. I have to admit, this has been a lot more fun than I thought."

"And, it's not over," Raphael shouted over the crowd. "We'll be heading over to see Niki in action, next. I'm really looking forward to it."

"Me, too," Alex agreed. "I still can't believe they're letting him bartend as a pup."

"More like a barback than a bartender, at least so far," Luke corrected. "But, still, yeah, I have to admit they were amazingly open-minded. I just hope it's all working out, for Niki and for the bar."

"So, Alex," Raphael grinned over his beer. "How are you liking your toga, you know, the one you called me a 'fucker' for designing? You seem to know how to use it when your husband is in the crosshairs."

"Yeah, I have to admit, it has its advantages."

"I wonder who that guy will be beating off to tonight, you or Greg?"

"Both of us, I hope." Raphael rewarded that not-so-humble quip with one of his signature kisses to Alex's cheek. It left a pale pink imprint that only enhanced Alex's image as a vulnerable sex slave.

They decided to head out before finishing their beers, eager to see how Niki was doing. Greg pulled his phone out of his boot top and ordered a Lyft. Even though it was Halloween, and even though they were all, even Alex by now, exhibitionists to one degree or another, they weren't sure MUNI was ready for four essentially naked revelers.

By the time their car had arrived and navigated through traffic to SOMA, it was approaching eleven p.m. The bouncer at the door offered them free admission if he could take a selfie with them. Alex was the last of the four to enter, making it too easy for the bouncer to fondle his bare ass on the way in. Yet another example of the danger ... or wisdom ... of Raphael's costume design, depending on your perspective. Once inside, they stood as a group to get their bearings. House music made it difficult to talk, and the bar was at, or more likely over, legal occupancy. Nevertheless, it took no effort to spot Niki behind the bar.

He wasn't washing glasses. He was pulling drafts, and the line of guys waiting for him to pull theirs was longer than the other two stations. Clearly Pup Niki was in demand. Every time he handed a beer to a customer, he barked, and every time each customer would do a lame, but heartfelt attempt at a howl in response. How had this become a 'thing' so quickly? Niki wasn't just working. He was performing, and it was obvious he was having a blast. Every time he turned his back to open the register, his tail would wag wildly, further energizing the customers sitting at the bar. True, Niki's pup hood offered him anonymity, still, it was mind blowing to Raphael and Luke that he was this at ease in a crowd, basically naked, cage clearly visible in the sheer jock. The guy who would never let another gym bunny even see a hint of his enviable cock, was the center of attention, and loving it.

The conquerors and their sex slaves spotted Steve sitting on a wall bench away from the bar. They squeezed their way through the crowd in order to join him, stopping along the way to hug Jake, who was on his regular stool at the end of the bar, dressed in his standard bar attire: harness, boots and codpiece jock, beachball belly on full display. Greg once again offered to order beers for them, and for Steve, and he and Alex made their way to one of the other bartenders who was in less demand than Pup Niki. Besides, they wanted to surprise Niki as a group, if possible.

"Okay," Luke said to Steve, once they reached him. "This is beyond my wildest hopes for Niki."

"No lie," Raphael seconded. "He's a totally different person!"

"Pup, Raphael," Steve laughed. "He's not Niki, your brother, when he's here. He's Pup Niki, the flirtiest, sexiest, most exhibitionist, and I might add, the most popular bartending pup in town."

"Why didn't you tell us?" Raphael scolded. "We'd have come down sooner."

"Yeah!"

"It's happened really fast. He was an overnight sensation. The owners have already given him a raise, and between us, I think the other bartenders are jealous. Niki's tips are outrageous."

Greg and Alex approached with the beers. "To Niki," Luke toasted. Glasses clinked all around.

"To Steve, for tipping us off to Niki's secret fetish," Raphael followed up. More clinks. "One that seems to serve him, and his customers, awfully well." They continued to watch Niki. The usually shy, unassuming cutie was reveling in the attention, giving each customer a personalized thrill, it seemed. It was hard to tell who was having more fun.

"I sometimes think guys buy beers they don't even intend to drink, just so they can interact with him, and have a moment with him," Steve said.

"The owners have to love that," Greg offered. Luke nodded. As they watched, one of the bartenders walked up to Niki, spoke briefly, and took over his station. Niki came out from behind the bar and started collecting empties. Half of the eyes in the place followed him and his wagging tail, and the sweet brown ass it was wagging from. That's when he finally spotted family. Niki rushed over, set the bottles and glasses he'd collected down and threw his arms around Raphael, then Luke, then Alex and Greg, then back to Raphael one more time.

"Niki!" Raphael shouted over the din. "You are amazing! They *love* you!"

"Yeah," Niki demurred. "It's a good crowd tonight. But look at you guys! Holy cow! You're all naked! Were you in the Castro like this?"

"Need you ask?" Steve laughed. "They're all over Instagram."

"Seriously?" Alex shrieked.

"Seriously. I'll show you later,"

"Are you having fun?" Luke asked, putting his arm around Niki's shoulders. Niki wrapped his arm around Luke's waist, pulled him tight.

"Yes. So much fun. And I have you to thank for it. Thanks for talking the owners into giving me a chance. This job is a dream."

"I'm sure they're just as happy about it as you are," Luke replied. "All the credit goes to you."

"Thanks. It sure beats steaming lattes in a nerdy polo shirt."

"I'm kinda jealous," Alex said as he pulled Niki out of Luke's grasp for another naked chest to chest hug with Niki. "I wish I could work in just a sheer jock like you."

"Said the guy who wouldn't even get naked at Folsom," Greg laughed.

"I've evolved!" Alex protested, smacking Greg's biceps. "Just wait 'til next year, mister."

"I'll make you a deal, Alex." Raphael said, wiggling his eyebrows. "I'll show up at work tomorrow in a sheer jock if you will."

"Tempting, Raphael. Very tempting," Alex laughed.

"Thanks for coming down, guys. Please come more often. I better get back to work." Everyone gave Niki a heartfelt hug. He'd have gotten his share of kisses, too, but the puppy hood made that impossible. Greg tweaked his pup tail as he started to walk away, resulting in a couple of barks from Niki as he looked back over his shoulder. As he neared the bar, Niki stopped at Jake's stool, bent down and nuzzled Jake's belly. Jake patted Niki's ass in return.

Everyone was in good spirits, having seen how well Niki was doing. They finished their beers, bestowed a succession of hugs on Steve, waved to Jake, and headed for the door. Tomorrow was a workday and it was already very late. As they neared the door, Luke spotted a poster promoting an upcoming event, and smiled.

Outside, Raphael and Alex were standing in a weary embrace, already longing for their respective beds as Greg was thumbing his phone to summon their Lyft. Luke squeezed Greg's cock, still on display in his net mesh body suit and quietly said, "How would you feel about getting even with Alex and Raphael for the dare they sprung on us tonight?"

"I'd love it. I have no idea what you have in mind, but count me in. Especially if means an equal measure of exposure."

"I'll text you tomorrow."

It had been a memorable evening, as Alex and Raphael had promised. Everyone was all smiles on the way home. Even the driver, who was sitting next to Greg.

Thirty-Two

OKAY, WHERE WERE WE?

THE FOLLOWING SUNDAY FOUND Luke and Raphael lounging on the couch, reading and noshing as usual. After the late night of Halloween earlier in the week, they'd all decided to pass on a beach day Saturday. Besides, Karl the Fog was more persistent than usual, so it probably would have been too chilly anyway. Halfway through his bagel, Raphael's phone rang, announcing a call from Angel.

"Hey, Angel, how are you?"

"Good, you?'

"We're fine, thanks. How's Mama?"

"She's good. She'd appreciate a call from you."

"I know. Thanks for the nudge. We'll call her later."

"Better not use Facetime, or else put some clothes on first."

"Gee, I hadn't thought of that. Thanks, little brother. Is that why you called, to scold me?"

"No. Actually, I was thinking about Niki. You said you were going to talk with him. How'd it go?"

"Oh, wow, Angel, I'm so sorry. I totally blew off getting back to you. We've been kind of busy here."

"Well, I assumed no news is good news."

"Definitely. Niki's ... fine. It all went really well. He's ... well ... he's much happier. We had a very emotional encounter ... all of us, Luke, Steve, Niki and me. It was good. Really good. Damn, Angel, I feel terrible for not getting back to you sooner. I mean, you deserve all the credit for forwarding that text."

"So, he's okay with you and Luke, I don't know ... exploring the fringe?"

"What?"

"Sorry, I don't know how to verbalize what you and Luke are up to. So, he's okay with it now?"

"Angel, I can honestly say Niki and I are closer now than we've ever been. And, again, I owe it all to you and your sharing things about his feelings for me that I was too oblivious to realize before. He's good. Really, really good. We're all good. Sorry for leaving you in the dark."

"No need to apologize. I'm just relieved that things are better now. Maybe I should make an effort to come up and see you guys. It's been a while."

"I'm sure Niki would love that," Luke interjected, scooting up next to Raphael so he could see Angel on screen.

"Glad to see you're both still living leathered and naked. Just so it's not only Raphael."

"It's always both of us, most of our friends, too," Luke laughed. "You should try it."

"Who says I haven't?" Angel shot back. "Maybe not as often as you guys, but, oh, well, whatever. Listen, you guys take care. I'll touch base with Niki, now that I know things are cool. Love you!" Angel rang off.

"Should we warn Niki?" Luke asked.

"On it," Raphael replied as he typed a text to Niki. "I don't know how much Niki wants to reveal to Angel, but it's up to him. Angel's as open-minded as they come, so sooner or later, I'm betting he'll get an earful."

"Or an eyeful." Luke laughed. "Maybe we should invite Angel up for one our Tuesday dinners."

"Or not. Although it probably wouldn't shock him. After seeing that pic that Niki sent him, he probably has a pretty good idea of what we're into. And, he probably doesn't care."

"Good. We'll put him on the list."

"Ha, ha. More coffee, please, Sir." Raphael batted his eyes at Luke as he held up his empty cup.

Tuesday evening finally arrived, along with the sadness everyone felt knowing that someone other than Ricky would be delivering dinner once again. Opening the door wasn't nearly as much fun as it had been with Ricky on the other side, despite the fact that whomever was there was at least bearing dinner. Everyone was gathered around the coffee/dinner table munching on cheese and crackers and kalamata olives when the doorbell rang.

"I'll get it," Alex said, as Raphael was struggling with a reluctant wine cork. Alex headed around the corner and opened the door. "RICKY!!!!" he shouted, bringing everyone to their feet, and to the door. Not only was Ricky holding out two bags of food, but it was a naked Ricky, with a brand new haircut. Greg took the bags out of Ricky's hands as Alex, Raphael and Niki smothered Ricky with a group hug. They pulled him into the apartment and closed the door.

"Did you drive your scooter over here naked?" Alex asked hopefully.

"Oh, thanks for reminding me. No, my clothes are outside. I wanted to make an entrance. I'll go get them."

"I'll get 'em," Luke said. "Don't you go anywhere near that door." Ricky looked chagrined, but chuckled. Once Alex, Raphael and Niki finally relinquished their holds on Ricky, it was Steve and Greg's turns, one after the other. Then Luke returned with Ricky's bundle, which he placed on the floor, away from the gathering. It was his turn to welcome Ricky back. They embraced, rocking back and forth a moment, then Luke bent down and planted a major kiss on Ricky's lips. When they parted, he said, "Ricky, you bad boy! You scared the shit out of us." He squeezed Ricky again, then they separated and everyone assumed their normal places. Yes, finally, Tuesday dinner felt normal again.

"Guys ... I'm so sorry. I've been going through a lot."

"We all have," Raphael said. "We've missed the hell out of you. Before another minute passes, hand me your phone."

"What?"

"Your phone. Unlock it and hand it to me, pleeease." Ricky could tell Raphael wasn't kidding around. He got up from his spot between Alex and Raphael and retrieved the phone from his pants. He handed it Raphael as he sat back down. Raphael punched the screen for a few seconds, until his own phone beeped. He handed Ricky's phone back to him, picked up his own phone from the table and spent another minute thumbing his own screen. That's when everyone else's phone responded.

"There," Raphael said triumphantly, sliding his phone under the coffee table. "Now we all have Ricky's number. You'll never be able to run from us again, muchacho." He put his hand on Ricky's thigh, something he'd missed doing for weeks, and said, "Don't you even try."

"Don't worry, amigo. I promise I'll never do that again." By now Luke and Steve had unpacked dinner and everyone began dishing it up and eating.

"So, Ricky," Luke said, seriously but gently, "please tell us what happened. You have no idea how worried we've been. What exactly did you mean when you said you've been going through a lot?"

Ricky set his plate aside and sighed. "I'll try. It's a lot. After I left here, after you unlocked the chastity cage, I went home and stayed in my room for two days. I was so depressed. I questioned everything, you know? Would Juan ever want me back, no matter what I might do? Could I even be a good leather boy for him, if he did? Was it worth risking getting beat up, or worse, for being a queer chastity boy? If I even am a queer chastity boy? 'Cause, you know, most of my family is going to be just like Julio ... the roommate who threatened me. I probably can't be Juan's leather boy and my dad's son. So ... what do I do? I was a mess. Totally. So, finally, I just kind of put everything out of my mind as best I could. Just worked, and avoided my fucking roommates.

"Then last Sunday, I couldn't stand it any longer. I went to the beer bust. You know why. To see if Juan was there, and who he was with." Ricky stopped talking. Everyone was holding their breath.

"Well, was he there?!" Alex demanded.

Another heavy sigh from Ricky. "He was. I don't think he saw me. I didn't want him to see me. Not yet. You see, that's when I decided I *do* want to be his leather boy. While I was there, he talked to a couple different guys, but he was alone. He's still single, guys. I want him back so much! I'll do whatever you think I should do. Anything!" He turned to Raphael, put his hand on Raphael's thigh and said, "Lock me up, Raphael. *Please*, lock me up!"

Faster than Speedy Gonzalez, Raphael was up, in the bedroom, and back with Ricky's Holy Trainer.

"Stand up, leather boy, so I can take care of this handsome unlocked cock," Raphael urged. As he slid the cock ring over Ricky's cock and balls, Alex reached up and supportively rubbed Ricky's thigh and ass.

"It's so good to have you back, Ricky," Alex sighed.

"You be careful, Ricky," Niki warned, crawling over to Ricky on all fours, despite that fact that he wasn't in pup gear yet. He'd be getting 'dressed' after dinner for his shift at the bar. "Don't let that asshole see you caged again."

"I'll be careful, Niki," Ricky smiled, patting Niki on the head, then roughing up Niki's multicolored mohawk. "I tried to get a haircut just like Raphael's this afternoon, but the barber didn't understand what I wanted."

Raphael held the chastity tube against Ricky's cock ring so Alex could slide in the key. As Ricky sat down, once again safely locked up, Raphael offered, "Luke, why don't you fix Ricky's high 'n tight tonight? He'll look great with it, don't you think?"

"He will indeed," Luke agreed. "I'd love to. As soon as we're done eating, we'll do that."

"Cool." Ricky smiled. "Man, I missed you guys. I don't deserve you."

Raphael reached out and took Ricky's chin in hand and turned Ricky's head to face him. "Ricky, stop saying that. You do deserve us. Whether you like it or not, we're family now, you and us. It's what we do, so get used to it."

"Raphael's right," Greg said. He got up from the couch and came around to where the locked cock contingent was sitting. He sat down behind Ricky, put his hand on Ricky's shoulder and announced, "Ricky, Alex and I want you to move in with us. You need to get out of that apartment as soon as possible."

"Oh, thanks, but I ... I couldn't impose. That's really nice of you."

"Ricky, we're not being nice. Like Raphael said, we're family now," Alex said. "We have a second bedroom that we're using as an office slash storage room slash black hole for stuff we don't know what else do to with. It would look so much better as your bedroom."

"You're welcome to stay as long as you want, Ricky," Greg continued. "To be honest, I don't think it will be that long before you move again ... in with Juan. But until then, you're living with us. And, don't even try to argue about it. It's settled."

"Dios Mio! I can't believe you guys. Seriously?"

"What does it take to convince this guy he's finally where he belongs?" Greg asked rhetorically. He draped both his arms over Ricky's shoulders, his hands halfway down to Ricky's killer abs, as Raphael and Alex anointed both cheeks in brotherly kisses. Ricky, choking up, was speechless for the moment.

"Ricky," Luke called for his attention. "How much stuff do you have to move?"

"Not a lot. My bed, a little dresser, clothes, some books."

"If all of us helped, how many trips would it take to carry everything out?"

"Well, considering how many muscles you guys have, I'm guessing one. It's not a lot. Why?"

"Are you thinking what I think you're thinking?" Steve asked.

"Yeah. Ricky you've spent your last night in that hellhole. We're moving you tonight."

"Hey!" Niki interjected. "I want to be in on this. Let me see if I can show up late at the bar." He headed into the kitchen with his phone, while Steve used his to check on the nearest Zipcar van. Meanwhile, Alex and Raphael were conspiring between themselves. Greg was still holding onto Ricky, rubbing his abs from behind. Ricky looked like he'd just won the lottery. Niki returned, all smiles, "It's a slow night. I have the night off!"

"I got a van three blocks away that should be big enough," Steve reported. So, everything was set. Until ...

"Guys." Raphael grinned, sitting next to Alex, their arms around each other's necks. "Alex and I have decided that this should be a move that the roommates from hell will *never* forget."

Luke looked at Greg, rolled his eyes, then addressed Raphael and Alex, "What have you cooked up now, boys?"

Alex took the stage. "After we get the van, we're going to stop at Steve and Niki's and our places. Luke, you and Greg are going to be wearing your Halloween see-through body suits. Raphael and I are going to be harnessed. Period. Niki will be pupped out, and Steve, I'm sorry, I'm not sure what you should be wearing, but what you're wearing right now looks good to me."

"I can be harnessed," Steve laughed.

"Perfect!" Raphael applauded. "Ricky, we don't want to make any more trouble for you, especially since you're caged again, so you should put your clothes back on."

"Oh, man ..."

"Better safe than sorry, Ricky," Luke advised. "You guys. Do you really want to do this?" The unanimous answer was affirmative. While Luke and Raphael put on their outfits, such as they were, Steve dressed and headed out to collect the van. Forty-five minutes later, the van, holding seven conspirators, only one of whom wasn't naked, pulled up in front of Ricky's building. They trooped up the stairs, each carrying a couple of empty trash bags, with Ricky leading the way.

He opened the door, and entered the living room where two stocky men were sitting on a couch, a couple of feet apart from one another, watching what Americans call a soccer match. A third man, thinner and younger, sat away from them in a separate side chair. All three were drinking from bottles of Modelo. They barely looked up at Ricky, that is, until his entourage followed him into the room. Ricky was tailed by Luke in his body suit, then Raphael, proudly, flamboyantly, caged and harnessed, then Greg ala his bodysuit, followed by a naked Alex doing his best to out flamboy Raphael (if only he'd had time to apply those killer eyelashes), then Steve in his harness and nothing else. Niki, in all his glorious pupness, took up the rear. It took less than thirty seconds for the parade to cross the room and enter Ricky's bedroom, but what a memorable thirty seconds it was. During the parade, one of the guys on the couch held his bottle up to his mouth, but though his mouth hung open, the bottle never moved. Only his eyes moved, following what he saw, but couldn't believe.

"That was amazing!" Ricky stage whispered after closing his door.

"No time to waste," Luke urged. "We need to be packed up and out of here before they call for reinforcements."

"You think they will?" Raphael asked.

"Let's not find out, baby. Move!" And, move they did. Clothes and bedding flew into bags. Greg and Steve upended the platform bed as Luke pulled drawers out of the dresser, and picked it up. In less than five minutes, they were loaded and ready for Act II. Ricky laid his house keys on the floor and picked up the last dresser drawer. This time he was near the rear, just ahead of Niki.

Just as Luke was about to open the door, Ricky called out, "Wait! Amigos, I really want to do this." Everyone turned to see him rip off his shirt and shorts ... and his boxers. The caged, naked leather-boy-in-the-making was ready to make his exit. "Okay, let's go!"

The three roommates, not understanding what was happening, had not moved. Everyone in the entourage grinned at each of the clueless roommates as they exited. When Ricky reached the middle of the room he stopped, causing Niki to nearly run him over. He reached into the drawer he was carrying, grabbed his boxers and tossed them on the couch, between the two brutes. "¡Adios, pinche cabrones!" He turned to the third roommate, winked, and said, "¡Buena suerte!" Niki barked and wagged his tail on his way out the door.

Another twenty minutes later they and Ricky's belongings were safely inside Alex and Greg's (and for now Ricky's) apartment. Steve pulled on sweats borrowed from Greg and headed out to return the van. The rest moved what they could out of Ricky's new bedroom, to make room for his bed and dresser.

"We'll clean this up tomorrow, Ricky, but at least you'll be able to sleep tonight," Alex said.

"No worries, Alex. I'll be fine. I still can't believe you and Greg are doing this. I'll never be able to repay you."

"Ricky. Remember what Raphael said ... we're family now." He planted a big one on Ricky's cheek. "Just having you here, safe and sound, is payment enough." After putting Ricky's bed and dresser back together, everyone settled in the living room, just as Steve returned and flung off Greg's sweats. Alex and Greg headed into the kitchen and re-turned with glasses and a bottle of Schramsberg sparkling wine they had stashed in the freezer when they stopped in for their 'moving gear' earlier. Greg eased the cork out with a 'maiden's sigh' and poured. Everyone raised their glasses to Ricky, who was beaming. "Welcome home, Ricky," Alex cheered.

"Home," Luke piped up, "where the buffalo roam, and the leather boys can stay naked and caged all day." As Raphael groaned, Luke asked, "Say, Ricky, what do you know about the guy who was sitting alone, nearer the door?"

"Mateo? Not much, really. He always keeps to himself. He's never been mean to me, or anything, but, you know, we're just roommates, were just roommates. By necessity, not friends. Not family, like this."

"Well, I couldn't help but notice the tent pole he'd erected after seeing us."

"Yeah, I noticed that, too," Greg agreed. "It was pretty obvious, even with the baggy pants."

"What are you guys talking about?" Ricky asked.

"Boner, silly. He had a boner," Alex laughed.

"Do you think he might be gay?" Raphael asked.

"Don't know. I really don't know him that well. Maybe. I've never seen him with a girl, but ..."

Before Ricky could continue, his phone beeped. He looked down, looked up at the others and grinned. He went back to his phone for a minute, then announced, "That was a text from Mateo."

"Annnnd?" Alex asked.

"It says ... I'll translate, 'Julio threw your boxers in the trash. I got them out. Let me know if you want them back."

"Oooooooooooh," Raphael and Alex said in unison.

"Interesting," Steve said. "Luke, you may be on to something." Ricky was busy texting.

"What did you say? What did you say?" Raphael begged.

"I texted, 'No, amigo, you wear them. My gift to you.'" His phone immediately beeped again.

"What did he say?" Alex asked. Ricky looked up from his phone, grinning.

"He said, 'Okay. Thanks. Take care.' Then a smiley emoji."

"He's sooooooo gay!" Raphael hooted. "You had an ally and didn't even know it."

"I'm not sure *he* knew it," Ricky countered. "I don't think he's ever acted on it, if he is gay."

"Hmmm," Raphael said. "We'll just have to ..."

"Stop. Right there, Mother Teresa," Luke admonished. "We have our work cut out for us getting Ricky back in Juan's arms. Mateo can take care of himself. If he comes asking for help, that's one thing, but until then, he's on his own. Back me up, here, guys. To Ricky and Juan." Luke lifted his nearly empty glass, as everyone joined him.

"To Ricky and Juan!"

Thirty-Three

RICKY'S FINISHING TOUCHES

LUKE FINISHED EMPTYING HIS glass and put it down. "Ricky, it's getting pretty late. How about we do that high 'n tight tomorrow night, or next Saturday. Hopefully it'll be another beach day."

"Whenever is good for you, Luke. Thanks. Do you really think it'll look as good as Raphael's?"

"I'll do my best, Ricky."

"You'll look sexy as hell, Ricky," Raphael promised. "Not that you don't, already."

"Come on, sweet talker, let's go home and go to bed," Luke said, snuggling up to Raphael. "It's been another long day."

"Yes, Sir." The group broke up then, hugs were exchanged, and everyone headed for their respective beds, happier than they had been in weeks.

The weekdays flew by, as they always do. Alex and Raphael touched base every day at work on how Ricky was adapting. Trying to show his gratitude, Ricky had become housekeeper, laundress, chef and bottle washer in the apartment. He had even surprised Greg and Alex by treating them to dinner one night.

"We keep telling him to stop, but he's so happy to be somewhere safe, where he can run around naked and caged. He says he's auditioning for his life as Juan's leather boy. He's having a blast, so we can't fault him. We just feel guilty that he's doing it."

"Hey, enjoy it. Like Greg said, it probably won't be for long. Juan will take him back the first chance he gets."

"I hope so, for Ricky's sake. But, you know, I'll miss having him around."

"You can get a puppy."

"Or, Mateo."

"And I'm the one they call Mother Teresa?"

"Well, he was kind of cute, don't you think?"

"I honestly didn't pay that much attention. I was focused on the thugs. But I'll take your word for it. Hey, ask Ricky when he's free for you and me to take him shopping for his leather boy look. The sooner we get him suited up; the sooner we'll get him married off."

"Good idea. He's busy almost every night with DoorDash. How about Saturday late morning, before the beach ... if the fog cooperates?"

"That'll work. Let me know."

And so it was that the three locked cock boys found themselves at Mr. S on Saturday. All three were in caged cock tees, and Raphael and Alex wore their leather shorts to set the mood for Ricky, Raphael's with the laced-up codpiece and more broken in than Alex's more 'street worthy' pair.

"What do you guys recommend?" Ricky asked as they perused the selection of assless chaps, assless shorts, codpiece shorts, codpiece thongs and jocks, not to mention the selection of rubber gear. The possibilities were overwhelming to him.

"I think less is more, like Luke said," Raphael advised. "You want to be as much of a blank canvas for Juan as possible. A sexy, enticing, irresistible canvas, of course, but we don't want to go overboard. Let him decide, with you, what kind of leatherboy you're going to be. I already have an idea, actually the perfect idea, of what you should wear above the waist when you approach him, and you already have those boots I gave you. And you're already caged, although Juan will probably replace the one you're wearing now with a metal one at some point. So, really, we just need to settle on bottom gear. Assless chaps? Or codpiece shorts? Or, rubber? Does Juan like rubber?"

"I don't know. Let's try these." Ricky held up a pair of lace up codpiece shorts, similar to Raphael's.

"Okay," Raphael said. "I'll hold them while you take off your pants."

"Here? Aren't there, you know, fitting rooms?"

"Yeah," Alex offered. "Over here."

"No," Raphael stopped him. "Those are for wannabes. Strip right here, leatherboy. That's what I do."

"That's right," said the sales rep, as he walked up behind Ricky. "Welcome back, Raphael."

"Hey, Rob, good to see you. I can't believe you remember me."

"I never forget a chastity cage," Rob laughed. "I see you're still wearing the collar. Nice shirts, guys, by the way."

"Thanks. Yeah, the collar, like the cage, is permanent. In fact, obviously, we're all caged. Ricky here needs something to help convince his ex to take him back and make him his leatherboy." Alex was clearly taken aback at Raphael's familiarity and openness with Rob. Ricky didn't know what to think.

"Let's do it," Rob smiled. "Ricky, let's see what you have to offer. Take off those pants." Ricky hesitated.

"Like this, amigo," Raphael said, as he stripped off his shorts and stood, arms crossed, proudly displaying his cage. Then he reached over, took the codpiece pants that Ricky was still holding from him, and said to Rob, "Maybe he needs your help."

As Rob started to reach for the button on Ricky's pants, Ricky relented and unbuttoned them himself. He slid them down and pulled them off over his shoes. "Part of the leatherboy training?" he asked Raphael.

"Si," Raphael smiled as he handed the codpiece pants to Rob. "Now, hand me your shirt." Ricky made a pained face, but Raphael simply held out his empty hand, silently requesting Ricky's tee. Since no one came to his rescue, Ricky finally relented and pulled the tee up and off, and handed it to Raphael.

"Okay, turn around for me, Ricky," Rob instructed. "Again. Okay, very nice! You should never wear a shirt, Ricky. So, you're auditioning to be someone's permanent leatherboy, right?

"Yes, Sir," Ricky replied.

"Let's try something a little different. Follow me." Rob, followed by two bottomless leatherboys, one completely naked, and a third still clothed, made his way to another section of erotic wear, mostly textiles. He took a pair of black Airtex Sport shorts off the rack and handed them to Ricky. "Try these on."

Ricky pulled them on. The shorts were only slightly more discrete than the body suits Luke and Greg had worn for Halloween. Ricky's cage and ass were clearly on display through the net like fabric. At Rob's urging Ricky did a 360, then another one. Both Raphael and Alex made affirmative ooooohing sounds.

"I know you're auditioning for a leatherboy position, and these aren't leather, but, with that cage and that ass, you look pretty damn desirable in these. What do you think, guys?"

"Juan doesn't stand a chance!" Raphael exclaimed. "You look amazing, Ricky! Come look." Raphael proceeded to replicate his own experience at Mr. S, many months earlier, and took Ricky's hand and dragged him to a nearby mirror, with Rob and Alex trailing ... both enjoying the view. Ricky was impressed with what he saw. Indeed, his baby blue cage was clearly visible behind the material. As was his bare ass.

Rob reached down and said, "There's this handy little feature, too." He unzipped the all-around zipper that totally exposed Ricky's cage and ass crack. "You don't even have to take them off to provide your partner full access."

"What do you think, Alex," Raphael asked.

"Let me put it this way," Alex smiled. "I'm getting a pair for myself."

"Would you like to try on a pair, now?" Rob asked. "I'll hold your shorts for you."

"Sure," Alex replied, relieved to finally be joining his fellow leather-boys in a little exhibitionism. "I have to say, the service here is top shelf." He handed his shorts to Rob and lead the four back to the rack of Airtex shorts, where he tried on a pair in the Army color. Both Raphael and Ricky approved. "This way, when we go out in them, we won't look like total twins," he kidded Ricky.

"Yeah, because we look so much alike otherwise, amigo," Ricky laughed. He was already relaxing despite being on full display in a retail store. The leatherboy training was going well, probably aided in great part by his new supportive and clothes-free surroundings at Alex and Greg's home.

"Will you gentlemen be wearing these out?" Rob asked.

"If it was dark out, absolutely." Alex replied as he peeled his new shorts off. "But, maybe not today. What about you, Raphael? Are you getting a pair?" Ricky had stripped his Airtex off and was pulling his pants back on.

"No, not today anyway. I kinda prefer less coverage than these shorts offer," he smiled and winked at Rob. "Thanks for your help, Rob. You made the right recommendation for Ricky. He'll blow Juan away."

"Glad to help. And always glad to be of service to proud and dedicated leatherboys such as yourselves. It was a pleasure meeting you Ricky, and you Alex. And, good to see you again, Raphael." Raphael hugged Rob, then the caged contingent carried their loot to the cashier, where Alex insisted on paying for Ricky's shorts.

"Don't argue with me, Ricky," Alex admonished. "Good leatherboys never argue. They just say, 'Yes, Sir. Thank you, Sir." Ricky looked at Raphael for support. Raphael shrugged his shoulders and made a wry face.

"He's got you there, amigo. Say it after me ... 'Yes, Sir. Thank you, Sir.'" So, Ricky did.

The three were headed back to Raphael and Luke's place, Ricky in the middle, holding hands with both Raphael and Alex, whose free hand was holding the bag with their promising new purchases. This was old hat for Alex ... he'd long ago learned you didn't walk anywhere with Raphael without holding hands, but it was new to Ricky, who had only held hands with them on a secluded beach. He thought he should feel self-conscious, especially since all three were wearing caged cock t-shirts, but Alex and Raphael were so matter of fact, so comfortable, and no one around them gave them a second look. After a couple of blocks Ricky just enjoyed the feeling. Of being himself, out in the open. Of being with men who loved him and did not care who knew it.

"So, is this everything we're going to do to make me ready for Juan?" Ricky asked. "The cage, the shorts, your boots, Raphael? I know Luke wants me to be ... what did he call it? An open canvas?"

"A blank canvas. He's right, we want Juan to have the most say on your transformation. Remember, Luke is going to finish up your high 'n tight as soon as we get back, and I have a plan for what you should wear with the shorts."

"A harness?"

"No, something more provocative. When are you planning to make your move?"

"Tomorrow, at the beer bust, if he's there. I'm so nervous, but I want to get it over with, you know?"

"Whoa. Tomorrow, huh?" Alex said. "I guess you'll be ready once Luke shaves you." As much as Alex wanted Ricky to fall into Juan's arms, he was still hoping it would not be quite that soon.

"In that case, we ought to make one more stop." Raphael said. "I don't think it'll do too much damage to your beautiful canvas."

"What are you thinking?" Alex asked,

"Ricky, I think you'd look adorable with a tiny little septum ring like Luke and I have. What do you say?"

"I'd love it, Raphael! I've actually wanted one, ever since I saw yours, but I didn't want to, you know, be a copycat."

"Hey, as your designated mentor, I wouldn't consider it copying me at all. More like emulating. Or, worshipping." Raphael laughed at his own faux egoism and planted one on Ricky's cheek. "Seriously, though, I think it would be the cherry on the Leatherboy Ricky Sundae."

"I bow to your superior knowledge," Ricky kidded back. "Take me to your piercer." The three immediately detoured toward Jake's shop. Hopefully he could squeeze them in, since the septum would be quick and easy. If, that is, he had the jewelry on hand. As they entered, they saw no one waiting, a good sign. Jake's assistant, a young trans man, came around the corner at the sound of the door.

"Hey, Raphael, how's it going?"

"Actually, very well, Oliver. I know we don't have an appointment, but we were hoping Jake could fit us in. These are my friends Alex and

Ricky, and we were hoping to get a little septum ring done for Ricky today, like mine and Luke's." Raphael needlessly pointed to his own piercing.

"Jake will be done with his current client in just a few minutes, so that shouldn't be a problem. Let's look at what piece of jewelry you want."

"I want the same as Raphael and Luke have," Ricky spoke up. "Tiny and cool."

"Tiny and cool. I like that," Oliver laughed. "I'm going to use that if you don't mind." Ricky smiled. "I do have a suggestion, though. Raphael's is stainless steel, so it looks like silver. But, for you, I'd recommend gold colored niobium, to go with those little gold ball earrings you have."

"Very cool!" Raphael agreed. "With your skin color, that'll be adorable." He put his arm around Ricky's waist and pulled him close as they stood at the display case. Oliver rummaged through one of the drawers below, then finally came up with a small gold colored ring the same gauge and diameter as what Raphael was wearing. He placed it on a black velvet pad and handed it to Ricky.

Ricky eyed it a moment, then turned to Raphael and asked, "Should I, really?"

"Have I ever given you bad advice?" Raphael grinned, then, without waiting for an answer turned to Oliver. "We'll take it." The locked cock contingent had barely had time to sit before Jake's client came out and settled up. Oliver stepped back to brief Jake, who immediately came out and greeted them, giving Raphael a familiar hug. After introductions, all four went into the back.

"I normally don't perform for an audience, Alex," Jake said over his shoulder as he settled Ricky on the table, "but we'll make an exception for Ricky, here. This is going to look really nice on you," he continued, addressing Ricky. "I assume you want it positioned like Raphael's, just touching the septum, not hanging down any."

"Yes, Sir, just like Raphael's." Since this was Ricky's first piercing with him, Jake was his gentle, reassuring self. Raphael watched intently, holding Ricky's right hand while Alex, holding his left, closed his eyes at the moment of thrust. Ricky hardly reacted, wanting everyone to see how good a leatherboy he could be. It was less traumatic than he expected.

"That's it?" he asked.

"That's it, young man. You're as much a trooper as Raphael here. All done."

"Ummm, wait, Sir. I was wondering..."

"Yes?"

"How would it be if I also got a little labret, to match my earrings?" He turned to Raphael with a concerned look on his face. "That wouldn't do too much to the canvas, would it, Raphael? I really think Juan would like it."

"Ricky," Raphael squeezed Ricky's hand, "it's really about what you want. It can't all be about what Juan wants. You're going to be his leatherboy, not his property."

Ricky turned back to Jake. "It's what I want." He then delivered a smile that no one, including Jake, could deny. Seriously, Alex thought, Juan really doesn't stand a chance, does he?

Thirty minutes later, after Raphael had insisted on paying for the piercings, and Ricky almost objected before he remembered to say, "Yes, Sir ... Thank you, Sir," they were on their way.

"There's just one thing about these piercings that I'm worried about," Alex said. "I mean, you *do* look adorable, Ricky ..."

"But what, amigo?"

"Jake said you'll want to be careful kissing for the next couple of weeks. If you approach Juan tomorrow, I predict you're going to be in a heap of pain ... on the spot. He's probably going to kiss you into next week." Both Ricky and Raphael broke into laughter. They laughed for half a block. Then, when he caught his breath Raphael turned to Ricky.

"He's right. You're fucked."

"God, I hope so," was Ricky's reply.

Luke and Greg were waiting for them when the three finally arrived for Ricky's high 'n tight. To help make up for their unplanned delay, they entered bearing lunch. The three immediately stripped to join Luke and Greg, who had to agree it had been worth the wait. Alex briefly modeled his new shorts, prompting a sloppy wet kiss from Greg, before allowing Alex to strip back down again. As they ate, Raphael explained that they'd moved quickly on the piercings because tomorrow might be the big day for Ricky.

"Well, we all know Juan will take you back, Ricky," Greg assured, "but I think you should go slow on moving in with him. You should probably take things verrry slow, ease into it. I'm thinking maybe move out in a year or so." Ricky laughed.

"I promise I won't run away, amigos. *If* he takes me back, I will insist we still do Tuesday dinners and beach days when we can. You are my family, now. You aren't going to get rid of me that easy." Alex leaned over and gave Ricky a hug. He really was going to miss him.

It didn't take long for Luke to 'fix' Ricky's flattop. Rather than doing it in the tub, as he and Raphael did each night, he put Ricky in a chair in the living room so they could all talk and watch the transformation. Had he not been caged, they'd have seen Ricky's appreciative boner as a bonus. Having Luke, who was naked himself, of course, touching him so intimately, along with the warm lather while on display, made an erection inevitable. Damn, it felt good.

"You know, guys, I hadn't said anything, but guess what? I haven't come since the first time Raphael locked me up."

"Not even while you were gone and unlocked?" Greg asked.

"Nope. At first, I was too depressed. Then, I felt an obligation to see if I really could 'be locked' long term, even though I wasn't locked, you know? So, it's been almost a month."

"How does it feel, Ricky?" Raphael asked, grinning.

"I'm so horny, I could suck every one of you guys off. Right here, right now!"

"Okay," Greg laughed. "he's ready for Juan."

"Yeah," Raphael agreed. "But is Juan going to be ready for him?" Then, just to torture poor Ricky, Raphael scooted over to the chair he was in, got up on his knees, and sucked Ricky's cage into his mouth, while reaching up for his nipples. That brought the house down, and nearly destroyed Ricky's one month of abstinence.

"You are so mean," Ricky scolded Raphael. Then, to everyone's surprise, he looked up and said, "Okay ... who's next?"

"Damn!" Luke exclaimed, "You *are* horny!" He rubbed Ricky's head one last time with the towel, and said, "All done, handsome."

Finally, it was time to head to the beach, which they all hoped just might be their last chance to offer Ricky the opportunity to publicly display himself and his cage before his debut with Juan.

Thirty-Four

⸺◦─────◦⸺

GREG'S REVENGE

IT HAD BEEN A full Saturday, the shopping, the piercing studio, the shaved high 'n tight session and the trip to the beach. Everyone was beat, and Ricky still needed to put in a few hours of DoorDash deliveries. He'd showered and put on street clothes, and stopped to hug Greg goodbye before heading out to work. Alex was in the shower, and Greg was about to join him.

"Ricky, how late do you plan to work tonight?"

"I don't know, it always depends. Ten, maybe eleven. The orders usually dry up by then."

"Can you keep a secret?"

"Until I met Juan, my whole life was a secret, so, yeah, I think so." Ricky grinned. "What's up, amigo?"

"You know how Raphael and Luke like to challenge each other with dares?" Ricky nodded expectantly. "Well, you can't say anything to Alex or Raphael, but Luke and I are going to spring one on them tonight. After what they did to us on Halloween, it's our turn to put the spotlight on them."

"But weren't they practically just as naked as you that night?"

"Well, yeah, but that's beside the point. One good dare deserves another, and this one is going to be a doozy. Anyway, if you're free around ten, we'll be at Niki's bar. You should come by. It's going to be fun. Maybe you can test out those new shorts I haven't seen on you yet."

"I'll try. Thanks for clueing me in. But I'm saving the shorts for tomorrow." Another hug and Ricky was off, and Greg joined Alex under the shower. As they toweled each other off, Greg casually mentioned his plans for the evening.

"A gym gear theme?" Alex repeated. "That's kind of lame, don't you think? What would we wear?"

"Duh. Gym gear ... workout shorts, tank top, tights, you know, gym gear. Besides the real reason to go is to see Niki in action again. It was really busy Halloween, so we didn't have much time with him. I know Luke and Raphael are looking forward to it."

Meanwhile, at Luke and Raphael's: "I know Greg and Alex are looking forward to it. And, besides, it'll be the first time in months that I'll wear shorts instead of a kilt in public. Nobody will recognize me."

"Shorts on you ... that is radical. But, gym gear night? Really? I don't think Alex even goes to a gym that often, does he?"

"Don't know, but I know they're eager to see how Niki's doing."

"Luke, I'm kinda beat. You sure?"

"Let's take a nap ... a nap nap, not sex." He wrapped his arms around Raphael and sank his tongue deep in Raphael's mouth and tongue wrestled with him for a moment. He knew how to distract his locked cock boy, how to ignite his need to submit. It only took a moment. Raphael sighed and pulled Luke tight. When their lips finally parted, Raphael looked up into Luke's blue eyes.

"Okay. Take me to your bed, Sir." Luke smiled, and obliged.

Luke and Greg's plan was for Greg and Alex to order a Lyft, then pick up Luke and Raphael a little after nine-thirty, with an estimated arrival at the bar a little before ten. As Raphael was picking through his gym clothes, Luke made a strange suggestion.

"Baby, instead of a regular jock, why don't you wear this under your gym shorts." He handed Raphael a black sequined thong.

"Why? That's silly. Even I wouldn't wear that to the gym."

"You're not going to the gym, baby. Maybe I'll rip off your shorts on the dance floor and show off your sexy ass. Please..."

"Okay, but then you have wear this under your shorts." He handed Luke a mesh thong, much like the body suit he'd worn for Halloween.

"Fine. Which caged cock shirt will you wear?"

"The maroon one. It'll look good with these shorts."

"Perfect," Luke smiled. When Raphael dived into the back seat with Greg and Alex, he was wearing nearly the same outfit as Alex, who had elected to wear his caged cock tee as well. Luke sat up front with the driver, and he and Greg exchanged smiles. Right on time, they arrived at the bar, greeted the bouncer, and entered to see ... no one else in gym gear.

Instead, the DJ was announcing contestant number two in the night's amateur strip contest.

"What the ..." Raphael turned to Luke. "You said it was gym gear night."

"I must have gotten the dates wrong," Luke lied convincingly. Past dares had been good practice for good natured deception. "Geez, what an idiot. Oh, well, at least we won't get hot dancing later. Let's go say hi to Niki." Raphael didn't even have a chance to question further as Luke took him by the hand and led him over to Niki's station. Greg and Alex followed. Niki came around briefly for hugs all around, then returned to his station to pull four Anchor Steams for them. Steve walked up and initiated another round of hugs.

"I wondered if you guys might come down for the stripper contest."

"Luke said it was 'gym gear' night," Raphael whined. "That's why we're dressed like this. Pretty lame, huh?"

"Raphael, many words could be employed to describe how you guys look, but 'lame' isn't one of them. At least you and Alex are both wearing signature t-shirts. Nothing lame about that." Alex beamed. He'd slowly been wearing his caged cock tees more and more, and enjoying sending the subtle message to those 'in the know.' He hadn't caught up to Raphael's level of openness yet, but slowly ... slowly.

"Actually, I guess watching strippers is more fun than looking at guys dressed for the gym ... it's not like we don't see that every week anyway," Raphael brightened. Luke smiled and nodded. The five moved away from the bar and watched contestant number three. He wasn't bad, and the crowd was enthusiastic, cheering him on.

As he finished his performance, Luke took hold of Raphael's shoulders, leaned closer to be heard over the crowd and said, "Don't hate me, baby." That's when the DJ announced, 'our next contestant, give him a big hand, is Raphael!' Raphael's beautiful almond eyes shot daggers at Luke. "Welcome to your next dare, baby."

"Raphael!" the DJ announced. "Where's Raphael?" Luke turned Raphael by the shoulders and walked him through the crowd up to the end of the stage. He raised his arm to signal to the DJ that 'Raphael had arrived.' As Raphael slowly ascended the steps at the side of the small, make-shift stage, he looked back at Luke, who was smiling and wiggling that stupid eyebrow. "Here he is," the DJ announced. "Let's hear it for RAPHAEL!"

The music started, and Raphael took center stage and began to move, trying to emulate what he'd seen other strippers do in past shows he'd seen. Unfortunately, performing on stage, especially dancing, was not among Raphael's many enviable talents. So far, though, his face, his high 'n tight, his squat-built thighs descending from his tight gym shorts overshadowed any fault one might find in his dancing, and the crowd was appreciative. And, eager, of course, to see more of him. Though nervous,

Raphael was thinking clearly enough to calculate that if he took about two minutes between stripping off his shirt, then his shorts, he'd only be exposed in the sequined thong for about a minute, since the previous contestant had only had to dance for about five minutes. In due time he peeled off the caged cock tee as sexily as he could and tossed it behind him. He turned away from the crowd to display his inked back, and that amped up the cheers and whistles. To make it easier, he decided to imagine he was performing just for Luke. In a way he was, because Luke was right down in front, clapping with the music, laughing.

By the time he was ready to peel off the shorts, he saw Alex and Greg had joined Luke and they were also clapping. Alex, was hooting, jumping up and down, obviously delighting in Raphael's predicament. Bastard. Wiggling his ass as best he could, Raphael peeled off the shorts, revealing the thong. He turned his back again to showcase his ass, and again, the cheers and hoots and hollers notched up another level. Meanwhile Alex raised both arms as he danced along, enjoying the show just as much as the rest of the crowd, and that's when he felt hands on his thighs and under his arms. Greg and Luke were lifting him up! In celebration? He turned to see Greg laughing, then bobbing his head toward Raphael. What the? As Alex flailed his arms, Raphael, one step ahead of Alex in realizing this was a dare for both of them, grabbed Alex's left arm, and with Greg and Luke's help, pulled Alex up and onto the stage. Seeing Alex was wearing a tee that matched the one Raphael had stripped off, made it clear to the crowd this was a stripping duo, even before the DJ announced, "Here's Alex, the other half of our fourth contestant." Alex was as surprised as Raphael had been, and had had even less time to prepare. He shot a 'who's idea was this' kind of look at Raphael, who looked down at Luke and Greg, who were enjoying the show way too much for their own good.

That's when Ricky finally arrived. He was not expecting to see his locked cock brothers doing a strip tease in a leather bar, but then, again, Greg had sort of clued him in. He grinned, looking around for Greg and Luke, and finally spotted them all the way in front of the crowd, right next to the stage. He pushed and shoved his way through the enthusiastic, and in some cases inebriated, crowd to finally squeeze in between Greg and Luke.

"You made it!" Greg shouted. Luke grinned, put his arm around Ricky's shoulders and pulled him in for a side hug.

"Enjoy the show, Ricky!" he laughed. Meanwhile, on stage, Contestant Number Four's five minutes would soon be up, and Raphael didn't want to be the only one who'd fully stripped, so as Alex started to dance, he reached over and pulled his tee up by the waist. Alex obliged and raised his arms so Raphael could pull it all the way off. The crowd loved it ... one guy stripping the other! Freed of his shirt, Alex really began to boogie. Makeup wasn't the only skill he'd learned doing drama in school. He'd been in a few musicals, and he knew how to move. Raphael immediately felt outclassed, and did his best to mimic how Alex was dancing. The crowd liked his moves, too, the cheers continuing.

But unfortunately, Alex wasn't taking off his shorts. This was a stripping contest, after all. Raphael was still more exposed than Alex, and time was running out. He didn't want to be only one bare-assed on stage in this truly evil dare, so he did what anyone would have done. He squatted down, reached up and yanked Alex's shorts to his ankles. The crowd went berserk. We're talking jet engine decibel levels. Alex put his hand on Raphael's shoulder as Raphael helped Alex step out of the shorts to avoid tripping. Raphael, smiling now that they had both stripped, looked up and discovered why the crowd was so energized. Alex was completely naked, flashing his cage at a couple hundred horny guys.

And Alex was not amused. Okay, Alex was pissed! But the crowd was ecstatic. Raphael immediately stood up and resumed dancing, showing Alex a 'sorry!' face, since talking was impossible.

Luke leaned over Ricky's head and shouted into Greg's ear, "Didn't you tell him to wear a jock?"

"I didn't think I'd need to. Who doesn't wear a jock to the gym?"

"Alex."

On stage, Alex was still moving well, not knowing what else to do. Surely the music would stop now. Please! Raphael felt guilty, even though he had acted innocently enough. He couldn't put Alex's shorts back on him while they were both dancing, so he decided the only decent thing to do, the only way he could make it up to Alex, was to ... rip off his own thong. The crowd was out of control now. Saturn Five launch decibel level with two caged and naked men on display. Alex grinned for the first time. He grabbed Raphael, pulled him in and planted a big kiss on his lips. Another first for the crowd at an amateur strip contest.

Behind the bar, Niki and the manager were watching the show. They had nothing else to do ... no one was ordering drinks. All eyes were on the show. Niki leaned into the manager and shouted, "Isn't it illegal to be naked? Isn't that why I have to wear this sheer jock?"

"Do you see any cops here?" Niki's puppy hood shook a definite 'no.' "Besides, the customers are having a great time. And, now that I think about it, with those chastity cages on, technically they're not completely naked."

"Then why am I wearing a see-through jock?"

"Fair question. Let me think about it. We'll talk."

Raphael was surprised that Alex was seemingly okay with being naked in front of a couple hundred rowdy, horny men, now that he'd stripped down himself. Apparently, for Alex, there was something to the 'strength in numbers' adage. What he did know for sure was that they'd passed that five-minute mark a long time ago, yet the DJ showed no interest in ending their set. Raphael decided to push the limits in hopes of bringing things to a close. He pulled Alex into another cage to cage embrace so he could shout into his ear what he had in mind. Alex nodded and smiled. As they broke the hug, Alex turned his back to Raphael, who dropped to his knees and buried his face in Alex's ass, pantomiming a rim job as Alex sashayed away. Ricky's hands flew to his mouth, eyes wide as he looked back and forth between Greg and Luke, who were hardly able to stand up. This was going *so* much better than they ever could have imagined. Their guys were slaying the crowd.

Okay, Raphael thought, this has gone on long enough. He raised up, and when Alex turned to face him, he pulled him close and shouted more instructions. Alex nodded. They broke apart, danced a few more seconds, then turned to the crowd and bowed, then turned their backs to the crowd and bowed again, displaying fully two immensely fuckable asses, one tanned white, one naturally brown, both heartbreaking. Then they raised up, Raphael took Alex by the hand and they headed for the stairs, DJ be damned.

Greg, Luke and Ricky were waiting for them at the bottom of the stairs, and a good thing, too. While half the men headed to the bar, the other half wanted to mob Raphael and Alex. As the DJ lowered the volume, Ricky was the first to speak.

"You guys were awesome!"

"Alex ... I'm soooo sorry," Raphael said, pulling him into yet another embrace, but finally one where they could actually communicate. "I thought you'd be wearing a jock."

"That makes three of us," Greg chimed in. "Alex, I'm sorry, too. Seriously, I just assumed ..."

"Okay," Luke offered. "Everybody is sorry. Really, Alex. That wasn't our intention. But ... you have to admit, Mr. Drama Grad, it made for one helluva show!" To head off any objection, Luke leaned in and planted a big one on Alex's cheek. "Seriously, Alex, you have some killer moves."

Before Alex could issue any individual or group condemnations, the DJ announced, "Time to choose tonight's winner! Let's get our contestants back on stage. Come on back up so we can vote on tonight's winner!" It took a couple of minutes, but soon all five men were back on stage, two in thongs, one in a jock and two, cock locked and naked, holding hands as usual. "Everyone in favor of Contestant Number One, let's hear from you." Polite applause. "Contestant Number Two." Ditto, along with a couple of wolf whistles. The same for Contestant Number

Three. Finally, after a very pregnant pause, probably because the DJ knew what was coming, "Contestants Number Fo..." and before he could finish, the crowd exploded. No applause meter necessary. Raphael felt badly for the first three, especially since they had willingly entered and probably had rehearsed and everything. So, he let go of Alex's hand and stepped over to the nearest contestant and gave him a big hug. Alex went to Contestant Number Two, and before it was over, everyone on stage got a hug from everyone else. The hugs didn't necessarily make losing to two caged guys any easier to accept, but their hugs were not a bad consolation prize.

The DJ started another house track, then walked over to hand Raphael an envelope with the cash prize. "You guys can decide how to split the $200 prize. You certainly earned it." Raphael and Alex thanked him, bestowed hugs on him, then turned to grab their clothes from the back of the stage. Which was bare. Empty.

"Hey!" Raphael yelled at the DJ. "What happened to our clothes?" As Alex continued searching, the DJ came back over and squatted down between Raphael and Alex. It didn't take long for the three of them to exhaust all the possibilities.

"Sorry, guys. This happens sometimes."

"What happens?"

"Someone wanted a souvenir of tonight's sexy strippers ... that would be you two. They'll get off on wearing your clothes."

"Just so they don't get off *on* our clothes," Alex pouted.

"Well, I can't promise that won't happen," the DJ smiled, not feeling as much regret as Raphael and Alex were. "Sorry, guys. Really."

Alex and Raphael descended the stairs to rejoin Luke, Greg and Ricky. "Someone stole our clothes," Alex announced.

"Are you kidding me?" Luke was pissed. "What kind of lowlife does that?"

"I believe it," Ricky offered. "You kidding me? Half the guys in here want to have sex with you two right here ... right now! Getting your shorts was the next best thing any of your fans could hope for."

"Hear that, guys? You have fans," Greg grinned. "It's stupid, yeah, but not surprising, I guess. Next time, toss the clothes to us. We'll hang on to them for you."

"Like there's going to be a next time," Raphael asserted. "My stripping days are over. If there is a next time, just remember, Greg. It's *our* turn for a dare."

"No repeats on the dares, baby" Luke laughed.

"Since when? I don't remember that in the contract."

"Since now. Read your addendum. The one I just wrote."

"Uh huh. Well, since we are still *completely naked*, can we please go home now?" Raphael pulled Alex close and gestured at both their bodies, not that he needed to make the point any clearer.

"Ricky, I assume you rode your scooter down?" Greg asked.

"I did. I came straight from my last delivery."

"Then let's head to our place for a drink, somewhere we can all be naked, so our celebrities here don't feel so all alone. I'll get a Lyft for the rest of us." They headed for the exit, which took a while since many of the customers wanted a hug or at least eye contact from the bravest strippers they'd ever had the good fortune to enjoy. Once outside, where it was cooler and much quieter, Raphael and Alex wrapped their arms around each other for warmth and comfort. Luke and Greg stood guard, since some customers still wanted a piece of the night's stars. Just before the Lyft arrived, the manager maneuvered through the crowd to get Raphael's and Alex's attention.

"Raphael, Alex ... I'm Brent, the manager. You guys were outrageous! Truly! We've never had a contest like you guys gave us tonight."

"Thanks," Raphael tentatively responded.

"Yeah, thanks," Alex agreed.

"Listen, guys, I'd like a few minutes of your time when you can. I'm here every day after three. Any day you can come by, please, could you do that?"

"Are we in trouble?" Alex asked, pulling Raphael a little closer.

"No, not at all. Not at all. I really don't want to get into it here," the manager cocked his head toward the somewhat unruly crowd. "Ten minutes. Please. As soon as you have time. Have a good night." At that, he headed back into the bar.

Mercifully, the Lyft pulled up and Luke ushered Alex and Raphael into the back seat and slid in behind them as Greg climbed in the front. After all the noise, the commotion, the twenty minutes of dancing, it was a welcome, quiet, warm, comfortable environment at last. At first, no one spoke, not even the driver, who had to wonder ... what the hell?

After a couple of blocks, though, Raphael broke the silence. In a sing-song attempt to mimic Luke he said, "Here, baby, wear this sequined thong under your gym shorts." Then, in his normal voice, "I. Am. So. Dense."

"Well," Alex calmly offered, "at least someone told you to wear something under your shorts."

"Who doesn't wear a jock under their gym shorts?" Luke countered.

To which Greg and Raphael both responded, "ALEX!" Raphael continued with "Dammit. That thong wasn't cheap!"

"Baby, you can buy a new one with your winnings," Luke laughed. "Listen, this was supposed to be fun. Greg and I had no idea Alex was going commando, obviously you didn't either, Raphael. It was a shock at first, yeah, but you know what? You guys ended up blowing everyone away. You put on a show they'll be talking about for years. I'm proud of you both."

"Yeah," Greg chimed in. "You two have set the amateur stripper bar so high, no one will even try to beat you."

"They're trying to make us feel better about being stark naked in front of two-hundred horny guys, at least one of whom is a thief!" Alex said. "Feeling any better, Raphael?"

"Nope."

Luke leaned across Alex and kissed Raphael's right ringed nipple. He looked up at Raphael, who was trying to look imperious, and said, "I'll help you feel better later, baby." At that, Raphael had to smile as he noogied Luke's mohawk.

When they walked into Greg and Alex's apartment, Ricky was already there, naked, cage on display, and smiling. On the coffee table was a platter of churros and pastries.

"Hey, amigos. I stopped at my favorite panadería on the way home. I thought you maybe worked up an appetite." Raphael and Alex both surrounded him with a hug of gratitude while Luke and Greg peeled off their gym gear. Everyone sat and dug in.

"You know," Ricky said, licking half a pound of sugar from his lips, "this is gonna sound silly, maybe, but I felt really proud standing there with you after your act, you know, being one of you guys in front of all those other guys who wanted to be with you. Like I was with celebrities or something, except you were gay celebrities, naked caged celebrities. I don't know, it just made me feel so good ... so good to be with you, so good to be me."

As usual when they were together, Ricky was sitting between Alex and Raphael, which made it easy for the two of them to physically respond to what Ricky had said. They both leaned over and planted sugar-coated kisses on his cheeks.

"Ricky." Greg said in a serious voice, "That doesn't sound silly at all. You are a really good guy who has had to put up with a lot of crap, and now hopefully that's all in the past." Ricky flashed him one of his shy, adorable smiles. "I have two wishes for you. One, is that you soon have a life as happy and sexy and fulfilling as Alex and I and Luke and Raphael have. You deserve it. You probably don't realize it yet, but you are just as deserving of 'celebrity' as any of the rest of us. Which is why my second wish is that no matter how madly you and Juan fall in love ... and get married and have lots of beautiful babies ... that you will always, always be a part of our lives. Por favor, amigo?"

"You guys...." Ricky was now blushing. "Thanks. Really." It was late, the platter was now empty, and Alex bounced into the bedroom and returned with a pair of shorts and a sweatshirt for Raphael to wear home. Luke was pulling on his gym gear.

"Thank you, Alex, I'll return these tomorrow when I bring Ricky's Juan-slayer top over, but I can't wear this," Raphael said, handing the sweatshirt back. "There's no caged cock on it."

"Baby, I'll allow this one exception," Luke laughed.

"No, Sir. I have a perfect record, and I intend to keep it that way. It's not that cool out, I'll just wear the shorts." Alex took the sweatshirt back, headed into the bedroom again, and returned with a caged cock tee. He handed it to Raphael, and took his last bow of the night. Raphael bestowed a signature cheek kiss on him. "Locked cock brother to the rescue. Thanks, Alex." Hugs ensued, then Luke and Raphael departed.

Alex, Greg and Ricky cleared the coffee table and headed off to bed. Alex was in the bathroom as Ricky and Greg stood at their respective bedroom doors. "Excited about tomorrow?" Greg asked as he gave Ricky his goodnight hug.

"Totally. I've wanted to do this for a really long time."

"Think you'll be able to sleep?"

"Probably not," Ricky smiled. "Gotta try, though."

"You're welcome to sleep with us tonight if you want. It'll probably be the last night you sleep here. Fingers crossed, anyway."

"Thanks, that's sweet. I don't want to keep you guys up."

"Okay. But, you're welcome, Ricky." One last hug and they headed to their beds. Alex was under the covers already. Greg hit the john, then crawled in next to Alex. They made out a little, but mostly just kissed and cuddled. It really had been a long, tiring day. After about twenty minutes, as Alex was dozing off, Ricky slid in between them on top of the covers.

"My last chance to share your bed, eh, amigos?" he whispered.

"Get in here," Greg smiled, lifting up the covers. Ricky slid in. Alex wrapped an arm around his waist as their cages clicked. Greg wrapped another arm around his waist, as his cock nestled into his perky, brown ass crack. And contrary to previous concerns, all three were asleep in no time.

Thirty-Five

RICKY'S AUDITION ... FINALLY

SUNDAY ... VICTORY OVER Juan Day ... finally arrived. Ricky, not surprisingly, was the first one up. He had coffee waiting, and fresh fruit bowls out and pancake batter ready to hit the griddle.

"Ricky," Greg said, "It's a good thing you're ambushing Juan today. A few more mornings like this, and we'd have to adopt you permanently. This looks great."

"Yeah," Alex seconded. "Greg never makes pancakes for me."

"Like I said before, I can never thank you guys enough for letting me stay here. I'll never forget it."

"Listen to him," Alex smiled. "He's already talking like he'll be sleeping in Juan's bed tonight."

"He's probably right." Greg replied. "I mean, look at him. Have you ever seen a more eligible leatherboy in your life? Naked, caged, the haircut. The piercings. Ricky is adorable and Juan is doomed."

"Hmmm. Would I be more adorable if I had a high 'n tight and piercings?"

"Alex, if you were any more adorable, I'd need a pacemaker."

"You guys are so funny," Ricky said as he slid the plates in front of Alex and Greg. "I just hope you're right about Juan."

"Well, if we aren't, at least we can look forward to pancakes every Sunday, right, Ricky?"

"Yeah, if I can see the stove through my tears." Ricky joked. "I'm too nervous to eat."

"Here," Alex said, sliding his plate between his and Ricky's places. "You can help me eat mine. Just a bite or two."

After breakfast Greg volunteered to freshen up Ricky's regulation high 'n tight if he wanted. Ricky was all for it, and although it probably took Greg twice as long as it might have taken Luke, the result was just as pleasing. Both Greg and Alex rubbed the shaved sides and back of his head once Greg was done.

"Have you rehearsed what you'll say when you walk up to Juan?" Alex asked.

"Oh, maybe a hundred times. You know .... "

"Good. You don't want to stumble around. You don't want to give him the opportunity to say anything but, YES! or whatever the right answer to your opener is. Do you want to rehearse with me?"

"Oh, I'd be too embarrassed. But, thanks, Alex. Really. I want Juan to be the first to hear my words, if that's okay." Alex put his hands on either side of Ricky's face and kissed him on the forehead.

"I get it. You'll be great," he assured Ricky. It was still late morning, with hours to go before Ricky could expect to meet Juan at the beer bust, and Greg could tell he was pretty wound up. He didn't want Ricky, and Alex for that matter, to obsess until mid-afternoon arrived.

"Ricky, have you ever hiked up to Corona Heights?" The question surprised both Ricky and Alex, since it seemed to come out of nowhere.

"Oh, sure, a long time ago. We used to ride our bikes up there when I was a kid."

"Listen, since I'm pretty sure Juan won't let you out of his clutches for the next month or two, why don't we all go up there so I can get a picture or two of the three of us with the city in the background. Something to remember you by until we get to see you again." Alex thought that sounded really dumb, but he also knew Greg wouldn't suggest something like this without a good reason. So, he seconded the motion, and the three dressed and headed out. As they walked, Greg and Alex got Ricky to talk more about himself, about growing up in the Mission, navigating the challenges of being queer in the Latino community. It helped take his mind off this afternoon, and that was the whole point of the outing. They joined a few others at the top of Corona Heights, and Greg took his time picking the right spot for them to pose. He took far more pictures than necessary, but no one complained. As they were reviewing the shots on his phone, it beeped with a text from Luke. He and Raphael were asking them if they wanted to get lunch somewhere before getting together for the final phase of Operation Leatherboy Ricky ... namely the top Raphael had insisted on providing. Ricky still claimed to have no appetite, so they settled on Fable for some light fare. Raphael and Luke arrived first, and snagged a table on the back patio.

"Are you going to let me see this 'top' you've been so secretive about?" Luke asked as they waited, sipping Mimosas. Raphael shook his head, flashing an evil grin.

"No one gets to see it, until it's on the body of San Francisco's next heart-breaking leatherboy. Trust me, it'll be worth the wait."

"Well, at least I don't have too much longer to wait. Here they come now." Greg, Alex and Ricky filed in, and Greg explained what they'd been up to that morning while the waiter delivered three more Mimosas. Luke complimented Greg on his barbering skills.

"You going to do Alex next?" he kidded.

"Only if he asks," Greg replied.

"I was thinking more along the lines of Niki's multi-colored mohawk," Alex joked. "You know, more in keeping with my colorful personality."

"Don't tempt me," Greg said, roughing up Alex's hair. "I'd love it if you did."

"I will if you will," Alex countered, laughing.

"You're on."

"No ... you know I was kidding."

"I wasn't."

"We aren't Raphael and Luke, Greg. Are we?" Raphael and Luke were looking on with interest. Was this an effort on Greg's part to further urge Alex into becoming more of a kinkster? Or, just talk? It was hard to tell. Raphael decided to change the subject.

"As soon as we're done here, let's go back to your place so Ricky can model his "Fuck Me Juan, Fuck Me Now" leatherboy outfit for us all."

"Yeah, I still haven't seen him in those new shorts," Greg pouted.

"Not to mention this mysterious top that Raphael hasn't even let me see," Luke added. "What if we don't approve?"

"Oh, you'll approve, all right," Raphael asserted. "The question is, will you let Ricky audition with Juan, or will you try to keep him all to yourselves?"

"Do I get a vote on this?" Ricky grinned.

"No," was the unanimous response.

"Oh, okay, amigos." The joking was over, as was lunch, and the five of them made a bee line to Greg and Alex's. Everyone was eager for the impending runway show. Once there, Alex and Raphael pulled Ricky into the bedroom and closed the door, even before stripping. That's how eager they were to dress their protégé. All three stripped, they helped Ricky into his boots and Airtex shorts, then Raphael pulled his creation out of his shoulder bag. He helped Ricky wiggle into it, then stepped back to admire it.

"Fuuuuck!" Alex whispered. "It's perfect, Raphael. Just like the Halloween costumes, you nailed it. Ricky, what do you think?"

"Muy sexy! You did great, Raphael!"

"Let's go show off our creation, Alex." Raphael and Alex walked into the living where Greg and Luke were patiently waiting. "Gentleman," Raphael stiffly announced, "may I present the future husband of Juan,

Ricky Soto!" Raphael and Alex stood aside, and Ricky entered, beaming. This was Greg and Luke's first view of Ricky in the skin tight see-through Airtex shorts. They alone were stunning. But Raphael's top definitely completed the look. It was a white caged cock tee that had been altered into a crop top that ended just below the bottom of the cage graphic, showcasing Ricky's mind-blowing abs. The tee had been sewn along both sides, to make it fit Ricky like a glove, as skin tight as the cage-revealing, ass-revealing shorts. Basically, it looked like Ricky's outfit had been painted on.

Both Greg and Luke rose to their feet. Greg started, then Luke joined him in applause. Although Ricky was the only one in the room actually wearing anything, he was arguably the sexiest of them all in that moment.

"Raphael," Luke exclaimed, "you were right. It was worth the wait. You did it again! Ricky, you look like a million bucks!"

"A trillion bucks," Greg countered. "I love how your cage is visible, subtly, but visible, still. And, that crop top, where did you find that, Raphael?"

"It's custom. I had the same friend who did Alex and my togas alter one of my tees. She did a great job, didn't she?"

"I'll say. Alex, you should have her alter a couple of yours, too." Greg suggested.

"Sure, right after I do a hundred thousand sit ups ... and *still* not have abs like that."

"So, guys, do you think I'm ready for Juan?"

"Oh, yeah, Ricky," Luke said. "You guys did fantastic. I wouldn't change a thing. I can't wait to see the look on Juan's face when he sees you."

"What?" Ricky reacted. "No, no, no. I don't want any of you there. I mean, you know, if he doesn't want me back, I don't want you to see me ... fail."

"No, we want to be there for you!" Raphael cried. "Don't you want our moral support?" He went to Ricky and took his hand in both of his own. "We want this as much as you do, Ricky." Ricky just shook his head no. Suddenly the cheery mood in the room had fled.

"How about this, Ricky," Greg said, as he, too, walked up to Ricky and put his hands on both of Ricky's shoulders. "How about Alex and Raphael go with you to the Eagle. You'll want to wear something over your sexy shorts anyway, and they can take your street shorts off you at the entrance, and then wait outside. We all know Juan and you will be leaving together, and at that point you won't care if everyone can see your cage or not. If the worst happens ... and we know it won't ... they'll be waiting outside with your street shorts. And, they'll text us, and we'll come down ... and we'll all get drunk."

Ricky pondered Greg's suggestion, then finally said, "Okay. But I go in alone. Please?" Raphael nodded.

Alex squeezed in under Greg's arms and embraced Ricky. "If that's what you want." Everyone agreed, even though everyone disagreed. This was, after all, Ricky's moment. They all took places in the room to wait until time to initiate Operation Leatherboy Ricky. Alex made a pot of tea and put out cookies. They debated the odds of being able to do a beach day the following Saturday. Alex modeled his own pair of Airtex shorts, then Raphael tried them on. Anything to kill time. Finally, two-thirty crawled around.

"If we walk instead of taking MUNI this would be a good time to leave," Raphael suggested. Ricky jumped up.

"Good idea. Get dressed, amigos." He stood by the door, hand on the knob, waiting for Raphael and Alex to dress. It didn't take them long, and soon they were at the door. Ricky opened it.

"Umm, don't you want to put these on before we leave?" Alex asked Ricky, holding out the street shorts. Ricky was still in just his runway outfit.

"Oh, thanks Alex." Ricky pulled them on. "'I'm not too nervous, am I?"

"No more than the rest of us," Raphael said as he took Ricky's free hand. "Okay, let's go." As they departed, Alex looked back at Greg and Luke and blew an air kiss. Once on the sidewalk, he took Ricky's other hand and off they went, not quite skipping, but certainly with plenty of air in their steps. Conversation during the thirty-minute walk was minimal. Ricky was undoubtedly still rehearsing his opening lines in his head. Pretty much anything Alex or Raphael could have offered had already been said. They were just grateful to be with Ricky, holding his hands and providing moral support. Neither could bear the thought of what they might possibly say if things didn't work out. Finally, the three arrived at the Eagle. Men, many in leather or Levi's, were entering in ones and twos. The trio stopped a few steps away from the entrance. Ricky slid Alex's shorts off and handed them to him. He hugged Alex, then Raphael and tried to smile.

"Sure you don't want us to go in?" Raphael asked one last time.

"I'm sure, but, again, thanks. I'll be fine, guys." Then he turned and entered.

"He left before I could wish him luck," Alex protested, folding up the shorts into a tiny bundle.

"He doesn't need it," Raphael assured, hoping to himself that he was right. Raphael took out his phone and pulled up his stopwatch.

"What are you doing?"

"Timing our entrance. I figure ninety seconds should be about right, don't you think?"

"We're going in?"

"Damn right. Ricky may get a vote, but he doesn't get the only vote." Raphael flashed that evil grin. "You don't want miss this, do you."

"What do you think? That's why I brought my ID." Raphael pocketed his phone and they headed in. Back at Greg and Alex's, both men had their phones out and ready. Raphael hadn't said anything about ignoring Ricky's request, but it went without saying that Raphael and Alex would be incapable of waiting outside the bar.

"I wish we were there, too," Luke said.

"Me, too, but Alex and Raphael are both shorter than us and better able to blend in. Less likely to spook Ricky, in case he has to scout the place to find Juan. It's going to be crowded."

"Makes sense, but still ..."

"Do you want to head down there ... just in case?"

"No, Raphael and Alex can handle anything. If there's anything to handle. We may all be worked up for nothing. What if Juan isn't even there?"

"Maybe we should head down there. If Juan's not there, Ricky's going to be mobbed by a hundred or more horny leather men who will think they've finally found the love of their life."

"Yeah, good point. If Juan is there, he's doomed. If not, Ricky's doomed. Doomsday at The Eagle." Speculation ended at that point, when Luke's phone sounded a text alert from Raphael. Luke looked expectantly at Greg, as he picked up the phone and unlocked it. "It says, 'Juan's here. Stand by.'"

"Like we have a choice..."

Back at the Eagle, Alex and Raphael had entered the courtyard and claimed a spot against an outside wall and craned their necks, trying to spot Ricky, who was not the tallest guy in the crowd. Raphael spotted him first, by following the swiveling heads of the guys checking Ricky out. "There," Raphael pointed. Alex nodded. Ricky was making a slow, but uninterrupted march toward a small group of obvious leather guys. Alex and Raphael had no idea what Juan looked like, but Ricky seemed pretty focused, so they assumed Juan was there. As Ricky neared the group, a tall, handsome man with a neat, black mustache, wearing an open leather vest over a bare, taught chest turned in time to see Ricky. A look of amazement and delight filled his face. That's when Raphael sent his text. If only they were close enough to hear ...

"Excuse me, Sir, but I am here to apply for the position of your permanent, caged, leatherboy. If, Sir, the position is still available." Ricky's face was intense, not smiling as he had rehearsed, but his voice was strong and even. Juan put down his beer, his smile widening as he placed his hands on both of Ricky's shoulders looking Ricky up and down. And up and down, taking in all the details of Ricky's transformation. It took place in a matter of seconds, but to Ricky, it seemed much longer. Juan still hadn't spoken, so Ricky said, "Please, Sir..." Before he could utter another word, Juan placed a finger over Ricky's lips to silence him. He then pulled Ricky into an all-encompassing embrace and held him there. Neither of them knew it, but many eyes in the courtyard were on them. Ricky had attracted plenty of attention walking across to Juan. Now he was in the arms of this handsome Latino guy ... just like that? WTF? Ricky didn't move. Didn't talk. Didn't breathe. He wrapped his arms around Juan's back and listened to Juan's heartbeat ... or was it his own heartbeat? He savored the smell of Juan's bare flesh. He wanted to melt into him right there. Finally, Juan pulled Ricky out of the hug enough that their eyes could meet. Finally, Ricky was smiling.

"Querido," Juan finally said, "I've been holding the position open ... for you." He then pressed his lips to Ricky's and that's when hearts fluttered in half the men in the bar. Some because they wanted Ricky for themselves, some because they wanted Juan, and in two because their efforts had succeeded. Raphael turned to Alex, slung an arm around Alex's neck and planted a big one on his lips, too.

"You know," Raphael said, when they pulled apart, "that kiss had to hurt Ricky a lot with that new labret."

"I don't think he minded, do you?"

"Nope. Alex, they're gorgeous together. Oh, look out, they're leaving." Raphael and Alex did their best to blend into the foliage, as Juan turned Ricky around and, hands on each of Ricky's shoulders, walked behind Ricky as they headed for the exit. Neither of them seemed aware of anyone else in the place as they walked. Ricky looked beatific. Juan looked fulfilled. Everyone else looked at Ricky, then at Juan, then back at Ricky. WTF?!?

Once they were gone, Alex slumped against the wall. All the tension, the worry, the hopeful anticipation drained immediately from his body. He looked at Raphael and said, "I don't know about you, but I need a beer." Raphael laughed, feeling the same relief as Alex, and indicated he'd take care of it. He returned, handed Alex his, then put his own beer down and pulled out his phone again. He put it down a few seconds later.

"That was quick. What did you text?"

"An emoji ... two guys holding hands. They really need to create more leather oriented emojis."

"Yeah. Here's to Juan and Ricky," As their glasses touched, Luke was reaching for his phone.

"YES!" he shouted, jumping to his feet. Greg joined him, and they hugged, jumping up and down. They had tension to release, too. "We need to celebrate! Let's see if Steve and Niki want to come over, too. I'm going to run out and get a couple bottles of bubbly from the corner store. Be right back." Luke was out the door, before realizing he was still naked. He lamely knocked seconds later.

Greg, taking advantage of Luke's oversight, stood on the other side of the door. "Who iiiisss it?"

"Your worst nightmare if don't open the door." They both laughed as Greg admitted Luke. "Okay, that's a first. And, I thought Ricky was funny earlier. Maybe we are spending too much time naked."

"Never. You were just excited and happy." Luke dressed and headed out again.

Back at the Eagle, Raphael and Alex were finishing up their tension-relieving beers when a guy wandered up. "Hey, can I ask you guys a question?" He was a nice-looking Asian guy, horn rims and spiky hair, slim but not skinny, in skinny-fit jeans and deep V-neck showing off his hairless chest.

"Sure. I'm Raphael, this is Alex."

"Vincent. Nice to meet you. I couldn't help noticing that you both are wearing the same t-shirt, kinda like the shirt on that amazing guy who was here earlier in the see-through shorts. Do you know him?"

"We do, yeah. Why?" Alex asked guardedly, wondering what was to follow.

"I thought so. Are you in some organization or something?"

"Not exactly. We all share a particular trait that we're kind of proud of." Vincent nodded and waited to hear more. His expression was one of curiosity and interest, not judgment, so Raphael continued, pointing at the graphic on Alex's shirt as he talked.

"This is a cage. This is a rooster, also known in the vernacular as a cock. It's a caged cock. Like this." He pulled the front of his shorts down to display his Looker 01. Not to be outdone, Alex pulled the front of his shorts down, too.

"Wow. I'd love to know more. I noticed the 'cage' on that other guy ... everyone did. So, I just had to ask, since you guys are wearing the same shirt." Alex and Raphael pulled their shorts back up and smiled.

"It's a movement, Vincent. Maybe you should join." Raphael teased.

"Maybe I should," Vincent teased back. "Maybe I should. Hey, thanks for being so nice. Sorry to bother you. Take care." And with that, Vincent was off.

"Well, Alex, our missionary work here is done. Let's go home and fill Luke and Greg in on all the gory details." Raphael put his arm around Alex's waist and they headed for home.

Thirty-Six

THE FAMILY GROWS

SUNDAY EVENING WAS, PERHAPS thankfully, anti-climactic. Steve and Niki did join Greg, Alex, Luke and Raphael at Greg and Alex's over wine and pizza. Everyone got up to date, and Niki showed off his latest dive into the pup life, small paw print tattoos, near his cage. He'd wanted them ever since BPOS, and Steve had finally agreed. Niki figured they'd amp up his tips even higher at the bar. Raphael, who had helped Niki by recommending Peg for the session, agreed. His own ink had certainly been well received at the beach, the gym, and that god-awful strip contest.

Which brought up another subject that had been all but forgotten, what with all the preparations and worry about Ricky and Juan.

"Niki," Raphael asked, "do you have any idea what your boss, Brent, wants to see Alex and me about?"

"Huh?" Niki responded. Although Sundays were usually one of his total pup days, no speaking, pup hood and so forth, he'd made an exception tonight, in celebration of Ricky and Juan's reunion.

"He came out of the bar while we were waiting for our ride after the strip contest, and said he wanted to meet with us. I thought maybe you knew why."

"No, no idea. He did talk a lot about your guys' performance though. I guess I haven't had a chance to tell you how incredible it was. I loved it! You were both awesome, especially you, Alex. You danced like a pro! Guys were talking about it the rest of the night."

"Yeah, see, if you want to get noticed all you have to do is get stripped naked in public. If I walked into that bar in my street clothes, no one would care."

"Alex," Niki continued, "it wasn't only because you were naked. They liked your performance, both your performances ... the dancing, kissing, the rimming, the cages. No one's ever seen a strip act like you two gave.

Afterwards, I asked Brent why I have to wear a sheer jock if you can dance naked, and he couldn't come up with a good answer. He said something about the cages meant you weren't really naked, but he didn't come right out and say it would be okay for me to be naked behind the bar. After all ... I'm caged, too."

"Niki!" Raphael exclaimed. "Wait, you, Niki, Niki of the famous steam room towels, you want to bartend naked? In a room full of gay men who aren't naked?"

"Maybe. I'm just exploring my options."

"Unbelievable. What have we done?" Raphael laughed.

"Well, you know," Steve offered, "he might as well be naked with those see through jocks he wears."

"Well, more power to you," Alex said, raising his glass in a toast. It was the first toast of the evening that hadn't been proposed to Juan and Ricky.

"I wonder if we'll see Ricky Tuesday night," Luke mused.

"We better," Alex said, "I bet we won't see him before then, probably."

"You think?" Raphael elbowed Alex. "You saw the look on both their faces when they left the bar. They may not come up for air for a month. Or, two."

"Man, I wish we'd been there," Greg whined. "Whose idea was it for only Alex and Raphael to go with Ricky?"

"Yours!" Alex and Raphael teased.

"Dammit. Since when does anyone listen to me, anyway."

"Guys," Luke soothed, "we'll get to see Ricky when he's ready. This was all our idea, remember? He's where he belongs right now, and for that we should be grateful. Hell, we should be proud. We did good."

"We sure did," Raphael seconded, as he raised his glass in yet another toast to Ricky and Juan. "We did good."

Raphael was deep in a project in his cube Tuesday afternoon when Alex came up behind him and put one hand on Raphael's shoulder and dangled his cell phone in front of Raphael's face with the other. Raphael took the phone and read the text on the screen: *'Don't order dinner tonight. I'm bringing a surprise. XOX.'* It was from Ricky.

Raphael spun his chair around and handed Alex's phone back. "A surprise, huh? Gee, I wonder what it could be, Alex."

"I'm betting it's about six feet tall, has a mustache and a sexy voice."

"We haven't heard Juan's voice, Alex."

"A boy can dream, Raphael. Besides, you *know* he has a sexy voice. Everything else about him was sexy."

"Yeah ..." Raphael said wistfully, remembering the sight of Juan walking Ricky through the crowd. "I was hoping we'd see them tonight. This is great. I'm going to text Luke now. Thanks! See you later, Alex." Raphael immediately texted Luke, who texted Steve, who texted Niki. All that was left to do was to wait. When Luke got home, Raphael was in uniform, harnessed and flying around the apartment with a dust cloth in one hand, spray polish in the other. The vacuum was out as well, and a fresh bouquet was on the dining table, the one that never seemed to get used as a dining table.

"Hey!" Luke greeted Raphael on his way to the bedroom. "Since when do we do housekeeping on Tuesdays, Hazel?" Raphael followed him into the bedroom and pulled Luke into a hug before Luke could strip, once again reveling in being naked when Luke wasn't. As soon as they parted, Luke stripped and pulled on his harness. Afterall, they were having family over for dinner.

"I just wanted to do a little touch up. Juan's never been here. Luke, I'm so excited to finally meet him."

"We'll, at least you've *seen* him. He's a total mystery to most of the rest of us. I have to say, I'm happy they're coming over. It would have been easy for Ricky to blow us off tonight, considering they've only had a couple of days together."

"He probably wants to show Juan off to us. Besides, we really are his family now, and they belong here."

"Eventually, yeah, but they have a lot of catching up to do. In bed and out. Don't get me wrong, I'm glad they're coming. I'm eager to meet this guy, too."

Raphael was putting away the vacuum when Steve and Niki arrived and stripped. In honor of their new guest, Niki had limited himself to just a chest harness, pup tail, and of course the permanent collar. Steve sported a similar chest harness as well. Raphael had hardly opened a bottle of white before Alex and Greg arrived. They stripped down to reveal their matching chest harnesses. Everyone was present and harnessed, in what passed for formal attire in this setting. Ready to meet the man of Ricky's dreams.

In due time, the doorbell rang, then Ricky and Juan entered on their own, before anyone could leap up to answer. Both were holding bags of food. Ricky, obviously excited and beaming, announced "Hi, guys, we're here! This is Juan!" He immediately put his bags on top of the ones Juan was holding and began to strip.

Juan could only laugh. "I see you've trained him well."

Luke was first to Juan, followed immediately by Greg. They took the bags out of his hands, and Luke extended his to shake Juan's hand. "I'm Luke, this is Greg." Greg, too, shook Juan's hand. Raphael was next up. He also shook Juan's hand, but, of course, he didn't stop there. Raphael threw his arms around Juan and held him tight. Juan, realizing Raphael wasn't going to release him anytime soon, put his arms around Raphael and squeezed. Raphael reached up and planted one on Juan's right cheek. "Welcome to the family. I'm Raphael."

"I figured you must be," Juan smiled. "And you must be Alex," he said as Alex put his arms around both Juan and Raphael, planting a kiss on Juan's left cheek.

"We're so happy you're here, Juan," Alex said. "Like Raphael said, welcome." Alex then leaned over to Raphael and said, "See! I told you he has a sexy voice!" Juan laughed again as Alex released his embrace. Juan looked over to where Steve and Niki were sitting, Steve on the couch, Niki at his feet.

Niki barked, then smiled and said, "Good to finally meet you, Juan." Steve stood, walked over to Juan who was still half in Raphael's embrace, and hugged the both of them.

"You'll find we're something of an affectionate group, Juan," Steve grinned. "Can I get you some wine?"

"That's fine by me ... on both counts," Juan replied.

Ricky walked over, put an arm around Juan's waist, leaned over and stage whispered to Raphael, "Didn't I tell you he was the best boyfriend ever?"

"Well," Raphael said pseudo-seriously, "it's pretty hard to tell with all these clothes on. What do you think we should do about that?" Raphael began unbuttoning a bemused Juan's shirt. Ricky immediately loosened Juan's belt and unbuttoned his jeans. Juan didn't resist, but just smiled at Ricky. He was loving this new uninhibited leatherboy version of Ricky, and appreciating the environment that had obviously been instrumental in his transformation. It was clear Ricky felt at ease with these men, and most importantly, at ease with himself. Already, Juan was feeling at ease with them, too. Once Ricky and Raphael had completed their task, Steve handed Juan his glass of wine and offered him a place to sit in a side chair. He sat, and Ricky immediately took his place, cross legged on the floor between Juan's legs, his borrowed baby blue Holy Trainer conspicuously on display. Juan placed a hand on Ricky's shoulder. It was obvious to all that Ricky was right where he belonged.

"Let's unpack dinner and eat while we interrogate Juan," Luke announced to the group. Juan laughed, and Ricky tilted his head back to wink at Juan. "It was awfully nice of you to bring dinner, you two."

"Are you kidding? We owe you a thousand dinners for all that you guys have done for us," Juan announced.

"We figured you'd expect Mexican," Ricky said, "so we brought Mediterranean instead."

"Oooh, La Mediterranee," Alex cooed as he began pulling containers out of the bags. "I love it." He and Raphael began arranging food on several platters on the coffee/dining table.

"Good choice," Greg agreed. "We haven't had Mr. DoorDash bring us Mediterranean food since when, Ricky?"

"Since forever," Ricky laughed. Looking up at Juan again, "They called me Mr. DoorDash before they knew my real name." He took a plate of food that Raphael handed him, and immediately passed it up to Juan. Clearly, he was indeed well trained. Soon everyone was munching, sipping and relaxing.

"Well, Juan, I guess I'll start the interrogation," Steve announced. "How did you two meet?"

"Funny thing. Ricky was my Mr. DoorDash."

"Noooo!" Raphael exclaimed. He was sitting closest to Ricky, and he reached out and slapped Ricky's thigh. "I thought we were your only stalking victims."

"Hey, you're the one who dragged me into your house and ripped my clothes off. Who was stalking who?"

"You did what?" Juan grinned, looking at Raphael.

"He's exaggerating. A lot. And, he's changing the subject. Or, maybe I was. Anyway, tell us more about you and your Mr. DoorDash."

"I hope this doesn't sound like the cliché gay porn delivery boy plot, but it really was. The first time Ricky delivered I was intrigued. He was so damned adorable. He had such an irresistible smile. But, I thought, too bad I'll never see him again. But, of course, I did. After about the third time he delivered, I figured something was up." At that, Juan put a hand on the back of Ricky's neck and squeezed, eliciting a moan and smile from Ricky. "So, I took a chance and ordered extra food the next time. Sure enough, it was Ricky at the door. Remember that night, Ricky?"

"Oh, yeah." Ricky's 'irresistible smile' spread wider across his face.

"I took the food from him, with one hand, took his free arm in my other hand and pulled him into the apartment."

"Just like I did!" Raphael laughed. Ricky joined in and clapped.

"Looking back, I can't believe I did that. Hell, he could have accused me of false imprisonment. But fortunately, my instincts were vindicated."

"So ... did you guys...?" Alex asked.

"Oh, yeah," Ricky grinned. Juan grinned, too. They didn't share any further details, but they really didn't need to.

"I was going to ask if you guys enjoyed the food," Alex dead-panned. Raphael looked at Alex as if he'd spoken in Arabic. "I'm kidding, Raphael!"

"I think that delivery is still in the fridge somewhere, Alex," Juan replied.

"So, Ricky is a serial stalker. Good to know." Greg intoned. "You might want to encourage Ricky to find an alternate occupation, Juan. Just for peace of mind." Juan laughed at that, and Ricky rolled his eyes.

"Hey, Greg, my stalking days are over. I found my man, and I found the best amigos I could ever wish for."

"Speaking of which," Juan said, raising his glass, "here's to the sexiest dinner party I've ever had the privilege to enjoy. Here I am sitting a room with seven other naked men, four of them caged, six harnessed, two collared, one with a pup tail ... and two with the bravest declarations in ink I think I've ever seen. Here's another cliché: 'it doesn't get any better than this.'"

"You're so right, Juan," Greg said, raising his glass in response. "We are so fortunate to have found one another."

"Will you be able to join us every Tuesday night, Juan?" Raphael looked appealingly at Juan. "Ricky doesn't have a choice. He owes us big."

"We both owe you big, Raphael. I mean that. I'm so grateful to all of you. Ricky's told me about how you gave him the courage ... and the sexy outfit ... to seduce me again. How you helped him lose his fear about exploring his sexuality." Juan then paused to break into laughter. "And, he told me about how you helped him move. Man, I wish I could have seen that. It must have been epic."

"Oh, it was. I think those two thugs are probably still sitting there, beer bottles half-way to their open mouths, not knowing how to react," Luke said. Raphael nodded vigorously in agreement.

"And, of course, I'm so grateful to you, Greg and Alex, for taking Ricky away from that nightmare."

"It has been our pleasure. Seriously," Alex piped up. "Has Ricky told you he only has to stay with us twelve more months to fulfill his pancake contract?"

"No. Really? Hmmmm. I may have to talk to my lawyer about buying him out of that contract." Alex pretended to be crestfallen.

"So, Niki," Juan changed the subject. "I hear you're the most pupular bartender South of Market."

Niki would have blushed if his complexion had allowed. "I'm doing okay, thanks. And, just like you and Ricky, I owe that, and my 'transformation' to these guys, too."

"I'm looking forward to seeing you in action. Puppy play can be a lot of fun."

'It is. You should come down. Of course, I don't totally pup out at work. You should come over to our place sometime and see the real 'pup Niki' in action."

"Don't worry," Steve patted Niki's mohawk, "he doesn't bite. He sucks ... but he doesn't bite." Niki arffed in affirmation.

"Juan, we've been taking Ricky to Marshall's Beach on Saturdays to get him comfortable being caged in public," Raphael said. "Can he still come? And, will you come, too? It's a lot of fun."

"Well, first of all, Ricky doesn't need my permission. And, yeah, I'll come when I can. I'm on call every other Saturday, but sure, when I can."

"On call?" Steve asked. "What do you do, Juan?"

"I'm an OR nurse."

"Whoa!" Alex exclaimed. "Seriously? That must be intense."

Juan laughed. "It can be. Mostly routine, but there are days ..."

"Ricky, you didn't tell us you were in love with the next best thing to a doctor!" Niki kidded. "You've been holding out!"

"Well, you know ... it just didn't come up." Ricky wrapped an arm around Juan's calf and kissed his knee. "I just have good taste in lovers ... and friends."

No one could argue with that.

Thirty-Seven

Brent's Proposition

As Raphael and Alex began gathering plates after dinner, Raphael had a sudden realization. He ducked into the bedroom, then returned and kneeled down beside Ricky at Juan's feet.

"Juan, Sir," Raphael intoned, "it is my great pleasure to present to you this most precious treasure which has been in my family for, well, nearly a year." Raphael, now the center of attention, bowed his head and held out a small black jewel box.

"Why, thank you, Locked Cock Boy Raphael," Juan played along. "May I open it now?"

"You may, Sir." Juan ceremoniously opened the box, smiled, and pulled out a set of keys.

"Ricky's been locked for some time now, and I thought you might need these for periodic hygiene and shaving sessions," Raphael said as he sat back and resumed his non-acting persona.

"Thank you, Raphael. "Would you like me to return the cage to you now?" A panicked look came over Ricky's face.

"Oh, please, no!" Raphael sat back up. "This is Ricky's cage now, and unless I'm totally wrong, he has no desire to give it up. Ricky?" Raphael had turned to Ricky.

"Please, no, Juan. Raphael, I get hard every time I think about the fact that my cage was your first cage. If it's all right with you, I'd like to wear it permanently." Ricky flashed that adorable smile, and Raphael leaned over and delivered a kiss.

"Nothing, and I mean it, nothing would make me happier, Ricky." Raphael then looked back up at Juan. "Thus, the keys for you, since this cage has to come off for hygiene every now and then."

"Ummm, well, to be honest guys," Juan said to the room, while rubbing Ricky's high 'n tight, "Ricky's free time will almost certainly involve more than just soap and water. You see," Juan cleared his throat, "although it's true I love the idea of Ricky becoming my permanently caged leather boy, like half the rest of you in this room, the truth is … I love sucking Ricky's cock just as much as I love him sucking mine." Ricky's smiled widened as he first looked down at his own caged cock, then looked back up at the room.

"He's pretty good at it, too," Ricky said, then tilted his head back to flash a grin at Juan. Again, Niki barked his approval.

"Then it's settled," Raphael sat back again. "Your journey as Juan's Locked Cock Boy is assured as you permanently wear the baby blue Holy Trainer, which first adorned the world-famous Luke's Locked Cock Boy!"

Ricky slapped Raphael's thigh and laughed, "You guys are so funny …"

"And, humble, Ricky," Alex joined in. "Raphael, you are so humble."

"I am, aren't I," Raphael laughed back. "But seriously, I'm honored that Ricky bones up thinking about the provenance of his cage."

"Okay, mutual admiration society, I think it's time for us to call it a night," Steve announced. "Time to get this pup to his job." Niki barked in agreement. Everyone began to stand and, reluctantly, dress.

Alex stopped by Raphael's cube Wednesday to see if they could go to lunch together, something they now tried to do once a week or so. Raphael agreed, and they headed to Rosa Mexicana. Over lunch, Raphael posed a question.

"I suppose we ought to meet with Brent, Niki's boss, soon. What do you think?"

"Oh, yeah, I forgot about that. I guess we should, for Niki's sake. Any idea what he wants?"

"Not really. I guess there's only one way to find out. When is good for you?"

"Let's get it over with. How about this afternoon, after work? It's kinda on the way home."

"Okay, come get me when you're done."

So it was that later that same day, Raphael and Alex walked into the Powerhouse in broad daylight. It seemed weird. The last time they passed through that door, they were naked and surrounded by newly minted fans. And they had Luke, Greg and Ricky there for support. As they walked through the door, the weirdness continued, as the bar was nearly deserted at this hour, with only a few diehards on hand. They approached the bar and asked to see Brent. The bartender disappeared momentarily, then reappeared and showed them to an office door they'd never noticed before. Brent stood up from his office chair and greeted them.

"Hey, it's the famous Raphael and Alex! Come in, come in ... I really appreciate you guys coming by. Have a seat. Can I get you something to drink?" Both demurred.

"We're just curious why you wanted to meet with us," Raphael said. "I realize we went a little too far with the stripping, but it was accidental. I thought Alex was wearing a jock ..." Brent raised his hand to stop Raphael in mid-sentence.

"Guys, I didn't ask you hear to reprimand you. I meant it when I said your performance was unlike any we'd ever seen before. You blew everyone's minds. I never realized how ... I guess 'captivating' is the right word ... chastity is for so many guys. I began to realize it when Niki joined us, and guys started falling all over themselves just to buy a beer from him. I mean, the pup thing is part of it, but I think his chastity cage is just as much of his appeal. Then, when you guys stripped down ... well, you were there, you heard the crowd. They went nuts!" Raphael and Alex looked at each other. The compliments were nice, but they still didn't know why they were here.

"So, it's okay that we ended up naked on stage. We didn't get the bar into trouble?" Alex asked.

"It's more than okay. Listen, I have a proposition for you. I'd like you two to do regular shows for the bar, once a month, twice a month would be better! Two shows a night, fifteen to twenty minutes each. I'll pay you each three hundred dollars a night. We'll promote it on social media at first, with posters in the bar. Something like, 'The Chastity Brothers, Live on Stage.' You'll fill the place, trust me. What do you say?"

"No," Alex responded, without even looking at Raphael. Brent's face fell. He looked hopefully at Raphael.

"No?" Brent repeated. "But ..."

Alex cut him off. "I suppose we should be flattered, but we're professionals. I don't mean professional dancers, I mean we have real jobs, day jobs. That performance wasn't even our idea. We were tricked into it."

Brent sat silent a moment. He looked again at Raphael, who was still quiet, looking down at the floor. "Raphael, you haven't said anything," Brent prodded.

Raphael sat upright and looked directly at Brent. "How many customers can you accommodate at once?"

"Oh, no..." Alex moaned.

"Max capacity is two hundred-twenty."

"And what do you usually charge for cover with a live show?"

"Nooo, Raphael ..." Alex whined.

"Depends. Five to ten bucks."

"Well, I haven't spoken with my associate here, but ..."

"No, Raphael. No!"

"Here's our counter offer. Two shows, once a month. You don't pay us a dime ..."

"What!? Raphael!"

"You charge a fifteen dollar cover and that ... and any tips we get ... are donated to the Trevor Project. And you promote that donation in your social media campaign and on the posters." Raphael sat back and waited.

"Raphael. You're talking between three and five thousand dollars a night. That's a hell of a lot more than the six hundred I offered you."

"It is. It's for a good cause. Ask Niki."

"Wow." Brent pondered Raphael's offer. "I'd look like a real prick if I said no, wouldn't I?" Raphael didn't say a word. Brent ran his hand through his hair, looked at Alex, then back at Raphael and blew a burst of air through his clenched teeth. "Okay." He looked again at Alex. "Alex?"

"Fuck!" Alex looked at Raphael, who flashed that 'never to be denied' smile at him. "So, I'd be the prick if I say no, right?" Raphael slowly nodded. "Fuck." Alex sighed heavily. Raphael reached over and took Alex's hand and squeezed.

"You can teach me how to dance, Alex."

Despite the fact that Alex was shaking his head no, he said, "All right. Yes ... but with one more condition."

"You guys are killing me! Okay, Alex, what is it?"

"Two hundred dollars per show to cover the cost of the costumes that we'll have to replace, since your customers have Very. Sticky. Fingers. Hell, we'll just toss our thongs into the crowd and save them the effort."

"Seriously?"

"Take it or leave it. That's my final offer." Now it was Alex's turn to sit back and wait.

"If you guys were anybody else, I'd be showing you the door right now. You negotiate even better than you strip." Brent looked up to the ceiling for counsel, then back at Alex. "Is the second Saturday of the month good for you?" Alex nodded.

"We'll see you then," Raphael said, extending his hand. The three exchanged numbers. "We'll raise a lot of money for the Trevor Project. It'll be great PR for your bar."

"It will indeed, Raphael. Alex." Brent reached out and shook Alex's hand. "We'll sell a few drinks, as well. Thank you, guys. Thank you."

As Raphael and Alex stood to leave, Raphael said "Oh, one other thing, Brent." Brent braced for another demand, and looked at both expectantly. "Just a question, and you don't have to answer if you don't want to. Since you're having Alex and me perform naked but caged, why does my brother Niki have to wear a basically transparent jock behind the bar?"

"Niki is your brother?" Brent looked surprised. "So ... chastity runs in the family?" Raphael grinned.

"Yeah, kinda, I guess. He used to be very self-conscious about being so well endowed, but we've been working on getting him over it. And, we've made pretty good progress. It might help if he could be on full display here. He actually feels more confident with the cage."

"Huh. I'm still learning about the ins and outs of this chastity stuff. He did bring it up, now that you mention it. Listen, don't say anything to him. I'd prefer to keep these conversations just between Niki and me."

"Of course. I understand."

"The difference between you guys and Niki is that, one, he's an employee and you're not, and two, he's waiting on customers and you're not. So, for the most part, I'm inclined to have him keep the jocks on, even though his caged cock is fully on display even with them. I might make an exception now and then, I don't know. I do want to keep Niki happy. Fair enough?"

"More than fair. Thanks for explaining, Brent. I appreciate it."

"So, Niki's your brother. I'd have never guessed."

"Yeah, it surprises a lot of people. Niki's the reason we're doing this for the Trevor Project. Niki's very important to me."

"Well, he's important to me, too. You guys have a good evening."

That night, as Luke was shaving down Raphael's high 'n tight, with both men nestled into position in the shower, Raphael revealed his and Alex's upcoming debut.

"You see, baby. I've said before you have what it takes to be a great dad. You care about queer kids you've never even met."

"I'm sure you do, too, Sir. You just haven't said so in so many words. Look how great you've been with Niki and Ricky ... hey, I just realized ... they'd make a great pop music group, or maybe better yet, a great *pup* music group." Raphael's laugh failed to drown out Luke's groan. "Anyway, I'm glad you think it's a good idea. It remains to be seen how popular 'The Chastity Brothers' will be. We may well be a one-month wonder, and that'll be fine with me, and especially Alex. He's not too thrilled about this, but he did agree to do it."

After they'd finished shaving and showering, Luke and Raphael were lounging on the couch when Luke's phone alerted a text from Greg. Luke read it and laughed. "It says, 'Thanks, guys, Now I'm married to a stripper. There goes my reputation. Does this mean I'll have to buy all my clothes at Knobs from now on?'"

Raphael laughed, too, "Text back: 'You had a reputation?'" Luke nodded and texted. His phone soon beeped again.

"He says, 'Bitch ... that's Alex talking.'" Luke put the phone down. "You know, I'll bet Alex is secretly excited to do this. It's a chance for him to work on his dance moves. He really was good up there."

"He was. I made him promise to rehearse with me. I want to dance at least half as well as he does. Okay ... one fourth as well as he does."

Luke crawled across the couch and pressed his body on top of Raphael's as his tongue dove for treasure. As their lips parted, Luke said, "Nobody is going to pay any attention to your dancing, baby. I promise. Come on. Let's go to bed."

Thirty-Eight

─◦━━━•━━━•━━━◦─

LAST BEACH DAY?

"BABY, SATURDAY MAY BE our last shot at the beach for a while," Luke said Thursday evening, looking up from his tablet. He and Raphael were lounging on the couch, post dinner, pre-shave & shower, feet playing with each other's crotch. "The long-term forecast looks pretty wet."

"Well, we always need the rain, so I guess we can't complain," Raphael replied as he reached for his phone. "I'll text everyone to see who's up for it. It may be Juan's day off ... I hope so." After a couple of back and forth texts, Raphael put his phone down. "Looks like everybody will try, including Steve and Niki."

"Niki!" Luke looked up and smiled. "Good for him. I know he doesn't enjoy it that much."

"He likes the beach and the surf, but, yeah, he doesn't worship the sun as much as we do. We used to go sometimes as kids and watch the sunset. That's still his favorite beach time, I think."

"This is cool, all eight of us. Remember when Alex dreaded the idea of being caged and naked in public? First the beach, then Halloween, then the strip contest ..."

"Uh, the strip contest was not exactly voluntary, Sir." Raphael said, giving Luke his evil eye.

"Well, he certainly rose to the occasion. And, now you two will be doing it on a regular basis. That's what I call progress."

"I guess. Which reminds me, I should talk to him tomorrow about when we can rehearse. And, we need to get some sleazy tops and thongs, too. And tear-away shorts. Where the hell do you buy tear-away shorts?"

"Google it."

Raphael reached out for Luke's tablet. As Luke leaned forward and played with Raphael's feet, Raphael surfed a bit. "These all look pretty boring. I guess our best bet is to have my favorite seamstress create something for us. Looks like Alex and I may be making another trip to

Britex. If we're going to create a following, sequins and shimmery lycra are definitely called for."

"Don't forget to polish your cages."

"Yes, Sir! Would you like to polish mine for me right now?"

"I would. I would, indeed." Luke stood, reached down to take Raphael's hand and led him into the shower.

Luke, Raphael, Steve, Niki, Alex and Greg all took MUNI to the Presidio together, while Ricky and Juan were riding Ricky's scooter to the Battery at the top of the cliff overlooking Marshall's Beach. Raphael had thought to bring an extra caged cock t-shirt for Niki, so all three caged cock brothers could be in unison, and in uniform.

"I can't believe I haven't given you one of these before, Niki," Raphael apologized. "I guess I'm so used to seeing you naked or pupped out that it didn't even occur to me."

"Hey, no problem, Raphael. But, thanks. I'll wear it to and from the bar sometimes. That'll be cool. Thanks." Unfortunately, there wasn't any skater dude on MUNI to impress. They did get a couple of smiles from guys walking in the opposite direction on the hike from the MUNI stop to the trail head. It could have been the shirts, or it could have been the sight of six guys, holding hands, clearly enjoying one another. They spotted Ricky's scooter when they turned into the small parking lot at the trail head.

"Cool! They did make it. This is going to be a fun beach day," Alex exclaimed. Fifteen minutes later, after tramping down the trail, they finally made it to sea level and started walking toward the Golden Gate. Niki was the first to spot Ricky waving at them from a spot near the cliff. He, Alex and Raphael began running to the spot Ricky and Juan had staked out, while Luke, Steve and Greg, who were wearing the backpacks, followed up.

"Amigos!" Ricky yelled as they sauntered up. "What took you so long?"

"MUNI," Alex smiled. "But we're here now!" Alex didn't even protest that the spot Juan and Ricky had picked was surrounded by plenty of other men. In fact, he was the first of the newcomers to strip. Raphael looked knowingly at Luke, who winked. Progress, indeed. Especially since Ricky was already naked and unabashedly caged for all to admire. Juan stood and gave each newcomer a hug, with Ricky right behind him. Already, it seemed, Juan and Ricky were a natural part of the family.

Once the blankets were spread, clothes disposed of and the oiling of the bodies ritual was completed, the group was ready to relax. After Luke's timer had beeped for the second time, the four caged amigos joined hands and headed out for a surf walk. Steve and Luke handed out water from their packs to Juan and Greg, and the four admired the view.

"At the risk of repeating myself," Juan said to the group, "I'm still grateful for what you all did for Ricky, and for me. It's been an amazing week for us. It's painful to have to leave him each day to go to work." His voice caught as he repeated, "Thanks."

"He's an amazing guy, all right," Greg said, reaching over and rubbing Juan's shoulder comfortingly. "We loved having him around. He deserves to be happy, and you, more than anyone, make him happy."

"Well, it goes both ways, for sure," Juan smiled.

"So, Juan ... none of my business," Luke posed, "but, have you unlocked Ricky yet for cleaning and ...?" Steve and Greg both laughed. Juan looked directly at Luke and smiled.

"Yeah. Last night. The 'and' was good ... for both of us."

"Just checking to make sure you're taking good care of our Ricky," Luke smiled back. The conversation continued, with Juan learning a bit more about everyone. About Raphael and Niki's brotherhood, Luke's and Niki's mohawks, Steve's handling of Niki's puppyhood, Alex and Raphael's strip act, which lead to more discussion on Raphael and Luke's dares, which explained their audacious tattoos.

"I'm impressed that you two trust each other enough to vow to never turn down a dare," Juan said. "Would you do that, Greg? Steve?"

"We've both actually been pulled into it a couple of times," Steve confessed. "So, yeah. Putting Niki through Obedience School was more or less a dare, wouldn't you say, Luke?"

"Sure. And, Greg and I were the victims of what Raphael calls a mutual dare at Halloween. You survived, Greg."

"I admit I wasn't too thrilled at first, but in the end, it was a blast. It seems to me the dares are always meant to stretch the other guy, not to hurt him. To take things beyond a comfort zone, but not too far. So, yeah, if Alex wanted us to start doing dares, I might be up for it."

"Up for what?" Alex asked as the caged contingent appeared out of nowhere, and plopped down next to their respective better halves.

"Up for dares, sweetheart. How was the surf?"

"Cold and wet. Can I have some of your water?"

"Guys," Steve interjected, "those guys over there by the volleyball net. They've stopped playing and started eating. I was watching them earlier. Looks like fun. Wanna ask if we can play a game while they eat?"

"Sure!" Alex jumped up. "Cages versus the free cocks!"

"That won't be fair!" Niki protested. "They're all taller than we are."

"Niki," Alex countered, "our cages give us special powers. Trust me, cages versus free cocks."

"Alex ..." Greg started to say. Alex gave Greg a dirty look, so Greg backed off. "Okay ... cages versus free cocks it is. If we can even borrow the ball."

"Come on, Raphael, let's ask." Alex commanded. Clearly, he was even more enthused than Steve. Alex and Raphael headed over to the group, with Ricky tailing them. As they approached, with Alex in the lead, Raphael naturally took Ricky's hand. "Hey, guys," Alex greeted the group. They were unwrapping sandwiches, opening containers of salads. "Would it be okay if we borrowed your volleyball while you eat ... just a quick game. You guys looked great out there, by the way."

"Hi," a guy with a man bun and an abundance of muscles responded. "Sure, why not." He tossed the ball to Alex, who caught it with one hand and tucked it under his arm without even looking at it. That was Raphael's first clue that Alex had talents beyond dancing and make-up. "Have fun."

"Awesome," Alex replied. "Thanks. You guys are great." He turned, put his arm around Raphael's shoulders and the three walked toward the net. As they walked away, one of the group turned to the ball handler and said, "What the hell? What's with their dicks?"

"I don't know, but let's just watch while we eat."

Steve led the rest of the group from the blankets to the net, Caged Cocks on one side, Free Cocks on the other. Since Alex had the ball, he dispensed with the traditional coin toss, and stepped behind the serve line to serve the first volley. Everyone took their places and looked to Alex, who powered the ball over and into the Free Cocks' court. Luke set, Steve palmed and Juan spiked the ball into the Caged Cocks' court. Even though he was furthest back, Alex pounced, set the ball before it hit sand and Ricky palmed it over the net. Juan met and returned the ball, but by now Alex, ignoring all protocol, was at the net and spiked it between Juan's feet.

One, nothing, Caged Cocks. It was more fun to watch than to relay here, but long story short, the Caged Cocks pummeled the Free Cocks. Twenty-five to six. Throughout the game, Greg held his tongue. Ricky was delirious, having expected Juan to out-jock everyone. He threw his arms around Alex and leapt up wrapping his legs around Alex's waist, almost bringing Alex to his knees. Raphael and Niki joined the party in a victorious group hug. The four Free Cocks on the other side of the net just stood there and watched.

"We've been hustled, haven't we, Greg," Luke said. It wasn't a question.

"Varsity team captain. Division champions. I wanted to warn you, but, hell, I thought we'd have a fighting chance." Greg put a consoling arm around Luke's shoulders. "It was kind of a David and Goliath moment, don't you think?" By now the caged cocks had joined the free cocks on the other side of the net, consoling and congratulatory hugs and kisses were exchanged.

"That was fun!" Niki exclaimed.

"Yeah!" Ricky agreed. "We should do this again."

Juan, who was still holding Ricky in a close embrace, laughed and said, "Next time let's try playing by the rules, eh, Alex?"

"What? What do you mean?" Alex laughed

"You know what I mean, 'captain,'" Juan smiled. "Well played, though. It was fun competing against a pro, I will say."

As the group headed back to the blankets, Raphael and Niki walked the ball back to the guys who owned it. "Thanks so much, guys. We really appreciate you letting us play," Raphael smiled as he tossed the ball back to the muscled manbun guy.

"No problem. It was fun watching you play. Say, can I ask you guys something ... something personal?"

Raphael and Niki looked at each other briefly, suspecting they knew what was coming. "Maybe. Depends," Raphael answered. "I'm Raphael, this is my brother Niki. What did you want to ask?"

"Hey, Raphael ... Niki, I'm Marco. Have a seat." He motioned for them to share his blanket. As he scooted aside, Raphael and Niki could easily see that his pubes were tightly trimmed, but not exactly shaved like theirs. He was wearing a cock ring and had a prince albert piercing poking out of his foreskin. Not caged, but definitely not 'vanilla.' Raphael and Niki sat, both cross-legged, cages clearly on display. The other guys were listening in, but trying not to be too obvious about it. "We couldn't help but notice that four of you are wearing those things on your dicks. What's that all about? Not judging, just curious ... if you don't mind."

"These are chastity cages," Raphael smiled, lifting his Looker 01 away from his body, then letting it fall back. "Niki, Alex, Ricky and I are caged. We don't have access to our cocks. We're each caged for a different reason, but for the most part its permanent. In my case, for instance, it's to prove my devotion to my fiancé. Likewise, my collar ... it's permanent, too. Niki's cage and collar are part of his pup persona. You may have seen him behind the bar at the Powerhouse."

"Oh, yeah!" one of the other guys interjected. "I didn't recognize you without your pup hood. You're awesome, dude!" Niki smiled shyly.

"You said yours is to prove your devotion to your fiancé, Raphael," Marco continued. "Is that a dom/sub thing?"

"Not exactly. Like Ricky, the guy in the baby blue Holy Trainer, that's a brand of chastity cage, well, we're both total bottoms to our partners. I was caged to prove my devotion as my fiancé's leatherboy. Ricky is Juan's leatherboy. But, it's not typical dominance or submission, no sadism or masochism, no pain, that kind of stuff. I do what Luke's asks, but Luke also does what I ask of him. We think of it as mutual ownership."

"That's cool. And, you don't mind having your dick caged?"

"Nope. Luke's cock is the only cock I want. You can see my tattoo." Raphael raised up on his knees to display his ink. "That's who and what I am. Luke's tattoo above his cock says, it all: 'Raphael's Cock.' His cock is my cock."

"And, you're 'Luke's Locked Cock Boy.'"

"Exactly."

"How often do you take the 'cage' off?"

"Never. Like I said, it's permanent."

"Fuck! Seriously?"

"Yeah."

"So, you never get hard?"

"I get hard all the time. We all do. And, it feels great when I do. My cage has a tube that goes up inside my cock, so when I get hard, my cock is squeezed from inside and out." Marco's mouth fell open in amazement.

"But you can't ... you know ... jerk off. You never come."

"I come all the time. Just about every time Luke fucks me. Believe me, I'm not sacrificing anything. Neither are Niki or Alex or Ricky. If anything, being locked up has made our lives better."

"It's certainly made mine better," Niki agreed. "I don't ever intend to let Steve unlock me."

"Wow. I was feeling sorry for you guys out there..."

"Don't. If anything, we feel sorry for anyone who hasn't experienced being caged. Listen, we better get going. Thank you again for letting us borrow your ball. You're really great guys." Raphael and Niki stood. Marco stood as well and extended his hand. Niki shook it, then Raphael did, then pulled him into a hug. "Thanks again, Marco" As Raphael and Niki walked back to their blankets, they could hear Marco and his friends immediately start chatting.

"You're kind of a missionary, Raphael," Niki said.

"Is that a good thing?" Raphael asked.

"It's not a bad thing, Raffie." Raphael wrapped his arm around Niki's waist and pulled him close. It was good having Niki close again.

Thirty-Nine

APPRECIATION FOR THE LOGICAL FAMILY

THAT NEXT WEEK RAPHAEL and Alex made their way to Britex after work. They knew they'd need more time to browse than the toga trip required, so exploring the store over the lunch hour, even an extended lunch hour, didn't seem feasible.

"What are we looking for exactly?" Alex asked as he and Raphael poked and prodded various bolts of fabric.

"I wish I could say," Raphael absentmindedly responded. "I guess we'll know it when we see it. It needs to be tacky, sexy, flashy and cheap. We'll be spending more of our budget on the sewing than the fabric."

"Are we having her make everything? Tops, shorts, thongs, leggings?"

"We can buy cheap thongs. And leggings would hide too much, don't you think? I'm thinking just breakaway shorts and tops ... tanks and maybe V-necks. Something easy for us to rip off of each other. Niki said one of the things guys were wild about was me stripping you, so for the most part we should strip each other, don't you think?"

"I like that idea, Raphael. Stripping you in public ... "

"I like that idea, too!" said the same clerk from their last visit as he approached. "Welcome back, gentlemen. How was your Halloween?"

"Exactly as planned," Raphael smiled.

"Yeah, we were all over Instagram," Alex agreed. "Raphael is a genius when it comes to public exposure."

"I'll just bet he is," the clerk laughed. "And, how can we help you charming young men today?"

"Well, oddly enough, we're planning costumes for even more exposure," Raphael confided. He briefly explained their upcoming extra-curricular endeavor.

"Oh, my. The second Saturday of the month, you say? I'll be sure to clear my calendar. How exciting ... and all for a worthy cause. Nudity and charity all in one pretty package. I am impressed. But, more importantly, we must make sure your audience is impressed, which of course they will be once the costumes come off. If you don't mind my saying so." The clerk chuckled. "I can tell by your smiles, you don't ... okay, boys, follow me."

The 'expert' as Alex and Raphael had come to think of him, efficiently presented them with more options than they could digest. Who would have ever thought Britex would stock so many stripper-perfect fabrics? Maybe none of them qualified as 'tacky,' but there was plenty of flash, plenty of sexy. Meshes, sequined, sheer, faux leather, they had it all.

"How many tops and shorts are you thinking, boys? And, do you want to be in matching outfits, or mix it up for each performance?" His questions were informed and thoughtful, and as before, he had ideas neither had even thought of at this point. The more they talked, the more ideas flowed. Besides tear away shorts, they decided on mini-kilts (Luke will love that idea), loincloths and mankinis. In the end, they walked out with enough fabric, or so they hoped, to make enough disposable outfits for three shows ... six performances total. Neither really expected their careers as The Chastity Brothers to go beyond that.

"I'll get this stuff to my friend, Allyson, in the next day or so, to give her enough time to make at least four outfits for our first performance," Raphael said as he and Alex strolled toward Market Street, hand in hand, each carrying a big Britex shopping bag. "Do you care which fabrics we start with?"

"Heck, no. We'll be tossing these clothes into the audience within minutes of putting them on, so who cares? Talk about 'fast fashion.'"

"Good point. I'll let her decide. When can we start my dancing lessons, Alex? I have to get better than I was. Way better."

"How about this Saturday, since the beach is out. Come over to our place, bring Luke if you want, and he and Greg can play audience."

"Okay, but no Luke. Not yet, just you and me until I feel more confident."

"You were fine before. With your definition, and your ink, and that face ... nobody will care how well you dance, Raphael." Raphael laughed, then planted one on Alex's cheek.

"If that was designed to bolster my confidence ... it worked. Still, I really want to be better."

"You will be. And it will be easier than you think. I coach almost as well as I spike a volleyball."

"Well, in that case, one lesson ought to do it."

"We'll see, Raphael. Maybe two in your case ..."

"Bitch." They wormed their way through the commute crowd into the Powell Station and boarded an outbound train to the Castro and, ultimately, their waiting men.

That evening, after dinner, before shave and shower time, Raphael sat at the rarely used dining table with his tablet and drew up several concepts for the outfits. The more direction he could provide Allyson, the better. Luke walked up behind him and slipped his hands under the shoulder straps of Raphael's harness and tugged while looking over his shoulders. He knew that would put pressure on Raphael's butt plug and likely spur an erection in his cage. Which usually led to an impromptu 'nap.' Raphael put his stylus down and reached around without looking to grasp Luke's conveniently located cock. Yep, tumescent, as he suspected. Raphael slid out of his chair, onto his knees, and swallowed 'his' cock to the root. Luke let out a long, grateful sigh and began massaging the ever so slightly stubbly sides of Raphael's head.

"I love you, Sir," Raphael whispered as he pulled away from Luke's now full-blown hardon. "And you taste so good."

Without letting go of Raphael's head, Luke kneeled down and locked lips with his locked cock boy. They tongue wrestled just long enough to make Raphael as hard as his cage allowed, Raphael moaning into Luke's mouth, the vibrations and the shared breaths further hardening Luke's cock. He moved his hands from Raphael's head and placed them under his arms and stood, lifting Raphael with him, lips still locked.

As Luke pulled back, freeing Raphael's lips and tongue, Raphael started to whisper, "Please, Sir ..."

Before he could finish, Luke finished his thought for him. "Yes, baby, I would love to fuck your brains out." And he did.

Saturday, Alex talked Greg into doing 'something' with Luke so he and Raphael would be able to practice without Raphael feeling too self-conscious. While Alex and Raphael worked on their routine, Luke and Greg decided to do something touristy. Greg had never seen the elevated park atop the Transbay Terminal, and that's where they headed. They were in no hurry, so they took a vintage streetcar downtown instead of the subway. As luck would have it, the first one to come was one of the cars from Milan, Italy. Greg had never ridden one of these, either.

"Jeez," he said as he and Luke took a seat. "This feels more like going to church than riding a streetcar."

"Oh, you mean the wooden seats? Yeah, they remind me of church pews, too."

"I like it. And the signage is in Italian. What a trip ... no pun intended."

Luke laughed. "Okay, I'll give you that one." As they rode, they talked about the loves of their lives, and how things had changed since Alex and Raphael had become good friends.

"Seriously, it took a threat to get Alex to go to Folsom that day. I'd bought the harnesses and codpieces as a surprise, and when I showed them to Alex, he looked at me like I'd lost my mind."

"What did you threaten him with to get him to wear them in public, no less? By the way, you both looked like you'd worn them all your lives when you walked up to us. You looked great."

"Oh, thanks. Well, first I put them on. That, turned him on immediately, a good sign, I thought."

"Yeah, always," Luke grinned. "I love turning Raphael on. Of course, it doesn't take much."

"That's what I'm talking about. Raphael and you have been such an influence on Alex, well, on both of us. We've become much more sexual, much more comfortable being sexual everywhere. I love how they hold hands wherever they go."

"You mean like this?" Luke reached down and took Greg's hand as the streetcar arrived at their stop at First and Market. "This is our stop." He stood, Greg stood, and still holding hands, Luke led him off the car.

"Is it cheating if we hold hands like this?" Greg asked. He sounded only semi-serious.

"Is it cheating when Alex and Raphael do it?"

"No. They love each other. So, no, they're not cheating."

"Well, I love you, too, both of you, so I guess that settles that."

"Ditto. See ... you two never stop encouraging us to push our own boundaries. It's kind of exhilarating sometimes. I've never told another guy other than Alex that I love him. Or held hands with him. I have to admit, Luke, it feels good."

"You're welcome." At that, just to pimp Greg, Luke leaned over and delivered a signature Raphael kiss on the cheek. Greg laughed, then returned the favor.

"I won't tell if you don't," Greg smiled.

"Are you kidding? It's the first thing I'm going to say when we get back! They'll be thrilled that we can be 'unlocked cock brothers.' Alex isn't the jealous type, is he?"

"No. I don't think so. He's always gotten all my attention. We've never had friends as close as you ... and the rest of our little family. Like I said, it feels good. It feels right. I feel very lucky."

"Me, too. Armistead Maupin calls it 'the logical family' as opposed to the 'biological family.'"

"The author of 'Tales of the City?' Yeah, love his books. I wonder if we could talk him into writing one about us?"

"'Locked Cocks of the City'? Why not. We could play ourselves in the movie."

"No, I want Armie Hammer to play me."

"Oh, and I suppose Timothée Chalamet will play Alex?"

"They are dead ringers, don't you think?"

"Now that you mention it ... yeah. You are a lucky guy, Greg."

"Look who's talking? We both are."

"No argument on that score, either." They crossed Mission Street.

"Whoa ... is that the Transbay Terminal? It looks like a giant space ship or something."

"Yeah. It takes up more than three blocks."

"And the streets just go right through it? Or, under it?"

"Yeah. Wait 'til you see the park on the roof." Luke and Greg entered the terminal and took a long escalator up, past the elevated bus level, on to the roof. They walked through the glass doors and back out into the great outdoors. And, Greg thought, it really was great.

"Wow. How many stories up are we?"

"Three. But it feels like you're in the Botanical Gardens in Golden Gate Park, doesn't it?"

"Yeah. Except we're surrounded by skyscrapers. It's weird, but cool. Trees, plants. Yet, you can look into the windows of skyscrapers ... almost touch them."

"Yeah, let's check it out." As they walked, still holding hands, Luke explained some of the exotic gardens as they passed them. Other couples, families, tourists and office workers walked with them and in the opposite direction, all enjoying the peaceful setting. As they approached the bus fountain, Luke slowed their walk until – whoosh – the fountain sprang to life. "Every time a bus passes by below us, it triggers this fountain."

"I love it. I have to bring Alex here. He'll love it, too." They stopped at one of the little heavily planted cul-de-sacs and sat down on a bench. Another gay couple was sitting on another bench across from them, sipping coffee, quietly chatting. One had his arm around the other's waist. "Lovebirds," Greg said, nodding to them. "God, I love this city."

"So, we now know you love Alex, you love me and Raphael and Niki and Steve and Ricky and Juan and this city. You've got a big heart, Greg." Luke squeezed Greg's hand. "But seriously, I'm glad for you, and for Alex. And, I'm glad we live in a time when the two of you can actually be husbands."

"I know. Sometimes I can't believe it's real. I know I've asked before ... are you two any closer to getting married?"

"Damn. That's what I forgot to do ... get married!"

"As Ricky would say, 'you're funny!' I didn't mean to put you on the spot."

"You didn't. You know, it was Raphael who proposed to me, who gave me this ring. Maybe it's my place to make some wedding plans."

"You'll know when the time is right."

"We're basically married now. I was so happy when Raphael dared me to move in with him. Speaking of dares, you never did finish telling me how you got Alex to go to Folsom bare-assed and in leather."

"Oh, yeah. I got distracted by this handsome guy who wanted to hold my hand, for, like, forever..." Luke slid his hand out from Greg's and pretended to pout.

"Well, if that's how you feel."

Greg took Luke's hand back into his own. "I wasn't complaining, Luke. It's nice. Really." It was Greg's turn to plant a Raphael cheek kiss. The couple across from them, no doubt assuming they were lovers, smiled and waved their coffee cups in a toast toward Greg and Luke. "Hey, I guess we make a believable couple."

"I'd do you."

"What!?! Luke..."

"Just kidding ... or, am I?"

"Where was I? Oh, yeah, how I got Alex nearly naked at Folsom. I wish I could say it was a dare, but we didn't know that was a thing, back then. I just threatened I'd unlock him for a month if he didn't go."

"A whole month? He probably would have gone blind after that."

"It was the most severe motivation I could think of. He blanched when I said it. He folded and agreed to go rather than risk being unlocked. Funny, these locked cock boys, huh?"

"Funny wonderful. Funny sexy. Funny can't live without 'em."

"Yeah. That's the truth."

The other couple stood and joined hands as they started to walk away. One turned back and said, "Have a nice day!" Greg looked at Luke and grinned.

"See ... you've corrupted yet another innocent gay couple into your daring plot of queer displays of public affection."

"Bwww haaaa haaa," Luke laughed menacingly. "Come, not so innocent victim, let us return to our dancing lovers and see how they're doing."

"Think they'll perform for us?"

"Well, you do have a pretty persuasive threat in your arsenal. One I'd never dare to use on Raphael."

"Well, now that Alex is locked in a Looker, and the keys are at Mr. S, I think that threat is no longer in the arsenal. Maybe I could threaten to shave my head in a mohawk."

"I'll do it for you. Just say the word."

"Don't tempt me." Greg planted another Raphael cheek kiss. Luke smiled and thought this had been a really good afternoon. Greg was beginning to loosen up, just as Alex had. The family was growing even closer, and that felt really good.

Forty

ALEX COMES CLEAN

WHEN GREG AND LUKE walked through the door, music was still throbbing and Alex and Raphael were still dancing, their backs to the door, intent on their moves. Greg slowly eased the door shut so their presence wouldn't yet be detected. Luke put his arm around Greg's waist as they stood in the doorway to the living room aka rehearsal hall. Raphael and Alex were totally naked, Raphael not even harnessed, so the view was as inviting as ever. Alex was still clearly in the lead, barking out moves periodically, with Raphael just half a beat behind. Actually, he was keeping up pretty well, and his moves were definitely smoother, more natural, and even sexier than before, if that was possible. Luke's heart fluttered a bit, and he longed to bury his face in that beautiful, sweaty brown ass. If Greg hadn't been there, he probably would have. Eventually, Alex and Raphael spun around, presumably to flash those asses at their imaginary audience, and both stopped cold at the sight of Greg and Luke.

"Hey!" Raphael smiled. "How long have you been there?" Alex picked up a remote and killed the music. Luke let go of Greg and moved to his sweat slicked lover.

"Just long enough to fall in love with you all over again," Luke cooed. "Looks like Alex is turning you into a first-rate dancer." While Luke was seducing Raphael, Alex had fallen into Greg's arms.

"We've been working our butts off!" Alex said breathlessly. "Raphael is a slave driver." He and Greg locked lips. Afterall, it had been hours since they'd last seen one another.

"Well, we don't have a lot of time before our first performance," Raphael justified. "I want to wring every last dollar out of our fans that we possibly can."

"Well as far as I'm concerned, you're ready for your close up, Raphael," Alex replied, handing Raphael a towel. "Maybe one more short session and we'll be good to go." Alex turned back to Greg and asked, "So what did you guys do?"

"Luke taught me how to corrupt innocent gay couples in a public park," Greg teased.

Raphael sat down on the floor, cross legged, then reached up for Luke's hand and pulled him down to join him. "This ought to be good. Tell us everything."

"Somebody's exaggerating," Luke said. He leaned over and licked sweat off of Raphael's pierced pec. 'Yummm, baby you taste extra good. But seriously, all I did was force Greg to hold my hand the whole time we were out, Raphael and Alex style."

"Really?" Alex exclaimed. He put his arms around Greg's waist and looked earnestly into his eyes. "So, big boy, does this mean you'll start holding my hand everywhere in public now?" Greg smiled and nodded.

"I think I'm ready, yeah. It was actually kind of fun at times. Empowering."

"So, what else did you two handsome men do when our backs were turned?" Raphael inquired, attempting Luke's eyebrow trick.

"Well, we did kiss a few times," Greg confessed. Raphael and Alex looked wide-eyed at each other.

"Alex," Raphael said conspiratorially, "I think our men are finally revealing their secret love for each other. What ever shall we do?" Playing along, Alex let go of Greg, dropped to the floor, crawled over to Raphael, pushed him onto his back and French-kissed the fuck out of him. That wasn't exactly what Raphael had in mind, but he certainly didn't resist. As Raphael and Alex sat back up, Raphael, looking more pleased than stunned, could only say, "Huh."

Luke was looking amused, and a bit curious, perhaps. Alex motioned Greg to come over and sit down next to him. Alex put his hand on Greg's thigh. Oddly, both Greg and Luke were still in street clothes, as they hadn't had time to decide whether Raphael and Luke were staying awhile or heading home.

Alex was looking down at his cage, and all eyes were on him. After a moment, he raised his head and looked each of the others in the eyes, ending with Greg. "I apologize if I was out of line just now."

"No apology necessary," Raphael responded, putting his hand on Alex's thigh. "I think we all know we all love each other. Don't we?"

"Well, actually, Raphael, today was the first time Luke and I said it to each other," Greg affirmed. "But, yeah. We do."

"Guys, I may regret this," Alex began. "And, I don't want to do anything to ruin what I consider the most fulfilling friendships I've ever had in my life. But ... I'm going to say it anyway." Alex took a deep breath, then continued. "I want the four of us to have sex together. There. I said it. I've felt it for a long time. But now I've said it. I just thought you should know." At that, Alex crumpled into Greg's lap. Greg ran his hand through Alex's hair, and looked over at Luke. Luke looked pensive, a look that was hard to read. Raphael rubbed Luke's thigh, then reached over and massaged Alex's naked hip, then slid his hand down around Alex's ass. He rubbed his ass a moment, then pulled his hand back into his own lap.

"Is that a dare, Alex?" Raphael asked, looking at Luke, again with the attempted eyebrow trick. No one else said a word.

Finally, Alex pushed himself up into a sitting position. He pressed himself against Greg, put his arm around Greg's waist, and in a very low voice asked Greg, "Does that seem wrong to you?"

"No, love. I totally understand. I know you love Raphael, too."

"I'll never love anyone as much as I love you, Greg."

"I know. Nor I anyone more than you. Forever and always." Alex exhaled a long, deep sigh. "It's okay, Alex. It's okay to love Raphael and Luke, too." Alex turned to Raphael. Beautiful, exotic, buzzed, shaved, caged, pierced and inked Raphael. Raphael, who was everything Alex had gradually come to admire, and envy and emulate. And, love.

"Yes, Raphael, it's a dare."

Raphael looked at Luke for guidance. They both were thinking the same thing. That it would be wrong to refuse a dare. But, did Alex, and even more to the point, did Greg think the same thing? Luke smiled and nodded at Raphael. Raphael looked back at Alex, who actually looked miserable right now. He moved back next to Alex, raised up on his knees, and took Alex's head in his hands and pulled him against his chest. Naked sweaty skin on skin. He held Alex there a moment, looking into Greg's eyes ... looking for some kind of reaction from Greg. Greg looked over at Luke, then back at Raphael. He smiled and nodded at Raphael. Raphael nodded back. He lowered himself back down level with Alex, who looked longingly into Raphael's almond eyes, seeking some kind of response. Hoping, fearing, anxious. So anxious he was nearly nauseous.

Finally, Raphael smiled, leaned forward, put his hand on the back of Alex's head and pulled him into a long, wet, kiss. Both men's cages strained with desire, a long ignored, long denied desire. Neither wanted to end the kiss, and for a long time neither did. Finally, slowly, Raphael pulled away. He looked at Alex, who's eyes remained closed, his lips still parted, the tip of his tongue still resting on his lower lip, still not wanting the kiss to end. Precum dripped out of the nozzle of his Looker. Raphael looked down at it, then up at Luke, then Greg, both of whom were watching silently, waiting to see what Raphael would do next. He collected a dab of Alex's precum on the end of his finger and deposited it on the tip of Alex's tongue. Alex smiled, opened his eyes and licked his lips. "Sorry," he whispered.

"Don't be," Raphael smiled. "Perfectly natural. I'll take it as a compliment." Alex gave a short laugh. "Alex ... we accept your dare."

Forty-One

NIKI HAS A POSSE

LUKE REACHED HIS ARM over and squeezed Alex's shoulder. Alex turned to him, wondering if Luke was upset. Instead, Luke smiled warmly.

"Alex, that was very brave of you ... thank you for being so honest with us. Look, we're not puritans here. Obviously." Alex exhaled another short, relieved snort of acknowledgement. "We don't live by the rules and mores of the majority of society. But, on the other hand, Raphael and I don't go around fucking every hot guy we encounter, and I know you and Greg don't either." Alex shook his head in the negative as Greg finally sat down behind him and put his arms around Alex's waist to hug him close. "In fact, even before Raphael proposed, we were completely monogamous. I can assure you I will never, and I mean never, do anything to risk my relationship with Raphael. He is my everything. Hell, it's his cock hanging between my legs." At that, Luke lifted the hem of his kilt to illustrate his point ... and his tattoo. Alex nodded. "But that said, I also know the friendship and love the four of us share is special ... and rare. So, yes. We accept your dare." Alex smiled and nodded again, apparently still not comfortable saying anything further.

"Raphael and I should go now, so you and Greg can talk, so Raphael and I can talk, too. We'll need to figure out what we are and aren't willing to do together. Sex is and should be fun and exciting. I want anything we do to bring us closer together, and not tear any of us apart. I've seen that happen, and you probably have, too. Agreed?"

"Agreed," Alex finally spoke. "I love you guys too much to risk losing you." He took Greg's hands that were resting above his cage into his own and squeezed. "All of you."

Luke leaned forward, and for the first time since he'd known him, he kissed Alex. A long, gentle kiss. Then he moved forward past Alex's head and kissed Greg. A long, maybe longer, gentle kiss. Then he sat back, pulled Raphael to him, put his arms around Raphael, just as Greg was doing with Alex, and kissed the back of Raphael's neck. He looked at Greg and asked, "Are we good?"

"Never better," Greg replied. Luke stood up, pulling his naked leather boy into a standing position with him.

"Why don't you get dressed, and we should go for now. Unless you want to go home like this." Raphael hugged Luke, then let him go.

"Tempting, Sir, but I think I'll dress." He ruffled Alex's hair as he walked past, then Greg's in turn. In some indescribable but deeply felt way everything had just changed among them. He felt a closeness to both Alex and Greg that he hadn't felt before. It felt good. When Raphael returned from the bedroom, dressed, Alex, Greg and Luke were all standing near the door. Greg was closest when Raphael approached. Should he? Would it be awkward now not to? Oh hell, what the heck, he put his arms around Greg and kissed him. Greg held him tight.

When he released Raphael, Greg smiled and said, "I guess it's okay to say, 'love you, Raphael.'"

"Love you, too, Greg." Raphael then embraced the still naked Alex. "Love you, Alex. And, again, thanks for opening up." Alex looked happy and a little chastened at the same time. Meanwhile Luke was kissing Greg goodbye, he then pulled Alex into a hug, Alex's head buried in his chest.

Luke leaned down and locked lips one more time with him. When he pulled away, he looked at Greg and said, "You're right ... he's a good kisser. Not as good as Raphael, but not bad!" That broke the tension and Alex pushed Luke away in faux disgust. "It was a fun day, Greg," Luke continued. "Thanks for going along ... with everything." Greg smiled and nodded, his arm around Alex's waist, as Luke and Raphael departed.

At first on the walk home Luke had his arm around Raphael's shoulders. Raphael kept nudging into Luke's side, forcing more contact than they'd otherwise feel. Then, he put his arm around Luke's waist, not wanting any distance between them. Finally, Raphael spoke. "Wow."

"Yeah, wow." After another silence, "Are you okay?"

"Yeah, I'm okay. I guess I shouldn't be surprised. I mean, Alex and I have been very physical with each other for a long time now, holding hands, hugging, kissing. But it was just locked cock brotherly stuff. Not 'I'm falling in love with you stuff,' ... at least for me."

"I've always loved seeing you two so close. And, I think Greg has, too. But the question is, can we have sex as just sex with them, and not have it make Alex fall even deeper in love with you? I've never considered sharing you with anyone, baby, and I've never wanted to stray from you either. Did we speak too soon, just to comfort Alex?"

"I don't know. I guess we need to think on it. I kinda wish Alex hadn't said anything but I guess it's good he did. Now we know."

"Yeah, let's give it some time and think on it." By now they'd arrived at home. "So, baby, you're still nice and salty. How about I lay you out on the bed, give you a tongue bath, then we 'nap' for a while before our shave and shower?"

"Yumm. Yes, please, Sir." Raphael began pulling Luke's shirt off of him before they even reached the bedroom. In seconds both were naked and prone, and true to his word, Luke started at Raphael's feet and licked his way all the way up to Raphael's landing strip, with a long, long layover at his lips.

Several interesting events took place over the following few days.

On Sunday

Despite the workout Raphael had experienced on Saturday, perfecting his dance moves with Alex, he and Luke decided to hit the gym since they'd missed their Saturday workout. At one point, when Raphael was at the end of his fourth set on the bench press, Luke, spotting, urged him on by saying, "Three more reps, stripper boy ... think of your fans." Instead, that ended the set as it caused Raphael to start laughing. They finished the workout with thirty minutes of cardio, then headed to the locker room to strip, then steam. There were three other members already lounging, so Luke and Raphael sat on a top bench, nestled together. Soon a couple of other guys entered that they didn't recognize. Either new members or maybe tourists. The new guys took seats on a lower bench on the other side of the steam room and began talking in low voices. A few minutes later, Steve entered and sat below Raphael, greeting him and Luke. Then Niki entered. The new Niki. The caged Niki who no longer hid his manhood behind a towel.

Before he could even make it to Steve's side, one of the new guys erupted, "Shit. What's wrong with your dick?" Niki and everyone else looked at him to see what was up. The guy was looking directly at Niki ... directly at his cage. Niki tried to ignore him, moved over next to Steve and sat down. "What the hell? What is that on your dick, man?" He turned to his companion and said, "Stupid fucking queer, man." He hadn't finished his sentence before Raphael was off the bench and landing in front of the guy, with Luke and Steve right behind him.

"If there's something wrong with his 'dick,' then I guess there's something wrong with my 'dick,' too." Raphael's cage and the tell-tale tattoo above it were directly in front of the guy's face. The guy looked up at

Raphael but before he could say anything else, Raphael continued, "The only stupid one in here is you." That's when the guy stood up, but before he could make a move, the three other members were up and right behind Luke and Steve. One of them said, "I suggest you get your sad ass out of here before we show you what 'fucking queers' are capable of."

The pathetic excuse of a man did his best to look menacing, then said to his companion, who looked more than a little worried, "Let's get out of here." As soon as they exited, Steve went back to Niki, pulled him into a sideways hug and whispered into his ear. Luke headed out of the steam room as Raphael and the other guys also gathered around Niki.

"I'm fine guys. Believe me, I've faced far worse than that. But, thanks for taking him on. I could have decked him, you know." One of the other members laughed and mussed Niki's mohawk.

"Yeah, we know, but we like sticking up for our Pup Niki," the member asserted. Raphael sat down on the other side of Niki, thigh against thigh. He squeezed Niki's biceps, but didn't say anything. Luke came back, pulling the towel from around his waist as he sat down next to Raphael.

"They've been escorted from the gym. They were on a day pass which has been voided." He turned to Raphael. "And, you, Raphael, what were you thinking?"

"I wasn't. But nobody disrespects my Niki."

"Yeah," one of the other members chimed in.

"Besides, I was counting on all you guys to bail me out." Raphael laughed. "We 'fucking queers' kind of had them out numbered. How the hell did they get in here in the first place?"

"It doesn't matter, baby. They won't be back." Luke put his arm around his feisty locked cock boy and planted one on his cheek, Raphael-style.

On Monday

As luck would have it, Monday morning Raphael and Alex arrived in the lobby on their way to work at the same time. Ordinarily Alex would have shown some sign of affection – a hug, a shoulder squeeze, on occasion even a manly rub of the back of Raphael's shaved head. But today he just said "Hey, Raphael." As they rode up the elevator with several others, Raphael could tell Alex was still a little freaked out about Saturday. Apparently self-conscious about his confession. Maybe even more self-conscious than he had been Saturday. This would never do. Although their desks were on different floors, Raphael exited the elevator with Alex, who first looked surprised, then immediately guilty. He gave Raphael a weak smile.

"What's up?" Raphael asked as they stepped into the empty corridor. "What, no hug?"

"Raphael, I ..." Alex was at a loss for words. So, Raphael, being Raphael, leaned in and kissed him. That produced the desired effect. A big, shy smile.

"Alex, stop ... just stop beating yourself up. Stop questioning whether you said the right thing or not. What's important is you said it. You spoke from your heart ... and maybe your locked cock ... but the important thing is you were honest. Now, if you're going to be weird from now on, I'm going to be pissed. Okay? Just relax, and please, let's just take things as they come, and treat each other like we always have. Promise me." He looked intently into Alex's eyes. When Alex looked down at his feet, Raphael reached under his chin and lifted his face back up so their eyes met again. "Don't pull away, Alex."

"Okay. As usual, you're right and I'm being the weird one. The scared one. I'm sorry. I don't want to pull away from you, far from it. I just ... don't want to have damaged what we already have."

"You haven't, okay? I just kissed you ... at work. I've never done that before. So, I'd say we're good. No damage. Come get me for lunch, or I'll come find you and kiss you in front of your whole department, IT Boy!" At that, Raphael turned and headed for the stairs to avoid an awkward wait for the elevator. He knew how to make a dramatic exit.

As Alex watched him go, he sighed, then muttered, "Will I ever be as brave as you ..."

Then On Tuesday

As usual, everyone was gathered at Raphael and Luke's. The only change to the routine, of course, was that when Ricky showed up with dinner, he would no longer be sitting between Raphael and Alex. This night, just for fun, or maybe to further cement his status as Juan's locked cock leather boy, when Raphael opened the door, Ricky, for the second time, was already naked. Raphael gave a whoop! and pulled him through the door.

"Look, everyone! DoorDash has gone clothing optional. Finally!" Raphael and Alex took the bags from Ricky and began pulling dinner out and setting it up. Juan stood up and pulled Ricky into a hug. Then a kiss. Ricky sat down, cross legged, between Juan's legs.

"Did you ride over here naked this time?" Niki asked.

"No. Oh, shit!" Ricky jumped up and ran to the door, then returned with a backpack he set down just inside the door. "I stripped before I rang the bell, like before. Forgot. Man, if someone had made off with this, I *would* have ridden home naked."

"I'd have ridden with you," Niki offered. "Still will, if you're up for it."

"Niki, you have come such a long way," Raphael teased. "That cage has really brought out your inner nudist, hasn't it."

"Maayybee. Or, maybe it's just spending every night naked at home or here with you guys, or all but naked working behind the bar. Now that I think about it, clothes aren't much of a part of my life anymore."

"Well," Steve said, "we're all the better for it." He winked at Luke.

"So, you guys have gone clothes free at home, too?" Luke asked.

"Pretty much. Saves on laundry."

"What about you guys," Raphael addressed Juan and Ricky. "Do you have a dress code?"

"Funny you should ask," Juan replied, massaging the shaved sides of Ricky's now permanent high 'n tight. "Ricky and I have been talking and exploring how we want our relationship and our roles to grow. We're kind of in negotiations right now, so don't be surprised if we show up here looking more and more like you, Luke and Raphael. Ricky really wants me to collar him."

"That's cool," Raphael smiled. Maybe he was something of a role model for yet another budding leather boy. His cage grew a little heavier thinking about it.

"Oh, guys, guess what?" Ricky asked rhetorically. "I got another text from Mateo."

Alex and Raphael simultaneously went "Wooooooo." Then Alex asked, "What did he say?" Ricky went to his backpack and rummaged for his phone. He plopped back down between Juan's legs and retrieved the text.

"'Thanks again for the boxers. I like sleeping in them.'" Alex, Raphael and Niki all shrieked. "'I hope you're doing ok, amigo.'"

"Well, that clears up any remaining doubt, doesn't it? He likes sleeping in *your* boxers?" Greg said.

"Yeah," Alex agreed. "He's gay. So, what did you text back?"

"I just got the text a little while ago, so I haven't yet. I wanted to get your guys' opinion." And everyone had one, including Raphael.

"Why don't you invite him to the Powerhouse Saturday night, to see the premier of The Chastity Brothers?"

"Oh, yeah, that's this Saturday? Good idea," Juan encouraged.

"Can't guys. Mateo is only nineteen, and he's DACA, so he has to be careful, you know. No fake ID."

"Seriously?" Luke said. "That sucks. Well, listen, he's welcome here, if you think he can handle the dress code."

"That's not a bad idea, Luke," Greg offered. "He'd get to know charming, and strikingly handsome, gays who represent different lifestyles ... leather, puppy play and more traditional roles right away. Expand his horizons in a non-threatening environment."

"Oh, so now I'm 'traditional,' huh, Greg?" Alex snarked. "Dammit, that does it. Luke ... I want you to give me a mohawk tonight!"

"I'll be happy to, Alex, but only if your strikingly handsome husband gets one, too," Luke laughed. "But, Greg's right. Mateo's young, inexperienced and right now he's finally reaching out. He needs a friend, an ally ... a gay ally. A bar would be the worst place for him to get his feet wet. Here's what I think. Ricky, you should invite him to lunch or dinner with you and Juan. Let him see how happy you are with Juan. If he comes out to you, then invite him to a Tuesday dinner with us, explaining how we all live. If he's cool with that, bring him. If not, that's fine. At least he'll get to spend time with two amazing guys that he can relate to. If not then, then maybe over time, as he continues to think about you two, he'll contact you again for more."

"I think that makes perfect sense," Juan nodded. "Let him determine when he's ready to explore and to what extent. We don't know how much, if any, experience he's had."

"Okay, amigos. How's this sound, 'I'm doing great. Wanna have dinner with me and my boyfriend next week?"

"Perfect," Raphael smiled. "How could he resist?" Ricky was already thumbing his reply without waiting for any more input. As Alex and Raphael were collecting dishes after dinner, Ricky's phone chimed. Everyone stopped and focused on Ricky. He unlocked his phone, read the text and smiled. "He says, 'Just say when' followed with a smiley face."

"Good job," Juan squeezed Ricky's shoulders.

Alex, who was standing next to Raphael, both holding used dishes, put his free arm around Raphael's waist, pulled him close and said, "The family grows."

"Maybe," Luke offered. "We'll see. But Ricky it appears your memorable moving day wasn't such a bad idea, after all."

"Yeah," Ricky grinned. "I feel good."

Once dessert was eaten and the last of the wine was poured, Greg and Niki dressed to get Niki to work on time, then Ricky and Juan departed on Ricky's scooter. As Alex was pulling on his sweat pants he turned to Raphael.

"I read the memo today about the company holiday party. Are you guys going?"

"Oh, yeah," Raphael replied. "Luke, this year it's going to be at the Ohana floor in the Salesforce Tower!"

"You're kidding! That'll be very cool," Luke said.

"I'm not keen on company parties," Alex frowned.

"Oh, man, you guys have to go," Luke replied. "We had only been dating a few months when Raphael took me last year and everyone was so nice, and the food and entertainment were first class. Besides, guys, it'll be at the Ohana floor!"

"What is that?" Greg asked.

"It's the sixty-first floor of the Salesforce Tower," Raphael enthused. "A spectacular three-hundred-sixty degree view. You guys have to go. Seriously."

"Sounds pretty cool to me," Greg nudged. "Is it formal?"

"Nah," Raphael said. "Business casual. Alex can wear his favorite cocktail dress."

"Bitch," Alex scoffed. "I was thinking maybe my Halloween costume."

"I will if you will," Raphael countered. "You know I will."

"I have no doubt. So, you guys really think it'll be fun?"

"I promise," Luke assured. "With or without your cocktail dress."

⟨⟨◦———————◦⟩⟩

Forty-Two

INTRODUCING THE CHASTITY BROTHERS

RAPHAEL TEXTED ALEX ON Thursday morning with the news that Allyson had finished their costumes for their strip act. In fact, she'd finished them all, so they had several options to choose from for their premier. At his first opportunity Alex stopped by Raphael's cube to confer.

"So, when do you want to try them on?" Alex asked as he squatted down next to Raphael.

"I'll pick them up on my way home, so, tonight, or whenever. We should practice stripping each other, at some point, so we don't look awkward on stage."

"Why don't I just come with you. We can take care of it all tonight."

"Come get me when you're ready to leave."

Perhaps to show Raphael that everything was back to normal, Alex took Raphael's hand as soon as they exited the office building and headed home. 'Good,' Raphael thought. 'I'm glad that's behind us.'

Allyson had their outfits arranged in what she thought made the most sense visually. "So, there are twelve outfits, total," she explained. "Tank tops and V-necks, shorty-short-short shorts, two loincloths and two very mini-skirts. Plus, two mankinis as we discussed. Good luck deciding how you want to put them together."

"Everything looks great, Allyson," Alex cooed as he inspected each item. "Very sexy. And very functional with these little hidden Velcro tabs. It'll be easy to strip Raphael."

"Yeah, that's the sad part, Allyson," Raphael moaned. "They're so cute and sexy, but they won't be on us for long."

"Well, hon, that's the whole idea behind strip tease, isn't it? 'Take it off ... take it all off!'" Then she laughed and dangled one of the mankinis in Raphael's face. "You boys will look fabulous with and without them on."

"Don't be surprised if you get requests for more orders from our fans," Alex smiled. "These would make great club wear." Allyson laughed again and began putting everything in a shopping bag. Raphael took out his wallet and handed her several bills. She put them down without even counting.

"Depending on how popular we are, we may be back to you for more outfits in a couple of months," Raphael warned. "Alex has been coaching me, but I'm far from the dancer he is."

"Hon," Allyson countered, "with these outfits and your bodies, nobody is going to be judging your dance moves. Right Alex?"

"That's what I keep telling him, and that was before I saw these," Alex said, holding up the shopping bag, "You're the best." Alex and Raphael each hugged her, and headed out and headed home. They ended up at Alex and Greg's where they immediately stripped and started trying each item on. The only problem was everything looked great, so it was hard deciding what should go with what. They had fun ripping the shorts, loincloths and the miniskirts off each other while dancing their practiced routines. Even with the ordinary lighting in the living room, they noticed how their cages were visible under the mostly sheer fabrics. Under the spots at the bar, they would no doubt sparkle.

"You know," Raphael proposed, "Maybe we should not bother with thongs. One less thing to mess with, just keep the bottoms on a little longer before we strip each other completely naked. That way we tease them more with the cages semi-visible. What do you think?"

"Works for me. After all we are 'The Chastity Brothers' not the 'Thong Brothers.' So, I'm thinking we never want to be wearing the same thing together. Act One, me in shorts, you in loincloth. Act Two, me in miniskirt, you in shorts."

"I was thinking the same thing. You V-neck, me tank top, etcetera. If we ditch the thongs, your cage will be on display the whole time in this miniskirt. Maybe wear the mankini with the miniskirt."

"No, no, no. Where is your fashion sense, Raphael? Mankini with shorts. Jeez."

"Actually, I've never seen a mankini worn with anything, except maybe a smile."

"True. Maybe we save the mankini for mingling with the crowd after the performance."

"Oh," Raphael moaned, "I was hoping to mingle completely naked."

"Raphael, remember the immortal words of P.T. Barnum ..."

"Yeah?"

"'Always leave them wanting more.' We should only be naked while on stage. We should be modestly dressed in the mankinis when mingling. Hey, that's it!"

"That's what?"

"You want to collect tips for the donations, right?"

"Absolutely."

"Well, that's when we collect them ... while mingling in the crowd. If we're tossing our costumes into the crowd, and then are naked on stage, they have no way to 'stuff tips' in our costumes while we're dancing. But they can stuff plenty of cash into the mankinis when we're pressing flesh as it were, after the performance."

"Genius! Of course! The DJ can announce that before the performance. That way they know to expect us to mingle, and if we plant enough kisses in the crowd, and shake our cages and bare booties, nobody will be able to refuse us. Damn, Alex, you really are a showman."

"It's worth a try."

"I knew the mankini idea was a good one."

That's when the door opened and Greg made his entrance. "Wow. The only thing better than coming home to one naked man is coming home to two naked men!" He walked over and pulled Alex into a 'welcome home' kiss. Then, he turned and kissed Raphael, but without the embrace. Everyone was still testing boundaries, Raphael guessed.

"We've been trying out our Chastity Brothers costumes. What do you think?" Alex slipped on the miniskirt and twirled.

"I think you should wear that to dinner tonight," Greg smiled. "Or, do you think it's just a bit too matronly?"

"If it was any shorter, it'd be a belt," Raphael laughed as he climbed into one of the mankinis. "We're thinking of mingling with the crowd after each performance in these, so they have somewhere to stuff tips."

"Yeah, good idea," Greg kidded. "That ought to hold at least ten, twenty bucks. If you had pubic hair, it would be showing."

"Well," Alex countered, "what doesn't fit, we'll hold in our hands."

"I was kidding. I really do think you're on to something. Guys would love a chance to get cock to cage with you two. I can't think of a better way to supercharge your tips."

"Exactly," Raphael agreed.

"I have to say, I'm amazed at how into this strip act you two are, considering the first one was forced on you."

"We wouldn't be doing it if Brent hadn't agreed to let us make it a fundraiser. Besides, it'll be good therapy for Alex here, and his Entrenched Modesty Syndrome."

"Are you kidding me?" Alex protested. "Umm, the beach, Halloween, for Pete's sake. Do I have to go to work naked to convince you I'm over that?"

"Well, you know my answer to that."

"Yeah, I sure do ... 'I will if you will.' That's where I draw the line. At least for now." Both Greg and Raphael laughed at that subtle promise of someday, maybe someday.

While Greg headed into the bedroom, Raphael and Alex decided on their costumes for Saturday night, and Raphael stuffed his into his shoulder bag. He pulled his clothes on, gave Alex a hug and kiss and yelled goodbye to Greg, who came out in harness and nothing else to hug Raphael goodbye. Another reminder of how much influence Raphael and Luke had had on those caught in their orbit.

Just for fun, Raphael was wearing the mankini when Luke got home that evening. "Feeling overly modest?" Luke joked before pulling Raphael into a 'welcome me home' embrace and kiss.

"Sorry for not displaying my cage for you, Sir, but I wanted to show off one of our Chastity Brothers outfits."

"Very becoming, baby. Don't move. Let me get comfortable. then you can model all of them for me." Luke stripped, harnessed up and was back in a flash, where he found Raphael in one of the sheer loincloths. "Now that is sexy!"

"Thank you, sir. How big a tip do you think this will generate?" Raphael pushed Luke into a sitting position on the couch and sat on his lap. Luke reached under the flimsy loincloth and began massaging Raphael's balls. Raphael closed his eyes and moaned as Luke took one of his pierced nipples into his mouth and sucked. A drop of precum landed on his hand. He pulled it out, licked it clean and with his other hand, guided Raphael's head so their lips met, sharing the nectar. As their lips parted, Luke finally answered.

"I predict your tips will exceed the cover." Raphael smiled.

"I hope you're right. Let's eat, then shave and shower so you can fuck me. All this sexy modeling has made me horny."

"I'm not all that hungry yet," Luke grinned, wiggling his eyebrow. He stood, pulling up Raphael with him, then guided him into the bedroom. The shaving would have to wait, too.

Saturday night Luke and Raphael walked to Greg and Alex's, where the four of them got a Lyft to the bar. They arrived a little after nine-thirty, so they could be ready for their ten o'clock performance. They were met with a line outside. Since Alex and Raphael were both wearing caged cock t-shirts, the door attendant didn't even need to see the pass Brent had provided to them.

"We've been at occupancy since eight-thirty, guys, so you'd better put on a good show," he said. "I've never seen it like this before."

"Gosh, no pressure now," Alex groaned as they entered.

"You'll be great," Greg assured him. Raphael and Alex headed to Brent's office to check in with him, while Greg and Luke got in line at Niki's station. The place was indeed packed. Once they got to the head of the line, Niki had already spotted them and drawn their beers. Luke pulled out his wallet.

"On the house," Niki shouted over the music and crowd. "Since you're Chastity Brother's Posse."

"Busy night?" Luke shouted back as he took the beers from Niki.

"Insane. Brent's going nuts. He thinks maybe he overdid the social media promotion." Luke and Greg moved away from the bar with their beers.

"I'm glad it's like this, though," Luke said to Greg. "Alex and Raphael put a lot of work into this, so they deserve a full house."

"Well, they certainly have that. And, then some. The show's about to start and you saw the line out front. There are going to be some disappointed men."

"Yeah. We'd have been out of luck if we weren't 'posse.' Luke and Greg clicked glasses at that thought. Luke's phone vibrated a text. He pulled it out and read. "Damn. Ricky and Juan are stuck in line. Let me go talk to the bouncer." A few minutes later, just before showtime, he returned with two honorary posse members. Hugs and kisses were traded.

"How did you manage that?" Greg asked Luke.

"Ask Ricky."

Ricky grinned and put his arm around Juan's waist. "Luke had me show him my cage ... to prove I'm one of the Chastity Brothers. And I said this handsome man is my owner."

"So, are you going to be up on stage tonight, Ricky?" Greg joked.

"Only if I'm invited," Ricky joked back. That gave both Luke and Greg an idea. Their eyes met and eyebrows danced. "Oh, shit!" Ricky responded. "I was kidding. I was kidding."

Luke put an arm around Ricky's shoulders and squeezed. "Don't worry. Tonight's program is all planned out. Right, Greg?" Ricky didn't seem convinced and gave Juan a 'please protect me, Sir' look. Juan leaned down and planted a kiss on the shaven side of his head. Then he looked at Greg and smiled. Ricky put his other arm around Juan's waist in a not so subtle plea for protection. That's when the DJ faded the music and announced the beginning of the show.

And what a show it was. Alex started out in V-neck and shorts, Raphael in tank top and loincloth. The crowd loved what they saw even before any stripping had started. Once their shirts were off and tossed into the crowd, the excitement grew. Raphael's back ink generated lots of cheers. But, of course, it was when Raphael ripped Alex's shorts off that things really got crazy. Everyone wanted him to rip Raphael's loincloth off, too, but Alex put that off just to torture everyone. Finally, ten minutes in, off it came, and the crowd had what it came for, two naked, caged, sweaty, dancing bodies to admire and lust after. If only they could touch them. But at least the Chastity Brothers were able to touch each other, and touch they did. They kissed. They hugged, they faux humped one another while dancing. At one point, Alex squatted down and licked each of Raphael's perky, sweaty ass cheeks. That got a rise from the crowd, some of the whom had been waiting three hours for the show. They certainly didn't feel cheated. If only ...

And then, as the music lowered, Raphael reached down and picked up a small ball of something and handed part of it to Alex. Then the two unfurled the balls and slipped into their mankinis in unison, turned their backs to shake their booties one last time on stage before walking to the end of the stage and down the stairs. The 'if only' moment had arrived as the DJ announced the opportunity to thank the Chastity Brothers in person. Luke and Greg moved through the crowd to their men. They each made a show of stuffing bills under the straps of the mankinis, where they'd be visible to the crowd. Raphael and Alex proceeded to mingle, smiling, kissing, hugging and best of all, collecting tips. Greg and Luke were never too far away, just in case someone tried to get too friendly. The mingling could have gone on for a long time, but, as preplanned, the DJ amped up the music after ten minutes, and the Chastity Brothers headed back to Brent's office/dressing room.

Five minutes later, they were back, in shorts ... street safe shorts, and caged cock tees. Their posse had both water bottles and beers ready for them.

"That couldn't have gone better," Greg enthused. "They loved you."

"Yeah, everyone seemed to like it," Raphael agreed. "Best of all, they were pretty generous, too."

"What was the haul?" Luke asked.

"Over five hundred bucks," Alex beamed. Juan reacted with a shrill whistle.

"That's awesome, amigos," Ricky chimed in.

"Just wait until Ricky gets up there with you," Luke teased. "He volunteered."

"No, I didn't! I did *not!*"

"That's not how I heard it," Greg laughed. Ricky ducked behind Juan.

"I'm happy," Raphael smiled, putting an arm around Alex's shoulders, "If the second show tonight does as well, along with the cover, we should pull in between two and three thousand. Not bad for a night's work, eh, 'brother?'"

"Not even that. More like an hour's work." Alex planted one on Raphael's cheek.

Actually, between the two shows and the mingling, and the dressing again, it was just over an hour's work. And the total take, with cover, was over three thousand dollars. Everyone, including Brent, had a very good night.

Forty-Three

I Can See for Miles

LATER THAT WEEK, LUKE and Raphael were in position in the shower, Luke shaving Raphael's high 'n tight to regulation specifications. Raphael was silent, eyes closed, enjoying the sensation of the warm water, the glide of the razor over the sides and back of his head, Luke's legs wrapped around his waist. The feel of Luke's breath on his denuded scalp as Luke concentrated on his task.

Once Luke had finished the shaving, he untangled himself from Raphael in order to reach the clippers so he could touch up Raphael's landing strip. All routine now, but still erotic, especially with the memory of how this was the act that began their increasingly challenging displays of devotion to one another. Their dares.

As they changed places so Raphael could shave Luke's mohawk, Raphael cleared his throat and spoke. "I've been thinking."

"I thought I smelled something burning." Raphael bonked the top of Luke's head with the soggy wash cloth.

"Okay, fine. Never mind."

"No, tell me. Tell me, baby."

"Um, well, you remember we sort of told Alex we'd have sex with him?"

"I remember. It wasn't 'sorta.' We said we would. So, we will."

"Well, they put out the list of birthdays for the month at the office, and Alex's birthday is coming up. The sixteenth. I thought we could surprise him with a sexstravaganza for his birthday."

"Sexstravaganza?"

"Yeah, look it up."

"I will. Meanwhile, enlighten me."

"I thought it might be fun to give Alex the kind of experience you gave me that night in Jake's dungeon. Without the piercing, and of course, he's already caged. But, if Greg's up for it, and I bet he would be, the three of us could 'torture' Alex. You know, blindfolded, in that suspension harness thing, playing with his body."

"Hmmm. Interesting. I like that it's more a play thing than a romantic sex experience. He's in love enough with you already."

"So you say. I still say we love each other, not we're 'in love,' but yeah, sex play. I haven't thought it through completely, but I wanted to see what you thought."

"Well, I like it so far. First, Greg has to agree. Second, Jake has to agree. Let me think about it, and I'll check with Jake. Why don't you check with Greg. The sixteenth?"

"Yeah. Of course, we don't have to do it right on his birthday. Greg may already have planned something. I'll text him tomorrow."

"Something to think about, baby. It's a good idea. Speaking of Alex and Greg, I assume we're all going together to your company holiday party this weekend."

"You are correct, Sir. Alex and I have been working on it."

"Working on it? What does that mean?"

"Well, Alex, the world-famous costumer, decided he should be in charge of what we're wearing. With a little input from me, of course."

"Should I be worried? How much input did he have for the Halloween costumes?"

"Not to worry, Sir. Nothing like that. I think you'll be pleased, amused even."

"Spill, baby. What am I in for?"

"I'm sworn to secrecy. All I will say is Greg will be more surprised than you." At that, Raphael licked the space behind Luke's right ear. Slowly. With a low moan. As he reached around from behind and found each of Luke's nipples. Then, reaching lower, his now upright cock.

"You can't distract me that easily, baby." Raphael began gently massaging Luke's erection with his right hand as he gently squeezed his nipple with his left hand. Then, for good measure, licked the back of Luke's freshly shaven skull. "Okay ... maybe you can. Nap time, baby ..."

Saturday evening, Alex and Greg arrived at Raphael and Luke's at six-thirty, as Alex had instructed. As usual Raphael and Luke were naked and harnessed. Alex and Greg each carried a carry-on bag, which they took to the bedroom where, out of habit, they both stripped and left their street clothes as well. They returned to the living room where Raphael had an open bottle of Zin and an artichoke dip waiting. After a cheery toast, they settled into their usual spots.

"So, Alex, I understand you are our dresser for tonight's performance."

"I am, Luke. I think you will be pleased. I can't take all the credit. Raphael helped a lot."

"Oh, really?" Luke looked suspiciously at Raphael. "He has been giving you all the credit for this dare."

"It's not really a dare, Luke. Just an opportunity for me to keep my costuming skills sharp."

"Costuming? Is this a costume party?" Greg asked. "Nobody told me."

"No, dear, it's business semi-formal/casual. You know ... San Francisco techie fashionable."

"What the hell does that mean?"

"I have no idea, but you know it when you see it. I decided, and Raphael agreed, that we should, well, make a statement."

"Oh, god. I'm flashing on Halloween."

"That's funny, Greg," Raphael laughed. "Luke said the same thing. No. You can relax. Nobody will see your cock. Unless they ask nicely, I guess."

"Maybe we should stop talking about it, and jump right into it," Alex suggested. "Raphael, let's get dressed first, then we'll dress Luke and Greg. You guys relax, we'll be back in a sec."

"Yeah," Greg smiled. "We've heard that one before. Luke, is there a Warriors game on tonight? We can probably watch the whole thing."

"Ten minutes, Mr. Smart Ass. Time me."

Fifteen minutes and forty-eight seconds later, Alex and Raphael opened the bedroom door and made their entrance.

"I was right," Greg pronounced. "It is a costume party."

"Greg, this is not a costume. This, my dear, is what fashion forward looks like." Alex and Raphael joined hands and twirled each other much as they had done, among many other things, on stage in their now legendary strip act. Except now they were clothed. Remarkably so. Each wore black satin knickers with knee high socks, one green, one red, for the holiday of course. They were each wearing one of Raphael's caged cock dress shirts and a bow tie, Alex in a green tie, Raphael's was red.

"Very ... festive!" Luke said. "Where did you find knickers?"

"There's an app for that," Alex laughed. "But, you two won't be wearing knickers."

"Thank goodness," Greg exhaled. "I was worried there for a minute."

"Come in the bedroom, so we can dress you two," Alex commanded. Luke and Greg rose and followed their never boring partners into the bedroom, where there, on the bed, were laid out knee length socks, two turtle-neck sweaters, one teal and one salmon-colored to mesh with the bow ties, and ... two kilts. Luke's family tartan and a black pinstripe. Luke bent over laughing.

"Not to worry, Greg. No knickers for you!"

"When will I learn to keep my mouth shut?" Greg picked up the pin-stripe kilt and looked it over. He looked at Alex and asked, "Seriously?" Alex and Raphael nodded.

"You might want to start with the socks," Alex suggested matter of factly. Greg sighed, sat on the end of the bed and did just that.

"Which sweater is mine," Luke asked.

"The salmon one," Raphael said as he picked it up and began helping Luke out of his harness and into the sweater. "It complements my tie."

"Of course. How silly of me." Luke then sat and began pulling on his socks. Once both men were dressed, Raphael and Alex stepped back and assumed the position of runway judges.

"What do you think, Raphael?" Alex asked, rubbing his chin. "Was this a good idea?"

"They. Look. Mahvelous!" was Raphael's decision.

"Agreed. We've done it again!"

"Greg, let me get a better look," Luke said, stepping back himself. "Hmmmm. Well ... Greg, turn around for me."

"Stop it, kilt boy. I look ridiculous and you know it."

"Greg, you look fierce. I mean it. These boys know their stuff."

"Yeah, right. Whatever. Alex, you said this wasn't a dare, but I'm going to make you a bet."

"Oh yeah?"

"For every snide remark I get tonight, for every critical look even, I get a blow job from you. All within a month. Thirty snarks, thirty blow jobs."

"Okay. I'll see your bet, and I'll raise you one, Mr. Smarty Kilt. For every compliment you get, you have to unlock and blow *me*."

"What?! Whoa! Alex!" Raphael exploded. "Really?" He and Luke exchanged knowing looks.

"Hey, Raphael, I'm a big boy. I've matured. Evolved. I bet I can handle being unlocked two or three times in month." Alex looked at Greg for validation. Greg still didn't look too amused.

Raphael kissed Alex's cheek. Then he turned to Luke, "I like my locked cock brother more and more every day."

"Both of them," Luke agreed. "Shall we head out and see just how many blow jobs we can rack up for them?" Greg shook his head, then stepped in front of the mirror to judge for himself. As he turned this way and that, Luke elbowed Raphael and both smiled. They were betting on Alex to win.

As the nattily dressed foursome was piling into the Lyft, Luke leaned over and whispered to Raphael, "When we get out of the car, play along with me. We're going to give Alex a leg up." Raphael nodded. Fifteen minutes later, as they climbed out of the car in front of the Salesforce tower, Luke innocently turned to Alex and asked, "Alex, you've been to the rooftop park here at the transit center, right?" Well, maybe not so innocently.

"No, not yet. Greg said it was pretty cool, but we still haven't made it down here, yet."

"Well, we're here now. Let's be fashionably not quite on time and take a stroll around the park. I haven't seen it at night yet, myself."

"Yeah, let's do!" Raphael enthused, as requested. "I haven't seen it at night, either." Then, without waiting for further discussion, he took Alex's hand and headed into the ground level of the behemoth transit center. Luke looked at the Greg, reached out his hand, and said, "Come on. Just like old times." Greg shook his head, but took Luke's hand as the two followed the boys in knickers into the center. Before they even made it to the three-story escalator, they got their first hit.

"Nice kilts!"

A tight smile crossed Greg's face. Not surprisingly, it was only the first of many. As the four strolled around the park, they rarely traveled more than thirty feet before an accolade was offered.

'Love the kilts! ... Awesome, dudes ... Rockin' the kilts ... and frequently ... Nice kilts!' There were even a few comments directed at their escorts, such as 'Whoa, knickers? You is stylin,' men.'

At about the halfway point in their walk, Luke asked Alex, "What do you think of the park, Alex?"

"It's beautiful. Kind of surreal ... the setting, but it's really cool."

Luke then asked, "Have you been counting?"

"Oh, yes. Twenty-eight. So far." Alex turned to look back at Greg and Luke and smiled. A big smile. Then he licked his lips.

Greg turned to Luke and said, "You bastards. That's why you wanted us to come up here, isn't it?" Before Luke could respond, an older couple walking in the opposite direction passed by as the woman said, "Lovely kilts, boys."

"Twenty-nine!" Alex grinned.

"Actually, it's thirty, Alex. You missed one when were on the ground floor." Luke couldn't help himself. He reached over and pulled Greg into a hug. "You brought this on yourself, 'kilt boy.'"

By the time they'd completed the circuit of the park, the count stood at thirty-four. As they approached the foot bridge to the Salesforce Tower Greg earnestly asked, "Is it always like this?"

"To be honest," Luke said, "Not quite like this. I think we got more than the usual affirmations because there were two of us in kilts, and maybe also because we were accompanied by two beautiful creatures in knickers and bow ties. They helped attract more than the usual attention. But, yeah, two, three, four times a day someone lets me know they like seeing me in a kilt. You'll get used to it."

"What does that mean? Oh, you mean for tonight."

"Maaaybee. Or maybe, now that you've experienced one of the benefits of kilt wearing, you just might give up pants, too."

"Benefits? What other benefits? And, not likely."

"I guess we'll see, won't we? Alex, what do you think about a kilted Greg?"

"I think he looks adorable. You both do. We all do." He planted a kiss on Greg as they stepped into the elevator and began their ascent to the Ohana Floor and the festivities awaiting them.

"Okay, that was a self-directed compliment," Raphael offered, "since Alex is the one who dressed us."

"Well, based on our park focus group, I'd say he deserves it," Luke smiled. "I've learned to always bow to Alex's fashion sense."

"You're welcome." Alex grinned. The elevator door opened and there before them was a fabulous party in the making, with an even more fabulous view across the room. The four immediately walked to the nearest spot along the continuous floor to ceiling glass.

"Wow."

"Didn't I tell you?" Raphael nudged Alex. "Aren't you glad you came?"

"This is awesome. Yeah, I'm glad. For a lot of reasons. You were right."

"Let's walk around and check things out," Luke suggested. "The view isn't going anywhere." He took Raphael's hand and began to stroll, with Alex and Greg following. As they worked their way around the floor that circled the entire building Raphael introduced Luke to several colleagues he hadn't met before. They encountered a few who did remember Luke from the previous year's party. Alex had a bigger task, as none of them had met Greg, though some had heard about him. Alex continued counting as several people complimented both on their fashion statements.

When asked, more than once, if he was Scottish, Greg replied, "Just enough." That always garnered a smile. The four made their way to one of the several bars, where they happily obtained glasses of sparkling wine. "Schramsberg," Greg noted. "They don't scrimp, do they?"

"No, dear," Alex teased with a smile. "And to think you'll get to enjoy it twice." Raphael burst out laughing.

"Yeah, Alex, you'd better start collecting on that challenge tonight. You've got a long way to go."

Luke, wanting to steer the conversation in a more socially acceptable direction, raised his glass, "A toast. To three of the most important men in my life. I love sharing moments like this with you." They clinked flutes, making sure to make eye contact with each clink, then sipped. They continued on, sampling food here, then there. They chatted with colleagues, meeting a new spouse or partner here and there, stopped to enjoy another perspective on the view now and then, and found more sparkling wine once their glasses were empty. This time Alex proposed a toast.

"To my husband Greg, who always resists, but always ends up 'rocking the kilt' in the end of every wild idea I throw his way." Clink, clink.

"May I join this toast?" It was Cynthia, the CEO, who had walked up to the group. "Raphael, you look smashing tonight, as do you, Alex. And, Luke, right?"

"Yes, Ma'am."

Oh, please, call me Cynthia. You look astonishing, Luke. Is that a family tartan?"

"It is. In fact, this was my grandfather's. Raphael was able to arrange for me to have it."

"That's our Raphael for you. And, Alex, this must be your husband, Greg?"

"Yes." Alex seemed slightly awed that Cynthia remembered Greg's name.

"Yes, I'm Greg. It's so very nice to meet you, Cynthia. Thank you for inviting us to this amazing party. It's spectacular."

"You're very welcome, Greg. Thank you all for making it a more memorable event. I appreciate how much thought you put into your fashionable attire. I wish more San Franciscans were as stylish as you four."

"There you are," said a woman dressed in a black pencil dress and what was probably a genuine emerald pendant. She stopped next to Cynthia and put her free arm around Cynthia's waist. She, too, had a wine flute in her other hand.

"Alex, Greg, this is my wife, Patricia. Patricia, you remember Raphael and Luke."

"I do indeed. But, Raphael ... and Luke, you've both changed your hairstyles, and Luke, you've grown a handsome beard, haven't you?" Raphael and Luke both nodded.

"Great to see you again, Patricia," Raphael said. "I love that dress."

"Thank you dear, but I must say, the four of you are absolutely brilliant! Aren't they, Cynthia?"

"I was just saying exactly that. You can see why we're so successful. We have the most creative and, dare I say, bold people working with us. Not everyone could pull off this look."

"Actually, Cynthia, the credit for tonight really goes to Alex. He was our fashion guru," Raphael smiled, then bowed toward Alex, who actually blushed.

"Good to know, Raphael. Patricia, we should consult Alex before the next symphony gala, don't you think?"

"Absolutely."

"We should mingle, but before I go, I did want to tell you how proud I am of your charity work, Raphael and Alex." Alex and Raphael looked at each other, eyes widening.

"Excuse me?" Raphael asked, his voice cracking.

"Yes. A little bird told me about your fund-raising endeavor for the Trevor Project. Very impressive. And I wanted to remind you to meet with HR. We match contributions to approved charities, and the Trevor Project is certainly one of them. They can help you with the paperwork. Please don't miss out on that opportunity." She smiled at each of them, took Patricia's hand and turned away to mingle.

"That was interesting," Luke exhaled.

"No shit!" Alex said. "Oh my god, Raphael! I didn't know Cynthia was gay!"

"You didn't? Everyone knows."

"Except. For. Me!"

"Well now you do. The real question is, how much does she know about our 'charity work?' And, more to the point how did she find out?"

"She said 'a little bird.'"

"Yeah, and I think I know where to find this little bird. Luke, you and Greg mingle. Alex and I are going to go strangle a little bird." Raphael turned on his heels, and Alex jogged to catch up. They did about a half circuit of the Ohana Floor before Raphael said, "Aha. Target spotted. Follow me." He walked up to two young men standing at the window wall, looking out at the bay.

"Clifford!" Raphael greeted one of them with forced enthusiasm. Clifford turned away from the window. "Raphael. Hi!. And, uh..."

"Alex. I'm Alex, in IT."

"Right, sorry. This is Ryan. Cool pants, guys." Raphael and Alex shook hands with Ryan.

"Knickers, Clifford. They're knickers. So, Clifford. You didn't happen to say anything to Cynthia about Alex and my fundraising activities for the Trevor Project, did you?" Clifford suddenly looked pale. Raphael cocked his head in an unstated question.

"Umm ..."

"Clifford, how much did you tell her?"

"Oh ... Raphael, I may be the 'intern' but I'm not stupid. I just said you two won a dance contest and they liked you so much they invited you back to perform more shows to raise money for the Trevor Project."

"And, who was the 'they?'"

"I just said one of the gay bars." Raphael and Alex said nothing and waited. "Guys, I didn't say you were stripping or anything. Jeez, give me some credit. Look, I'm sorry if I fucked up, but I thought she'd be pleased that you were doing charity work on your own time." Another pause with no reaction from Raphael or Alex. "Look, I'm sorry." He genuinely looked sorry. Ryan looked very uncomfortable.

"So, you're telling us everything you said. The Powerhouse wasn't mentioned. Stripping wasn't mentioned. Locked cocks weren't mentioned."

"I swear."

"Okay, then," Raphael relaxed. "Remember, Clifford. What happens outside of work is private. I have no problem with you watching us strip, with you knowing our cocks are caged. That means you're contributing to a good cause. But it stays private. Okay?"

"Sure. Okay. I promise." Clifford finally smiled again. "But, can I say this one last thing since we're not really in the office?"

"What's that, Clifford?"

"You guys are fucking hot together." Ryan did a spit take all over Clifford's sport coat.

Raphael took Alex's hand, and as they turned to leave, he said over his shoulder, "Thanks, but we already knew that."

Forty-Four

NIKI WHO NOW?

LATER, AS THEY RODE down the elevator after saying their goodbyes to various colleagues, Greg pulled out his phone to summon a Lyft. They only had to wait a couple of minutes by the time they reached sea level. The word was probably out that there was a good-sized party coming to a close. Luke held the back door open as Raphael, Alex and Greg slid in the back, then he climbed in next to the driver, who took one look at Luke and said, "Nice kilt, man!"

Greg groaned.

Luke turned to say, "Alex, you can add eight more to the count ... while you and Raphael were off bird hunting."

"Thanks, Luke, but I decided to cap the count at sixty. That's two per day, and I think that's plenty, don't you Greg?"

"Yeah. Sure. Sounds good. I guess I should be grateful, huh?"

"Oh, come on. You know we both love it. I'll ... I'll drink lots of cranberry juice." Raphael let out a whoop as Luke turned back to face forward.

"So, Greg," Luke continued, "how many kilts should we order tomorrow when I come over to help you shop online?"

"Oh, is that what we're doing, Luke?" After a moment's pause, "Well, maybe one." Raphael whooped again. "I'm not going pants free ... I'm still wearing pants to work, but ... this was eye-opening, I have to admit." Alex reached up under Greg's kilt and grabbed his cock as he turned toward Greg. Greg smiled and turned to Alex as the two fell into a two-mile kiss. Raphael let out a long, audible sigh. This had, indeed, been an eventful evening.

"Have you heard from Jake?" Raphael asked Luke Sunday afternoon as he was putting the finishing touches on the raspberry topped cheesecake he'd decided to make for Tuesday's dinner. Sunday was about the only day he had time lately to indulge his cooking skills. Luke was paying bills at the dining table, not nearly as much fun as what Raphael was doing.

"Let me check again." Luke unlocked his phone. "Yeah, he says just say when, he has nothing planned for the dungeon."

"Perfect. Greg was just planning dinner out, but he's more than willing to reschedule that if we want to kidnap Alex on the sixteenth. He sounded pretty enthusiastic, actually."

"No doubt. I think he's really enjoying how our influence is rubbing off on Alex. I'm willing to bet they'll both be naked at Folsom next year."

"Should we bet 'drinking from the tap?'"

"Baby, I'll drink from the tap, any time, any day, no betting required."

"Then, get in here, Sir, I have to pee!" So, Luke did, and Raphael did. Followed by an herbal tea kiss. A really, really long one.

Luke had resumed opening envelopes when he said, "Huh. What's this?" Raphael walked up behind him and put his hands on his shoulders to see what 'this' was. It was a formal looking stylish envelope addressed in calligraphy to both of them. Luke slit it open and pulled out an announcement card and read it. "How bizarre." Raphael took it from Luke's hand and read it again.

"Why is Niki inviting us to dinner with a formal invitation?" Luke asked rhetorically. Raphael handed it back to Luke, then sat down in one of the chairs.

"Jeez, I hope he doesn't have bad news of some kind. Or, maybe he got a promotion at the bar ... that's probably it! He'd be pretty jazzed about that. Or, maybe Steve got a promotion."

"Well, I'm glad I found it today, mixed in with the bills. The invitation is for tomorrow. Which makes sense since that's one of his days off. Should we call or text to find out what's up now?" Raphael pondered a moment.

"Let's not. Since he chose an old school way of inviting us, let's wait. Where's dinner?"

"Poesia. Italian, and not cheap. It must be good news of some kind."

"Luke, on second thought let's text Steve and find out what's up."

"Don't, baby. Remember how we drove Niki crazy the week before Obedience School? We owe it to him to let him have his way over this ...

whatever 'this' is." Raphael sighed. Then stood up and kissed Luke on the back of the neck, just below the tail end of his mohawk.

"You're right. That's fine. I don't need to sleep tonight anyway."

"Drama queen."

"Said the man who only wears skirts."

"Kilts! And, I do it because of you, remember." On cue, Raphael reached up and rubbed his steel collar and smiled. He didn't even have to say why as he returned to the kitchen.

"Hey, baby, you distracted me with your bladder. If we're going to celebrate Alex's birthday this week, we need to come up with a plan."

"Agreed. We don't want to be fumbling around and end up making a lame mess of it. What you did with me was amazing. I mean ... look at me now."

"Look at both of us. We're not the same men today. Any regrets, baby?" Raphael returned from the kitchen and leaned down to whisper in Luke's ear.

"Is that a trick question, Sir?" Luke shook his head no. "I would think the tattoo above my locked cock says it all, Sir. Now, Sir, I've finished my cheesecake. May I suck you off? Or, do you have more bills to pay?"

"The bills can wait." Luke stood, picked up his locked cock boy and carried him to their bed for a 'nap.'

Monday evening Luke and Raphael shaved and showered each other as soon as they got home, in order to be ready for Niki's mysterious dinner date. They then walked to Poesia, where they found Niki and Steve already seated, a bottle of sparkling wine chilling. As soon as Luke and Raphael were seated a waiter approached, looked knowingly at Niki, who nodded. The waiter pulled the wine bottle from the ice, opened it, poured, then retreated.

Niki raised his glass, the other three hoisted theirs. As they held them in anticipation of a toast, Raphael looked intently into Niki's eyes as Luke was looking at Steve, seeking a clue. Steve smiled knowingly, yet mischievously. Finally, Raphael said, "Say something!"

"I have an announcement to make," Niki teased.

"My arm's getting tired," Raphael prodded.

"I'd like to introduce your future brother-in-law, Steven Phillips." Finally, glasses clinked.

"You're getting married?!"

"Congratulations, Niki, Steve," Luke enthused. "I'm so happy for you."

"When? When's the date?"

"We haven't set one yet, Raphael," Steve said. "Soon. Very soon, right Niki?"

"Yes!" Niki grinned, wiggling in his chair. If he'd been wearing his tail, it would be wagging out of control. "There's something else I want to share." He reached into his sport coat pocket and handed Luke and Raphael each a business card, which read:

Niki Maricel Raphael Angel Malaluan-Phillips
PupTender Extraordinare
San Francisco CA

Raphael looked up at Niki, open mouthed, literally. Niki beamed. Luke put his arm around Raphael's shoulders and confirmed the obvious, "You changed your name?"

"Yes, Luke. I did it so I'd be ready when we got married. I wanted to honor the people who rescued me, and gave me the life I love so much. And, I wanted to take Steve's name, too."

"God, Niki, I think I'm going to cry," Raphael sniffed. "Wait 'til Mama hears."

"She already knows. I told her first. Like you, she cried. She said, 'You've made me so proud. You've always been my favorite son.'"

"She did not!" Raphael protested, suddenly laughing.

"Well, the first part's true. She said she was very proud that I would take her name as my second name. And, Malaluan as part of my last name. Then she made me cry."

"Yeah, she does that. Niki, I am so honored." Raphael was gazing into Niki's eyes. "Does Angel know?"

"Mama's probably told him, but we haven't talked yet. I want them at the wedding."

"Of course." Raphael looked at Steve. "Best brother-in-law ever! I know I've always called you family, but now it'll be legal, too!" He raised his glass to Steve, and the two clinked glasses again.

"I can't imagine marrying into a better, more loving, more interesting family," Steve toasted. "It's kind of a dream come true." At that point the waiter approached, poured more wine and handed out menus. Dinner, as delicious as it was, was doomed to play second fiddle to Niki and Steve's announcement.

It turned out the cheesecake was not the highlight of Tuesday night's dinner. As hard as it was for him, Raphael waited until everyone was eating to ask, "Niki, Steve, do you have something you would like to share with everyone?"

"Subtle, baby," Luke grinned. Raphael ignored him.

"Go ahead," Steve deferred to Niki.

"Steve and I are getting married, guys!" Alex, Greg, Juan and Ricky all jumped up and climbed over Luke and Raphael to hug the betrothed. A few kisses were tossed in as well.

Once everyone was seated again, Alex said, "Finally, we won't be the only married old fogies in the family. When's the date?"

"Soon," Steve replied. "We haven't finalized the details yet."

"Guys, Niki also legally changed his name," Raphael announced. "Henceforth you can call him Niki Maricel Raphael Angel Malaluan-Phillips!"

"That's a mouthful," Greg laughed. "Don't they have a character count limit?"

"Nope," Niki beamed. "When I explained why so many names, the judge just smiled. She said, 'Good for you.'" Everyone went back to eating for a moment, then Ricky twisted around between Juan's legs. He reached up with his left hand and toyed with the 2-gauge PA poking out of Juan's foreskin as he looked up coyly at him.

"When we get married, I'm going to take your last name, Papito." Juan smiled, reached down and brushed Ricky's regulation high 'n tight.

"Oh, is that so? I guess I must have missed the proposal, mijo." Ricky giggled and turned back around to face the room.

"Raphael?" Ricky asked. "How long have you and Luke been engaged?" Raphael looked at Luke as he swallowed his bite of gnocchi.

"Hmm, almost a year, isn't it, Luke?" Luke nodded. Raphael, of course, knew exactly how long it had been. To the day.

"Maybe you should make it a double ceremony," Ricky innocently suggested. Juan put his hand on Ricky's shoulder as if to silence him. Alex, on the other hand, raised up on his knees as he put his plate down and clapped his hands.

"Out of the mouths of babes," he exclaimed. "You should do it!" He looked at Luke, his eyes begging for an affirmative answer. Then he bent down to Raphael next to him, "Could there be a better time?"

"Well," Raphael said after a pause, "we don't want to horn in on Niki and Steve's big day."

"Are you kidding me?" Niki shouted. "Raffie! Nothing would make me happier!"

Steve put down his plate, stood up and walked over to Raphael, then bent down to say, "Don't let your little brother down." He looked up at Luke and continued, "How about it, Luke?"

"Well," Luke deadpanned. "These days a year *is* an awful long time to be engaged, don't you think, baby?"

"Sure is," Ricky asserted. Juan gave up and just squeezed Ricky's shoulders in affirmation. Raphael got up and bounded over to Luke, jumped in his lap and kissed the daylights out of him. Suddenly, it wasn't just Niki and Steve's moment any longer. Not that anyone, including Niki and Steve, minded. When Luke finally released his hold on Raphael, Raphael got up and sat down in front of Ricky, put his hands on the shaven sides of his head and pulled him into a similar breath defying kiss. When he released Ricky's lips, he looked up at Juan and winked.

"Thank you, Ricky." He brushed his hand across Ricky's fabulous abs. "Your beauty is exceeded only by your uncanny wisdom." He kissed Ricky again on the forehead, then returned to Alex's side, where it was Alex's turn to embrace him.

"What just happened?" Raphael asked the room. "Are we really getting married?"

"Yes, you are!" Alex confirmed. "And I insist that I get to be your wedding planner!"

"Here we go," Greg said.

"What?" Juan asked, looking at Greg.

"If they let Alex plan their wedding, well, let's just say, it won't be boring."

"We were thinking of a simple ceremony at City Hall," Steve stated.

"Oh, no, that will never do," Alex argued. "City Hall?"

"Have you been to City Hall?" Luke asked.

"No ..."

"I think that's perfect," Raphael insisted. "Alex, City Hall is amazing. It's like Versailles. Well, kinda. It's beautiful."

"Yes, it is," Steve continued. "Besides, we wanted to honor the thousands of gay men and women who were married there in 2004, in defiance of the laws. They helped move the country to marriage equality. We owe them."

"Exactly," Luke agreed.

"I think you've been overruled," Greg said to Alex. "Are you ready to resign?"

"Hell, no. Four of my brothers are getting married. I still get to dress them. And, I'm in charge of the reception. I won't take no for an answer."

"I see what you meant," Juan laughed. Greg nodded helplessly. "Reception? What's happening?" Raphael whined. "Alex, relax." "Raphael, this will be our wedding present to you four. Right Greg?" Greg sat back, sighed and said, "Wake me when it's over."

Forty-Five

A DARE WITHIN A DARE

BETWEEN THE EXCITEMENT OF his and Luke's impending wedding with Niki and Steve, and coordinating details with Greg and Luke regarding Alex's birthday kidnapping, Raphael was having trouble concentrating at work. Hell, he was having trouble sleeping. Since he always slept wrapped in Luke's arms, that meant Luke was having trouble sleeping, too.

"Baby, you need to relax. Everything is going to work out fine," Luke said as he pushed Raphael's head under the shower head for a last rinse during their morning going to work shower. "I don't think you stopped moving all night."

"Sorry, Luke ... Sir. Maybe I should sleep on the floor, like Niki does sometimes," Raphael said as he grabbed their towels and handed one to Luke.

"Huh uh. I won't be able to sleep if can't feel you breathing. Besides, I think everything is set for tomorrow night's seduction of Alex, so that shouldn't be worrying you. Going three days without sex is probably what's really messed up our sleeping."

"Hey, that was your idea. You wanted us to be especially horny. I know I'm primed." He pulled Luke into a damp full body embrace and kiss. "And ... from the feel of that growing erection you are, too."

"Feels good, baby. Don't move ..." Luke moaned.

"Any other time, I'd suck you dry right here and now, but it's for a good cause, right?" Raphael pushed Luke away and headed to the bedroom for his dreaded, but necessary street clothes. His favorite part of the morning was over.

When Alex stopped by Raphael's desk that afternoon, Raphael casually asked him if he and Greg had special plans for his birthday the following day.

"How'd you know?" Alex responded.

"Duh. It's right there in the company forum." He pointed to his monitor.

"Oh, yeah. I should read that more often."

"Yeah, you'd be surprised what you're missing," Raphael said only somewhat cynically. "So anyway ...?"

"Oh, Greg's taking me out to dinner. I don't know where ... he's planning a surprise."

"That's cool," Raphael smiled convincingly. "Luke and I will take you out for a celebratory drink this weekend, maybe."

"That'd be nice, thanks," Alex squeezed Raphael's shoulder as he headed off. While Raphael silently thought, 'Yes, my lovely, you'll have dinner, but not until we've had our way with you. Bwaa haa haaaa.'

The following evening, Luke beat Raphael home. He prepared a backpack with a few items he thought they should have for Alex's special night, including something even Raphael didn't know about. Alex wouldn't be the only one in for a surprise. It wasn't long before Raphael arrived, and Luke handed him a protein bar before he could even make it into the bedroom.

"I know we're having dinner after the dungeon, but you're going to need your strength. When was lunch?"

"I just had an açai bowl at my desk ... busy day. So, this is probably a good idea, thanks. Did you already get our supplies ready?" Raphael asked, indicating the backpack.

"Yep. We're good to go. Unless you want to change into something fresh, what you're wearing now should be fine for dinner later."

"I'm good. Let's head over to Jake's. Alex left about the same time I did, and we want to be there first." Raphael gave Luke an uncharacteristically brief kiss and the two headed out.

The plan was fairly simple, with plenty of room for improvisation as the spirit, and Alex's moans, would guide them. As they walked, Luke remarked, "We have just one goal tonight, Raphael. Make Alex feel good."

"Yep. I wonder if he can produce multiple orgasms?"

"Until I met you, I didn't think that was a real thing, baby."

"My super power."

"*One* of your super powers, baby. But an impressive one."

"Yes, Sir. But seriously, we should have checked with Greg. Does Alex come easily, or does he take a lot of build up? What are his triggers? Since he's caged, I assume he's mostly anal ..."

"He doesn't come easily, he's very anal, kissing turns him on, he likes to be spanked, and he really, really, really likes to suck cock."

"Oh. Okay, then. I, uh, guess you've done our homework."

"Would you expect any less of me, locked cock boy o' mine?"

"No, Sir. I bow to your superior spy craft." After a few more steps, "Wait. Spanking?"

"We all have our kinks, sweetie."

"Did you pack a paddle?"

"We'll be in a well-stocked dungeon, baby."

"Of course." A few more steps later, "Are we going to let Greg set the pace?"

"At first. I think we should take the lead at times. After all, Alex said he wanted to have sex with us. We shouldn't hold back. Do whatever seems right at the time. I have something in mind for the finale, actually."

"Ooooh ... what?"

"It's my surprise for you, too, baby. I think you'll like it."

"A dare within a dare?"

"Sure, let's go with that." Luke put his arm around Raphael's waist and pulled him close. Three days without sex was a looong time. Soon, they'd reached Jake's. They bounded up the steps and entered the code Jake had provided them and unlocked the front door. Once they'd entered Jake's apartment Luke headed down to the dungeon to prepare, while Raphael kept watch at the door for Greg and Alex. Meanwhile ...

Alex and Greg were walking from their place to 'the restaurant.' Or so Alex thought. Since he'd never been to Jake's, he had no idea their destination was in fact something quite different, but hopefully even more satisfying. As they neared the Victorian, Greg saw Raphael in the door before he whipped out of sight. As they came even with Jake's steps, Greg stopped, pulled Alex into an embrace and kiss, then said, "Alex, before dinner, I have a very special surprise for your birthday. Just do as I say, okay?"

"Oooh kaaay?" Before Alex could say another word, Greg pulled a blindfold out of his jacket pocket and slipped it over Alex's head.

"Hey!" Alex started to reach up to remove it. Greg caught both his hands and held them at his waist.

"Please, don't spoil the surprise, Alex. Just do as I say. You won't be sorry, I promise, okay? This will be a very special birthday, sweetie."

"This is too weird, Greg."

"Trust me, love. Now come with me. I'll lead you. We're going up some stairs."

Greg carefully led Alex up to the street door where Raphael was now waiting in plain sight. He held the door open for them, then carefully closed it behind them. He motioned to Greg which way to go, since he'd never been here either. Raphael had stripped while waiting, so he was barefoot now and able to follow soundlessly behind them.

"Greg, this really is weird ... and kind of scary. Where are we?"

"You'll see soon enough. Now, we're going down some stairs. Hold onto me ..." Luke was waiting at the bottom of the stairs, naked and harnessed. He moved aside as Greg and Alex finally reached the bottom. Luke had the lighting very dim, and he motioned to Greg where to guide Alex to stand.

"Alex, step up here ... just one step. That's it. Now turn around. Okay. Now. I'm going to undress you."

"What?! Wait ..." Alex started to reach for the blindfold again.

"Alex!" Greg grabbed both hands. "Please don't spoil the surprise. Okay, listen. I'll tell you this much. I'm about to make love to you in a way we've never done, okay? And I can't do it if you're dressed. Trust me. This is all for you, birthday boy. Okay? I love you." As he continued to hold Alex's hands, he pressed his lips to Alex's and pulled Alex's tongue deep into his own mouth. He held firm until Alex relaxed a little and his hands moved back down to his sides. Greg released his grip on Alex's hands, then his grip on Alex's tongue.

"Okay, good. Just relax. Let me do all the work and all the talking for now." Alex sighed deeply as Greg began undressing him. Once Alex was naked, Greg placed the sound canceling headphones Luke handed him on Alex's head. Enigma was playing in the headphones to help set the mood. Greg quickly stripped himself and pulled on the harness Luke was holding for him. Now the trick was to buckle Alex into a suspension harness Greg had never seen before without revealing that anyone else was in the room. Luke did a lot of hand gestures and fairly comical facial expressions, but Greg was a quick study. Soon Alex was laced and buckled in and ready for whatever was to follow. And frankly what followed is impossible to describe fully. At least as fully as Alex experienced it.

As Greg removed the headphones, Luke flipped a switch to channel the music to speakers, so they could all appreciate it. "How does that feel, Alex?"

"Weird, but I've said that a dozen times already. I still don't understand ..." Greg placed a finger on Alex's lips in a shushing gesture.

"You'll understand very soon, love. Just relax and enjoy every sensation." As Greg faced Alex and placed his hands on Alex's shoulders and gently massaged them, Luke and Raphael moved into position on either side of Alex. They squatted down and each began to massage Alex's inner thighs with one hand while each began massaging an ass cheek with the other. Had he not been bound in the suspension harness Alex probably would have shot through the ceiling.

"JESUS! What the fuck!" The boy next door knew how to swear. "Who is that?!"

"Relax, Alex. Enjoy the sensations. It's okay..." Raphael and Luke slid their hands up Alex's body as they stood, caressing his sides, his shoulder blades, his pecs, his nipples. After a couple of moments massaging Alex, Raphael moved into position where Greg had been standing and pulled Alex's bound body into an embrace, their cages meeting with a clink as he drove his tongue down Alex's throat. Alex resisted initially, then immediately recognized Raphael's taste and touch. Oh, my god, he thought, it's Raphael! Alex's stiffened body relaxed into the harness and he swallowed Raphael's tongue gladly, feverishly, wholly. He desperately wanted to reach his arms around Raphael's defined, pierced, torso, but, of course, he couldn't. Oh, my god, he thought again, I'm in bondage. I'm in fucking bondage with Raphael and Greg and ... and Luke? ... all making love to me. Oh. My. God!

As Raphael continued to face-fuck Alex, Greg moved around behind him and massaged Alex's neck and back. Luke lifted Alex's right foot and began to suck his toes, one by one. Alex moaned into Raphael's mouth. Damn, he wanted to touch Raphael! Greg had never seen Alex in bondage before, never seen another naked man making love to him, especially one as erotic, as exotic as Raphael. This was becoming as much a turn on for Greg as it was for Alex.

Greg moved his hands around Alex's body, playing with each nipple from behind, his erect cock painting a pattern with precum across Alex's ass. As Greg lowered himself, Raphael, still locked with Alex's tongue, replaced Greg's hands, massaging Alex's back. Greg began licking, nibbling Alex's ass. The moans intensified. Luke released Alex's foot and stood, reaching around Raphael to resume playing with Alex's nipples. As they hardened in response, Raphael released Alex's tongue and dropped down to inspect Alex's cage. It was crushing Alex's useless erection. As he'd hoped, precum was dripping from the Looker's spout. He licked up a sizeable gob, raised back up and delivered it into Alex's open mouth, coating Alex's tongue with his own cum. Tongue on tongue. As he did so, Greg spread Alex's ass cheeks and drove his own tongue into that special place that he knew so well. Alex bucked in reaction and surprise. Or was it ecstasy? Seemingly every part of his body was being made love to by the men he loved so much. Could this be real? And, please, could it last for hours?

While Greg tantalized Alex's pussy, Luke decided it was time to intensify Alex's experience. He wasn't sure about everything that Alex and Greg enjoyed together, although he was rapidly being educated tonight, but he figured he might as well take advantage of Alex's inability to resist whatever might come his way. He selected a couple of nipple clamps from Jake's collection and, while Raphael and Alex continued to breathe through each other's lungs, he maneuvered around Raphael to apply them to Alex's still hard nipples. As he slowly tightened one, then the other, Alex reacted. Luke decided to interpret his moans as pleasure, and slowly tightened the clamps. Once he decided he'd better not go any tighter for now, he returned to the wall and selected a well-worn paddle. Luke bent down next to Greg and brushed his ass to get his attention. Greg seemed to be in as much of a state of euphoria as Alex. He withdrew from Alex's rosebud, looked at Luke, who held up the paddle, then nodded. As Greg took the paddle and stood, Luke moved to the other side and slid his arms around Raphael's chest. Because Raphael was standing on the platform and Luke wasn't, his erect cock slid effortlessly between Raphael's smooth, hard thighs. Raphael pulled free of Alex's mouth and turned his head so Luke could whisper into his ear.

"You need to take a break, baby. Let me take over." Raphael smiled and nodded, and moved aside for Luke, who embraced the bound birthday boy as Raphael had been doing, wrapping his arms around Alex's torso, pressing his body against Alex as he licked Alex's lips with his tongue. Alex immediately sucked his tongue in, forcing their lips together tightly. He knew it was Luke, thanks to the feel of Luke's beard, but his enthusiasm was no less erotic, no less fierce, and for both, no less satisfying. Alex, was indeed a damn good kisser. After a couple of deep, shared breaths Greg struck with the paddle. Alex bucked and moaned into Luke's mouth. Greg struck again. Again. Again, timing the hits with the beat of Enigma. Alex never let go of Luke's tongue. His breathing quickened, sweat slowly dripped onto their locked lips. Greg continued, at a measured cadence. Alex's breathing quickened some more. Not having much experience (really none) with corporal punishment, Luke didn't know when enough might be enough. Watching from the sidelines, Raphael, too, was entranced. In any other setting, he would have felt compelled to intervene on Alex's behalf, but ... but Alex didn't appear distressed. Finally, Luke pulled his head back just enough to break the seal between their lips and asked, "Should we stop?"

"God, no, please, neither of you," Alex moaned. Luke's eyebrow did its thing, and his tongue plunged back in. He decided he'd defer to Greg. After a couple of minutes Raphael got up and squeezed between Luke's legs out of curiosity. Sure enough, precum was flowing from both Luke's free cock and Alex's cage. What the hell. He licked both, and then again, collecting a sizeable tantalizing amount, backed out again, then walked around to Greg, who was now sweating himself, and put his arm around Greg's waist to get his attention. When Greg turned, Raphael lifted his lips to Greg's and delivered his treasure. It was Greg's turn to moan as he pulled Raphael into a tight embrace. They shared Luke's and Alex's cum in a long, deep kiss that gave Alex a brief respite. When Greg broke away, he smiled at Raphael and mouthed, 'Thank you, baby' using Luke's pet name with him for the first time. Raphael smiled back, nodded and moved away.

Raphael wrapped his arms around Luke from behind, his cage pressed between Luke's thighs. Luke pulled free of Alex's mouth, turned around within Raphael's hold and whispered in Raphael's ear, "Take over, baby, I'll get the next phase ready." Raphael had no idea what that was, but he was eager to find out. As Luke stepped aside, Raphael again wrapped his arms around Alex's chest and back and plunged in. Alex cooed with appreciation as Greg resumed treating his ass like a bass drum.

Luke unrolled a large, thick black mat in the middle of the floor and positioned the backpack at one corner. What he was about to do was untried, just a concept, but if it worked, well, it would be fucking amazing. Literally. He walked back to the action, and put his hand on Greg's ass. Greg turned and he whispered in his ear a moment. Greg did a double take, then grinned and nodded in ascent. He put the paddle aside and stepped up behind Alex as Luke stepped behind Raphael and pulled him away from Alex, far enough away that he could whisper, "Baby, you need to go take your Master plug out."

"Are you going to fuck me?"

"No."

"Is Greg going to fuck me ... while you fuck Alex?" Raphael looked surprised, but not disappointed.

"No, baby. Alex is going to fuck you."

"What?! How?"

"You'll see in just a minute. Now, hurry."

As Raphael whipped into the lavatory on the other side of the stairs, Luke took his place in front of Alex, who seemed to be enjoying the attention he was getting from Greg. Alex was still wearing the nipple clamps. Luke tightened each one a last little bit, enough to see Alex react. Then, he ripped them off. Alex screamed. And, he swore. A lot. Luke put his hands near Greg's on Alex's sides, and gently licked each nipple.

Alex moaned in appreciation. Luke then licked Alex's left ear, just before saying in as low and sexy a voice as he could muster, "I'm told you like to be fucked."

"Mmm hmmm."

"I'm told you really like to suck cock."

"Mmm hmmm. Very much."

"Have you been a good boy tonight, Alex?"

"I've tried my best, Luke, Sir." That got a surprised look between Luke and Greg, who had to smile at Alex's response. Apparently, Alex was channeling Raphael.

"Good. Then we're going to take you out of the harness and give you a special treat. Would you like that?"

"Very much, Sir." As Luke and Greg began unbuckling Alex, Raphael returned. Luke motioned to Raphael to take hold of Alex, who was undoubtedly going to be unsteady on his feet. He'd been in bondage now for nearly an hour.

"Okay, Alex, we're going to help you down, and we're going to take off the blindfold at last." All three lead Alex off the short platform and onto the middle of the black mat and lowered him down onto his hands and knees. He started to sit up, but Luke stopped him. "Alex, we need you on your hands and knees, doggy style."

"Oh. Oooh!" Alex laughed. "Am I going to play with Niki now?"

Luke got down directly in front of Alex's face, and lifted the blindfold. Since the room was dimly lit, it wasn't much of a transition for Alex. Luke smiled and, looking Alex in the eyes, said, "No, Alex. No doggy play. You're just going to fuck Raphael." Alex's face telegraphed confusion. And surprise. Luke stood up, took Raphael's hand and guided him behind Alex, where he had Raphael get down on his hands and knees, his legs aside Alex's, their asses pointed at each other. Everyone but Luke was clueless. Until he pulled an implement out of the backpack, out of Alex's line of sight. Somehow, he'd wired two Sport Fucker Thunder Plugs together to fashion a two-headed dildo of remarkable proportion. Greg moved closer to inspect.

"Can Alex take this?" Luke whispered.

"Oh yeah. I think so. Where the hell did you get that?"

"Later. Right now, we need to lock these two up, ass to ass, before we let them suck us dry. Alex loves blowing you, right?"

"Oh yeah. I can't wait to see what you have in mind." Luke grinned and nodded. He retrieved a squirt bottle of lube from the pack, then got down on his knees between Alex and Raphael. "OK, boys, relax those sphincters." He liberally coated the plugs, then he lubed up Raphael while Greg did the same with Alex. Luke started with Alex, and Greg was right, he took the plug fairly easily. Once it was in, Alex, whose ass was still warm and reddened, wiggled the plug.

"That feels good. Is that a puppy tail?"

"No," Luke laughed. "It's about to feel a lot better. Now, hold still. Baby, back up a little." Greg guided Raphael as Luke lined his half of the plug up with his rosebud. "Ok, baby, a little more ... that's it ..." Once Raphael's plug was planted and his ass was pressed tight against Alex's, both locked cock boys moaned. Luke's idea worked. As Raphael and Alex explored the sensations of banging their asses into one another, producing prostate pleasing results in both simultaneously, Greg and Luke positioned themselves on their knees in front of their respective cocksuckers.

"Alex," Luke asked as he slid his cock into Raphael's waiting mouth, "have you ever been face fucked and butt fucked at the same time before?"

Alex probably answered in the negative, but with Greg's cock already past his tonsils, his response was too muffled to interpret. Raphael and Alex were experiencing sensory overload. A sizeable plug dancing on their prostates enhanced the sensation of feeling another locked cock boy's bare ass on ass, their legs rubbing together, all accompanied by the comforting familiarity of each man sucking his lover's cock dry. Although Alex had been the center of attention, all four men had been engaged in sex in one way or another all evening. Luke had no idea how long it would be before Greg or Alex might come. He decided not to worry about it and just enjoy Raphael's talented tongue.

In fact, Raphael wasn't sure how much longer he could hold off. Sucking Luke was reward enough, but Alex was driving that plug hard, and the sensation of Alex's ass rubbing his was a unique added trigger. He didn't want to be the first to come, but he really didn't feel in control anymore. When Greg suddenly announced he was cumming, that was all it took for Raphael to lose it, too. He had no choice but to manipulate Luke, in hopes they'd come together. As Luke shot, Alex continued to fuck Raphael with the plug. Overload, indeed.

Between the plug in his ass, the sensation of Raphael's ass against his own, and the familiar taste of Greg in his mouth, Alex finally came. And came. And came. Raphael steadied himself on his left hand and grabbed Luke's cock with his right, then licked it like the lollypop it was for him. He looked up into Luke's eyes and grinned, as he did his best to sound Luke's cock with his tongue. Luke pulled out, then lowered himself enough to allow him to slide his tongue into Raphael's mouth for a finale kiss. That's when a new thought occurred to him.

"Greg, let's roll them over onto their backs." He and Greg then carefully maneuvered Alex and Raphael, still locked at the ass, onto their backs. Luke then straddled Raphael, his free cock over Raphael's cage, his hands on either side of Raphael's shoulders. Now, he could lower his face and seriously kiss his 'baby.' Greg followed suit, so now Greg and Luke's asses were bumping as they enjoyed a final few minutes breathing through their locked cock boys.

When Luke finally pulled his tongue free, he said, "Should we separate you two, or would you rather keep your asses locked together all night like this?"

Alex moaned and smiled at Greg. "I'm fine like this. I've never fucked anyone with my ass before."

"That was amazing," Raphael agreed. "Luke, Sir, you're a mad fucking genius."

"I know," Luke replied. "But I have to give full credit to my inspirations ... our two beautiful locked cock boys." He leaned down and gave Raphael one more kiss. "But seriously, I think it's time we get you two cleaned up. Greg, you pull yours and I'll pull mine." Greg and Luke grabbed each lover by the shoulders and pulled in opposite directions. Alex's plug popped out first. Then, Luke reached down and eased Raphael's half of the plug out. Slowly, Alex and Raphael sat up, facing each other.

"You look like shit," Raphael joked. "Come on, let's go shower." He stood, reached a hand down and helped Alex, who had taken the lion's share of the night's punishment, to his feet. Okay, not punishment, reward. Most definitely reward. Raphael surreptitiously bent down once more, then Alex wrapped an arm around Raphael's waist and the two headed to the lavatory.

"Let's clean this all up, then we'll shower," Luke instructed. "We want to make sure Jake finds the place just the way he left it for us."

"Of course," Greg agreed. "We may want to do this again sometime."

"Next time we'll put you in the harness."

"I could probably handle that," Greg smiled. "This was undoubtedly the best birthday Alex has ever had. Well, except for the time I proposed."

"Yeah, that would be hard to top. And, funny you should say that."

"Why?"

"Because it was in this very dungeon that Raphael proposed to me."

"Seriously? Well, good for him. Good for you." Greg walked up to Luke and pulled him into an embrace. "And, let me say once again how much the two of you mean to Alex and me. We love you guys. Thanks again for making tonight happen for Alex ... and me."

"I don't have to tell you how much Raphael and I love you, too. We've really become a family, haven't we?"

"Yeah, and we're so looking forward to your and Niki and Steve's wedding. Especially Alex. He's been working his butt off."

"For a little reception? I hope he's keeping it simple ... you know, tasteful."

"Have you not met Alex? Simple? Tasteful, maybe. I should stop talking right now. But tonight was a hell of a surprise. You obviously worked your butt off, too. You did good, Luke."

"Thanks. Like I said, I had plenty of inspiration. Actually, I think it was Alex's butt that took the brunt of it tonight."

Greg laughed. "Yeah, the boy loves a good spanking."

"Who are you talking about?" Alex grinned as he and Raphael walked into the center of the dungeon. Both were clean and fresh, and still naked, as good locked cock boys should be.

"Baby, have you seen that double-headed butt plug? I thought it was right here," Luke asked, looking over at Raphael.

"Yeah, it's right here," Raphael slyly grinned. "And here." He put his arm around Alex's waist. Luke looked puzzled for just a second.

"So, you uh ..."

"Yeah, we uncoupled them, and put them to good use."

"Yeah, it feels so good, Luke, Sir," Alex laughed. "Thank you."

"You're plugged?" Greg asked, surprised.

"Yep. And the way this thing feels, I plan on being plugged more often now, just like Raphael." Alex pulled out of Raphael's arm and walked over to hug Luke. He reached up and kissed him one more time. "You probably didn't plan this part of the birthday surprise, but it really does feel awesome. Thanks."

Luke looked over at Greg and shrugged. "My bad, Greg. Now you're going to have to unplug your husband from now on before you can fuck him."

"I guess it's a small price to pay to have him happy, willing ... and ready."

"Okay, Greg, our turn to shower. You two locked ... and plugged boys ... get dressed, and we'll take Alex out for his well-earned dinner." Luke grabbed Greg's hand and headed to the lavatory. Fifteen minutes later they were out the door and on their way.

Forty-Six

EDGING THE CLOSET DOOR OPEN

SUNDAY MORNING RICKY WOKE first. Although they always fell asleep curled around each other, they always ended up apart by morning. Touching, but no longer in an embrace. At first, this disappointed Ricky, and in fact one morning as the two were stirring he had said so. As usual, Juan had been able to comfort him.

"Mijo, as long as I fall asleep in your arms, it doesn't matter how I wake up, as long as I wake up in bed with you."

"Si, Papito. I guess you're right. And as long as I have your cock to play with, I'm happy that you keep mine locked up, nice and safe." Ricky then began to fondle his favorite free cock. "I love you, Juan."

"And I love you, and I promise to keep you safe, and locked up ... except when I get hungry for your cock. You may not be permanently locked like Raphael and Alex, but you're still *my* locked cock boy, eh?" Juan leaned over and tugged on Ricky's baby blue Holy Trainer.

"Always and forever!"

On this morning, it was Ricky who was hungry for Juan's cock, so he gingerly slid away from Juan and crawled down the bed, positioning himself so he could swallow Juan's cock slowly. As true of many mornings, though still asleep, Juan was already hard, as Ricky was. Which was probably why he was already horny and frustrated and deeply in need of tasting Juan's cock. Juan always removed the 2-gauge PA before fucking Ricky and often before letting him suck, but Ricky took pride in deep throating Juan with the PA in place. It's what a good leather boy does, right? He peeled back the covers enough to reveal his prize and took all of Juan in one smooth dive. He tasted so good. It wasn't long before Ricky felt Juan's hand on his back, then sliding down onto his ass. As Ricky continued to serve, Juan massaged Ricky's balls, his taint, his pussy. Fully energized, Ricky lifted his left leg over Juan's body, to straddle him, and really began to suck. Not to be outdone, Juan raised his head grabbed either side of Ricky's ass, now perfectly positioned, and dove his tongue into Ricky's pussy. Both men moaned as each received pleasure from the other. What a perfect way to greet a Sunday morning. When Ricky could tell Juan was close, he freed Juan's cock, flipped around and drove his tongue into Juan's mouth.

"You tease," Juan said, once Ricky released him.

"I don't want you to come in my mouth this morning, Sir. I want you to fuck your locked cock boy until he comes in his cage for you."

"So ... you're giving the orders, this morning?" Juan studied Ricky's earnest face. "I kind of like that."

"Yes, Sir. I need you to fuck me."

"Very well. But, first, let me pee."

"Pee on me, sir. I want to be wearing your piss when you fuck me."

"Ricky! Where did that come from?"

"I ... it's just ... you know ... I'm ready, Sir. I so want to be your locked cock leather boy in every way possible."

"Ricky. I have no intention of ever letting you get away again. Ever. Okay? You don't need to prove anything to me ... your brave encounter with me at The Eagle that day was all the proof anyone would ever need. You don't need to worry." Juan pulled Ricky back down for a long, deep, sloppy kiss. When they pulled apart, Ricky sat up and smiled as he grabbed Juan's still hard cock.

"I'm not worried, Sir. I just want to wear your piss this morning. Please, Sir?" The look he gave Juan, that 'adorable' smile that produced so many DoorDash tips, worked just as well on Juan.

"If you insist, mijo. Let's go." Juan sat up and Ricky climbed on his back, arms around his neck, legs around his waist, and the two headed as one to the shower, which was destined to be golden this morning.

After the 'shower,' after Juan slowly, patiently fucked Ricky on the floor, kissing him, kissing and licking his piss flavored nipples, talking dirty, doing everything he could to get Ricky to come, he finally could hold off no longer and came inside Ricky. Ricky had spooled out a fair amount of precum, but still had not come. Juan collapsed on top of Ricky, kissing him apologetically.

"It's hard, isn't it?"

"What? This was easy."

"No, I mean it's hard to come caged."

"Oh. Yeah. But I haven't been caged that long yet. I'll get better, Sir, I promise!"

"I want you to come as often as me, mijo."

"No, Sir. My job is to make you come. To taste your cum. Even your piss. Prove my devotion to you."

Juan laughed, despite Ricky's seriousness. "Ricky, you're not a sex slave. You're my lover."

"I know, but I want to be the best leather boy ever. For you. For me. For Raphael and Luke and all the others. It's not a game for me, you know? One day I will be as good as Raphael." Ricky's expression was adorably confident.

"You're already better than Raphael ... you're *my* leather boy. And I wouldn't change a thing about you."

"Please. Sir I want to get so much better. I *need* to get so much better." The plaintive look on Ricky's face kind of bent Juan's heart.

"Okay, Ricky. We'll work on it together. Okay?" Ricky nodded, then smiled.

"I really, really love you, Juan."

"I know. Almost as much as I love you." He pulled Ricky into a sitting position. "Now, let's shower and go find some brunch."

They'd nearly finished brunch when Ricky's phone vibrated. "It's a text from Mateo. He wants to talk."

"Is that so ..."

"Yeah. What should I say?"

"Ask him to come over this afternoon. Let's finally find out what he's all about."

"Okay." Ricky typed a comment, including their address." A moment later, his phone buzzed again. "He'll be over at three, between shifts at the restaurant."

"This should be interesting, Ricky." Ricky nodded, and downed his last bite of chilaquiles.

At three on the dot, Juan's phone indicated a visitor was at the entrance to the building. He greeted Mateo, and told him to enter and take the elevator to the fourth floor. He unlocked the street door, then put the phone down. He and Ricky had debated if Mateo might be intimidated if they were in their typical attire, which, of course was no attire, or harness for Juan, collar for Ricky, and lately wrist and ankle restraints. Not that he'd been tied down yet, but he loved the feel of them. How they made him feel more submissive to Juan. His cage always got heavier when he wore them. And Juan's cock always tasted a little bit sweeter. At any rate, they'd decided to compromise, with Ricky in the outfit he'd worn to seduce Juan, see-through shorts and caged cock crop top. Juan was in bare-assed chaps and thong jock, and a mesh t-shirt. Ricky walked down the hall to greet Mateo at the elevator and escorted him back to their apartment.

"Mateo!" Juan greeted him when he entered just ahead of Ricky. "Nice to meet you. Welcome to our home."

"Gracias, señior." Mateo looked a little intimidated, maybe a little unsure if he was doing the right thing. Taking Mateo's cue, the conversation that followed was in Spanish.

"Mateo, call me Juan. Please have a seat." Mateo sat, looking around approvingly at the apartment. Ricky immediately sat next to him and squeezed his shoulder, wanting to show affection, but not certain how far to go. Juan flashed his bare ass as he walked away into the kitchen and returned with three Modelo Especials. "I know you're only nineteen, but I'm guessing you've had a beer or two, am I right?"

"Yeah," Mateo grinned, a little more at ease. "One or two, Juan."

"It's so good to see you again! How are you, Mateo?" Ricky asked intently, after clinking bottles with Mateo. "I mean, really. You good?"

"I'm okay." He didn't sound totally convincing. Ricky decided to try another tack.

"What did the guys say after my amigos and I left with all my stuff?"

"Oh, man ... you fucked them up good." Ricky squealed and slapped his thighs, then squeezed Mateo's thigh.

"What did they say?"

"Well, they called you all kinds of names. But they really didn't know what to think. Deep down, I think they had more respect for you than before. You were very brave, Ricky. So brave."

"Well, I did have a pretty impressive posse with me, don't you think?"

"Impressively naked, yeah. I was speechless, Ricky. Like I said, you fucked them up good. You blew their minds ... and their budget. They had to scramble to find a new roommate." Ricky nodded, then decided to approach the elephant in the room.

"You may have been speechless, but your cock had plenty to say, Mateo."

"¿Qué?" Juan was watching and listening, letting Ricky guide Mateo.

"A couple of the guys saw your boner as we left, Mateo. It was pretty obvious."

"Seriously? Oh, fuck! I wonder if anyone else did."

"Did they say anything to you? Have they been treating you okay?" Then, Ricky decided to come right out and say it. "Have they figured out you're gay, too?"

Mateo set his beer down and stared at it a moment. Then he turned to Ricky and said, "I don't know. Maybe. Does it show?" Ricky pulled him close, an arm around his shoulders.

"No, Mateo, it doesn't show. But I wish it did. I wish you were happier about being gay ... like we are."

Juan finally spoke. "Mateo, tell us about yourself."

And, so, Mateo did. Haltingly at first. But into his second beer, he was more relaxed, more at ease with both Ricky and Juan. He talked about the challenge of entering school at age five, having only been in the US for a year and never having seriously interacted with anyone speaking English. About being cautioned to avoid anyone in authority. About the pain of seeing more than one relative deported. Of the tenuous but still heartening relief when DACA was instituted. And, after observing Ricky over time, of his gradual recognition of his own sexuality.

"I really have a ... had a ... crush on you, Ricky." Mateo looked over at Juan as he said this. "I always thought you were so sweet, so sexy. But I was afraid to say anything in case I was wrong about you."

"Well," Ricky laughed, as he stood up, his cage on full display behind the Airtex shorts. "As you can see, you weren't wrong. I'm a bona fide queer boy ... just like you!"

"Not like me. Not at all. I ... I'll never be as brave as you."

"I wasn't brave either, Mateo, until I met Juan. Then, after I lost him, it was Raphael, Greg, Luke and the others who made me realize I really did deserve love. Juan's love." Ricky walked over, leaned down and pulled Juan into a deep kiss as an impromptu visual aid. He walked back, sat down and again put his hand on Mateo's thigh. "We can help you be brave, too, if you want."

"You make it sound easy."

"It's not easy, amigo. But, it's worth it. Look at me ... at us, now. I've never been happier. You deserve to be happy, too."

"Yeah, I do. I do." Mateo smiled meekly. Juan got up, sat down on the other side of Mateo and put his arm around Mateo's shoulders as Ricky had done. This time, interestingly, Mateo leaned into Juan, putting his head on Juan's chest and one hand on Juan's thigh. Juan looked over at Ricky who was grinning, then winked.

"It's settled, then," Juan said. "Do you work Tuesday evenings?"

"Yeah, why?"

"You need to change shifts with someone, Mateo. Tuesday nights are very important for Ricky and me, and for you, too. Can you do that?"

"I'll try." Juan patted Mateo's thigh, then stood up.

"Good. Let us know. If you can, meet us here at five-thirty."

"¡Estupendo! Now, I have to get back to work." Mateo stood, and Ricky, more confident now, pulled him into a tight hug. When he released him, Mateo turned and put his arms out to hug Juan. Juan pulled him in, again looking over at Ricky, who seemed very pleased.

"Off you go," Juan said as he let go of Mateo. "Don't work too hard, and we'll see you Tuesday." Mateo smiled, nodded and walked to the door.

He opened it, turned and waved as he said, "Tuesday!" Then he was gone. Ricky jumped for joy. He really did jump, then he pulled Juan into a fierce hug. Then he looked up and pursed his lips, begging for a well-deserved kiss.

"Nice job, mijo. You were great."

"Yeah? Well, I don't think I'm the only one Mateo has a crush on anymore. He really likes you, Papito."

'What's not to like, mijo?" Juan laughed. "I'm not used to drinking beer this early in the day. I think, maybe, we should take a nap. Sound good?" Ricky just nodded and started pulling his crop top off as he headed to the bedroom.

Forty-Seven

MATEO'S 'INITIATION'

TUESDAY EVENING ALEX AND Greg were walking hand in hand to Raphael and Luke's for dinner. Alex had made a detour on the way home from work to pick up a special treat, macarons from Chantal Guillon in Hayes Valley, and he was careful not to jostle them too much.

"What inspired you to get the cookies?" Greg asked.

"It may sound silly, but they're kind of a bribe ... well, more like a lubricant. I'm ready to start finalizing some of the plans for the wedding, and I want everyone feeling as happy as possible when I spring some of the plans on them. A festive touch, I guess."

"Aren't you supposed to be planning a little reception, not a wedding?" Alex looked at Greg is if he'd just accused him of a felony.

"This is going to be the wedding of the century. They are not going to get away with a 'simple' ceremony in City Hall."

"Isn't that what they want?"

"That's what they *think* they want."

"But you know better."

"Of course I do."

"Just checking." They walked a bit further before Greg asked, "And I'm going to be involved in this major production at some point, aren't I?"

"Oh, yeah. Big time."

"Juuust checking ..."

Juan, Ricky and Mateo arrived after everyone else, bearing the food. Juan had once again insisted on treating, since they were bringing a guest, not that Mateo wouldn't be welcomed by everyone with open arms. Naked open arms. Juan wasn't sure how Mateo would react, but he'd seen the group in all their glory when Ricky moved out, so it hopefully wouldn't be a shocker. As was now custom, they didn't bother to ring the bell upon arrival and walked right in.

"Hey!" Raphael greeted them, jumping up from his spot on the floor. Alex stood, too, and both approached Mateo. Two naked, caged guys, Alex in chest harness, Raphael, collared and in full body harness, not quite obscuring his locked cock tattoo above his cage. Raphael stuck out his hand to Mateo and said, "Hola, Mateo. ¡Bievenido!"

"Hola, amigo," Mateo smiled, taking in Raphael fully for the first time. He'd been just one in the crowd at the apartment, but now he was life size. Actually, bigger than life. As Alex extended his hand, Raphael took the bags from Juan so he could join Ricky in disrobing. Ricky was already half naked.

"Mateo," Raphael said as he carried the food into the living room, "my Spanish is not the best."

"So my English," Mateo smiled.

"It's okay, amigo, we have Juan and Ricky if we need help, right guys?" Raphael assured. Raphael then made introductions of everyone while Juan and Ricky unpacked dinner. Mateo took a spot on the floor nearest Ricky as soon as he sat down. Mateo was still fully dressed and clearly somewhat in awe of the men around him. As everyone ate, they chatted about this and that. Mateo was keenly aware of how comfortable everyone was in a setting he'd barely ever even fantasized about. Not only were they naked, some harnessed, some collared, some caged, but everyone was comfortable touching one another as if they were all lovers or something. Right next to him Ricky was nestled in between Juan's shins, with Juan periodically rubbing Ricky's head or shoulders when he'd made a joke or a comment about something he and Juan had done. Raphael and Alex seemed especially close, touching thighs, hands often on each other ... on the back of each other's neck, a leg, arm wrapped around the other's waist, and once a kiss after a comment he didn't fully comprehend. Even the buff guys on the couch, Greg and Luke, were sitting thigh against thigh, not two feet apart like his roommates. They often touched, too. And then Niki, the cute black guy with the crazy mohawk and the dog collar, periodically affectionately licked the cheek of his lover. Must be a 'puppy' thing. Weird, but sexy hot at the same time. And, that's what this whole dinner was, sexy hot. Yet, everyone acted like it was just normal. Everyone but him was naked. Everyone but him had a lover present. Everyone.

As Alex and Raphael began clearing things, Ricky quietly turned to Mateo. "Do you like our friends, Mateo?"

"You are all so sexy, Ricky. I can't believe it's real. You do this every week?"

"Yeah. We sometimes go the beach and run around naked, play naked volleyball."

"You're kidding! That's loco!"

"Crazy fun," Juan interjected.

"What's crazy fun?" Raphael asked as he and Alex returned from the kitchen with herbal tea and Alex's macarons.

'The beach," Juan smiled. "Hey, those look like fun, too."

"Alex brought macarons for dessert," Greg announced. "I think he said they're a bribe or something."

"A bribe?" Luke eyed Alex as he reached for a macaron. "What's going on, Alex?"

Alex chewed on a lavender black currant macaron as he eyed Luke back, grinning as he chewed. "I've been doing a little preplanning for your wedding, and I wanted to run something past you before I go any further."

"Oh, that's right," Steve said. "As I remember we somehow hired you to throw us a reception without actually hiring you ... unintentionally ... against our will. Whether we like it or not, isn't that right, Luke?" Mateo was suddenly confused. Was Steve marrying Luke? But didn't Raphael introduce Luke as his fiancé? Was Niki Steve's lover or just his puppy?

"Be nice, Steve," Niki slapped Steve's shoulder. "I think what Alex is doing is very sweet." Niki turned to Alex and said, "Uh, what exactly *are* you doing?"

"Well, I'm still in the early stages, but what I wanted to clear with the four of you tonight, was the date. I've made a preliminary reservation for your ceremony in the Mayor's Balcony for Valentine's Day. Will that be okay?"

Raphael looked at Luke, who looked at Steve, who was looking at Niki. No one protested. Actually, everyone smiled. Raphael pulled Alex into a sideways hug. "Valentine's Day! How romantic! A date!" He jumped up. "We have a date!" Luke stood and he and Raphael embraced as Steve and Niki followed suit. Mateo looked at Ricky still not fully comprehending.

"Luke is marrying Raphael and Niki is marrying Steve. A double ceremony."

"Ah. Si. ¡Fenomenal!" Mateo broke out into a wide smile. Luke looked down, saw his reaction, and reached down. Mateo reached a hand up, and Luke pulled him to his feet and pulled him into an embrace with Raphael. Not surprisingly, Raphael in the midst of his joy joy, planted a big one on Mateo. Mateo didn't resist. He looked at Luke to be sure it was okay with Luke, who followed suit with his own lip lock. Wow. Now they're kissing me, Mateo thought. Like I'm already family or something. Before the thought had fully sunk in, everyone was in a monster embrace and by the time it was over, everyone had kissed everyone, including Mateo.

As they broke apart, Raphael took both of Mateo's hands and looked him in the eyes. "Mateo, have you had a good time this evening?"

"Dios Mio, amigo, si! This was amazing for me. And, I am so happy you are getting married! I am so happy for you."

"Thank you, Mateo. Will you come again next Tuesday?"

"I hope so, Raphael. I really hope so." Raphael pulled him into a one-on-one hug, then planted a peck on his cheek.

"Good. Next Tuesday, amigo! And, no pressure, but ... maybe you will take off your shirt next Tuesday?" Mateo looked a little confused. "Or, you can take everything off if you would like that better. It's kind of a rule here." Mateo got it. He grinned shyly, looked down at his feet, then back up into Raphael's eyes.

"Si, amigo, naked is okay." Raphael grinned back at Mateo. Juan grinned, too. He should have known Raphael had a way of talking almost anyone out of their clothes. Raphael dropped back down to the floor, and soon everyone followed suit, returning to their spots.

"I thought you were working on a reception, Alex," Luke said as his right hand fondled Greg's thigh, totally in a brotherly way, despite how close his hand was to Greg's cock. He turned to Greg while still addressing Alex. "It sounds to me like you have expanded your mandate to cover the whole day. Are we in good hands?" Greg laughed.

"Luke ... all of you," Alex addressed the room, "You won't be disappointed. Your wedding and your reception are in the best of hands." He raised both hands and talked to them as he continued, "These hands will make your wedding day legendary!"

Luke looked over at Niki and asked, "Did we order 'legendary?'" Niki barked. Then grinned.

"I can hardly wait to see what Alex is cooking up. Legendary sounds good to me." He looked at Raphael, and said, "Raphael?"

"Niki, you are already legendary, so, I guess ... legendary it is." He looked at Luke and made a 'so there' nod with his head. Luke sat back in defeat.

"Legendary sounds so far away from 'a simple ceremony.'"

"Luke, Luke, Luke ..." Greg turned to him. "A lot of Raphael has rubbed off on Alex, and I seem to remember you saying once that no one can say no to Raphael. Well, welcome to Alex Two Dot Oh. The good news is Alex knows his stuff. I'm with Niki ... I can't wait to see what your wedding day will be."

"It will be legendary!" Ricky exclaimed. "I'm so excited. Can I help, Alex?" Alex immediately produced a mischievous grin, and nodded very slowly.

"I have big plans for you, Ricky." Ricky beamed. Mateo smiled and for the first time tonight grabbed Ricky's thigh and shook it in celebration. Most everyone else looked confused.

"Big plans? For Ricky?" Raphael probed.

"I've said too much," Alex said as he stood. He spread his arms as though preaching to the crowd. "Thank you all for electing me Wedding Planner of the Year. You won't be sorry." Luke leaned forward and put his head in his hands in mock grief, as Greg patted him on the back.

"You get the easy part, Luke," Greg consoled him, "You just have to show up and follow instructions. I have to live with him for the next few weeks." Luke just shook his head.

Forty-Eight

RICKY'S TRIGGER

A COUPLE OF TUESDAYS closer to the big day, Alex had made progress. He'd worked discretely for the most part, but had to ask for some information, like Angel's number so he could ensure Angel and Mama could attend. They'd be driving into the city. Besides the four grooms, Greg and Alex who would witness, and Angel and Mama, Luke's and Steve's parents would be flying in. Juan, Ricky and Mateo would also be there. The biological family and the logical family.

Alex had made hotel reservations for Mama, Angel and Luke's and Steve's parents, for the night before and the night of the ceremony. The ceremony itself would be late afternoon, followed by dinner at Waterbar. Dinner under the shimmering Bay Lights on the Bay Bridge seemed appropriately romantic. And fitting for the biological family.

Then, there would be the 'reception' after that, for the logical family ... and a few others. Keeping that a secret was going to be the challenge, especially considering how Alex had to rely on social media for some of the planning. Other aspects of the planning, though, were face to face. It was during this Tuesday dinner that Alex took Ricky aside, into the bedroom, and closed the door. He told Ricky what he was planning, the whole affair, and swore him to secrecy. That was the easy part. Then he described the role he wanted Ricky to play, He was fully prepared for Ricky to say no.

"Me? Alex, you chose me?"

"You are the perfect man for the job."

'Wow. How many people will be there?"

"A couple hundred probably."

"Dios Mio. I don't know. I mean with you guys it's one thing..." Alex, who was facing Ricky with a hand on each of Ricky's taut hips, let him ponder, no pressure. Ricky continued looking into Alex's eager eyes, clearly torn.

Then, just a little pressure. "Ricky. You. Will. Be. Legendary."

"Yeah! Okay!" Ricky smiled. "For Raphael, for Niki, Steve and Luke ... yes! I'll do it!" Alex pulled Ricky's hips into his own, cage to cage, and shared a grateful kiss.

"Thank you, Ricky. Thank you. Don't say a word, okay?"

"Are you kidding. I'm not spoiling *this* surprise."

Hoping no one had noticed their little tête-a-tête, of course, was a lost cause. It had taken longer than Alex intended and everyone looked up as they returned to their spots. Ricky settled into his, between Juan's shins, and next to Mateo's naked thighs. Yes, Mateo had been true to his word to Raphael, and he'd duly stripped the next Tuesday, and again tonight. As was true with every new recruit, he'd acclimated quickly, and already seemed at ease. He actually felt less conspicuous than he had the first night, when he was the only one clothed. Being next to Ricky and Juan had helped a lot.

"We miss you, amigo," Mateo teased.

"Yeah, Alex," Raphael accused. "Whatever were you plotting in there? Hmmmm?"

"As if you didn't know," Alex replied. "All in good time, my dear, all in good time."

"Is everything about this wedding, reception or whatever it is you're planning a secret? It's our wedding, after all."

"All secrets will be revealed in due time. I might be ready to reveal more at next Tuesday's dinner, I promise."

"Thank you," Luke said. "It's a little unsettling not knowing what's what ... not even knowing what we're wearing."

"Oh, well if you must know, you will be wearing your family tartan kilt, of course."

"What about me?" Niki asked, putting an arm around Steve's waist. "What are we wearing?"

"Okay, I'll tell you this much, guys. Since the ceremony is in a very formal, iconic setting at City Hall, I want you to be stylish as hell. Luke, as I said, will be in family tartan. Niki, you and Steve will be wearing leather jodhpur pants, and all four of you will be wearing matching Renaissance shirts, so no ties."

"You seem to be forgetting something, 'my dear'," Raphael intoned.

"Oh, yes. You, my dear, and your allegedly handsome brother will both be wearing family sarongs. Angel has already picked them out for the two of you."

"Cool!" Raphael said. "I haven't worn one in ages. I'll bet Angel hasn't either. That's a great idea, Alex ... a sarong will complement Luke's kilt."

"Didn't I tell you, you were in good hands?" Alex replied smugly. "You four are going to look spectacular, five counting Angel."

"So you've been plotting with Angel behind our backs?" Luke joked.
"Not plotting, coordinating."

"I like the idea of Raphael in a sarong, though," Luke relented, then turned to Niki and Steve. "What do you guys think?"

"I have no idea what a jodhpur is, but if Raphael and Angel are wearing sarongs, I'll wear whatever," Niki consented.

"I know what jodhpurs are, and you'll look pretty sexy, puppy," Steve cooed. Then, looking over at Alex, "Where the heck are you going to get leather jodhpurs, not to mention renaissance shirts?"

"I have sources," Alex smiled, even more smugly.

"He's not just a drama queen, Steve, he's a former college drama student, too," Raphael offered. "I'm betting he still has contacts."

"Wow, beauty and brains," Greg laughed. "Bingo, Raphael."

"First of all, I was an engineering student ... drama was extra-curricular. And secondly," Alex turned and put his face an inch away from Raphael's, "who taught me the benefits of being a drama queen, Queen Raffie? Huh?"

"Actually, Alex, I think of Raphael more as a Princess than a Queen," Luke half-joked.

"Fine, you can both suck your own cocks tonight. This Princess ... Queen is having none of it." Raphael dramatically turned away from Alex in a campy pout.

"See! What did I tell you?" Alex laughed as he pulled Raphael into a sitting hug. "Now that's how a drama queen sounds."

Mateo was obviously enjoying the kidding, campy, totally queer atmosphere the evening had devolved into. He was quiet, as usual, but beaming. Juan reached down and squeezed his shoulder. Mateo looked up in response.

"I'm really glad you're here, amigo," Juan smiled,

"Yeah, Mateo, we're all glad you're here," Steve affirmed from across the room. He got up and walked over and sat next to Mateo, putting his arm around his waist. "How are things back at the apartment for you? Everything okay?"

Mateo smiled bravely. "Is okay, si."

"Nobody is giving you a hard time?"

Mateo paused. "No. Not much. I keep to myself." He looked around the room. "Is not like this, amigos." He smiled again at Steve and gingerly put his arm around Steve's waist. Steve pulled him close to show it was all right to do so. Meanwhile Greg and Alex were communicating telepathically, their eyes locked for a moment.

"Mateo," Alex said, as he scooted over in front of Mateo and Steve. He squeezed Mateo's thigh, the one next to Steve. "We still have Ricky's bed in our second bedroom. Why don't you move in with us, like Ricky did? You can live like this full time, sweetie." Mateo looked surprised and uncertain. He turned to Ricky who nodded furiously.

"¡Hazlo!" Ricky insisted, shaking Mateo's other thigh that was rubbing up against his own. "Do it! Alex and Greg are wonderful. You can have my bed for as long as you want ... forever! You'll be able to live naked and totally gay all the time! Do it! Juan and I will come over and make pancakes on Sundays!"

"He makes great pancakes, amigo," Alex encouraged. "And I can practice my Spanish with you and I'll help you with your English. Everyday. I promise."

"Mateo," Luke spoke up. "You'd better do it. Alex gets very grumpy if he doesn't get pancakes at least once a week." Mateo looked concerned, until Luke continued, "I'm kidding, Mateo. Alex never gets grumpy. But I think you should take them up on the offer."

"Okay, amigos, I let you know. Okay?" Mateo was overwhelmed. This was a lot to take in, and he needed to think about it.

"Mateo," Greg leaned forward, "don't worry about anything. You can pay us half the rent you're paying now."

"Half?!" Mateo was stunned. "I let you know!" he said more forcefully. It was obvious he'd probably already decided, but needed some time. Speaking of time, it was time to end the evening. As everyone stood and prepared to leave, Greg turned to Luke.

"He can stay rent free, but I don't want him to feel like a charity case. What do you think?"

"I think you made the right call. A suggestion ... put whatever rent he pays in an account, and when he finds a lover, and you know he will, it can be a going away gift for him."

"Great idea. Thanks, Luke. Perfect."

That Thursday night Mateo texted Ricky and asked to come by. Ricky was busy with deliveries, but promised to be home by nine, and invited him to come over then. He then texted Juan to be sure it was okay.

'Sure, mijo. Pretty sure I know why.'

'Si. So happy for him. & Greg & Alex' Ricky ended up finishing around eight-thirty, got home and stripped to match Juan, although Juan was wearing his chest harness. They intended to get a body harness for Ricky, but just hadn't found time to get over to Mr. S yet. If Ricky got his way, the harness wouldn't be their only acquisition on that visit. Ricky, who hadn't come in weeks due to his insistence on having his next orgasm only from Juan fucking him, was beyond horny. So, while waiting for Mateo, he busied himself with sucking and teasing Juan until Juan's phone announced Mateo at the street door. Juan released the door lock, put down his phone and tried to rise.

"Stay put, Papito, he knows the way. You taste too good to stop now." Ricky swallowed Juan's cock and resumed pleasuring the two of them until there was a knock at the door. Ricky released Juan, lifted his head and yelled, "¡Adelante cariño!" Mateo started to enter, saw Ricky's head buried in Juan's crotch, and started to back out.

"Ups ... perdón," Mateo apologized.

"Hey, come back here," Ricky yelled as he turned around between Juan's legs, smiling his adorable smile. "I was just making my Papito happy while waiting for you."

"Bueno," Mateo smiled back as he entered and gingerly closed the door. "Sorry is so late." Juan peeled himself away from Ricky and stood, motioning Mateo to the same spot he'd occupied on his last visit.

"Have a seat, I'll get us a beer." He returned with three, handing the first to Mateo, then returning to his seat, where Ricky was patiently awaiting his return, so he could snuggle in between his shins. "You can get naked, too, if you want ... might as well get used to it if you're moving in with Alex and Greg." Juan held up his bottle in an air toast. Mateo followed suit, took a sip, then stood and stripped.

"This is maybe really weird, but ..." Mateo confessed. "You make it seem so normal. To be naked. To be excéntrico. To be queer."

"Mateo, it is normal," Juan affirmed. "Forget all that macho shit you've had rubbed in your face all your life, all *our* lives. There are many normals, and this is one of them." He punctuated his point by leaning down while lifting Ricky's head with one hand and kissing him deeply. He released Ricky and sat back, while Ricky gave Mateo a satisfied smile. "When are you planning to move, and can we help?"

"That's why I wanted to see los dos ... both of you. If I will live with Greg and Alex, I am to make my English better, no? Anyway ... I want to ... but it will be so different. I don' really know them ..."

"Mateo, when they took me in, I didn't know them very well, either, and they made me family right away. You will love them, I promise."

"Yes, but you had experience being gay, Ricky. You know what you was doing ... like when I come in now ..." Mateo gestured toward the door.

"Wait a minute," Juan said. "Are you saying you're a virgin?"

"Si, virgen." Mateo looked sheepishly at Juan. "Not like Ricky and you. I don' really know how to do sex." Ricky, taking a cue from how he imagined Raphael would have reacted, got up, walked over to Mateo and knelt down at his feet. He placed his hands on both of Mateo's thighs as close to his crotch as he dared and looked into Mateo's eyes.

"Mateo, Greg and Alex will not ask you to have sex with them. They're not like that. They will love you and take care of you like family ... you will be family ... you *are* family, now ... to all of us, but they will not take advantage of you. ¿Entendido?"

"I understand. Thank you, Ricky. I maybe feel better now."

"Mateo," Juan came over, too, and knelt at his feet, putting an arm around Ricky's shoulders. "were you worried they would expect sex from you in exchange for staying there?" Mateo didn't say anything verbally, but his face made his answer obvious. He didn't want to come right out and say it. "You have been the victim of abuse, haven't you?" Mateo looked away and sighed, still silent. Finally, he nodded his head sideways, not exactly yes or no, then looked into Juan's eyes.

"Not bad, Juan. No rape or anything, but in the restaurant lots of words, looks, guys touching my face, my butt, wanting me to go home with them, but I say no."

Juan bent his head down and kissed Mateo's thigh, just below where Ricky's hand was resting. "Good. I'm not surprised ... you are a very sexy guy, Mateo. I'm glad you were able to protect yourself. You've been fortunate."

Mateo smiled and placed a hand on Juan's shoulder. "Maybe too ... fortunate ... amigo. I still waiting to learn how to fuck." At that, Ricky burst into laughter and sat up straight, pulling his hands free of Mateo's thighs. He turned to Juan, putting both arms around Juan's tight waist. Juan turned to him.

"Papito, let's show Mateo how it's done. Please fuck me in front of Mateo." He turned to Mateo, again putting a hand on Mateo's thigh. "Would you like to watch, Mateo? He's very good. You will learn a lot." Juan was the one to laugh at that, as he pushed Ricky away in mock disgust. Ricky lifted himself back up, jumped up, ran into the bedroom and returned with a towel and the lube bottle. He squatted down behind Juan, put his mouth next to Juan's ear and whispered in his most sexy voice, "I'm serious, Juan. Let's show Mateo how it's done."

"There are a thousand ways to do it," Juan demurred. "I don't think we have that much time."

"Let's show him our favorite." Ricky jumped up, moved the small coffee table out of the way, spread the towel, laid down on his back and threw his legs up, wrapping his arms around them to present himself. He turned his head sideways toward Mateo and Juan, both of whom looked a little stunned. "Fuck me, Papito. Pleeaasse."

Juan sighed, turned to Mateo and said, "Well?" Then he looked down to see Mateo's erection, then back up into his eyes. "There's my answer. Okay, then, Mateo ... watch and learn." Juan moved over to Ricky, crawled between his legs, put both hands on either side of Ricky's shoulders, leaned down and swallowed Ricky's tongue. Within a couple of minutes of deep kissing Juan was impressively hard. He raised up on his knees, reached down and unscrewed his PA. He lubed up Ricky, then himself, looked back over at Mateo who was grabbing his erection with one hand, and smiled. Mateo smiled back, but didn't let go of his own hard cock. Juan returned his gaze to Ricky, his adorable caged leatherboy ... his apparently exhibitionist caged leatherboy, and he entered Ricky, purposely slowly since this was part love making, part demonstration on how to do it right. Mateo was about to find out how verbal Ricky could be when fucked. As Juan massaged his prostate, he moaned, he sighed, he begged, he shouted proclamations of undying love. At times Juan silenced him by alternately burying his tongue in Ricky's mouth, or extracting Ricky's tongue into his own. Juan drooled into Ricky's open mouth and licked it back up. He picked up the pace hammering Ricky's ass, then slowed it to a gentle pump. As had been the case lately, Ricky was drooling precum from his Holy Trainer onto his unbelievable abs, making Juan hungry to taste his leatherboy's cum. So hungry.

Juan looked over at Mateo just in time to see him blast his own cum all over his chest and stomach. He, too, became verbal. Juan leaned down as he pumped hard, and said, "Mateo just came for you, Ricky." And that was the trigger that had been missing. Ricky let loose with a roar as he came all over himself. Juan, grateful, thrilled, relieved and proud, came as well, pumping Ricky's ass full of his Papito's cum. Since this had become a performance, Juan decided to make the most of it. He pulled out, lowered Ricky's legs to the floor, then knelt forward and lapped up every drop of Ricky's cum and precum. Then, he crawled forward and shared it all with Ricky in a long, grateful, happy, deep kiss. Then he collapsed on top of Ricky, licked his face, his ears, his chin, all of which were nice and salty, then he moved down to lick each of Ricky's rock-hard nipples. Then, for what he thought would be an apt finale, he pulled Ricky into a sitting position and maneuvered him over to Mateo.

"Look, mijo, Mateo brought dessert." Juan collected some of Mateo's cum on his forefinger and dramatically licked it off. Ricky followed suit.

"Yum! Mateo, you taste really good!" Ricky proclaimed.

"Have you tasted your own cum, Mateo?" Juan asked. Mateo shook his head, not quite believing what he'd just witnessed. "Here, try it." Juan collected another sample and held his finger up to Mateo's lips. Slowly, the tip of Mateo's tongue emerged. Just barely. Juan raked his finger across it, just before it disappeared behind Mateo's kissable lips. Juan smeared the rest on those lips, bringing Mateo's tongue back out to wipe his lips clean. As Mateo smiled and gave a funny little laugh, Juan and Ricky took turns licking Mateo's belly clean, pausing every few seconds to kiss and share what they had found.

When they sat back, Mateo was still hard. And beaming. "Did you learn anything, amigo?" Ricky asked, a little hoarse.

"Si, amigo. Si, si, si. Gracias. Dios Mio. Si."

"I learned something, too, Mateo," Juan smiled, pulling Ricky close. "My little leatherboy loves an audience."

"I blame Raphael" Ricky laughed. Then, still keeping Alex's secret, "And, Alex!" Then, turning to Mateo, "Let us know if you need any more lessons, amigo." Juan pushed Ricky away and laughed as well.

"School's out, mijo. Mateo has graduated!" He picked up his luke-warm beer and gave an air toast to Mateo and Ricky, "Here's to your first time coming with another guy ... two guys! I'm glad it was with us."

"Si. Same for me." Mateo picked up his bottle and air toasted back.

Forty-Nine

MATEO MAKES HIS MOVE

JUST IN CASE, AND hoping it would make it so, Greg and Alex were putting the finishing touches on the conversion of their second bedroom into an actual bedroom. Ricky's stay, as enjoyable as it had been, had been so brief that the room had still been half bedroom, half storage room when Ricky fell ... well, pushed himself ... into Juan's arms. This weekend some of the stuff went to Community Thrift, some to a couple of other charities, and some to a long talked about, but never quite acquired, storage locker. They were ready for Mateo, if Mateo was ready for them. This was all done around regular obligations and Alex's new extracurricular activity ... the 'reception.'

"I don't know why you keep calling it a reception," Greg posed early Tuesday evening. "Do you think it's fair to spring something like this on them ... on their wedding day no less?"

"Greg, their entire love lives, at least Raphael's and Luke's, are based on surprises. They call them dares, but they're surprises nevertheless. And, think about it. Niki's whole persona today is the result of a lifechanging surprise by Steve and ... dum de dah! ... Raphael and Luke. If we didn't surprise them, they'd think we don't love them anymore."

"That kind of sounds like rationalization to me, to get to do what you're going to do anyway, but, okay. It maybe, kinda, sorta has a teensy tiny basis in fact."

"Gee, what do you really think?" Alex snarked. Greg took Alex's face in his hands, to deliver a casual, husbandly kiss.

"I really think you're amazing. Nobody else would ever go the lengths you're going to, to fete Luke, Raphael, Steve and Niki the way you are. I just hope they appreciate everything you're doing ... that all your co-conspirators are doing. This isn't going to be easy to pull off."

"It's all in the planning, darling. I have spreadsheets to prove it."

"I have no doubt. Anyway, time to head over to Raphael and Luke's. What should we wear?"

"What you're wearing now looks good." Both of course had stripped upon arriving home earlier.

"I will if you will. You know I will."

"Are you channeling Raphael tonight? If it was warmer out, maybe I would."

"Would not."

"I would, my darling, daring stud. I've evolved, remember?"

"I'm going to remember this moment, Alex. And, hold you to it."

"Yeah, you do that." Teasing over, they pulled on sweats, took one last look at what they already considered to be Mateo's room, and headed to dinner.

Alex and Greg arrived only moments before Steve, who walked in before Alex and Greg had finished stripping.

"Where's Niki? Did he have to work early?" Alex asked.

"He's coming. He's with Juan."

*"With Juan?" Luke spoke from the living room. "Is Juan getting some puppy tips from Niki, for training Ricky?"

Steve laughed. "No, I don't think Ricky's pup material. I don't know what's up. I'm sure we'll find out when they get here. All I know is Niki texted to say he'd meet me here after helping Juan." Ten minutes into a wedge of St. Andre and a bottle of Pinot, the front door opened, and voices came from the other side. In walked Niki, then Juan, then Mateo. Among them they carried four boxes and three large shopping bags, which they carried directly into the bedroom, before returning, closing the front door and ripping off street clothes.

"Lucy, you have some 'splaining to do." Raphael directed to Juan. Juan looked confused for a moment, then laughed, turning to Mateo.

"He's doing his Ricky Ricardo impression, Mateo. If you laugh, maybe he'll stop."

"Since when do you channel Lucille Ball characters?" Niki asked, helping himself to cheese and crackers.

"Since I have three gorgeous Latino men in my house, Ethel." Raphael replied.

"I think I'd rather be Fred, but, whatever." Niki sidled up next to Steve, bestowing a 'hello, I'm back and I missed you' kiss.

"So, what's up, guys. Seriously." Raphael would not be ignored. Alex and Greg had surrounded Mateo by now, and were conferring in low tones.

"Somebody tell me what's up, dammit," Raphael insisted.

"Do you really have to ask, baby?" Luke walked over to Raphael and wrapped his arms around him from behind while facing Mateo, Alex and Greg. "Is tonight the night, Mateo?"

"Si, but I wanted to wait until Ricky is here." Mateo beamed. "Si ... yes ... I accept to live with Alex and Greg."

Raphael was out of Luke's arms and wrapping his around Mateo, who completed the embrace. Raphael then hugged Alex, then Greg while bouncing up and down. "This is ... so perfect!" Then, he bolted toward the kitchen, exclaiming over his shoulder, "We need to celebrate!" While he was putting a bottle of Schramsberg in the freezer to chill, Ricky arrived, food bags in hand. Luke took the bags from Ricky, who began shedding his clothes. Once done, Ricky planted a kiss on Juan, then made a point of not so casually sauntering over to the coffee/dining table to help himself to some cheese. Raphael returned from the kitchen and let out a whoop.

"Ricky! Nice harness. Oh, and let me see ... you have a collar now, too!" Raphael pulled him into a locked cock brotherly hug. "How do you like them?"

Juan answered for Ricky, "He won't take the harness off ... he even sleeps in it. The collar of course, won't be coming off. And, oh by the way, the collar was not my idea.'"

"Hey, I slept in my harness, too, before Luke moved in. It was my way of having him with me."

"I think it's Ricky's way of having you with us, Raphael," Juan suggested. "He made a point of telling Rob ... Ricky's on a first name basis with the guy at Mr. S, if you can believe it ... that he wanted the same harness you have. They had to custom fit it, but now it's his."

"When did you get it?" Alex asked, running his hands along the chest straps, and 'accidentally' brushing across Ricky's nipples.

"Saturday. It was kind of a celebration," Ricky smiled. "I finally came from Juan fucking me." Ricky didn't share all the details of that night.

"Awesome!" Raphael congratulated Ricky. He glanced over at Juan who looked just as happy about it as Ricky. "So ... was it what you'd hoped it would be?"

"Dios Mio, Raphael, it was maybe my best orgasm ever." Ricky looked over at Juan, then back at Raphael. "You know what I mean, right?"

"I do, muchacho. I'm happy for both of you." He looked over at Mateo, to urge him to share his news with Ricky. "Mateo ..."

"Ricky, I move in with Greg and Alex tonight! Juan and Niki help me get my stuff from the apartment while Julio and Tomás were at work." Ricky and Mateo hugged, then Ricky pulled Greg and Alex into a group hug before turning to Mateo while still holding onto them.

"You're going to be so happy there, Mateo. These guys are the best." Greg and Alex just smiled, each with an arm around Ricky's shoulders, enjoying the moment.

"Perfect timing, Mateo," Alex said. "Your room is ready for you. I hope you like pink sheets." Mateo looked confused. "I'm kidding ... I'm kidding." Mateo laughed, pretty sure he got the joke. Alex then turned to Ricky, "You were serious about the Sunday pancakes, weren't you, Ricky?"

"Damn straight ... I mean ... right!" Ricky laughed at his own lame joke. He was basically giddy over Mateo's news, and a little thrilled to be modeling a harness and collar just like Raphael's.

"So, the harness and collar were a celebration, Juan?" Luke asked. Ricky moved back into Juan's arms. Everyone had been standing, and now they started to assume their regular places.

"Yeah, the harness was something we'd been meaning to get since Ricky didn't have one. The collar ... well, he twisted my arm over that. Him and Rob. You should have been there. He actually told Rob he deserved to be collared because he was going to be the best leatherboy ever."

"I might have something to say about that," Raphael challenged, smiling all the while. "What do you think, Luke? Sirrrrrr?"

"Is there such a thing as Best Leatherboy Emeritus?" Luke suggested, looking over at Juan. "As far as I'm concerned, it's a tie. I wouldn't change a thing about either of you."

"I'll drink to that," Juan raised his wine glass in an air toast. "Here's to the best locked cock boys, leathered and otherwise, in the world!" That got everyone's glass in the air.

"Mateo, do you think your old roommates are going to be pissed?" Greg asked. "Julio was pretty rough on Ricky."

"Maybe ... but they know many people. Someone will take my place."

"Mateo was paid up through the end of the month, and I left a little money to get them well into next month," Juan volunteered.

"Juan!" Mateo reacted. "No, you should not have."

"Don't worry, Mateo. I just don't want them to have any hard feelings about you. It's better this way, muchacho."

"If they have half a brain, they'll figure out Mateo's queer, and they'll be glad he's gone anyway," Alex said as he scooted over and rubbed Mateo's thigh. "You're where you belong now, and that's what matters." Then, looking up at Juan, "That was a cool move, Juan. I'm impressed."

"Thanks, Alex. And thank you both, again, for doing this for Mateo. I wish we had more room ..."

"I'm glad you don't," Greg said "It makes us happy to do our part for our little family here."

"Guys," Steve interrupted the lovefest. "Why don't we open these bags and eat? I'm guessing my pup here worked up an appetite lugging that box here from Mateo's apartment." Alex and Raphael leapt up and started unboxing and serving.

"I guess we got distracted, huh?" Raphael apologized. "So much fun news tonight, eh, collared brother?" He handed a couple of plates to Ricky, so he could hand one off to Juan ... or Mateo. In fact, in pursuit of Best Leatherboy Ever recognition, he handed both plates off. Raphael handed him another for himself and said, "You have learned well, grasshopper." Then, he kissed him on his landing strip.

While everyone was chowing down, Raphael turned to Alex and said, "So, Alex ... you promised more info on this reception you're planning. Our big day is not that far away ... so spill." Mateo looked confused.

"That means tell us everything, amigo," Ricky 'splained. Mateo smiled and nodded. Joining the family was improving his English already. Even if it wasn't textbook English.

"Hmmm," Alex raised his eyes to the ceiling, as if seeking enlightenment. "What to tell ... what to tell." Raphael just stared and munched. Alex continued to munch as well, and despite himself, smiled a little too devilishly.

"Raphael," Luke offered, "maybe this would be a good time to find out if Alex is ticklish."

"Good idea!" Raphael put down his plate and raised up on his knees.

"No, no, I'll talk, I'll talk," Alex scooted away from Raphael, and toward Niki. As Raphael sat back down and resumed eating, Alex returned to his side. "I'm not trying to be a jerk, guys, it's just that I know you like surprises, and I'm working on making your wedding day as awesome as I can. Trust me, okay? Let me have my secrets for now. You'll see, feel, experience it all in exquisite detail soon enough."

"Exquisite detail?" Niki asked. "Now I'm really curious ... and maybe a little worried." Steve rubbed his mohawk in a comforting gesture, but nodded in agreement.

"Isn't there anything you can reveal, Alex?" Steve asked. "I've never heard of anyone having a surprise wedding."

"Hmmm. Well, I've already told you about the actual wedding ceremony, what you'll be wearing, and who'll be there, so technically, the wedding won't be a surprise." He paused a moment, then continued, "Okay. How's this. I've actually planned two receptions. One for right after the ceremony for you four and family. Not really a reception, but a nice dinner. To celebrate with your loved ones, so, kind of a reception. Then, the parental units will take a limo to Feinstein's at The Nikko, which is where they'll be staying, so it'll be classy and convenient."

"What is Feinstein's?" Ricky asked.

"Michael Feinstein's nightclub. Very cool. Nice touch, Alex," Juan approved.

"Sounds very nice, Alex," Raphael agreed. "Mama and Angel will be impressed."

"Angel won't be going to Feinstein's. He'll be at the other reception, the one for you four, and a few others."

"Oh?" Raphael asked curiously, looking over at Niki, then up at Steve. Luke came over and sat down behind Alex and Raphael.

"Aaaannnnnd?" Luke asked, putting a hand on each locked cock boy's shoulder. "We'll be going toooooo...."

"Aaaannnnnd, that's all you get," Alex turned to Luke and smiled smugly. "All you need to know is that after dinner, your parents will be entertained, and so will you."

"Oh, man!" Niki exclaimed. "We were so close ..."

"If I may." Greg stood up, taking over the floor. Alex gave him a 'please don't' look. "This guy," he joined Luke behind Alex and put his hand on Alex's other shoulder, "has been working his butt off to create an event you'll never forget. He knows how much you like surprises, and he knows how much you appreciate surprises that blow your minds. He knows how much work each of you have put into creating such surprises yourselves. This is his wedding gift to the four of you. Trust him. Let him blow your minds. I, for one, can't wait for your wedding day."

"Well," Luke said, letting go of Alex and wrapping his legs and arms around Raphael from behind, "when you put it that way, I guess we should stop badgering Alex and just be grateful. Eh, baby?" He kissed the back of Raphael's smooth head.

"I guess you're right. Dammit."

"Sorry, Alex," Niki said softly. "And, thanks. Really. Thanks." Then he looked up at Steve and barked.

"So, there's nothing we can do to help?" Steve offered. "And, yes, indeed, thank you for all you're doing, Alex."

"You're welcome." Alex leaned back into Greg's arms. "I'm not doing this all alone, so I don't get all the credit, and no, all you need to do is promise me one thing." Then, once again, he stopped talking and looked at Raphael. And waited.

"What?! What do we have to promise, O Master of Surprises?" Raphael snuggled deeper into Luke's arms. Alex leaned forward and looked at each future husband one by one.

"Promise you'll do whatever I ask you to do when the time comes. No matter how strange it may seem. Can you do that?" Niki looked up at Steve, as Raphael and Luke did the same.

"Sure, Alex. Whatever you say," Luke volunteered. Alex looked at Steve, who nodded. Niki barked. Twice. Alex then looked into Raphael's eyes. The eyes of the guy who surprised him on his birthday by butt fucking him with a double headed plug, one that both now happened to be wearing as they sat.

"I promise. I owe you that," Raphael quietly consented.

"Thanks, guys. I won't let you down."

"Mateo," Raphael said as he stood up, "we're going to celebrate your move with a toast of sparkling wine. Want to help me?" Mateo jumped up and the two of them headed into the kitchen and returned with the chilled bottle and nine flutes. "Our family has grown to the point that I can't carry all the wine glasses anymore," Raphael joked as he and Mateo returned. Mateo helped clear a spot on the table so they could set the glasses down.

"That's not a bad thing," Greg offered.

"Not at all," Steve agreed. "I have to admit, I really look forward to all of us being together every Tuesday."

"And Sunday," Ricky chirped. "Pancakes, every Sunday at Alex, Greg and Mateo's place." Niki nodded and smiled, as Raphael began pouring sparkling wine.

"Alex, Greg and Mateo's place," Alex repeated. "That has a nice ring to it, don't you think?" He picked up a glass and raised it toward Mateo. Everyone else followed suit. "To Mateo's new life."

"To Mateo!" everyone chorused. Mateo looked up at Juan, who was beaming at him, then to the rest of the group.

"Gracias a todos!" he said shyly, then, "Thank you ... every ... one?" Ricky nodded, rubbing Mateo's thigh.

"As always, I wish I could stay longer, guys, but duty calls," Niki said as he stood, set his empty flute on the table and headed to the bedroom to put on his mesh thong, then the street clothes that would get him to the bar.

"We should probably do the same," Juan stood. "We need to truck Mateo's stuff over to the new place."

"Juan, you and Niki did your part," Greg also stood. "Alex, Mateo and I can handle it, right guys?"

"Si!" Alex responded, looking at Mateo and grinning. ¡Vámonos!, muchachos." That tickled both Mateo and Ricky. Juan gave Alex a thumbs up gesture. It was clear Mateo's presence was already leaving its mark on the family as another pleasant evening drew to a close.

Fifty

<figure>⟨◦ ⸺ • ⸺ ◦⟩</figure>

THE BIG DAY FINALLY ARRIVES

Two PANCAKE BREAKFASTS AND another Tuesday dinner later, and seemingly before anyone knew it, it was the week of the Big Day. That Monday Alex stopped by Raphael's cube mid-morning to check in.

"How are the butterflies, my little blushing bride?" he asked, placing hands on both Raphael's shoulders as he leaned over and cooed in Raphael's ear. Alex had shed a lot of inhibitions about displaying queer displays of affection at work in the months since Raphael had begun conditioning him. Finding out the CEO was gay herself, hadn't hurt.

"I have no butterflies," Raphael replied, spinning his chair around. "We're in good hands, or so I've been told." He reached out and took Alex's hands and pretended to examine them. "Yep, just like Allstate. What about you, Mr. Wedding Planner? How are your nerves?"

"Not bad, considering. I'm wrapping up a few loose ends, but everything's under control. I'm taking off Thursday, and Friday of course. What about you?"

"I'm taking off Friday, yeah, and doing just a half day Thursday. Angel and Mama are driving up and Luke's parents are landing Thursday afternoon, and we want to spend time with them before you take control of our lives on Friday."

"Back to my question ... aren't you a little bit excited, about getting married? Married, Raphael! You're going to be Luke's husband. Finally. And he's going to be yours." Alex crouched down and looked earnestly into Raphael's eyes. "Most guys would be jelly right about now."

"Maybe I'm in shock, but, no, Alex, I'm fine. After all we've done for each other, and meant to each other, the wedding seems like more of a validation of what we've already accomplished. It's not like olden times, when the wedding is the beginning of exploring life together." Raphael leaned forward and lowered his voice. "You know better than anyone that we've done our share of exploring already ... butt buddy." He sat back up.

"We've been living together for almost a year. I wear his collar ... and his cage. He wears my ink. This wedding is just the exclamation point on our bliss." Raphael paused a moment. "Okay, that sounded pretty stupid."

"Sounded pretty poetic to me, my LCB. What about Luke?"

"Oh, he's a mess," Raphael laughed. "Mr. Studly actually cried last night in bed."

"What? Why?"

"I don't want to get too personal. Basically, he was saying he can't believe it's happening. He puts on a good show as a leather stud, but not so deep down he's a romantic fool. It's one of the things I love about him."

"That's no surprise. Remember the flowers ... the bouquet that led to us to really get to know each other? That was about as romantic as it gets. You're a very lucky guy, Raphael. So's Luke."

"Yeah. Now, stop, or you're going to make me cry, too, right here in front of everybody."

Alex stood and pulled Raphael to his feet and embraced him. "You deserve this, Raphael. All of it. That's why I'm going to make sure your wedding is legendary."

"There's that word again. Alex, it follows you wherever you go. Just how legendary can a civil ceremony be?"

"Just. You. Wait. My lovely." Alex grinned as he released Raphael. As he walked away, Raphael sat, spun around in his chair, then kept spinning for a few seconds. He had to admit, he really couldn't wait. Were these butterflies?

The last Tuesday dinner in which there was only one legally wedded couple present was, for once, without any surprises. The topic of the wedding was front and center, but Alex held his ground.

"All you need to know for now is to be at Angel's room at the Nikko at three. That's where we'll get dressed. We'll meet the parents in the lobby at four, and we'll take two limos to City Hall. The ceremony is at four-thirty. From there the newlyweds and biological family will limo around town with bubbly served while the grooms point out sights to Steve's and Luke's parents ... basically killing time until you'll arrive at the restaurant for dinner at six."

"Where's dinner?" Niki asked, knowing it was fruitless, but he had to ask.

"Someplace worthy of you," Alex smiled. "After dinner, the parents, as I explained before, will take a car back to the Nikko, and the newlyweds ... god, I love saying that ... and Angel, will take a separate car to ..."

"Tooooo ...?" Luke implored.

"To an evening that will be ..." Alex tortured.

"LEGENDARY!" Raphael finished Alex's tease. Ricky clapped his hands and whopped, inadvertently drawing everyone's attention. He immediately pulled back securely between Juan's shins and tried to look innocent.

"Niki," Raphael said, "how easy do you think it would be for us to torture a few details out of Ricky?" Niki started crawling towards Ricky, barking all the way. Ricky grabbed Mateo and pulled him in front of himself as a shield. Mateo began laughing and pulled away, and crawled behind Raphael and Alex to head Niki off. The two began wrestling for dominance, much to the delight of everyone else. It was gratifying to see Mateo so at ease with the idea of wrestling another naked man. No one wanted them to stop, but soon both Niki and Mateo were laughing so hard they had to. As they separated and returned to their places, Raphael looked winsomely at Luke.

"So, everyone here knows what's happening on Friday except the grooms themselves?" Luke asked no one in particular.

Alex rose up and walked over to Luke on his knees, then sat back and placed a hand on Luke's thigh. "Luke, Sir, if it makes you feel any better, no one knows everything except moi."

"Not even Greg?"

"Not even Greg."

"What's this now?" Greg leaned across Luke's other leg to put his face closer to Alex's. "You have surprises for me, too?"

"For everyone, darling," Alex smiled. Greg sat back up and looked warily at Luke.

"Okay, now I'm getting worried. I've been here before ..."

"And, I'm feeling better already," Luke laughed. He looked at Raphael and did that eyebrow thing. "What do you think, baby?"

"I think there's no point in speculating. Alex has us right where he wants us. I have a feeling this wedding will be YouTube worthy one way or another. Legendary good or legendary disaster. If it's the latter, we do know where they live." Luke laughed at that and slapped Greg's thigh.

"Owww! Hey, I'm just an innocent bystander."

"Excuse me," Luke protested. "More like a co-conspirator. Raphael's right ... we know where you live."

Alex moved back behind Raphael and pulled him into a sitting hug. "No disasters, boys. Trust me."

"We do, Alex," Raphael said as he laid back until he'd forced Alex on his back. Then he rolled over so they were cage to cage on the floor. "We're counting on you." He planted a big wet one on Alex's lips, then rolled off him and sat back up, facing Mateo.

"Something tells me you're in on this too, amigo." Mateo smiled and looked away. Then, he looked back at Raphael, put a hand on Ricky's thigh, and nodded.

"It will be ... legendary!" Mateo pronounced, causing everyone to burst into laughter. Alex's English lessons were fully on display.

Fast forward to Thursday evening. Luke and his parents, Steve and his parents, Angel, Mama, Niki and Raphael enjoyed getting to know one another over a table full of tapas and more than one bottle of cava at Canela. Mama had insisted on sitting between two of her three favorite sons. Once the obligatory questions about Raphael's, Niki's and Luke's 'interesting' hairstyles were out of the way, the conversation focused on what everyone had been up to. The details of Niki's new job were adroitly avoided to spare the uninitiated. That could come later, if ever. By evening's end the future in-laws were all relaxed with one another, and looking forward to the upcoming ceremony.

City Hall. The Rotunda. Friday Afternoon. It's probably safe to say the arrival of the wedding party was the most Instagramable event at City Hall that day, thanks to Alex. Luke, in his tartan, fit right in. His dad, thanks to a little encouragement from Alex, was also kilted. Raphael and Angel were resplendent in their sarongs. Niki, Steve, Juan, Ricky, Mateo, Alex and Greg were all in matching jodhpurs, and along with the grooms, in maybe slightly too flamboyant shirts of the Renaissance. If anything, Steve's dad stood out in his gray suit. The moms at Alex's urging, held their own in various outfits of red and black, to complement the black jodhpurs and red carnations pinned to each man's shirt. The parents all marveled at the opulence of the setting, having never been in City Hall before. The party received more than a couple affirmations from admirers as they ascended the grand staircase en route to the Mayor's Balcony, where they were greeted with applause by the officiant.

"I must say, what a perfect way to end my day," the Mayor said. "You all are just fabulous!" Yes, Alex managed to arrange for the Mayor herself to officiate. He never revealed how he pulled that one off.

The ceremony itself was fairly standard, taking only about fifteen minutes. Rings and kisses and hugs were exchanged, a few tears were shed. The Mayor clasped each hand in congratulations, and the party headed down to ground level, all of whom were now bound together more tightly ... and legally ... than ever. As they neared the bottom of the staircase, Niki stopped and turned to Steve. He took Mama's hand in one hand and Steve's in the other.

"I'm now complete, thanks to both of you. My new name honors you, but now it also proclaims to everyone that you are a part of me." He looked over at Raphael and Angel. "All of you." Mama leaned in and kissed his cheeks, one, then the other.

"You will always be a part of me, too, Niki. Thank you again for the honor. I'm very proud to be your Mama." Then she smiled at Raphael and Luke, "I'm proud of all of you. This has been one of my happiest days ever. I now have five handsome sons to brag about." That got a laugh, and propelled the group back on track onward to ground level. Two cars were waiting at the curb, a massive limo for the grooms and family, another standard Lyft for the five co-conspirators.

"You guys really aren't going to join us for dinner?" Raphael pleaded.

"No, Raphael. This is your family reception. It's all set. We have ... we have some things we need to take care of. We'll see you later. Have fun." Alex kissed Raphael, then stood back as the driver opened the limo door. After the parents had boarded, Luke kissed Alex as he prepared to enter, as did Niki, then Steve. As Angel passed him, he, too, kissed Alex.

"What the heck ... when in Rome!" Angel laughed as he climbed in. Angel knew just enough about what was coming to know that kissing Alex would probably not be the gayest part of his evening. Alex's cage suddenly got heavier. Beauty ran wide and deep in the Malaluan family, and a kiss from Angel was unexpected, and very much appreciated.

As the limo pulled away, Juan said, "I didn't know Angel was gay, too."

"He's not," Alex smiled. "But he should be, don't you think?"

"Oh, yeah. Lucky you, kissing a straight boy. In broad daylight."

"Play your cards right, maybe you'll get a kiss from him, too, before the night's over."

"That's okay," Juan grinned, pulling Ricky, who already had his arm around Juan's waist, tight. "I get all my kisses from the Best Leatherboy in the World, right here." And, to prove it, Ricky leaned up and planted one.

"Okay, guys," Alex commanded. "Into the car. We have our work cut out for us. ¡Vamonos!, amigos!"

Fifty-One

L.E.G.E.N.D.A.R.Y.

DINNER FOR THE TEN members of the wedding party was as special as the ceremony at City Hall. Waterbar itself was a hit. Their table was at one of the huge windows overlooking the Bay. Everything was extraordinary, not just the food, but the service, the floor to ceiling aquaria, and, of course, the company. Maybe because of their non-traditional wedding attire, or maybe due to something Alex had communicated to the restaurant, the staff seemed unusually attentive. The Bay Lights installation on the Bay Bridge just beyond the windows began their dance shortly after they were seated, a further acknowledgement of their celebration. If the evening had ended then, it would have been a perfect day. But, of course, there was still more to come. So much more.

Luke's father discretely asked the server to bring him the check while everyone was mooning over dessert. "I'm sorry, Sir, I can't do that. The check has been taken care of." He looked at Luke, who looked at Raphael, who looked at Steve.

"Alex and Greg," Steve stated the obvious. "We're going to owe them dinner for a year."

"I guess when Alex says, 'you're in good hands,' he means it," Raphael agreed. "We'll figure out a way to get even, right Niki?"

"We have our ways," Niki grinned. Then he turned to Mama, "I hear you're all going to a fancy nightclub this evening."

"Yes, with my new friends and in-laws. May I call you in-laws?" she directed to Luke's and Steve's parents.

"Sounds fine to me, Maricel" Luke's mother agreed. "And what will you boys be doing?"

"We have no idea," Luke admitted. "Alex has some kind of surprise planned. If you don't see us by nine in the morning, send out the St. Bernards." Then he turned to his dad. "You wearing that kilt to the nightclub?"

"If you can wear kilts full time, Luke, I think I can wear one for one night, don't you think?"

"Feels good, doesn't it?"

"It does. Yeah. I can see why you do it."

"Actually, I don't have a choice, but that's a long story."

"You'll have to tell us that story sometime, Luke."

"Maybe after a couple of single malt scotches, Dad. It's a doozy."

"I'll look forward to it." Meanwhile Raphael's eyes, those dreamy, almond eyes, were widening with each exchange. How much had Luke had to drink? As they made their way toward the door, Raphael pulled Luke aside.

"How much are you going to tell him ... about us?"

"That day may never come, baby, But, if it does ... as much as I think he can handle. He just celebrated his gay kilted, mohawked, septum-pierced son's marriage to a beautiful sarong-wearing, collared man, sporting a regulation high 'n tight and matching septum ring. I think he's figured out most of it by now, all by himself. Oh, and there's his son-in-law's Black, mohawked, dog-collared brother to boot. Nothing about us is ordinary."

"As usual, you're probably right. He's cool, all right."

"Yeah, and he thinks you're pretty cool, too. Of course, everybody falls in love with you."

"I know. It's my cross to bear." That brought a hearty laugh, just as they exited the door.

"What's so funny, Luke?" Steve asked.

"Raphael. My husband is so funny." That was the first time Luke said it, and it brought a lump to his throat. Suddenly it was real. Husband. Raphael wasn't just his 'baby' any longer. He was his husband. He pulled Raphael tight against him as the group approached the waiting limo. Hugs and kisses were exchanged again as the 'boys' saw the parents off. Then, the five looked around for their ride.

"It's supposed to be a van of some sort," Angel announced.

"Why a van? There are only five of us." Luke questioned.

"Here it comes," Angel responded without answering Luke's question. It was indeed a big van. Once they climbed in, they found out why. Waiting inside for them, was Juan. Not just any Juan, but a Juan wearing only a black net racing suit, like the ones Greg and Luke had worn for Halloween. The van began to slowly move.

"Oh, no!" Steve exclaimed. "Now we know why our parents were sent off on their own."

"What the hell?" was all Raphael could muster as he looked at Juan, sitting in the last row of seats, grinning away.

"Hello, boys. My name is Juan and I'll be your escort this evening. Please do as I say and no one will get hurt."

Niki had to laugh at that. "Is that why you're here and not Alex? I could take Alex."

"Seriously, guys, I'm just here to help. I have a bag for each of you. Inside is your outfit for tonight. We don't have much time, so strip, put on your outfits, and put your clothes in your bag."

"I don't believe this," Raphael said. "Wait, what am I saying. Of course, I believe this. Alex is a monster, and *we* created him. This has 'dare' written all over it. On our wedding day, no less. Amazing!"

"Juan, can you tell us what's going on? Alex said he was planning a reception." Luke asked.

"I'm just following orders. Oh, wait, I do have something here to read." He picked up a note card from the seat beside him. "Ahem. And I quote, 'You all agreed to do whatever I ask of you when the time comes. The time has come.' End quote. Not me, Alex. You promised Alex. Strip boys." Juan's grin was back. After a couple of heavy sighs, they started stripping. As they opened each bag, there was more consternation, not to mention a fair amount of swearing.

"What the hell is this?" Steve asked, holding up the contents of his bag.

"It's my Halloween costume!" Luke exclaimed. "Remember? It's a see-through body suit, like what Juan is wearing." Then Luke opened his bag. "Quelle surprise! Here's my body suit. Alex must have gone shopping for you, Steve. You've got your own body suit, now."

"Swell." Steve was not amused.

"You were right about Alex shopping," Niki agreed, holding up a sheer white mankini dotted with gold and silver flecks. "This looks suspiciously like what Raphael and Alex wear at the end of their strip act."

"Yeah," Raphael agreed, holding a sheer white mankini of his own. "Juan, where are we going dressed like this? This is totally weird."

"I should have said no," Angel moaned, holding up his own net racing suit.

"Angel!" Niki exclaimed with glee, "Okay, this may make it all worth it ... to see you in that."

"I should have said no," Angel repeated. "The sarong ... sure. I've worn lots of sarongs, with and without Raphael. And, our dad. But this?"

Juan stood up, moved toward them and did a three-sixty. "This, Angel, is sexy. On you, double sexy. Now, strip."

"Once again, we see why Ricky couldn't get over losing Juan," Raphael grinned, in spite of himself. "Damn, you look hot, Juan."

"Not as hot as you're about to look, Raphael. Those mankinis were custom made to fit you and Niki. Hurry up, guys, you're running out of time." Considering how little they had to put on, it didn't take long for the wedding party to go from stylishly festive to all but naked. Juan helped them stuff jodhpurs and sarongs into their respective bags, just in time for the van to come to a stop. "We have the van for the evening, so just leave your clothes here. And follow me." This was the first time any of them had seen Juan in a racing suit. Maybe Alex planned it this way, maybe not, but anyone would have followed Juan anywhere at that point.

As they climbed out of the van, they found themselves in an alley, facing an industrial style steel door. Juan knocked on it three times, then waited.

"This just keeps getting weirder and weirder," Raphael moaned, his arm around Luke's waist. "Where are we, Juan?"

Before Juan could answer, the door slowly opened to reveal a stranger who instantly smiled. "We've been expecting you gentlemen. Please follow me." Juan took hold of the door so everyone else could enter ahead of him. They followed the stranger up a short flight of dimly lit stairs, down a hall, around a corner and onto what appeared to be a darkened stage. A stage? There was a heavy curtain before them, and behind them was a softly lit scrim, so it must be a stage. The space was decorated with a number of palms and many arrangements of alstroemeria, in a variety of different colors. Once they were all together, the stranger, referencing an index card much like the one Juan read from earlier, spoke again.

"Niki, Steve, Juan, please stand here." He indicated a spot further into the space. "Raphael, Angel and Luke, over here, please." He positioned each of the men in a line, facing the curtain, with about five feet between Luke and Niki. "Excellent. By the way, congratulations. I have to say, you're one very sexy wedding party. Now, don't move, anybody." Then he just walked away.

Raphael looked at Luke and said, "Weirder and weirder!" That's when Alex and Greg walked in from stage left. Greg was wearing a net racing suit, Alex was in one of the sheer gold and silver flecked white mankinis. Greg kept walking and stood next to Angel. Alex remained center stage, facing them.

"Okay, Alex ... what ... is ... going ... on?" Raphael implored. Alex smiled, then clapped his hands together, and bent at the knees in pure delight. He straightened up and cleared his throat.

"First, of all, you all look amazing." He paused, taking in each member of the group, pausing maybe just a little bit longer with Angel. He looked back at Raphael in approval.

"I promised you a reception, and there is one waiting for you in just a few minutes, but first, I wanted to make absolutely sure you really are married. I mean, I know you are, I was there. But I wanted you to have the opportunity to exchange your vows in a way a little less traditional and in a way far more fitting with how we live our lives. I wanted your wedding day to be ... legendary." With that, as Alex walked over to Greg's side, the curtain before them began to rise.

As it did, bright light flooded the wedding party from spots shining directly on them, making it difficult to see what was beyond the stage. But it soon became apparent that they were no longer alone, as a crowd ... a crowd? ... of people began clapping and hooting beyond the lights. Something Raphael and Alex were used to, right down to their current state of undress. But, given the circumstances, totally disorienting for all of them, nevertheless. They barely had time to look at one another for answers when a tall, radically outfitted, over the top nun in a wickedly accessorized habit, walked from behind them, through the space between Niki and Luke and on to the front of the stage. She turned to face them and motioned them to come toward her. Once they were only a couple of feet from her, she motioned for them to stop. She turned to face away from them and spoke to the crowd.

"Ladies and gentlemen, friends, family and lovers, thank you for joining us tonight. I am Sister Merry Evermore, of the Sisters of Perpetual Indulgence, and I have the great honor to join, in your presence, four very special young men in holy matrimony." At that, the crowd, which was slightly more visible from this new vantage point, cheered. There seemed to be hundreds of them.

"Before we begin, we seem to be missing a few members of the wedding party." Surprisingly, Sister Merry put her fingers to her mouth and issued a shrill whistle.

Luke leaned toward Raphael and whispered what had by now become the evening's mantra, "Weirder and weirder." Before Raphael could respond, Mateo, clad in a matching sheer mankini, walked on from stage left and took his place next to Juan. Right behind him trotted three human pups, while at the same time three more human pups trotted out from stage right, each threesome setting themselves down in front of each half of the wedding party. As good pups should do, they wore only puppy hoods, tails, collars and chest harnesses. Only two were caged, and one of the uncaged should have been. His erection was clearly visible from most angles. As if on cue, all six pups looked back up at Niki and barked.

"That's better," Sister Merry said above the din of the cheering, clapping crowd. Raphael took advantage of the commotion to lean past Angel toward Alex.

"Where's Ricky?" he asked, surprised to see Mateo with Juan, but no Ricky.

"It's okay ... he's here. Just wait." Raphael, relieved, straightened up and faced forward again.

"Love can be expressed in as many different ways as there are people," Sister Merry Evermore began. "Our four celebrants this evening are, to put it mildly, shining examples of that. These four men not only have devoted themselves to their individual partners, but they have in so many ways affirmed their love for other members of the wedding party as well. Not only are three of those before you brothers, but in substantial and everlasting ways, all of these men have grown to form a loving family, a chosen family. The wedding vows we are about to witness are mere legalities, in essence ratifying what has already come to pass. We are not creating new bonds this evening, we are, indeed, celebrating them."

Sister Merry turned to face the wedding party. Her wireless mic insured nothing would be missed by the crowd. "At this time, we'd like to witness each of you exchange vows with your partner. I know this celebration is a surprise for all of you, so you may need a moment to gather your thoughts."

"I'm ready," Niki surprised everyone. Steve squeezed his hand, knowing public speaking was not one of Niki's talents. Niki looked into Steve's eyes, having long ago found inspiration there. At Sister's urging, Niki and Steve took a step forward.

"I owe my life to four people, two of whom are on this stage, and one of whom is sadly departed," Niki proclaimed. "I owe my happiness, the joy in life I feel each and every day, to many on this stage, but most of all, to you, Steve, my love, my guardian, my husband. You hold the leash that guides my way. My love for you, as it should be, is unconditional." At that Niki turned to Sister Merry, as Steve wiped a tear from his eye with his free hand.

"Steven, have you any words for us?"

"Okay, that's a tough act to follow," Steve said, after clearing the frog from his throat. "Wow. Niki, I knew the day I met you, that it would be easy to fall in love with you. You had a smile, and still do, that pretty much renders me speechless. You have the biggest ... heart ... of anyone I've ever known, I would do anything for you, and I know there is nothing you would not do for me. You have proven that countless times already. Having you by my side makes life. Worth. Living. Nothing I've ever achieved has made me as proud as my privilege in being able, from this day forward, to call you my husband." A silly, shy grin worked its way across Niki's face. Steve started to bend down to kiss him, but Sister Merry intervened.

"Ah ... Ah ... no kisses yet, you two. We're not quite done." She turned to the crowd and stage whispered, "If I was marrying either one of these two, I'd be eager for a kiss ... and a whole lot more, too, but ... we must observe proper protocol. Don't you think?" The crowd roared its approval. She nodded approvingly and turned back to the wedding party.

"Raphael and Luke, please step forward." As they did, Steve and Niki, stepped back in line with Juan and Mateo. "Luke, what would you like to say to Raphael?"

Luke, who was already holding Raphael's hand, bent down on one knee, as if proposing. "One year and six weeks ago exactly, in the midst of you and me discovering just how exciting and adventurous and fulfilling a life together could be, you knelt as I am doing and proposed to me. Although we had only been together a few months, I already knew I had found the love of my life. So, I did not hesitate, not for a second, to say yes. Yes, I would marry you. Yes, I would devote my life to you. Yes, I would ask you to become my Locked Cock Boy. Forever, and always. You have never said no to me, and I have never said no to you. And I never will. I never would have dreamed that anyone could make me as happy, or as complete, as you do. Before you entered my life, I was nothing. With you, I am Raphael's husband. I am everything I ever could have hoped to be." Luke stood up, and with extraordinary difficulty restrained himself from kissing Raphael. He looked at Sister Merry, who again turned to the crowd.

"I don't know about you," she stage whispered, "but I don't know how much more of this I can take." She dramatically wiped a tear from each of her heavily made-up eyes. She turned back to Raphael. "Raphael, please be gentle with us ... we're all verklempt here." Someone in the crowd honked loudly into a hanky to reinforce the point. Raphael took Luke's other hand in his, so he was holding both.

"Luke ... Luke ... nothing I can say here ... or ever, will adequately describe what I feel for you. I am who I am because of you. You showed me how to be a man. How to be a lover. How to be part of a whole that I never dreamed I could be a part of. How to be outrageously proud to be ... Luke's Locked Cock Boy. With you in my life I am everything, and without you, I would be no one. I love everyone on this stage. But ... I am so very proud to say, I belong to you." Raphael looked to Sister Merry for permission to kiss Luke, but, dammit, she held up her forefinger, waving it to say not yet, you eager Locked Cock Boy. Not quite yet. She turned back to the crowd.

"And now ... may we please have the rings?" she pronounced dramatically. At that the lights ... all the lights, dimmed then went completely dark. In the back of the hall suddenly a faint blue glow appeared. About the size of a pickle. No one could tell what it was. Then, three spots illuminated a circle on the floor, a few feet ahead of the blue glow. Pachelbel's Canon in D began to play. After a few bars, the blue glow moved and suddenly a burst of light exploded at the locus of the spots. It was a form ... a man ... it was Ricky! Ricky, who was completely naked, coated head to toe, from landing strip to each and every toe, in gold and silver glitter that reflected back those spots in a million different directions. The only part not coated in glitter was his glowing, baby blue Holy Trainer. He was holding a small, black velvet pillow in both hands, on which rested four gold bands. The crowd erupted in gasps, cheers and applause. The wedding party was stunned. As Ricky stepped toward the stage in time with the music, the spots tracked with him and the crowd began to clap in time with his steps. Raphael had wrapped his arms around Luke, Niki was holding Steve and looking at Juan, who was beaming with pride. Mateo was clearly proud, too. And a little erect. Greg was hugging Alex, who was finally breathing a deep sigh of relief. No question about it, Ricky was spectacular; it had come off even better than he'd hoped. Ricky looked angelic. Ethereal. And, sexy as hell. He knew it, because Sister Merry Evermore was desperately fanning herself.

Ricky reached the steps leading up to the stage. Once he topped the stage, he knelt down on one knee, presenting the pillow and rings to Sister Merry Evermore. She looked at him in awe. She reached down and took the pillow, he stood and walked over and took his place between Juan and Mateo, each of whom put an arm around his tiny, glittering waist. Sister Merry looked out at the crowd.

"If I live to be as old as Methuselah, I will never ... ever ... officiate a wedding as epic as this." She turned to Ricky, "Young man, I should tell you, and I say this as a revered member of the order of the Sisters of Perpetual Indulgence, don't you ever let those gorgeous men holding on to you right now ever try to put clothes on you. If God had wanted you to wear clothes, he never would have bestowed upon you all that sacred glitter." Once again, the crowd erupted in applause and cheers. Sister Merry held up a hand,

"If I may ..." She turned back to the wedding party and distributed the rings, indicating to Steve which were his and Niki's, then to Luke which were for him and Raphael. Once the rings were slid into place on each husband's hand, she spoke again.

"Niki Maricel Raphael Angel Malaluan-Phillips ... whew! ... do you take Steven Phillips as your lawfully wedded husband, guardian and companion in life?"

"I do."

"Steven Phillips, do you take Niki Maricel Raphael Angel Malaluan-Phillips as your lawfully wedded husband?"

"I do."

"Raphael Malaluan, do you take Luke Mitchell as your lawfully wedded husband and keyholder for life?"

"I really, really do."

"And, finally, Luke Mitchell, do you take Raphael Malaluan as your lawfully wedded husband and Locked Cock Boy?"

"Of course, I do. Forever and always."

"Then in the power invested in me by the State of California, I pronounce you husbands for life! NOW, you may kiss!" As the crowd cheered, the husbands kissed, they really, really kissed, but they didn't stop there. By the time they were done, everyone on the stage, with the exception of the hooded pups, had kissed, which meant everyone, including Sister Merry Evermore, had glittery lips. And a few glittery bare chests. Hell, there was glitter all over everybody, and nobody minded a bit. Sister Merry turned one last time to the crowd.

"There is bubbly and glitter-free wedding cake at the back of the hall. Please enjoy yourselves, and, if possible, try to congratulate our newlyweds without getting too much glitter on yourselves." She led the way down the stairs off the stage, followed by the six pups, now on two legs, then the wedding party. One of the waiters, in a more conservative, if you could call it that, solid black mankini, met them at the bottom of the stairs with a tray of flutes filled with bubbly.

Fifty-Two

THE PROMISED RECEPTION

THE MEMBERS OF THE wedding party each took a flute from the mankini-clad waiter and clinked glasses, then sipped. Alex held his glass up again.

"A toast, before we scatter and mingle, please ... to the sexiest newlyweds anyone has ever laid eyes on ... to the unbelievably brave and willing ring bearer, who has set the bar somewhere in the stratosphere, and to the loving groomsmen, gay *and* straight, who cheerfully went along with this crazy scheme." The glasses clinked again, then they were drained. Another mindful mankini-clad waiter arrived to exchange glasses with each of them.

Ricky in all his glittery glory, had his free arm around Juan's waist, and Mateo had his free arm around Ricky's waist. Raphael moved over to him and kissed him on the lips again. "You were stunning!" Raphael affirmed. "And, look at, you. Sister Merry Evermore is right ... Juan should donate all your clothes. Clearly, you're totally at ease, spectacularly naked among all these people."

"Well, you know, it helps to be the star of the show," Ricky kidded. "Besides, you're all pretty much naked, too."

"So, what's the secret to the glowing cock cage, Ricky?" Niki asked, as he bent down and took it in hand to examine it.

"Little LEDs. Alex and Juan removed the cage, glued them to my cock and replaced the cage."

"Where's the battery?" Luke asked as he, too bent down.

"In my butt. See the wires?" Ricky lifted his left leg.

"That is so cool!" Niki stood back up and turned to Alex. "It makes me wish I wore a plastic cage so you could do the same for me. It would be a huge hit at the bar."

"Let me give it some thought, Niki," Alex agreed. "I'm sure there's a way to illuminate your steel cage. It would look great, wouldn't it? If there's room in your butt for the battery and your tail."

"No sweat," Niki laughed. "I can take 'em both." Steve nodded knowingly. The group began to disperse, to accept congratulations, and greet the many attendees, some of whom were in pup gear, some in various elements of leather attire, and some in more standard party dress.

"Peg!" Raphael exclaimed as he realized Peg and her wife were present. "It's wonderful to see you both." Luke joined Raphael and nodded.

"This was just amazing, you guys," Peg smiled, clinking glasses with each of them. "Your friend Alex really knows how to orchestrate a wedding. So much more than a wedding ... more like a happening."

"I get compliments just about every day on my tattoos, Peg. I'll always be grateful to you."

"Well, we're grateful to you and Luke, too. You'd be amazed at how many people linger over the photos of you two in our portfolio books. We've even done a couple for guys inspired by Luke's pubic ink. Guys who want their penises dedicated to their lovers. You're both inspirational." Not far away Alex and Greg were chatting with a couple of the regulars from Niki's bar when someone tapped Alex on the shoulder. He turned to see Cynthia, the company's CEO and her wife, Patricia, both tastefully attired as usual. He blushed as he turned to shake their hands.

"Cynthia, Patricia, what a surprise!" He considered creating a fig leaf with his free hand, but decided it was much too late for that.

"A surprise?" Cynthia mused. "But you invited us, didn't you? And I'm so glad you did. This was a wedding not to be missed, am I right, Patricia?"

"Yes, indeed. I understand you were the architect of this affair, Alex?"

"I had a lot of help."

"You are clearly a very dear friend to Raphael and Niki, and their new husbands," Patricia continued. "You are all very fortunate to have one another. And, the ring bearer. Truly inspired. Very clever. And perfectly executed. You must be very persuasive to get him to agree to participate so boldly."

"Actually, it was easy. He's family. All of us who were up there are family, like Sister Merry Evermore said ... chosen family. Except Angel, here, he and Raphael are biological family." Alex reached out and snagged Angel's arm as he was passing by, and introduced him to Cynthia and Patricia.

"You must be very happy for Raphael," Cynthia said. "And, if you don't mind my saying so, you look absolutely studly tonight."

Angel laughed, and grabbed Alex's biceps as he said, "I don't know about 'studly,' but this was all Alex's doing. I have to admit I wasn't very happy about wearing this when I first saw it tonight, but I guess Alex knew what he was doing. He managed to honor the life that these guys all enjoy together. It's really inspirational in a way. And, best of all, they all take such good care of each other. We, uh, had the privilege of being there for Niki years ago when he needed us, and it seems Raphael just keeps finding new people to rescue. I'm glad I could be a part of his and Niki's big day, as unconventional as it is," he looked down at his net encased body as he finished. Raphael and Luke appeared then, Raphael's eyes widening at the sight of Cynthia and Patricia.

"Cynthia ... Patricia ... heeeyyyy. Um ... fancy meeting you here!" Raphael turned to Alex with a questioning smile as he spoke. "Did you ... did you enjoy the ceremony?"

"Yes, Raphael. And, Luke. Very much. We were just complimenting Alex on what a spectacular job he did."

"It was a surprise to all of us. Obviously not to you..." Raphael wasn't sure how to handle this moment, naked and caged before the woman in control of his career.

"I'll admit, we were expecting something a little more ... conventional, but I'm glad it wasn't! I have a whole new measure of admiration for you and Alex. There's nothing wrong with going bold, eh, Patricia?"

"An evening to remember, indeed, my dear. Now let's let these boys mingle." As they turned and walked away, Raphael turned to Alex.

"Wow. The surprises keep coming!"

"Word got around. I didn't want Cynthia to feel snubbed. I never in a million years thought she'd actually come."

"Word got around?" Luke asked. "How did you get all these people here, Alex? I have to say I'm impressed."

"How much time do you have? An undercover social media campaign. Face to face. Email, texts ... I've been busy."

"Damn, I'll say," Raphael laughed. "And, you know, maybe it was fine that Cynthia was here. Now you can wear that mankini to work after all. We have no more secrets."

"We still have our secrets, butt buddy," Alex grinned. "But, yeah, it's good to know she can handle socializing with naked staff."

"Not just naked staff members, caged naked staff," Luke interjected. "She's one awesome lady."

"Yeah," Raphael agreed, just before Jake grabbed him from behind and spun him around for a big bellied hug and kiss. Not surprisingly, Jake was mostly naked himself, except for his ubiquitous body harness and leather codpiece, all of which showcased his impressive belly. As he chatted with them Niki walked up and started rubbing his belly admiringly. Steve joined the group, wrapping his arm around Niki's shoulders.

"Jake ... looking good!" Steve greeted him.

"Thanks. I might say the same ... in fact I will. You should wear that outfit to the bar from now on, Steve. Shows off your dedication to the gym. You all look irresistible tonight ... especially that ring bearer. My, my, my." He rubbed Niki's belly as he spoke. A secret ritual between them? Luke looked at Steve to see if he was paying any attention, but Steve was busy looking around the room.

"Steve, Jake makes a good point," Luke said. "Why not wear that when you join your puptender at the bar?"

Steve laughed, "Maybe for special occasions. I don't want to distract attention from that puptender. Like that would ever happen." As if Jake's mention of Ricky had sent a signal, Ricky, Juan and Mateo wandered up to the group. Mateo had definitely attached himself to Juan and Ricky, not knowing anyone else present, and still no doubt shy about public nudity.

"Mateo," Raphael said, leaving Luke's side and pulling Mateo into an embrace. "You were very brave tonight. Thank you for being a part of our celebration. You look beautiful."

"Thank you. You look beautiful always, Raphael. You all do. I'm so lucky to be here!"

"Did Alex threaten to throw you out if you didn't do this?" Luke joked. Alex barked a laugh.

"No," Mateo laughed. "He ask nice. What can I do. We are all amigos, no?"

"Well said," Steve agreed as he pulled Mateo out of Raphael's embrace and into his own. "We're the lucky ones, Mateo. Let me second Raphael's gratitude. Gracias, muchacho."

"Hey, guys. I just wanted to say congratulations and wow ... what a wedding!" A young guy who looked vaguely familiar joined the group, a little awkwardly.

"Thank you ..." Luke nodded to him, then looked at Alex for help. Alex made a 'beats me' look and stepped forward to shake his hand.

"I'm Alex ..."

"I know. Remember? I'm Ryan. I was Clifford's date at the company party. You and Raphael were upset with him for telling the boss about your strip act ... well not the stripping..."

"Oh, yeah. Right ... Ryan. Sorry," Alex looked over at Raphael. "Where's Clifford?"

"Um, I don't know. We broke up last week. But I already knew about this from him, and I thought it would be okay if I still came. I didn't want to miss a Chastity Brother's wedding." He looked from Alex to Raphael and back. "Gosh, I hope that's okay."

"It's fine. It's fine. Glad you're here. Having a good time?"

"Are you kidding? This is awesome. You guys are all so hot!" Ryan looked admiringly at Mateo as he spoke.

"Well, thanks for coming," Raphael smiled as Ryan turned and started to walk away. Good grief, he thought, is everybody I ever met here? As he turned back to Luke, Mateo grabbed his hand.

"He is cute," Mateo grinned. "You know him?" Raphael whooped and pulled Mateo back into a hug.

"No, not really, but I think you should get to know him." At that he yelled out "Ryan!" as he pulled Mateo away from Juan and Ricky. Ryan turned around in response as Raphael, with Mateo in tow, approached.

"Ryan, I wanted you to meet my amigo, Mateo. Mateo, this is Ryan. Ryan, hablas español?"

"Si," Ryan grinned. "Nice to meet you, Mateo. I love your outfit." As Ryan reached out to shake Mateo's hand, Raphael released his grip on Mateo.

"Gracias," Mateo shyly responded, looking back and forth between Ryan and Raphael, not quite sure what to expect. Raphael looked at Ryan and winked.

"Ryan, I don't think Mateo has had a piece of wedding cake yet ..." As Raphael turned to walk back to the group, Ryan took Mateo's hand and led him toward the buffet.

"You better not ship our Mateo off so soon," Alex scolded when Raphael returned.

"Not to worry, Alex. Ryan was dating Clifford, so he's probably a student at SF State, and in no position to take Mateo on full time. Mateo needs to start meeting guys his age, don't you think?" He pulled Alex in for a side hug. "Besides, he's the first guy Mateo's shown an interest in. You're not jealous, are you?"

"No. You're probably right. It's just ..."

"Have I told you yet how grateful we all are for what you've done here ... not just here, but all day. City Hall. Waterbar. Feinstein's. God, Alex ... you're unbelievable." Alex smiled as he looked deeply into Raphael's eyes. He took both Raphael's hands in his own as he did so.

"Raphael, I would do anything for you and Luke. You know that. Niki and Steve, too. It was absolutely a labor of love in every sense of the words. Maybe, deep down, I wanted to participate in a wedding I wish I had had myself. If I'd been brave enough then to have such a wedding. I've grown a lot since you and I became friends. You know that, Raphael. You engineered most of it. Consider it a small down payment on pay back. Besides, how else was I ever going to get to see your other brother naked? Damn, Angel's almost as hot as you, Raphael."

The lump that was forming in Raphael's throat instantly disappeared with that last sentence, and he had to laugh.

"Yeah, he's a good sport, isn't he? I wonder when he'll wear that body suit again?"

"Do us all a favor, and insist he join us for Tuesday dinner once in a while. Damn." Raphael laughed again and pulled Alex in for yet another hug and kiss.

"I haven't seen Niki lately, have you?" he asked Alex when they pulled apart.

"He's over there, with the other pups," Alex pointed to a spot across the hall, near the stage. Raphael started to head that way when Ricky joined him, still nursing his flute of bubbly. They joined hands.

"How many propositions have you had tonight so far, Ricky?" Raphael joked.

"I stopped counting at ten," Ricky laughed. "I'm thinking of dressing ... well undressing like this on my DoorDash runs."

"You should! People will start ordering all their meals from Door-Dash, and insisting on you to deliver."

"I know, right?" Ricky giggled. "I'll be able to retire in a year."

"In a month. Don't sell yourself short, sparkle boy," Raphael grinned, making Ricky giggle again as they approached what had become an ad hoc puppy park. There were several other pups sniffing around one another, besides the six who had been in the ceremony. Niki was in the midst of them, despite not being in his normal pup gear, except for the collar. Raphael squatted down and began petting one of the caged pups who'd been on the stage.

"Hey, puppies," he announced. "Thank you so much for participating tonight. You were all awesome!" The other five groomspups trotted over to get their share of attention. Ricky got down on his knees and began petting them, too. The pups were barking in appreciation, maneuvering for their share of attention from the sparkly human, apparently not willing to break out of pup mode to tell Raphael and Ricky that they were happy to have been of service. It was pretty obvious, though. A couple were sniffing Raphael and Ricky in places somewhat inappropriate for the setting. More giggles from Ricky. Raphael looked over at Niki.

"You wish you were in your pup hood and tail right now, don't you?" he needlessly asked. Niki nodded.

"Of course," Niki smiled wanly. "Oh well. Some of us are getting together in the pup park next weekend. Besides, Steve deserved to be married to the human me ... you all did. It's fine. More than fine. Tonight was perfect."

"It kinda was, wasn't it?" Raphael agreed. "You get the credit, Niki. I'm a married man tonight thanks to you and Steve."

"That glittery guy next to you was the one who suggested a double ceremony."

"I guess I owe thanks to both of you." Raphael stood, reached down and took Ricky's hand to lift him up. As they started back into the crowd, Raphael turned back to Niki and mouthed, "I love you." Niki barked in agreement.

"Have you tried the wedding cake?" Ricky asked.

"No! Let's check it out. Oh wait. Can you eat with all that glitter on your lips?" Raphael cautioned.

"Have you seen your lips?" Raphael licked his lip tentatively and realized some of his kisses had had consequences.

"Don't worry. The glitter on my lips is edible."

"Of course. Good ol' Alex ..." They headed straight for the buffet area. Before they could join the short line, a mankini clad waiter grabbed two plates and came around the line to hand deliver them.

"Now that's what I call service," Raphael said, taking his plate.

"All part of the service, Sir. And, congratulations," the waiter responded as he handed Ricky his plate.

"Sir. He called me, Sir," Raphael mused, making Ricky giggle again. "What will Luke say?"

"Probably something like," and Ricky tried to lower his voice, "'To me you'll always be baby.'"

"Yep," Raphael laughed. "Thank goodness, huh? We both have our Sirs to worship, don't we, amigo?"

"Yeah ..." Ricky replied a bit wistfully. "Raphael, do you think Juan and I will ever get married?" Raphael stopped munching on cake and put a hand on Ricky's shoulder.

"I can't guarantee it, muchacho, but let me put it this way. You two were made for each other. I knew that the moment you fell into his arms at the Eagle that day."

"You were there? You promised!"

"Of course, we were there. We'll always be there for you, Ricky. Just like we'll be there when you get married. Just don't ask Alex to be your wedding planner."

"Are you kidding? I want a wedding just like this. And I want *you* to be my ring bearer."

"Me? Gee, I don't know..."

"You owe me," Ricky grinned as he stepped back and gestured at his sparkling naked body.

"Oh, yeah ... I guess I do. Maybe. Wouldn't Mateo be a better ring bearer? He's so cute."

"He's too shy, Raphael."

"Today, maybe. But I think he has promise, Ricky. He's seemed pretty at ease tonight."

"Yeah ... well, I want you." Raphael laughed, put his free arm around Ricky's waist and walked the two of them back into the crowd. There were so many who wanted to greet them and congratulate Raphael. Including regulars from Niki's bar, not to mention Brent and all the staff. Raphael was stunned to learn he'd posted a 'closed for private event' sign at the bar so everyone could attend Niki's wedding. More than one suggested that Raphael and Alex should add the sparkly ring bearer to their strip act. Raphael pretended to think it was a brilliant idea just to pimp Ricky.

"No, thank you. I only do weddings," was Ricky's response. He did seem to enjoy the attention, though. And he was relieved when Juan strolled over and wrapped his arms around Ricky, telegraphing to everyone that Ricky, thank you very much, was taken. Very taken. Allyson was there too, much to Raphael's delight.

"I'm assuming you created these mankinis for Alex," Raphael complimented her, as they hugged.

"I did. He really put together quite a show. I'm proud to have had a small part in it. It looks damn good on you, by the way, if I do say so myself." Raphael laughed.

"I love it. I'll wear it for our strip shows at the Powerhouse, so it'll get more than one wearing."

"How have the costumes been working out for you guys?"

"Perfect!" Raphael praised. "Your designs have been much loved by our fans."

"That's what I wanted to hear. You all certainly live interesting lives. Judging by what's under this mankini, *very* interesting lives. You'll have to come by the shop sometime for a pot of tea and fill me in."

"I'll do that, Allyson. Thanks." They parted and Raphael finally found Luke again, who was talking with a couple of the regulars from the gym. They all chatted a moment, then Raphael pulled Luke away.

"Did Alex hack our phones?" he asked Luke. "How did he know how to invite them? He's never been to the gym."

"I'm guessing the word 'viral' applies here. He did mention social media." Luke pulled Raphael into a full body hug. He bent down and whispered into his ear, his lips teasing Raphael's ear as he spoke, "I'm ready to make love to my new husband. How about it, baby? How much longer should we stay?" Raphael turned his head to line his lips up with Luke's. Neither of them was timing the kiss, but it must have lasted a while, because suddenly Alex was there beside them.

"I think it's time you two got a room," he said authoritatively. Then he laughed. They pulled apart and gave him their best dirty looks. "I'm serious, though. The van is here, and it will take us all home. Sister Merry will announce our departure, then we can go, and the rest can stay and party. Follow me." He took each of their hands and led them back to the stage, where the rest of the wedding party was waiting. Had the kiss really lasted that long?

Sister Merry Evermore announced their departure, the crowd applauded one last time with a few chanting "Ricky! Ricky!" Ricky let go of Juan's hand and made a dramatic bow to more cheers, and they all filed off, stage right, down the hall, out the door and into the van.

"Now I see why you got such a big van," Steve said as they settled in. There were now ten passengers.

"We'll drop off Angel at the Nikko, then Juan and Ricky, then Niki and Steve, then Luke and Raphael, then finally Greg, Mateo and me." Alex announced, apparently still in charge.

"Where is my bag?" Angel asked. "I don't want to scare the tourists, wearing this into the Nikko."

"Yeah, your sarong is so ... nondescript," Luke kidded. "Here's your bag."

"Thanks. I'll risk the sarong if you don't mind. It is a Japanese hotel after all."

"Probably why Alex picked it," Raphael surmised, wiggling his eyebrows at Alex.

"Sure, whatever you say. That and the convenience of Feinstein's," Alex replied.

"Speaking of Feinstein's, I wonder how our parents' evening went?" Steve asked. Luke fished his cell out of his clothing bag.

"My dad sent a text a while ago. Says they had a nice evening, hopes ours is fun, too. He's inviting all of us to brunch at the Nikko tomorrow at eleven. All of us. That includes you, too, Mateo. How about it? Can everyone go?" No one objected. "I'll let him know the count."

As it turned out, only Angel bothered to pull anything on over his body suit before exiting the van. No one else needed to, since they'd be stripping down as soon as they got home anyway, and heading to bed. Except, maybe, for Ricky and Juan.

"Ricky," Alex advised as they pulled up in front of Juan and Ricky's place, "stuff a coffee filter in the shower drain to catch as much glitter as possible, or you might end up with a clogged drain. Use lots of warm water and shampoo on your body as well as bath gel. That should loosen the glitter." Ricky nodded.

"Are you going to leave the cage lit up like that?" Raphael asked with a grin.

"Hell, no," Juan replied. "I have other plans for his butt tonight. And, since the cage has to come off, I have some very special plans for ... you know. If it isn't too sore after we peel those LEDs off." That comment elicited a collective groan.

"Ricky." Alex said earnestly, taking his hand as Ricky stepped down from the van. "Gracias, amigo, you were amazing. No ... you were legendary." Ricky smiled, and reached up to press a bit more glitter onto Alex's lips.

"You're welcome. Alex. It was an honor. Really." Then, more loudly, "Bye guys! See you tomorrow!" Then, hand in hand, Juan and Ricky, sparkling under the street light, headed into their building.

"How the hell did you ever get Ricky to agree to be our naked ring bearer tonight?" Raphael demanded once the door slid shut. "He was incredible."

"He did it for you, Raphael. And for you, Luke, Niki and Steve. He felt he owed you for your help in getting him and Juan back together. He would have done anything for you guys."

"That's crazy. Seeing him and Juan together ... that's all the thanks we'll ever need." Luke said, pulling Raphael close, as he seemed to be shivering a bit, despite the heat circulating through the van.

"Agreed," Steve seconded. "But, I'm glad he did it. I have to admit I think my heart stopped when he stepped into that spotlight. When it comes to putting on a show, you are a genius, Alex."

"Thanks, Steve. But the truth is, I had some pretty amazing talent to work with. Ricky made it work."

"You're too modest," Steve said as he slid the door open and stood aside so Niki could climb out. "It seems feeble to say thank you, Alex and Greg, but really, thank you for the most extraordinary day of my life." Niki nodded, putting an arm around Greg's waist, then he barked, grinned, and barked again. As Greg slid the door closed, Niki and Steve headed up the stairs to their front door, and to yet another surprise in a day full of surprises.

Fifty-Three

─◦◦─•────────•─◦◦─

GIVING PUP NIKI AN OPENING

GETTING NAKED DIDN'T TAKE long, considering Niki was in a sheer mankini and Steve's mesh racer suit could be removed with the pull of one zipper. Which is exactly what Niki did, sliding the suit off Steve's shoulders and down to his feet, pausing to kiss Steve's now free cock, before shimmying out of his own outfit.

"There were a lot of pups there tonight," Steve said as he stepped out of his racing suit and pulled Niki into an embrace. Niki nodded then pressed his lips into Steve's. Neither seemed in a hurry to break the kiss, which prompted two erections, only one of which was visible. Finally, Steve pulled back far enough to be able to speak again. "I have a surprise for you, puppy, something I think we'll both enjoy." He led Niki into the bedroom and sat him at the foot of the bed, then turned and opened a dresser drawer and rummaged for a second. He turned around and presented Niki with a Neo K9 Hood.

"It's a new puppy hood, in a camo design to complement your mo-hawk." Niki immediately dropped to the floor on all fours, his human tongue panting in anticipation. He'd entered pup head space before Steve had even put the hood on him. "Let's see how this looks on you ..." Steve sat on the floor in front of Niki, his cock still standing at attention as he maneuvered the hood into place over Niki's head. "You look amazing, puppy!" Pup Niki barked excitedly. "Do you want your tail in, pup?" More barks. Steve lubed up, then inserted what they'd come to consider Pup Niki's sleeping tail, as the pup continued to pant enthusiastically. "I could tell spending time with all those pups tonight had pumped up your puppy hormones. This seemed like a good time to spring this new hood on you." Pup Niki barked affirmatively.

Steve moved around in front of Pup Niki again and took his head in both hands. "Another reason I chose this hood is this, puppy ..." He popped three snaps on the snout, releasing the cute snout from the rest of the hood, revealing Niki's sexy-sweet human lips. "Now I can kiss you while you're in pup mode, and, better yet, you can suck me more easily in puppy mode." Pup Niki barked even more excitedly, moved forward, and dived his mouth down onto Steve's rigid cock. After a moment of bliss, Steve pulled Pup Niki's shoulders up, releasing his cock from the pup's firm hold.

"Although you look pretty damn cute right now, it's been a really long day and I see a little glitter here and there on you. Probably on me, too. You can keep the tail in, but let's ditch the hood and shower, okay?" Pup Niki barked affirmatively again. After a shower that probably went on far too long, but certainly not as long as the one Juan and Ricky were probably laboring through at this very moment, Steve was toweling Niki off, slowly, carefully, enjoying the opportunity to be with him, just the two of them, after the long, full day of sharing him with so many other people.

"I'd like to spend the rest of the night with my human husband, if that's ok, Niki," Steve proposed. Niki laughed as he turned around so Steve could towel off his back and butt.

"I'd like that, too, 'husband.' My husband, Steve. Wow … it's real, isn't it? We got married twice today!"

"Which means if you ever get tired of me, you'll have to divorce me twice to get rid of me." Niki turned back around and took the towel out of Steve's hands so he could return the favor.

"Not to worry. I waited all my life to have someone to love, someone who would truly love me. It'll take more than two divorces to get rid of me. I love you, Steve, and I love our life together. More and more, it seems to always be full of surprises."

"You surprised me today … going first with your vows. That was very impressive, Niki. 'Unconditional love.' Nobody can ask for more than that." Niki leaned up and planted a fresh, glitter-free kiss on Steve's lips.

"Can I ask my husband to take me into our wedding bed now? I'm suddenly very tired." Steve took the towel out of Niki's hands and tossed it over the curtain rod as he led him out of the bathroom and into bed. After a few minutes of more kissing, Niki rolled over and let Steve pull him into their normal bedtime embrace. Niki's tail between Steve's thighs, Steve's cock riding just above where the tail exited Niki's butt. Steve draped his right arm over Niki's torso as he slid his left arm under Niki's neck, so Niki could clasp his forearm with his right hand. After a few sighs and deep breaths, Steve slid his right hand down to Niki's belly.

"Niki, can I ask you a question? It's a question, not an accusation, I'm just curious." Niki didn't respond at first, wondering where this was going.

"Of course. Always ... anytime. What is it?" Steve held his hand on Niki's belly, gently rubbing it.

"Do you also have a fetish about big bellies?" Niki barked a laugh, but didn't answer right away. "I've noticed you really like Jake's belly. I mean, it is a pretty impressive belly. And, somehow it looks good on him ... even sexy, I guess. Like I said ... I'm just curious. It's totally okay with me if bellies turn you on." Still no response from Niki. "Okay ... goodnight puppy." After a couple of minutes Niki wriggled free enough of Steve's embrace to roll over and face him.

"Boy, nothing gets past you, does it, my love. My guardian. My husband." Niki's eyes sparkled in the dim light as he looked squarely into Steve's. "Yeah, maybe I do get turned on by bellies. Mostly little bellies, I think. But, for some reason, Jake's is a turn on, too. And not because he's Black, like me. At least I don't think so. There's that guy at the gym, Latino guy who always wears pink shorts ... he has a sexy little belly. Is that weird? I mean none of us have a belly. I think Ricky's abs are sexy as fuck ... so it's not a mandatory. I'm babbling, aren't I?"

"Yes, you are, and I love it!" Steve gave Niki a quick peck on the lips. "You're always a man of so few words. I wish you'd talk more. I wish you'd share more of yourself with me, puppy. Haven't things between us been even better than ever since you were forced to own up to your puppy fetish? I wish you'd shared your belly fetish a long time ago, too. Niki, the more I learn, the more I love you. Okay?" Niki just stared into Steve's eyes another moment, reinforcing his 'man of few words' reputation.

"I guess I worry that you'll love me less if you know me more."

"Okay, Niki that's the craziest thing you've ever said. Like I just said, each revelation that, I guess, I have to drag out of you, makes me love you more. I love you ... the whole you. Every sexy, beautiful, kinky, weird, embarrassing little bit of you." Niki smiled and closed his eyes. "Niki if you want to grow a belly, that's fine with me." Niki's eyes popped open.

"Oh, I don't think you understand. I fantasize growing a belly on *you*." Totally out of character, Niki burst into laughter. "Okay, I said it. Out loud. And on our wedding night!" He pressed his lips against Steve's before he could respond. And kept them there trying to avoid the inevitable reaction. Finally, Steve broke the seal.

"Ooooh. Okay. Of course. If bellies turn you on, that would only make sense that I should have the belly." Per usual, Niki just stared, saying nothing. "Hmmm. How big a belly, puppy?"

"It's just a fantasy, Steve. You're plenty sexy just the way you are, gym body and all."

"Jake has a gym body ... and a belly. He's plenty sexy. How big a belly?"

"I don't know. Are you serious? You'd do that? Grow a belly ... for me?"

"Have you forgotten my wedding vow already? I said I'd do anything for you and I meant it. Luke and Raphael both branded commitments to each other on their bodies with permanent ink, Niki. I think I can add a few pounds to prove my love to you."

"Wow. I don't deserve you, Steve."

"Yeah, you do. You deserve all of me, even a little bit more of me, puppy." Niki laughed again at that, planted one more lip lock, then rolled over to settle back into their nightly embrace. Steve pulled Niki even closer, so they could each feel the other's breathing. It had been such a long, big day, it didn't take many breaths before both were sound asleep.

Brunch the following morning was a nice mix of logical and biological camaraderie. This weekend was the first time Luke's and Steve's parents had met and the first time they'd met Mama and Angel. There was no telling when they would all be together again, so they made the most of it. At one point, Mama, who was sitting across from Ricky, lifted her fork toward him.

"Ricky, you have a sparkle in your eyebrow. Very cute." Ricky, embarrassed, turned to Juan at his side. Juan laughed and picked the glitter speck out.

"I guess we missed one, Ricky," he said, as nonchalantly as possible. Luke's dad looked across at Luke who said nothing.

"Another long story, Luke?" he asked, smiling coyly.

"Very, very long." Luke laughed, then looked to Raphael, who smiled and looked across to Luke's dad and just nodded his head.

"Well, I'm glad you all had a festive evening. You deserved it."

"You are so cool, Mr. Mitchell," Ricky volunteered. "You all are," he looked around the table. "This was very generous of you to invite us." Raphael wanted so desperately to tell everyone what a spectacular contribution Ricky had made to last night's ceremony, but ... well, maybe another time. After several single malt scotches.

"We're just happy to be together with all of you," Luke's mom replied. "It makes us happy to know that our guys are surrounded by such good friends." Steve's mom raised her mimosa in agreement. Everyone else followed suit, except of course, Mateo, quiet little Mateo, who raised his virgin orange juice.

Once brunch was over, Angel and Mama and Luke's and Steve's parents checked out of their rooms. The group shared one last hug as the airport bound parents climbed into Alex's last contribution, a town car headed for SFO. A valet brought Angel's car around, and another group hug preceded his and Mama's departure.

"It was truly memorable," Angel smiled as he gave Alex probably the biggest hug of all. "You're a wicked, wicked man, Alex, but I wouldn't have missed it for the world."

"Thanks for being a good sport, Angel. You were awesome."

"Hey, I just did as I was told." Then Angel laughed, "Like I had a choice. Anyway, take good care of Raphael, Niki, Steve and Luke for me." Then, Angel turned and pulled his big brother into a hug and murmured into his ear, "I'm so happy for you and Niki. I'll try to get back up here soon ... on my own, so I can learn more about this, well, fascinating life you lead. I guess I have a lot of questions."

"Anytime, Angel. You're always welcome. You can stay with us next time." Angel laughed again.

"If I do, I guess I won't have to pack a lot of clothes, right?"

"Just that sexy bodysuit Alex gave you." Angel nodded and squeezed Raphael one more time. And with that he climbed in, and he and Mama were on their way.

"Is everybody headed home?" Greg asked. "Maybe we can get a van to take us all at once."

"No. More. Vans!" Raphael said emphatically. "I'll never fall for that one again."

"No more tricks, Raphael. Promise. At least for today," Alex assured. Nothing looked promising on Greg's app, so they walked, en mass, to Market Street and the Powell Street station. As they walked, Raphael maneuvered to get next to Mateo, and took his hand. Luke still had Raphael's other hand.

"Mateo," Raphael asked, "I'm glad you met Ryan last night. Do you think you'll see him again?"

"Si, yes. He is nice."

"Did he kiss you?"

"Raphael!" Luke scolded.

"I'm just looking after our boy," Raphael responded. "Mother Teresa worries." Mateo looked confused.

"Yeah ... he is nice."

"Good. You'll have to invite him to Tuesday dinner some time, okay?"

"Okay. We maybe go out Sábado ... Saturday? Yeah, next Saturday. He has many classes." Raphael squeezed Mateo's hand in encouragement.

"Mateo," Luke warned as he looked over Raphael at Mateo, "if he asks, don't let Raphael chaperone you on your date Saturday." Mateo didn't grasp all that, so Ricky translated. Mateo laughed.

"Si ... no chaperone!" Quiet little Mateo managed to get a laugh from everyone with that comeback. The nine of them filed into the station, headed for home. Even though it was barely mid-day on a Saturday, no one suggested doing any group thing as they rode an outbound L-Taraval. Everyone was still decompressing from the previous couple of days. As they climbed up the stairs at the Castro Street Station, Luke confirmed that everyone was good for Tuesday night, and that Vietnamese would be the menu. Steve volunteered to bring dessert. Hugs were exchanged in front of Soul Cycle and then everyone headed for their respective apartments.

As they walked home, Raphael casually said, "I wonder why Steve offered to bring dessert Tuesday? I usually make the dessert."

"He probably thinks it's his turn, I don't know," Luke speculated. "Do you think maybe we're monopolizing the dinners too much?"

"Are you kidding? If it wasn't for us, these poor guys would all be eating at home ... probably wearing clothes!"

"Oh, the humanity!"

"I KNOW!"

"Look at it this way, baby, it's one less thing for you to do." Raphael nodded, as they climbed the steps to their door, beyond which awaited a well-deserved 'nap.'

Fifty-Four

RICKY FOLLOWS THROUGH

LATER THAT EVENING, POST nap, post shave and shower and post a light supper, Luke and Raphael were wrapped around each other, watching a movie. Had it not been for the shave and shower and that 'nap,' and the fact they were naked and harnessed, collared and caged, someone might have accused them of already becoming a boring old married couple, sitting at home on a Saturday night. But they'd earned a night of rest after the events of the last two days.

"Oh, Angel promised to come up soon and learn more about Niki's and our 'lifestyles,'" Raphael suddenly remembered.

"That's good, right? He's interested. Open-minded. Heck, he was recruited into it yesterday."

"He probably has lots of questions, especially about the whole Pup Niki thing, and, well, all of our cages. We really never had any time to talk about any of that. It was just kind of thrust on him without warning. He's so cool to just take it all in stride."

"Well, he had a bit of a preview over the phone ... you and me naked and harnessed."

"True. But the cage and the tattoos ... must have been a surprise."

"Hmmm. Surprise. You mean like a dare? Something we haven't seen much of lately?" Raphael suddenly slapped Luke on the pec.

"Sir! You're right! When was our last dare? Things have been so crazy."

"Not sure it counts, but ... maybe Alex's birthday surprise?"

"Oh, yeah ..." Raphael looked a bit wistful. "That was pretty awesome. I wonder if he still wears that plug."

"He does. Greg told me. Just like you. One of my better purchases." Raphael planted one on Luke's lips, a longer one than usual. One that was interrupted when both phones chimed. Raphael reached for his.

"It's a group text from Alex. Reminding everyone that Ricky's making pancakes tomorrow at their place. Ten o'clock. Think this is going to become a thing?"

"Time will tell. If his pancakes are as good as his ring bearing, I hope so." Raphael nodded, then yawned, and snuggled close. "Tired, baby?"

"Mmmm mm." Luke pulled loose from Raphael's grasp, stood up and pulled Raphael to his feet, so he could scoop him up and carry him to bed. It really had been a demanding two days.

Raphael and Luke stopped at Molly Stone's for fresh berries and melon on their way to Greg, Alex and Mateo's place. They arrived just before ten, only to find they were the last to arrive. Apparently, Ricky's pancakes were already an irresistible draw. Luke pulled the containers of fruit and berries out of the bag and handed them over to Alex, who was acting as sous chef to chef Ricky while Raphael pulled off his street sweats, leaving Luke the only one still dressed, but only for a moment. Everyone but Ricky and Alex was seated around the kitchen island, sipping coffee and watching Ricky, hard at work. As the newly naked Luke slid into place next to Raphael, Alex placed a steaming mug in front of each of them. As if this was a Tuesday dinner, Luke, Raphael, Ricky and Juan were in full body harnesses, Greg, Alex, Steve, and Niki were in chest harnesses.

"I'm dying to see if these pancakes are as amazing as the Yelp reviews," Luke said after his first sip of Alex's brew. Ricky turned from the two griddles he had going, to laugh.

"Five stars, Luke, I promise!" he replied.

"They're pretty good," Niki volunteered. "I got to taste the test cake. Mmmm."

"Test cake?" Luke asked.

"The first pancake is always a tosser," Juan explained. "Until the griddle is fully seasoned and up to temp."

"Ah," Luke nodded. "The science of pancakes. I'm learning something new."

"What a minute," Raphael changed the subject. "Where's Mateo?"

"Ooooo la la," Alex grinned. "Our little Mateo has an overnight guest, and we haven't seen either of them yet."

"What!?" Raphael jumped off his stool.

"He texted us last night, and asked if it would be okay to bring Ryan home. It seems Ryan showed up at the restaurant near the end of his shift."

"I thought he said they might go out *next* Saturday," Raphael protested.

"Apparently Ryan couldn't wait," Alex replied. "Pretty sweet, huh? It was cute that Mateo wanted to clear it with us first."

"How long have they been in there?" Raphael wondered out loud. Luke looked at him curiously. "I mean ..." he lowered his voice to a whisper, "we don't really know much about Ryan, do we?"

"Baby, Mateo's a big boy, well, big enough to take care of himself," Luke admonished. "You should chill."

"You know," Ricky turned from the stove, "I think this is Mateo's first date ever ... and he scored!"

"Oh man!" Raphael was still in Mother Teresa mode. "Greg, Alex ..." Greg looked across the island at Raphael.

"Raphael, it's okay," he assured. "When he texted for permission, we put some condoms and lube on his dresser."

"Oh, that must have been subtle," Steve smiled.

"You'd have done the same thing," Alex said. "Any one of you would have. Amiright?" Alex began distributing plates of pancakes and fruit. Raphael sat back down, then stood back up and walked over to Ricky and mumbled into his ear. Ricky nodded, slipped out of the apron he'd been wearing for obvious reasons, and headed out of the kitchen. Raphael returned to his stool.

Luke leaned over and asked, "What are you up to?"

"Noooothing." Then, after he took a bite, he turned to Luke and said, "I'll bet they're hungry after all that ... exercise."

Before Luke could respond, everyone heard Ricky knock on Mateo's door. "¡Chicos, el desayuno está listo!" Ricky returned to the kitchen, picked up his plate and slid into place next to Juan.

"Aren't we supposed to be improving his English?" Juan kidded.

"It's early. First, coffee. Then, English," Ricky smiled, taking a bite. "Great berries, Luke!" As Luke was praising Ricky's pancakes, Mateo entered, sleepy eyed and well trained by now, appropriately not dressed. Of course, he probably hadn't been dressed to begin with. Alex jumped up, poured a cup, and handed it to Mateo.

"What time?" Mateo asked, willing to give his English a try even before his first sip.

"Breakfast time," Greg smiled, as he slid a stool in front of Mateo. "Where's Ryan?"

"I'm here," came a voice from around the corner, as Ryan entered, wearing boxers and a t-shirt.

"Ryan!" came the chorus from about eight voices. Alex once again got up and poured another mug, then walked over to Ryan. Ryan reached out, but Alex pulled the mug back. As Ryan looked at him curiously, Alex grinned.

"Our house. Our rules. Lose the clothes, Ryan. This is a clothing not-optional household. Right guys?"

"RIGHT!"

"But ... I mean ... seriously?" Mateo was looking on, not sure if this was a good thing or not.

"Ricky, what does Ryan have to do to get a pancake around here?"

"Follow Mateo's lead," Ricky responded as he dished up another plate. "Strip ... or starve."

Luke turned to Juan, "Your little leatherboy knows how to give orders, doesn't he?" Juan smiled.

"And I follow every one of them." That brought a smile from Luke and Raphael, who figured they fully understood the dynamic of Juan and Ricky's relationship. Ryan was still hesitating, as Alex teasingly waived the mug in the air.

"Look, Ryan, do you believe in fairness?" Alex asked.

"What?" Ryan didn't follow. "Fairness ... as a concept?"

"Fairness, as in you spent a good part of yesterday seeing everyone in this room naked, or damn near naked, and it's time you returned the favor. None of us is embarrassed, and you shouldn't be either. You'll be in very good company. Right, amigos?"

"RIGHT!"

"Mateo, tell your new boyfriend his coffee is getting cold," Alex continued, not giving in. Rather than saying anything, Mateo climbed off his stool, walked over to Ryan and pantsed him. Which produced a cheer from the spectators.

"Bravo, Mateo!" Greg yelled. "That's our boy ... a man of action!" Ryan stepped out of his boxers as Mateo pulled up the hem of his t-shirt. Once Mateo was finished, Alex handed Ryan his coffee at last, but before he could let go of the cup, Alex noticed, well, everybody noticed, that Ryan was suffering, if suffering is the right word, the same fate that Ricky experienced in his first naked evening with the family.

"See, that's why I didn't want to get naked," Ryan whined. "I can't help it!" Mateo, looking appalled, put his hands on Ryan's shoulders from behind to comfort him. His touch really didn't help the situation, as Ryan's erection wobbled from side to side. Alex, too, moved forward and put a hand on Ryan's forearm.

"Ryan, it's okay. It happens to all of us ... you just can't see it on us locked cock brothers. Seeing you like this is making me hard right now, in fact, but ... well, you can kind of tell, can't you?" Ryan looked down at Alex's Looker and, despite himself, had to smile. He looked back up into Alex's eyes. "See, it's okay. In fact, it's kinda cute. Now, come eat."

Mateo, Ryan and Alex took their seats. Breakfast proceeded normally, at least as far as what was considered normal for this family. Ricky split his time between eating and griddling more cakes, which were as popular as he'd hoped.

"Now you know why we do DoorDash for Tuesday dinners, Ricky," Luke said between bites. "Otherwise, Raphael would never sit down."

"I don't mind," Ricky responded, sliding another pancake onto Steve's plate. "I love cooking for you guys. I love us all being together." Then he looked at Mateo as he said, "This beats 24th Street, right, amigo?" referring to their previous apartment. Mateo grinned and nodded; his mouth too full to speak.

Niki raised his juice glass in a toast, "To us, our tribe, our pack, our locked cock family. I'm so happy we managed to find one another!" Glasses were raised in tribute. Eventually, one by one, each man finished eating, even Ricky.

"There's one last pancake," Ricky teased. "What am I bid?" Everyone groaned and passed. Everyone, except Steve, who held up his plate. As Ricky delivered, Niki put an arm around Steve's waist and planted one on his cheek. Steve turned to make it a real, lip on lip kiss. Ryan took note of their unabashed devotion.

"Thank you, guys, for including me in breakfast this morning, and for not giving me a hard time about, you know ..." he offered. "This is really nice. We don't get food like this at school."

"They probably make you wear clothes in the student union, too," Alex consoled. "You're welcome. I hope I didn't make you too uncomfortable earlier ..."

"I, uh, I mean, I kind of understood what was going on yesterday at the wedding, especially knowing you and Raphael strip for charity. But it seems like you all really live like this," he spread his arms to include the whole scene, "and ... well, I'm not sure I understand it." Everyone looked at Ryan, waiting for more. He looked down, paused, then realized suddenly he was drawing attention to his rambunctious penis. "Not that it's a bad thing." He looked up and smiled and made an 'I don't know what else to say' expression.

"Ryan," Juan spoke up. "I know what you're saying. Except for Mateo, I'm the newest member of this family, and even though I've been a participant in the leather community for some time, I was pretty surprised at first by how these guys live, and love and relate to one another. If I had to describe it, it's like they ... we ... live life quite literally the way some people just fantasize about how life could be. Once you realize that, it's perfectly natural. And, may I add, very much appreciated." Ricky leaned over and kissed Juan's shoulder in agreement.

"Even the chastity thing? I'm sorry, I'm not being critical. I mean, you guys are all like sex symbols. But, some of this is just a mystery to me. Again, I'm not saying it's bad, or wrong, I just need to get comfortable with it all, I guess. If, I guess, Mateo and I are going to see more of each other." He looked at Mateo who had been doing his best to follow the conversation. Mateo, smiled shyly and put his hand on Ryan's thigh, and looked into Ryan's eyes expectantly.

"Ryan, this is where you're supposed to kiss him," Raphael instructed. "Do it, or I will." So, Ryan did. Ricky clapped, and everyone cheered yet again. Ryan was clearly embarrassed. "Okay, Alex, make another pot of coffee. Let's adjourn to the living room and answer a few of Ryan's questions. It looks like Mateo might want to keep Ryan around ... at least for a while ... so we should probably bring him up to speed." Alex got busy while Ricky and Raphael bussed the dishes into the dishwasher. Everyone else headed into the living room.

Once everyone had found a spot, and gotten comfortable, Greg started things off. "So, Ryan, what is it you don't understand about this perfectly understandable family of ours." He paused a beat, then continued, "I guess we seem pretty unconventional to someone like yourself."

"And, thank goodness we are," Raphael volunteered. "So, yeah, Ryan, where do you want to start?"

"Hmmm," Ryan replied "Well, the obvious, I guess, the chastity cages. I'd never seen one before yesterday. Clifford told me about your strip show, but I had a hard time visualizing it. The reality is, well, kind of surprising. It's sexy, I guess, but I don't get it."

"Maybe it would help if each of our caged brothers explained why he's caged," Steve suggested. "It's different for each of them."

"Yeah, that'd be cool," Ryan responded. Alex returned from the kitchen with a carafe of coffee that he placed on the coffee table, that, for once, actually was a coffee table. As Greg reached for the pot and poured more for Luke who was sitting next to him, Alex sat down next to Ryan and spoke.

"Ryan, I can totally relate to your ... problem. Which isn't a problem at all. More like a blessing, but anyway, I was a chronic masturbator. I couldn't keep my hands off my cock. At home, in the car ... we used to live in the Midwest where everybody drives ... at my desk at work. I was always touching myself. And, every chance I got, I'd beat off to porn. I was addicted. I loved having sex with Greg, but at that time, I guess it just wasn't enough. Finally, Greg insisted we try chastity. I was furious at first. I hated the idea. I couldn't imagine not being able to touch myself." Alex stopped and took a long sip of coffee.

"Wow, I can't imagine that either," Ryan said. "How long did he lock you up?"

"It's been over three years, now. Looking pretty permanent." Both Ricky and Raphael whooped.

"Fuuuck," Ryan reacted. 'Oh ... excuse me. Sorry."

"You can say fuck, Ryan, it's okay," Alex patted him on the thigh. "Here's the thing, though. Within days, I was so 'fucking' horny, I couldn't keep my hands off Greg. Or my mouth. Or ... well, let's just say it saved our marriage. Our sex life has never been better. That's my story. Chastity saved my marriage. Niki, your turn."

"Gee, I don't know where to start," Niki said, addressing Ryan directly. "My cage is just a part of my once secret persona. Actually, a previously unattained persona, I guess. I can see I'm confusing you. It's a part of my pup persona, but I'm not going to bore you with all that."

"Bore me," Ryan interjected. "I'm fascinated. Those pups at the wedding were incredible. They never broke character."

"Well, maybe another time we'll get into that, if you want, but let me just say when you're in pup space, I mean really in pup head space, you're not playing a character. You're a pup. You think like a pup. You feel like a pup. So, you want to look like a pup. Anyway, back to the cage, I had to be locked up when I went to obedience school ... all us pups were locked."

"Obedience school!?" Ryan interrupted again. "Damn, you've got to tell me everything."

"Another time. I promise. These guys all know the story. The thing is, well, just like you are embarrassed by your involuntary erection, I was always embarrassed by the size of my cock."

"It doesn't look small to me," Ryan assured. Niki laughed at Ryan's innocent remark.

"Umm, it's not."

"Nine inches ... plus," Steve informed Ryan with wiggling eyebrows.

"Before, whenever people saw my cock, they stopped treating me normally. Again, a long story. The point is, I'm happier and more comfortable, locked up and small. Well, smaller. And, like Alex said, I'm a lot hornier now, too. Any complaints, Steve?"

"None," Steve sat back and took a sip from his mug. "Everything's fine. And, I know you can't see him in action at the Powerhouse yet, but when you turn twenty-one, we'll take you down so you can see how pupular this puptender is behind the bar there." Niki rolled his eyes at Steve's mangled compliment, but Ryan was fascinated.

Ricky, who, as usual, was ensconced between Juan's shins, turned and looked up at Juan. "Papito, you tell him my story. I want to hear you tell it." Mateo, apparently getting more comfortable with the group, moved close enough to Ryan that their thighs were in full contact. He put a hand on Ryan's thigh, which of course caused Ryan's erection to bounce. Mateo giggled in spite of himself.

"You know, Ryan, if we ever give you a nickname, it's probably going to be Boner Boy," Alex kidded.

"No, no ... Rigid Ryan," Raphael laughed. "Sorry Ryan. Really, it's cute. Makes us locked brothers a little jealous."

"All I can say is, you asked for it," Ryan defended himself, clearly not as self-conscious by now.

"Yeah, you guys ... stop being mean," Juan said. "Well, Ryan, like Niki, I'm not sure where to start. I will say I fell for Ricky the first time I saw him. I'll skip a bunch of details, too, but once we started seeing each other, I fell in love pretty quickly. Maybe too quickly, 'cause it wasn't long before I realized, at least I thought at the time, that maybe he and I weren't really suited for each other, despite how much I enjoyed being with him. I had long been interested in and a part of the leather community and a lot of things it entails. Ricky ... well, Ricky was unspoiled. A sweet kid who wasn't ready for the kinds of things I wanted to share with him. So, I made the biggest mistake of my life, at least I thought so at the time, and told him we should stop seeing each other. I thought he'd be happier with someone more ... well, more conventional. More vanilla."

"I showed you, huh?" Ricky laughed.

"Boy, did you. Ricky really should be telling this, but, basically these guys took him under their wing and turned him into the perfect little leatherboy. The day he came back and told me he wanted to be my leatherboy, was the most rewarding day of my life. To be honest, I figured the cage was a prop, like that amazing shirt you were wearing, and those shorts ... jeez, you should have seen him. This was at the Eagle, and every eye was on him."

"He's not exaggerating," Alex piped up. "We were there, Raphael and me. Just like Friday night, Ricky was the center of attention that day."

Juan continued, while rubbing Ricky's high 'n tight, "So, I figured in a day or two, the cage would come off."

"But it couldn't!" It was Raphael's turn to interrupt. "I had the key!"

"Not that it mattered," Juan said. "Even after we got the key, Ricky insisted and I quote, 'perfect leatherboys are always locked' ... and, I guess it's true, because he's the perfect leatherboy, and he's almost always locked."

"Yeah, it only comes off for cleaning and ... when Juan wants to suck me. But I haven't touched my cock in months!" Ricky proudly announced.

"Wow," was Ryan's response. "Months?" Ricky and Juan both nodded. "Wow. That's a great story. I'm really happy for you guys. You look so awesome together." Ricky grinned and kissed Juan's knee.

Ryan looked expectantly at Raphael, then Luke. "This is the best story time I've ever experienced," Ryan said earnestly. "This is really interesting. Chastity is so much more than I ever would have imagined, not that I ever gave it any thought before yesterday. Soooo, who's going to tell us the last story?"

"I'll start, but if I know Raphael, and I do, you'll be hearing from both us," Luke began. Raphael rolled his eyes. "It's similar, in a way, to what you just heard. Raphael was the innocent one, I was the more, well, the kinky one. I hadn't pushed it. Like Juan I was falling in love but I didn't want to do anything to spoil it. We just got to talking one night about who was more devoted to the other one. A little competitive maybe, maybe just dancing around the idea of admitting we were really getting serious about one another. Anyway, it sounds silly I know, but we decided our love could be measured by how willing each of was to accept a dare from the other. By the way, you probably wouldn't recognize the Raphael then, compared to today. But, once we got started with the dares, they just got more and more daring, so for better or worse, I went for broke. I tied him up in a dungeon, this is after shaving off most of his 'beautiful' hair by the way, and our friend Jake pierced one of his nipples and I locked a cage on him. He was blindfolded at the time, and we did some other stuff, but that's when he was caged the first time. Again, kinda like Ricky and Juan's story. From day one, Raphael took to becoming my locked cock boy like it was our destiny. He hasn't touched his cock since, and the cage he's wearing now hasn't come off in almost a year. We don't even have the keys ... just like Alex."

Ryan couldn't help himself. "Fuuuuuuuckk!"

"Ryan, that's a quick primer on why half the family have locked cocks. What else would you like to know?" Greg continued in his Master of Ceremonies role.

"Well, I guess now I understand why you're all wearing some leather. Also, sexy, by the way. But, um, why are you all naked like this?"

"You can blame Raphael and Luke for that," Alex spoke up. "They were naked, well Raphael was naked and Luke almost was, the first time Greg met them at the Folsom Street Fair. We found out they lived naked the first time we went to their apartment, and it just kind of became the norm for all of us when we went to their place for Tuesday dinner. Pretty soon, we were doing it all the time, too. We don't even think about it anymore."

"Yeah, they were my favorite delivery ... all those cute naked guys," Ricky grinned. "And, now I'm one of them."

"And, now I'm one, too, at least for today," Ryan looked down at his slightly more subdued cock. "This has been one helluva weekend."

"Are you weirded out?" Niki asked. "I mean, think about it, and it's not just the pup in me saying this, but why wear clothes if you don't have to? Are you cold, Ryan?"

"No."

"Is there a stranger here that you might offend?"

"Well, I don't really know any of you very well yet..."

"But, just yesterday you spent hours with all of us when we were naked, or all but naked, so ..."

"What our once shy pup Niki is getting at," Luke interjected, "is that clothes are an affectation. Our leather gear is an affectation. The collars, the cages, the ink ... all affectations. We're just happier eliminating some affectations and adopting others. Too weird for you?"

"No. I mean, it's a lot to take in, but I get it. I think. I guess if I have to get naked to see Mateo again, I can deal with that." He turned to Mateo and smiled, then pursed his lips. Mateo responded appropriately.

"Well, gentlemen," Greg wrapped things up. "Our work here is done. These two need to probably go make their bed. Or do something with it. Or in it." Ryan nodded and stood, reached down, pulled Mateo up and walked him out of the room. As soon as the bedroom door closed, Alex spoke.

"So," he posed. "Which one are we going to lock up first?"

Fifty-Five

Ricky's On A Roll

"Guess what Saturday is?" Alex asked Raphael over lunch on Wednesday. There they were, two married working guys, having lunch South of Market, pretty typical, right? Raphael's high 'n tight not that unusual. His septum ring, snug and discrete, pretty common, actually. The collar? A tasteful choker ... a fashion statement. The caged cock emblem on each of their polos? Yes, Alex had added to his wardrobe. Probably some new designer line, no doubt. If only their fellow diners knew what lurked beneath their khakis. Or, if they could overhear their conversation.

"I know. The third performance by The Chastity Brothers. Third and final?"

"Exactly. I'm torn. I mean, it's not that bad an ordeal. And, we have raised some pretty big bucks for the Trevor Project. On the one hand, I feel obligated to continue. Of course, after Saturday, we'll be out of costumes, so it would be a logical time to stop. Besides, I wonder if our fans are losing interest."

"I don't think so. We pulled in more money last time than the first. I assume that means word is still getting out and we had a lot of newbies in the crowd, but you're probably right that 'The Chastity Brothers' will run its course. So far, Brett seems fine with us continuing. I don't know ... maybe we need to do something new."

Alex put down his fork and picked up his phone. After he apparently sent a text, Raphael asked, "Making dinner plans with Greg?"

"No, something much more fun. Give it a minute." They continued eating, until Alex's phone chimed. He read the text, then, grinning, held the phone out for Raphael to see. The text was from Ricky. One word: *'YES!'*

"I couldn't see your text."

"I asked Ricky if he was ready to join The Chastity Brothers strip act. I remembered Greg and Luke joking about him joining us after our first official performance. Raphael, we'll wire him up again and blow the crowd away." Raphael put his chopsticks down and lifted his glass in salute.

"You really are an evil genius, Alex. That's brilliant! I'm surprised he said yes, though."

"I'm not. He got so much affirmation after the ceremony. I think he was only half-kidding when he suggested doing his deliveries naked and glittered. He's ready."

"Do we have time to rehearse with him?"

"I think we can do this without much rehearsal. I already have some ideas. Besides, with his abs and a glowing Holy Trainer, who's going to judge his dancing?"

"True that. Just tell me what to do. By now I've learned to trust you when it comes to putting on a mind-blowing performance. Tell you what, though. Let's not tell Greg or Luke, or anybody. In fact, let's ask Ricky to try to keep it from Juan ... let's surprise everybody."

"Now who's the evil one? I'll text Ricky again."

Juan had to work Saturday, so Raphael and Alex met at Juan and Ricky's place after claiming they had to work on some costume adjustments with Allyson. It wasn't a total lie. They took the leftover fabric with them to see what, if anything, they could conjure up for Ricky. The day before, Raphael had borrowed Niki's wedding mankini for Ricky to wear after the act, when they'd collect tips on the floor, as usual. They spent an hour, or so, rehearsing some dance moves; Ricky had watched them enough that he caught on pretty quickly. Then, they worked out the logistics of how to introduce him into the act. They decided Ricky would have limited, but very crowd-pleasing minutes at the end of the show. Next, they played with the leftover fabric, but there wasn't much of it. Nothing they could come up with really spoke to them. Finally, Ricky made a suggestion.

"Why don't I come on stage in my caged cock crop top and just a towel around my waist?"

'I love it!" Alex exclaimed. "You dance a minute, then Raphael and I rip off the towel. The crop is a teaser of what's to come."

"Yeah, but we'll have to struggle to get the crop top off," Raphael worried. "It's skin tight."

"No, Raphael, he keeps it on ... those abs and the glowing cage, and the crop top shouting 'caged cock.'" It's simple, sexy and oh so very Ricky!"

"Once again, you're probably right," Raphael enthused. "Ricky ... are you sure you're ready to be a stripper?"

"I already am a stripper, Raphael," Ricky grinned. "Your wedding was my first performance. I was naked all night in a hall full of clothed people. I can do this." Raphael squeezed Ricky's biceps and nodded.

"Good point, Ricky. So, now all we have to do is wire up your cock."

"We'll do everything but connect the battery," Alex suggested. "We can insert it just before the performance."

"You can put it in now if you want. I'll be fine. You guys are both plugged now, aren't you?"

"Yeah, but ..."

"Remember, Alex, I'm the perfect little leatherboy. I can handle it." Raphael clapped and laughed, then pulled Ricky into a tight hug.

"Juan is one lucky guy," Raphael said as he let Ricky free.

"I think we're all pretty lucky," Ricky responded. "Gee, I hope I can find the keys. Juan is in charge of them, you know." While Ricky searched, Alex pulled the special effects paraphernalia out of his backpack. Raphael had never actually seen the works before.

"Do you think it really is possible to rig up something like this for an open cage like Niki wears?"

"Oh, sure. We'd use even smaller LEDs, but, yeah. Whenever Niki's ready to try it, I'll order the stuff. He'll look great behind the bar ... even greater I mean. He's already a legend."

"As are we, Alex. As Ricky was last Friday. You're in the wrong business, Alex."

"This is just for fun. I like what I do at the office. Hey, Ricky! Can we help?"

"Found 'em!" Ricky returned, holding up the keys. "I should have looked in the bathroom first. That's where we always take the cage off for cleaning. Dum Dum Dum." Ricky handed the keys to Alex, then laid down on the floor. He knew this was going to take a while. And, he was determined to still not be the one to unlock the cage, let alone be the one to accidentally touch his unlocked cock.

Alex turned to Raphael as he inserted the key into the HT. "I feel so honored. I'm the only man, other than Juan, authorized to free this cock." Both Raphael and Ricky laughed.

"I should be filming this, right?" Raphael joked. Then he did, in fact, take a few pictures, for posterity, as Alex went to work. Forty-five minutes later the cage was back in place and Alex connected the battery for a test.

"Ooooohhh," Raphael imitated the unsuspecting audience to be. "Seriously, Alex, how did you ever come up with this idea?" As Alex lubed up the condom containing the battery pack, and propped up Ricky's legs on his shoulders to prepare for insertion, he looked up at Raphael and wiggled his eyebrows, even better than Luke could.

"You said it yourself, Raphael ... I'm an evil genius."

Several hours and two Flour + Water pizzas later, everyone but Juan was at the bar. He'd promised to be there in time for the second performance. Ricky was in the audience with Greg, Luke and Steve, looking perfectly normal in a standard caged cock tee and baggy shorts. Raphael and Alex were wrapping up their first set, naked, sweaty and beaming in the spot lights. As the music faded, their arms around each other's waists, the DJ hustled over and handed a wireless mic to Raphael, as planned. Then he returned to the controls and brought the music down to zero, and nodded to Raphael.

"Hey, everybody. Are you having fun?" Raphael spoke into the mic. He got an enthusiastic response. "So are we. We have a special challenge for you tonight. Are you up for that?" Another enthusiastic response. Luke and Greg looked to each other blankly. They looked at Ricky who mimed a 'beats me' look, which turned into a big grin the instant they looked back at Raphael.

"We have another performance at eleven, just about forty-five minutes from now, and if you can meet our challenge, we'll include a very special surprise ... one that I *know* you're going to want to see. So, here's the deal. My chastity brother Alex here is putting a liter jug at the edge of the stage. If you can fill it with dollar bills before eleven, we'll unveil that special surprise. But ... you have to fill the jar. Ones, fives, tens ... whatever you have. Remember, this is all for a really good cause. Right Alex?" Raphael handed the mic to Alex.

"Raphael wasn't kidding, guys. You do *not* want to miss this surprise, so open those wallets and fill the jar. We'll see you all back here at eleven!" He handed the mic back to Raphael, who moved to end of the stage and handed it back to the DJ, who immediately brought the music back up. Raphael and Alex exited stage right, down the short flight of steps and into the crowd. A couple of guys, one of whom was wearing Raphael's tossed tank top around his neck, tried to hand them tips, as had been the scenario in their previous performances, but they waived them toward the stage, and the waiting jar. They both headed for the office door and their clothes. Once back in shorts and caged cock tees, they joined the rest of the family.

"Excellent performance as always," Greg praised, pulling Alex close. "You guys sure know how to excite a crowd."

"It's actually pretty easy," Raphael said drolly. "All you have to do is take off your clothes."

"Yeah? If it was that easy, about hundred guys in this room would be doing it. You're too modest. So, what is this surprise you guys cooked up?"

"If we told you, it wouldn't be a surprise," Alex shouted over the crowd and music. "You'll see. Juan's still not here?"

"I hope he wasn't held up at the hospital," Luke said. "That would be a bummer, eh, Ricky?" Ricky was concentrating on his phone. He looked up and made an 'ok' sign with his left hand. "He's on his way, amigos." Then, he looked at Alex, widening his eyes to say, 'I can't wait!'

Time passed, a little beer was consumed, and soon it was time for Raphael and Alex to get ready for the last performance of the night. Juan still hadn't arrived. Alex and Raphael headed for the office as Steve, Greg and Luke continued talking. Just before eleven, Juan walked up, still in his scrubs.

"I hope I made it!" he greeted them, exchanging hugs.

"Talk about timing," Greg yelled. "They're about to start."

"Where's Ricky?" Juan asked, craning his neck around.

"He was right here a minute ago," Steve replied. "Maybe the john? He'll be back. Can I get you a beer, Juan?" Juan nodded absentmindedly, still looking around for Ricky. The music faded, and the DJ began to speak over it.

"The Chastity Brothers, the Powerhouse and the Trevor Project thank you for your generosity. You filled the jar, I mean you really filled it, so let's welcome back The Chastity Brothers, with a very special performance this night only!" He ramped up the music and Raphael and Alex stepped out from behind the curtain, Alex in a tear-away camo miniskirt and tank, Raphael in a loincloth and loose tee, arm holes down to his waist. For ten minutes they performed their synchronized routine, stripping each other slowly, hugging, kissing, bumping butts, tossing costume items into the crowd, driving their audience crazy. Finally, they ripped away the miniskirt and loincloth, generating the reaction they'd come to expect. As before, when their cages were revealed, the decibel level was topped yet again. The only one in the crowd not deliriously enthralled, was Juan, who was still missing Ricky.

Only a few seconds after Raphael and Alex had stripped each other bare, they jumped back from one another, then turned toward the curtain, their butts to the audience, and they beckoned with their hands. A spot hit the center of the stage between them, and out stepped Ricky. A third stripper! The crowd erupted. Ricky, his white caged cock crop top blazing in the spot, joined Alex and Raphael in their routine, perfectly synchronized. After about a minute he turned his back, Raphael and Alex grabbed his towel and pulled, revealing a perky, luscious bouncy little ass, which generated the expected ... and appropriate reaction. Until. The spot dimmed as Ricky spun around. Alex and Raphael each dropped to their knees, their arms extended toward Ricky and the glowing baby blue Holy Trainer. One guy fainted. Or, pretended to. We'll never know for sure. Even the DJ was dancing now. Shouts, howls, whistles, clapping, they did it all. All for Ricky.

Toward the back of the crowd, Luke and Steve were clapping Juan on the back. Juan didn't even notice. All he could see was a beaming, dancing, too fucking adorable for words ... perfect little leatherboy ... who had the entire crowd in the palms of his hands.

Alex and Raphael danced up to Ricky from each side and began pretending to manhandle him, making every man in the place wish, just for a minute, to be up on that stage, just for one minute, to touch that beaming, glowing, locked cock boy. After a hokey, leggy tribute to the Radio City Music Hall Rockettes, that made their cages bounce even more than usual, the set came to an end. As the music faded, Alex, Ricky and Raphael pulled into a sweaty group hug, then pulled apart and bowed deeply to the crowd. Then, without the benefit of the mic, Raphael shouted, "The Trevor Project thanks you! Pup Niki behind the bar thanks you! The Powerhouse thanks you! Alex, Ricky and I thank you! Thank you!" The three slipped behind the curtain, pulled on the mankinis stashed there earlier, and then they moved out into the crowd. By the time they made it to where their men were standing, Ricky's mankini was stuffed with even more donations, and both his hands were grasping more bills.

"Amigos! That was awesome!" he shouted over the crowd as Juan pulled him into a crushing embrace. "Were you surprised, Papito?" Ricky leaned up, demanding a kiss. Juan obliged.

"Surprised ... proud ... turned on ..." Juan looked at the rest of the family. "Was I the only one in the dark?"

"No, this was another Alex and Raphael ... and Ricky ... stunt," Greg assured. "Luke and Raphael have been a terrible influence on Alex and Ricky. You'd better keep your eyes wide open, Juan, you never know what might be coming next."

"Well, as long as I end up like this, with a perfect naked leatherboy in my arms, I'm not going to complain," Juan replied. Then, looking back into Ricky's eyes, "At least we won't have to spend an hour in the shower scrubbing glitter off this beauty tonight."

"Nope. Just unplug me and I'm good to go," Ricky laughed.

"Holy crap!" Alex cried out. He'd been pulling bills out of Ricky's mankini.

"What's wrong?" Raphael asked.

"Nothing," Alex held out the wad of cash. "Ricky pulled in over a thousand dollars just walking over here from the stage! There's even a hundred-dollar bill."

"Nice work, mijo," Juan pulled Ricky close again. "Somebody ought to get some special attention when we unlock him tonight to peel off those little lights."

"You should be proud," Luke agreed, knowing exactly what Juan was hinting at. "What made you guys decide to recruit Ricky tonight, anyway?"

"It was Alex's idea," Raphael explained. "We were thinking tonight might be our last performance, and we wanted to do something a little different. We figured, maybe, 'been there, done that' for The Chastity Brothers."

"I'm not so sure the Chastity Brothers have run their course," Steve offered. "Niki says guys ask every Saturday 'is this a Chastity Brothers night?' You might have to make Ricky a regular, though after tonight. You've set a pretty high bar, yet again."

"Orrrr ... maybe we introduce the Chastity Brothers' handlers ... the Amazing Greg and Luke!" Raphael countered.

"Orrrr ... maybe this was a good night for you to end things after all," Luke counter countered. "I declare a no-dare dare on that idea right now!"

"What's a no-dare dare?" Alex asked.

"Read the dare contract," Luke smiled, looking at Greg for support. "It's a dare vaccine. I just invented it. Now, who needs a beer?"

Fifty-Six

DARES HAVE CONSEQUENCES

The following evening, as Raphael was finishing Luke's mohawk, his cage occasionally brushing against Luke's back as he worked, both enjoying simply being wet and naked together, he broke the silence.

"That was interesting the other day, each of us telling Ryan about why we're locked up. What our lives are like. Lots of similarities, but differences, too."

"Yeah. Some big differences," Luke replied, less than enthusiastically, which gave Raphael pause.

"What do you mean?"

"Nothing, baby." Raphael put the razor down and maneuvered around so he could face Luke. He sat, his legs surrounding Luke's waist, cage to cock.

"Sir, sometimes I can read your mind, but not always. Not yet. What's up?"

"Nothing, baby. Nothing." Luke gave a weak smile before looking down at Raphael's cage, a distant look in his eyes. Raphael put his hand under Luke's chin and raised his head to face him squarely.

"Still not reading your mind, Sir." Luke stared into those loving, almond eyes and decided, what the hell. He breathed a deep sigh.

"Well, it's no big deal. It's just I've been thinking about how Juan occasionally sucks off Ricky." He fell silent for a moment, but didn't break eye contact. Raphael didn't either. "I guess part of me misses sucking you."

After another silence, eyes still locked, Raphael said, "Oh. I'm sorry. Sir. I didn't know."

"I know. I didn't want to say anything. I know how important it is for you to be permanently locked. Your happiness is my happiness."

"It doesn't sound like it to me. At the moment, anyway. So, you miss sucking cock. Jesus. I'm so selfish. Of course you do. I would!" Raphael reached out and pulled Luke into a hug. Luke breathed another long sigh.

"It's okay," Luke whispered, unconvincingly. Raphael pulled back and met Luke's gaze again.

"No, it's not okay. I totally understand. I can't believe I've been so self-centered. You're a gay man. Of course you miss sucking cock. Luke. Sir ... flash dare!" Luke's eyes brightened.

"Sir, it's still early. Your dare is to put on a kilt, head over to Eros, and Suck. Some. Cock!"

"What? Eros? Baby..." Raphael cut Luke off in mid-sentence.

"You. Eros. Now. And, don't come back until you've given your first blow job in ... what? Almost a year and a half!"

"Raphael, I don't want to go to Eros. I don't want to ..."

"Sir, it's a flash dare. It doesn't matter what you want." At that Raphael climbed out of his leg embrace of Luke, grabbed a towel and handed it to Luke. "Just make sure he's half as cute as me." He grabbed his towel and started patting himself down. "Oh, but don't let him suck you off. Save that for me for when you get back."

Luke shook his head, knowing there was no point in arguing. No point in trying to deny Raphael this flash dare. He really had only one option, and that was to do it. And, get it over with. He regretted even bringing the subject up.

Raphael didn't know what to think. Luke had been gone for two hours now ... no 'be home soon' text, no nothing. I mean, how long does it take to give a blow job? Even when a pro like Raphael stretched it out to torture the fuck out of Luke, thirty minutes was about the most he could hope for. Was this the one, last dare that Raphael would always regret? Was Luke in somebody else's bed right now? No, not possible. Was it?

Unable to take the agony any longer, and unwilling to cry uncle and text Luke, Raphael crawled into bed. He tossed and turned. He clicked on his tablet and looked to see if there had been some disaster on the block where Eros was located. Nothing. He laid the tablet aside, knowing there was no way he was going to fall asleep when he finally heard Luke open the front door. Raphael froze. Luke walked around the apartment expecting to find Raphael up. Slowly, he entered the darkened bedroom. He began pulling off his shirt and kilt as Raphael sat up and stared silently. Luke didn't look any happier than Raphael felt. Luke crossed the room and sat on the bed next to Raphael.

"I'm so sorry, Raphael. I'm ... I'm so sorry." Raphael's heart stopped.

"Was he really that good?" Raphael choked out.

"Who?"

"The guy you blew. Or, was it guys?"

"No." Luke sighed and took a very deep breath. "I didn't blow anybody. I couldn't. I just couldn't, Raphael. I only want one cock in my mouth ... yours. I failed, Raphael. I failed to do your dare. I'm the one to end the dares. I'm so sorry."

Raphael's heart leapt. He grabbed the morose Luke and squeezed with all the strength he could muster. He kissed one cheek then the other, then one shoulder, then the other. Then he found Luke's questioning mouth and dived in. Moments later, Raphael pulled his tongue free and said, "You've been drinking beer."

"Yeah. For the last two hours. I went to Eros, as you dared. But I couldn't go in. I just stood there and watched several guys go in. A couple of them cruised me, so that was nice. You know, the 'nice kilt' kind of cruising. But, Raphael, I couldn't do it. So, I went around the corner to the Pilsner and sat at the bar, drank beers and worked up the courage to come home and confess."

"Confess?!?"

"Yeah. I never thought it would be me to turn down a dare. I failed you, baby."

"Luke, you silly, silly man. Come here." Raphael pulled on Luke to get him the rest of the way onto the bed. Raphael maneuvered himself so that he was sitting facing Luke, with his legs around Luke's waist again. Locked cock against free cock. Arms around each other. Faces centimeters apart. "By 'failing the dare' you proved yourself a better man than most. You proved your devotion more than you ever could have if you'd completed the dare. You proved why I made the right decision to become your locked cock leather boy. To become your lawfully wedded husband. I chose wisely, Luke. Sir. God damn, Luke you scared the shit out of me when you were gone forever tonight. But I never should have doubted my Braveheart. I love you, Luke." Raphael paused, looked away, and then looked back into Luke's still contrite eyes. "I love you so much that I've made a decision that should make you very happy."

"I can't imagine you making me any happier than I am right now, baby." Luke was starting to choke up.

"Well, try this on for size, Sir. It's my job to serve you, and you long to suck my cock, so I am willing to give you permission anytime you want ... to suck my cock. Anytime. Sir."

"Anytime? But you hate being unlocked."

"You're right, I do. Because, more than anything I love being your locked cock boy." Raphael paused, continued staring into Luke's pale blue eyes and grinned. That evil, mischievous grin.

"What?"

"Well, there *is* a catch."

"Jesus." Luke sighed, a partly happy, partly suspicious sigh. "What?"

"You can unlock me as often as you want, suck me as long and as often as you want. I guess, deep down, I've kind of missed you sucking me, too. Just not enough to ever unlock. You can suck, and every time you do ..."

"WHAT?!?"

"As soon as you're done, you have to lock me right back up again."

"Ohhhhh. Okay. That's fine. I would have expected to, anyway."

"Annnnnd ... I get to lock you up for a week. And every night I get to fuck your brains out with the strap-on we got when your cock was healing from your piercing."

"We still have Brutus?"

"Oh, yeah. He's in the toy bag, right where you put him."

"Ohhhhhh kay. For a week?"

"Yes. Annnnnd ... you still have to go to the beach, the gym, wherever, locked and on display."

"Oh, come on. You can't be serious."

"Do I look like I'm kidding? I think it's a small price to pay for me to let you unlock me." At that Raphael began laughing so hard he let go of Luke and fell back on the bed. Going from fear and worry to offering Luke the gift he craved was making Raphael giddy. Luke untangled himself from Raphael's legs and stood up.

"I'm going to have to think about this. Meantime, I still haven't had my shower. May I have the pleasure of your company?"

"Absolutely, Sir. You go ahead. I'll be in, in a minute."

Luke luxuriated under the warm shower rotating back and forth, not soaping up too much, since that would be Raphael's job. He'd so dreaded coming home and admitting failure, but Raphael had made his failure a success. And, of course, Raphael had made everything all right. Raphael always made everything better than all right. Finally, Raphael joined him and began soaping down Luke's back.

"What took you so long?" Luke asked.

"Nothing ... I was just ordering your Holy Trainer."

"Seriously? You really are serious about this, aren't you?" Luke said as he turned around.

"Yes, Sir. Absolutely. I didn't want you to wait any longer than necessary for my first blow job." Raphael slid his tongue in Luke's waiting mouth. And, kept it there. He put his arms around Luke, who did the same, prolonging the kiss. When Raphael finally pulled his lips away, he grinned and said, "It'll be the same color as my first caged cock t-shirt, Sir."

"No!"

"Yes, Sir. Hot pink. Just think how jealous all the guys at the gym will be."

"Oh, man. We may have to just leave it in the case after all. I mean, it's been so long, I probably won't remember how to give a blow job anyway."

Raphael continued to grin as he tsked and said, "It's easy. Like riding a bike. Here, I'll show you." And he slowly dropped to his knees, his hands trailing down Luke's soapy chest, abs and finally his hips as Raphael inhaled his cock. As Raphael began what would no doubt be another of his signature oral performances, Luke leaned back against the shower wall.

"Dios Mio," Luke sighed, causing Raphael to laugh out loud, despite his mouthful of Luke. Luke reached his hands down to caress the ever so slightly stubbly sides of Raphael's head. He realized, once again, that Raphael was right. The guys in the steam would be jealous. Not of his pink cage, no, of course not. They'd be jealous because he'd be entering the room with his arm around the naked waist of the most Beautiful. Locked Cock Boy. In the World. And who could blame them?

It didn't take long for Raphael to take command and conquer Luke as he had so many times before, leaving his Braveheart spent, and grateful. Both were very tired after an emotion filled night. They toweled off and collapsed into bed. Luke pulled Raphael into their usual caress, Luke on the outside, Raphael's decorated back snug against Luke's chest, their legs intertwined. Raphael took a deep breath.

"Thank you, baby," Luke quietly whispered. "Thank you for not accusing me of failing a dare, even though I did."

"How could I?" Raphael whispered back. "Like I said, you proved your love, your devotion, and that's what the dares were all about." Then, after a long pause, "So, does this mean we're done with the dares?"

"Do you want to be done with the dares?"

Raphael stayed silent for so long that Luke thought maybe he'd fallen asleep, when he finally responded. "I hope not. Luke, think of what we owe to the dares. I'd never have become the man I am today if not for the dares. Nor would you be. Niki wouldn't have found his bliss if he hadn't texted Angel, and that was because of the dares. We wouldn't have amazing friends like Alex and Greg. And Juan and Ricky. He'd still be in that awful flat, longing for Juan." He fell silent again. Then, on the edge of sleep, he said, "Don't you think, Sir?"

"You're right, baby. It's been quite a ride." Luke reached his hand down and wrapped it around Raphael's cage. "Maybe I should write it all down, you know, for posterity. Something we can share with the grandkids." That got a sleepy chuckle from Raphael. "No, I'm serious, though. It could be fun. Maybe post it online somewhere. Or, better yet, write a book."

"You should. Nobody would believe it, but, yeah, you should." Then, Raphael rolled around in Luke's arms so they were now facing each other, chest to chest, cage to cock. He brushed his lips against Luke's, grabbed a little beard between his teeth and tugged playfully, then let go. "If you do, I have the perfect title for you."

"Oh, yeah? What is it, baby?"

"Double Dare."

"Double Dare ... hmmm. Yeah, I like it. Double Dare."

THANK YOU

I HOPE YOU ENJOYED following the exploits of Raphael, Luke, Niki, Steve, and the rest of this adventurous chosen family. If you did, first, I hope you will leave a favorable review with your favorite retailer.

Secondly, I hope you will seek out the sequel, *Double Dare II, A Shaman Appears*. It picks up where *Double Dare* ends, as the family bravely confronts the challenges presented by a global pandemic and the rise of the Black Lives Matter movement.

Double Dare III, Hiroshi's Gift, concludes the trilogy. In this third volume, members of the family face heartbreaking trials and breathtaking (literally) opportunities they never would have imagined.

You can find more information and links to all three books and interact with me at:

www.macinsf.com.

To pique your interest, a sneak preview of the first chapter of *Double Dare II, A Shaman Appears*, is included here. I hope you find it compelling enough to continue reading the trilogy.

ACKNOWLEDGEMENTS

I owe much to so many on my journey to where I am today. Too many to list here, a list you may not wish to read, anyway. No doubt you are more interested in reading *Double Dare II, A Shaman Appears*, right? Nevertheless, allow me to express my humble gratitude first to Ms. Conner, sophomore English teacher, who took me aside after class and told me I should become a writer. (After reading my short story to every one of her classes that day.) Teachers who inspire their students deserve pedestals. And better pay. Gracias, amigo, to Carlos Hickerson for perfecting my Spanish. I also owe a great deal to my early readers, too many to mention, for their encouragement and patience.

Deep gratitude must go to the countless authors whose efforts entertained, fascinated and intrigued me as a reader from a very early age, and who ultimately inspired me as a writer myself.

At lastly, to the men I've known and loved who inspired some of the characters in this trilogy. They are by no means 'too many to mention.' But each of them taught me much and left me a better man.

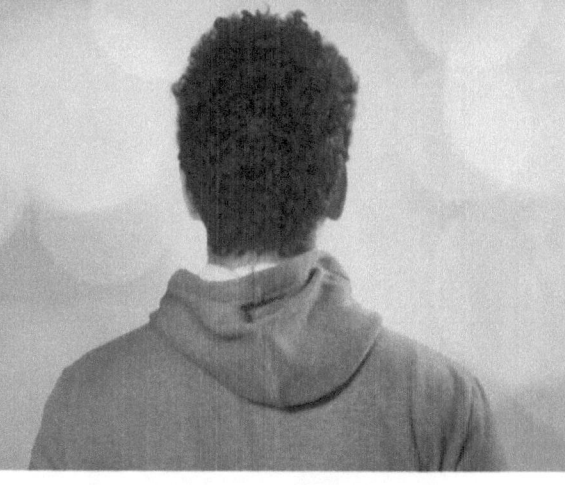

DOUBLE DARE II

A SHAMAN APPEARS

MICHAEL CURLESS

Three Thousand Miles, Give or Take

"HEY, BUDDY, YOU OKAY?" Juan, who had been leaning forward, head in his hands, sat up straight and looked up into Raymond's eyes. Juan's face mask was down around his throat, down for the first time in what ... more than twelve hours? Raymond's mask was still in place.

"I'm fine. Just really tired." Raymond sat down on the bench across from Juan, pulling his mask down as well.

"Yeah, a shift and a half of non-stop chaos will do that to you." Raymond looked intently at Juan to make sure it was just exhaustion that was responsible for Juan's posture. "You sure you're okay? Not that any of us are really okay."

"Well ... okay, considering. How's that?"

"Honest. Sounds honest. Good. None of us were ready for this, but at least some of us were more accustomed to dealing with all too frequent ER crises. What's your specialty back home?"

"OR. Yeah, this is a whole different world. Sure, we'd have an occasional crisis of our own. Gang shooting. Multi-car pileup. There was that horrible Asiana Airlines crash at SFO. But most days were pretty manageable. Mostly electives. Transplants. Joint replacements. Pretty routine. This is something else."

"You didn't have to do this, you know." Raymond leaned forward, resting his own head in his hands as he studied Juan. Juan looked across at Raymond, then slowly nodded without speaking. "You guys have this under control in California."

"That's why I came. You needed help, here in New York. The Bay Area was the first in the country to shelter in place, so we flattened the curve ... hell, we smashed it. Between that and the mandate to halt all elective surgeries, I wasn't really needed there. When I saw your governor asking for volunteers to come, when I saw how overwhelmed you guys were, I knew what I had to do."

"So, you're a fan of Andrew Cuomo, eh?"

"Well, not necessarily. He's not as handsome as our governor, but, you have to admit. He seems to be telling it like it is, which is pretty rare for a politician. Seriously, though, I felt like maybe I could help. And you guys needed help. Still do."

"No shit. None of us have been through anything like this pandemic before." Raymond sat back up, dropping his hands onto his lap, exhaustion evident in his face, too. "Thanks in part to you and the other volunteers who came, I feel like we're finally getting our hands around this. In case no one else has said anything, thanks, man. Really glad you're here."

"I appreciate it, but not to worry. I hear that about a dozen times a day. No thanks are needed."

"Good. I'm glad you know you're appreciated. You have a wife or girlfriend waiting for you back home in Frisco?"

For the first time, maybe all day, a smile graced Juan's face. He reached into the backpack next to him and pulled out his phone and pressed the power button. As it powered up for the first time since his shift started at five a.m., he directed his smile at Raymond. "No offense, but I have to set you straight regarding two parts of your question."

"Huh? Come again? Oh, was I prying? Sorry ..."

"No, no ... not at all. It's just, well, first of all, never say Frisco. You can say San Francisco. You can say Ess Eff. Or even, San Fran. But never Frisco."

"Why not?"

"I don't know. I don't make the rules. I just enforce 'em."

Raymond smiled back. Probably his first smile of the day, too. "Okay, got it. Ess. Eff. And, the second thing I need to be set straight about?" Juan held his phone up to show Raymond a photo of Ricky's beaming face.

"This is who's waiting for me. I'm, uh, not all that straight." Raymond leaned forward and studied the image, longer than Juan had expected. There really hadn't been time or opportunity for any of the staff to share much about their personal lives. From the minute they entered the hospital until the moment they dragged themselves out to go home, or in Juan's case, to walk to the nearby hotel where he quarantined himself each evening, there wasn't time or energy for much in the way of small talk. In fact, despite working side by side for several weeks now, saving lives and, all too often, not, this was the first time he and Raymond had had an opportunity to talk about themselves. Raymond finally leaned back and grinned a crooked smile.

"He's adorable."

"Yeah, he majored in adorable."

"Summa Cum Laude from the looks of that picture." Juan actually laughed, for the first time in days.

"I'll tell him you said so." Juan put the phone back into his bag. "What about you? Who's waiting at home for you?"

"My wife, Gabriela, and our six-year-old daughter, Mia."

"Those are both pretty names. Okay, your turn. Do you have pic?" Raymond nodded and fished his phone out of his locker. He handed it to Juan after a moment.

"Very sweet. Both of them. Let me guess. Is Gabriela Puerto Rican American?"

"Good guess, yeah. New York born and bred, though."

"The name gave it away. Looks like you did all right in the romance department, as well."

"I did. Of course," he said humbly, "Gabriela thinks she did okay, and Mia is sure of it." Juan laughed, indulging Raymond. "In a way, I have to say I miss them, too. By the time I decontaminate when I get home and feel safe enough to actually see them, it's basically time for Mia to head to bed."

"That's got to be rough."

"Not as rough as being three thousand miles away."

"Two thousand, nine hundred and two point eight miles away. Ricky calculated it."

"He misses you." Raymond's eyes showed some of the compassion he'd had so much practice exhibiting for the past two months. "You miss him."

Juan sighed and nodded. "Yeah, we Facetime every evening after I get off, and before he starts his shift. He's kind of a front-line warrior right now, too. But, yeah, I miss him. He ..." Juan's phone chimed, interrupting him. He pulled it out to see the call was from Ricky. "Speak of the devil. Here, I'll introduce you." Juan answered the call, but before he could say anything, Ricky greeted the entire staff locker room.

"Papito! I love you! I was worried you hadn't called yet. I ... oh, are you still at the hospital?"

"Uh, yeah, mijo, I'm here with my buddy, Raymond. We just finally ended our shift. Here, say hi to the most amazing ER doc I've ever worked with. Ricky, meet Dr. Raymond." Juan handed the phone to Raymond.

"Hi, Ricky. How are things in Ess Eff?"

"Crazy, just like there. Nice to meet you, Dr. Raymond. Is Juan doing a good job for you?"

"He's doing great ... we couldn't do it without him. In fact, we're thinking about keeping him here. Is that okay with you?" Raymond looked slyly at Juan as Ricky reacted as expected.

"No. No. No. No. NO! It is NOT okay with me, Dr. Raymond ... sir."
Ricky paused, then smiled that irresistible smile through the phone that
overpowered all gay men, most women and a sizable majority of straight
men.

"I'll forward your input to the staffing committee, Ricky," Raymond
earnestly replied, then he smiled into the phone. "Nice meeting you,
Ricky. Let me hand you back to Juan."

"Nice meeting you, too, Doctor Raymond!" Juan took the phone as
Raymond stood and began pulling off his scrubs to change into the street
clothes he'd drive home in, before stripping to shower and change clothes
yet again.

"I should go, mijo," Juan smiled wanly into the phone. "It's been a
long day. You be safe tonight. I love you."

"I love you, too, Papito, and I miss you *this* much!" Juan could see
Ricky spread his arms beyond the view of the phone's camera.

"I miss you more!" Juan ended the call, and looked sheepishly over at
Raymond who was pulling on sweats. "Sorry, Raymond. I didn't intend
to slow you down. Thanks for humoring Ricky."

"You kidding? After what we've been through today, it was kind of
nice to be reminded there are sweet, healthy, people out there who love us
and are waiting to help us return to normal once this is all over. Whatever
normal turns out to be." Juan slowly nodded. As he stood and picked up
his backpack, Raymond spoke again. "Listen, Juan, thanks for opening
up tonight. For sharing Ricky with me. We, uh, need to think seriously
about getting you back home ... to Ess Eff."

"I'm here as long as you need me, Raymond."

"I know. And I really don't want to see you go, but you've been here
almost a month. Don't worry about us; we'll find more volunteers." As
Raymond headed out, he turned and said, "Try to get some rest tonight.
Tomorrow isn't looking to be any easier than today." Juan smiled, nodded knowingly and waived Raymond off. He intended to get some rest,
but sleep? Sleep had been hard to come by lately. What little of it he got
was haunted by the pain, the tragedy and the loss that surrounded him
and all his colleagues every day. The virus wasn't just a killer. It was an
accomplished torturer, one that preyed not just on its victims, but on
everyone who tried to save them as well.

Ricky pulled up on the sidewalk at the foot of the stairs leading up to
Greg and Alex's front door and killed the engine to his scooter. He gave
two quick beeps on the feeble horn to signal his arrival. He waited for

Greg and Alex to pull on enough clothing to avoid irritating the neighbors. Soon Alex came halfway down the stairs, with Greg right behind. Alex, already masked, took a seat on a step as Greg slipped his mask in place and sat next to Alex. Ricky, of course, was helmeted, masked and gloved. He had just made his last delivery for the night.

"Who is that masked man?" Greg asked in what had become their standard greeting whenever Ricky stopped by.

"Why, it's the Masked Ring Bearer!" Ricky announced, sticking to script. Then, off-script he continued, "Like I could recognize you guys behind those masks ... and all those clothes."

"Yeah," replied Alex, "seems like forever since we were all together in one room, in all our naked glory. God, I miss that."

"We all do, Alex," Greg agreed. "At least I still get to live naked with you." Greg wrapped an arm around Alex's shoulders and pulled him close. "Think of our poor Ricky here."

"I know. Sorry Ricky, I guess I shouldn't complain, huh? How's Juan doing?"

"He says okay, but I can tell he's really, really tired. Things are pretty bad there in New York."

"I know. I've become addicted to watching Cuomo on cable news. I keep waiting for him to personally thank Juan for his contribution."

"Any day now!" Ricky exclaimed. "You know, I got to meet one of the ER docs tonight when I called Juan, and he said nice things about him. Asked if Juan could stay there permanently."

"Seriously?" Greg asked.

"He wasn't serious about keeping Juan, but he was very complimentary. Kinda cute, too. Dr. Raymond."

"How much longer do think Juan will be there?" Alex asked, tugging at his mask. "He's been gone a long time. You must be awfully worried about him. Hell, I worry about you, doing deliveries every day."

"I'm really careful, Alex. Don't you worry. But, yeah, I worry about Juan. A lot. The news is so scary I can't even watch it anymore."

"I understand," Greg said. "Me, I can't stop watching. I wish it was just a scary movie. But it's not." Ricky nodded meaningfully but didn't say anything for a moment. He looked tired. Tired and lonely.

"You shouldn't be going home alone, Ricky," Greg continued. "Why don't you stay with us until Juan comes home? You could sleep in your old bed. You shouldn't be alone." Alex smized as he put a hand on Greg's thigh.

"Yeah, just like old times, Ricky," Alex agreed.

"Where would Mateo sleep?" Ricky asked tentatively.

"Next to you, amigo," Greg smiled. "He hasn't been able to see Ryan for weeks. I'm pretty sure he could use a bed buddy." Ricky laughed.

"Um, pretty tempting, but I only sleep with Juan, you know. Besides, I can't risk infecting you guys."

"But you said you're careful," Alex protested.

"I am, but you never know. I'd never forgive myself."

Greg stood up. "Well, okay, but think about it. I'm sure Juan would think it's a good idea. Ask him what he thinks." Ricky nodded. "Thanks for stopping by, Ricky. We should let you go so you can go home ... and decontaminate."

"Yeah, I will. But are you guys hungry? My last pickup gave me a bunch of food they had left at the end of the night." Both Alex and Greg looked at each other, hesitating. "It's Thai."

"In that case ..." Alex approached Ricky's scooter as Ricky stepped away to maintain a six-foot distance. Alex opened the DoorDash bag and peered inside. "Whoa. That's a lot."

"Yeah, that's why I came over. Take all you want. I can't eat it all, you know, being lovelorn and all."

"God, I wish I could give you a hug right now," Greg whined. "This is so frustrating." Alex rejoined Greg, holding three good-sized black plastic, microwaveable take-out containers.

"This is a feast, Ricky. Thanks!"

"Don't thank me. Remember what Juan said ... we owe you a thousand dinners for everything you guys did for us. I think we're down to about nine hundred and ninety-five now."

"Nine hundred and ninety-six, Ricky, but who's counting," Greg countered, grinning behind his mask.

"Okay, sorry. My bad." Ricky climbed back on the scooter and fired it up. He slid forward to release the kickstand and waved, "Always good to see you, amigos. I love you!" Both Alex and Greg blew kisses through their masks, the best they could do given the circumstances. As Ricky rolled up the hill, Alex and Greg turned and headed up the steps. Greg put his arm around Alex's waist.

"We really can't complain, can we?" Greg asked rhetorically.

"I'm still going to complain. I miss 'normal' life. A lot! But, no, we're pretty damn lucky. I don't know how Ricky and Juan can stand it." Before they got to the top of the steps, Mateo, who had been working a late shift as an 'essential' worker at the restaurant, prepping takeout, raced up the stairs to join them.

"Hi, honeys, I'm home!" he crooned. "Was that Ricky?" His English was improving by the hour.

"It was. And this is dinner, sweetie, compliments of Ricky. Sorry you missed him." Greg opened the door and held it so Alex and Mateo could file in ahead of him.

"Yeah, I miss him," Mateo said. Both Alex and Greg looked at each other, not sure if Mateo had missed the point, or had gotten it and made his own in one succinct statement. Not that it mattered. They all missed each other. But at least there was Thai to eat, as soon as Mateo had stripped, showered and decontaminated.

Alex finished loading the dishwasher and joined Greg on the couch, cuddling up close, rubbing Greg's naked thigh affectionately. Mateo was sprawled on the floor, hands supporting his head, his perky butt occasionally twitching as he stared at the television. As usual Mateo had offered to clean up after dinner, but Alex insisted he chill after having worked much of the day. Mateo was the only one in the household who wasn't totally sheltering in place. Even though both Greg and Alex worked even more hours than they would have had they been able to commute to work, they were keenly aware of the risks Mateo took each day to insure he was doing his part financially. Greg turned to Alex and delivered a full-on kiss.

"Dinner was great. Thanks."

"Hey, all I did was reheat and serve. Ricky gets all the credit." Mateo rolled over on his side to face the couch, his head supported by his left hand.

"I have a question on Ricky," he said.

"About Ricky," Alex suggested. Mateo grinned.

"Thanks. About Ricky." As he spoke, he nonchalantly fondled his cock with his right hand. He'd fully adapted to living naked with Greg and Alex and no longer gave a second thought to how he lived now.

"What's your question?" Greg asked, enjoying the view.

"Juan has been away for one month now, no?"

"Yeah," Alex agreed. "Do you miss him?"

"Si. Yeah, and Ricky, and Raphael and Luke and everbody. But I am wondering ..." Mateo paused, uncertain if his question was inappropriate. Or, if the answer was obvious to these more experienced members of the family. He didn't want to appear too clueless.

"Well?" Alex prodded.

"Who is taking off Ricky's cage for his cleaning?" Greg and Alex both immediately turned to each other in surprise.

"Damn!" Greg exclaimed. "I hadn't even thought about that!"

"Me, either!" Alex let go of Greg and sat upright. "Geez, you're right Mateo." He pondered a moment. "Don't you think, considering everything, that he's doing it himself? He does know where Juan keeps the keys ... or at least he did."

"I don't know, Alex," Greg replied. "Ricky's pretty adamant about being 'the best locked cock leather boy in the world.' Unless Juan ordered him to, I'm not so sure he would."

"Well, I'm the only other person who's ever unlocked him, but Ricky hasn't said anything."

"Would we be out of line to check with Juan?"

"It's after midnight there. Hopefully he's asleep."

"Text him. He'll see it in the morning." Alex nodded and reached for his phone and started the text. Then he stopped, looked over at Greg then resumed.

"What?" Greg asked.

"I'm texting Ricky instead. The last thing Juan needs right now is to be worrying about Ricky's hygiene."

"You're probably right," Greg agreed. Mateo nodded and rolled back over on his stomach, pleased that his concern about Ricky's hygiene routine had been valid. Alex laid his phone down and resumed his cuddle with Greg. Maybe because of the topic they'd been discussing, Greg reached down and fondled Alex's Looker 01. At least Alex's chastity cage was designed to be permanent. He felt Alex harden inside the cage, as Alex let out a low moan. But not low enough.

"Maybe I go to my room," Mateo smiled as he looked over his shoulder.

"No, sweetie, you're fine," Greg grinned back at him. "Our Alex here is just letting us know he's finally relaxing after a long day." Alex's phone chimed, and he picked it up.

"Ricky." Alex unlocked and read the text. "He says he's okay. He's been using an ear wax squeeze bulb to keep clean. Not perfect, but good enough." Alex laughed. "He says he's still the best locked cock leather boy and thanks for asking." Alex looked over at Mateo, who was staring at Alex. "I guess our services are not needed, Mateo. That was a good call, though. Thanks." They traded smiles as Alex put down the phone, placed Greg's hand back on his caged cock and resumed his cuddle.

ABOUT THE AUTHOR

AFTER SPENDING MANY YEARS, maybe too many years, in the advertising game, sometimes writing copy for print, radio and television, which followed a period of feature writing for a periodical during his undergrad years, the author took a break from all that to take over a bed and breakfast, as one does. And where he collected enough anecdotes and personal stories to fill a six-story bookstore.

That was interesting.

Now, he's back to writing. And reading. Full time, as it were. And incorporating a few of the lessons he's learned on the path to the life he dreamed about living all those years when he was doing something else. He doesn't teach writing, like many writers. He just writes. Although he was privileged to sample the offerings at the esteemed University of Iowa Writers Workshop. Maybe it helped. You be the judge.